FORGED IN THE CHASMS OF DARKNESS

FORGED IN THE CHASMS OF DARKNESS

THE RECORDS OF ELESHAR, BOOK II

RICH INMAN

An Inman Media Group Book
Published by Inman Media Group LLC
https://www.inmanmediagroup.com

ISBN: 979-8-9926681-0-0

Cover designed and illustrated by Chandika Belie
Book designed and formatted by Rich Inman
Edited by Matt Miller & Rich Inman

First Edition: February 2025

This book is printed on demand. Each copy is uniquely manufactured.

To my amazing wife who believes in me, even when I don't believe in myself.

FORWARD AND ACKNOWLEDGMENTS

I humbly present to you *Forged in the Chasms of Darkness*, the second installment in *The Records of Eleshar*. Publishing *The Storm's Approach*, the first book in the *Records of Eleshar* series was a major milestone in my life and in my writing. It was the first book I truly felt was good enough to share, even if it wasn't the first one I published.

Let me explain...

I've been writing as a hobby for close to twenty years now, and for most of that time I'd been putting words on paper thinking they were fantastic. Unfortunately, the feedback I received wasn't so fantastic—or helpful. Nurturing the ability to tell a compelling story, especially in a genre as complex as fantasy, requires skill in many different areas: Plot development and character crafting, an above average vocabulary and grasp of the English language, time management, dedication, and the ability to write even when it's difficult and you don't feel like doing it. That reality means that when you need feedback to improve, you need it to be detailed. Unfortunately, when people give you feedback, it's usually quite generic.

"You need to work on your prose."

"The main character isn't believable."

"I don't understand what's happening."

"I couldn't read past a few paragraphs because the writing was so bad."

That's not a criticism of people who give that sort of advice, they're usually trying to help. And someone who knows what to do with that feedback can make great use of it. But that person wasn't me, and no one with the skills to help me had the time to sit down and tell me why my verbs were bland, what exactly made my characters stiff, or why my writing was "unreadable." To emphasize how inept I was, I had no idea what a story beat was for fifteen years!

So, I kept writing, being frustrated by feedback that I couldn't understand, and abandoning my stories when I didn't know what to do with them. In the meantime, I was building my career in technology, which consumed the time I had for writing. After years of managing technology projects, my time management improved. Finally, I could carve out time for writing again, and as a bonus I brought project management skills to my writing. I'd became intimately familiar with the emotional stages of complex projects: Excitement, frustration, apathy, avoidance, renewed focus, the mad dash to the finish line, and the odd sensation of finishing yet feeling like there's more work still to do.

Recognition of these perfectly normal project stages helped me practice wrapping up the plot threads I'd had so much experience starting but never finishing. But there was still something missing.

My writing remained sub-par. I knew it, even as I hoped others would read my works and rejoice at the gift I'd just given them, only to get the same feedback I couldn't process or learn from.

In the end, it didn't matter that I'd finished stories, because I didn't improve those foundational things that made them readable, relatable, and most of all *fun*!

It was 2021 when I'd finally decided to write *The Storm's Approach* (Titled *Unchained* at the time), the first book in a planned nine book series. When I look back at that decision, I still wonder why I hoisted this daunting task on the shoulders of future me. I'm sure it was an unfortunate byproduct of my blind ambition. Stupid past Rich.

But I digress...

I wrote three chapters of that book before I forced myself to stop. I could tell I was about to write the same terrible prose, stiff characters, wonky plot lines, and uneven story beats I'd been writing for over fifteen years. I knew if I was going to create a story epic enough to span nine books, they needed to be entertaining, and the text readable.

So, I switched gears and became a student. I watched every BYU lecture Brandon Sanderson posted on YouTube, then watched them twice. Then I watched videos from other authors, soaking in as much knowledge about the craft of writing as possible. I read books about plot, characters, grammar, punctuation, and finally prose. Reluctantly, I took a highlighter to my books, dissecting the prose of professional authors, desperate to learn where I was falling short.

A year later I came back to *The Storm's Approach*. I re-plotted it and started writing again. Thankfully, my efforts paid off! I was a better writer, and with my new skills, I finally finished the first draft.

But I knew I wasn't done. I had to edit that book, and I had to do it the right way. So, I spent time going through every editing round a traditional publisher would put their author's books through. Unfortunately, without the several thousand dollars necessary to hire the right editors, I was forced to do it myself.

If you've read *The Storm's Approach*, you'll know that it's not the most polished text out there. However, it's not the least, and for all its flaws, I'm very proud of the story I was able to tell.

Through the process of editing *The Storm's Approach* I found my writing improving dramatically. It forced me to confront and fix my mistakes. In fact, editing pushed me to a level I never thought I'd achieve, and it renewed my vigor for writing.

And so, I dove into *Forged in the Chasms of Darkness* and found myself going through the same improvement processes. My writing continued to improve, and I felt energized by those improvements.

More than that, I found in this book a way to release the pressure of the issues I'd been facing. Though I'm not schizophrenic like the main character of this book, I'd been dealing with severe depression while I was writing it. I decided to use my main character—who struggles with severe mental illness as an inherent character trait—as an outlet for my own difficulties, and, though I can't handle my problems with magic and a healthy dose of being awesome, my main character certainly could, and at times gave me the hope I was missing.

Pouring those struggles into the text resulted in a character more relatable and emotionally resonant than I could have even expected. The responses from my alpha and beta readers blew my mind. Not a single one of them had feedback on the writing itself—other than some basic typos and minor grammar issues. Instead, they gushed over the main character and how they related to his struggles. They cheered for his successes and rooted for him when all seemed lost. Zeriel was the hero my writing needed.

This book feels like the culmination of twenty years of effort finally producing that thing I'd been chasing: A story that moved people.

Now, let's move on to the people who helped me make this book possible. While I've done the majority of the work around this book (outlining, writing, editing, and editing, and editing, and formatting), there are key people that have provided invaluable insights and feedback that contributed to it significantly. In fact, this book wouldn't be what it is without them.

First, I have to thank my long-time friend Matt Miller. He work shopped the plot of this book with me, helped in key areas, then became an alpha reader. He's one of the reasons I'm able to bring these stories to you.

Second is Diran Ogunlana. I convinced him to become an alpha reader, and his input became invaluable in developing many of the most important plot points.

Thirdly, my beta reader Book Bassey. She was a fantastic find on a Goodreads forum who provided that much needed third party feedback I was looking for.

And finally, I would be remiss if I didn't thank you, the reader. I can't spend a lot of time and money on marketing these books, so they don't reach many people. Luckily, you've found it! And as I subscribe to the idea that a book isn't finished until it's read, you're the last step in this twenty-year journey. I put my characters, and my world in your hands. I hope you love them as much as I do.

CHAPTER ONE

Sneaking into the estate of a rich, pampered merchant should be
easy for an assassin. For Zeriel, it was anything but. Yes, he was
a member of the Te Et Sha, a group composed of the most powerful assassins across Eleshar, spoken of only in the whispers of those
who knew of their existence. Unfortunately, he held the position of
worst among them.

The infiltration was a long and arduous event for Zeriel, easily taking twice the time it would have taken his fellow assassins. Luckily, it
was a dark month, one of the thirty-day spans where the sun slept below the horizon. The darkness provided him with the cover he needed
to cross the expansive grounds of the estate without being seen. His
only obstacle was the soft light provided by the polychromatic bioluminescent plants of the estate's gardens.

Difficulty aside, he eventually made it inside his target's mansion
and to his bedchamber unseen. He listened at the chamber's door for
movement or voices inside. The hallway he stood in was lit by white
vine lanterns on shelves along its walls, each one darkened by a thin
cloth draped over it. The vines that grew from those pots glowed with
a pure white light, a hundred times brighter than any other plant on
Eleshar. It was a marvel of selective breeding achieved hundreds of
years ago by a man whose name Zeriel could never remember. The
coverings muted the lights, providing Zeriel enough darkness to cover
his infiltration.

A rumbling snore sounded from the other side of the door. Satisfied, Zeriel reached for the handle. Just before he touched it, though, a

man appeared next to him as if out of thin air.

He was shorter than Zeriel and his close-cut black hair had streaks of silver on the sides. His face had the sharp lines of cracked stone, and his dark green eyes shone with mischief. He always wore the same perfectly tailored dark blue doublet and black trousers. Lines of thread that glowed bright orange climbed the seams of his clothes. They created spiral box-like patterns that crisscrossed black lines in the same pattern. The man leaned on a waist-high cane topped with a golden ball that was inlaid with jewels of all sorts. He wore a flat-topped hat with a large orange feather stuck to the side and facing backwards. "Are you sure it's safe?" the man asked. "Maybe he's not the only one in there and that snoring is coming from someone else. I bet he's got a crossbow across his lap, waiting for you to enter."

Zeriel had known this man for over ten years. In their first meeting he introduced himself as Jekjarah, and at the time he had no reason to doubt the man was real. But it didn't take long before Zeriel discovered Jekjarah was just a figment of his imagination. Although he looked and sounded as real as any other person, Zeriel knew better. When he was in his early teenage years, he'd fallen deep into a shaft in his Clan's mine. Jekjarah appeared to him while he was stuck there waiting to be rescued. The hallucination brought voices along with him, though they never appeared to him as Jekjarah did. Instead, they tormented him with malevolent commands to hurt or kill himself, and constant lies and emphatic curses.

He'd visited many healers and shaman over the years. While they all gave a different explanation for his affliction—a mind fracture, that he was some ancient Void Walker, or that he was afflicted with something they called the curse of echoes—he quickly discovered that however they tried to define it, nothing would change the nature of what was wrong with him, and there was no cure.

With a sigh at the hallucination's doubt, he checked both directions of the hallway and saw no one. "He's alone in there, Jek," he whispered.

"But how can you be *sure?*"

Footsteps sounded from down the hallway, likely from a guard patrol. The noise forced Zeriel into action. He left the hallucination where he stood and swept into the chamber.

Just as he'd expected, a single man was sprawled out on a giant four-poster bed dressed in a brown night shirt and white nightcap. His covers were strewn about, and he faced the ceiling as he snored. The room was surprisingly plain for a man with so much wealth. A fireplace stood opposite the bed with a single potted white vine lantern on the mantle, covered to provide just enough light so one wouldn't stumble in the dark. A small four-paned window was set in the far wall with thin white curtains pulled to the sides. The only real decoration in the room was a giant portrait of the man himself hung over the fireplace.

Jekjarah appeared next to the bed, his arms crossed and posture hostile as he inspected the sleeping man. He turned toward Zeriel with a mixture of resignation and anger on his face and said, "I guess he was alone, after all." That expression immediately changed to one with wide eyes, and a manic smile stretched unnaturally across his face. "You're going to kill him now, right?"

Jekjarah's fast-shifting expressions didn't bother Zeriel. He was familiar with them by now and assumed it to be further proof of his own insanity. Instead of concern he actually shared the unrestrained glee Jekjarah displayed. The emotion pushed him to move, and he pulled a dagger from his belt. His fingers scraped along the tightly packed pouches also attached to the belt, tearing some of the skin of his knuckles, but Zeriel barely noticed. Death was the only thing on his mind.

A few steps. A hand over the man's mouth. A quick stab through his rib cage and into his heart. Exhilaration surged through his body. He reveled in the process and tried to extend the moments.

His target's eyes shot open in panic, pain, and fear. The reaction only served to enhance Zeriel's excitement. Blood seeped from the wound around the knife as the man thrashed in his futile attempt to fight, but it was in vain. Zeriel released the hilt of his blade and rubbed his hand in the man's blood. His other hand pressed harder on his target's mouth. With muscles strengthened far beyond any normal man's, it only took one arm to hold the dying man in place.

He brought the bloody hand to his face so he could inspect it.

"Let me see!" Jekjarah exclaimed. His face slid uncomfortably close to Zeriel's as he tried to get close.

It was an even shade of red across his palm. Intriguing lines cast by the subdued reflections of the lantern on the mantle played across its surface. He moved his hand to his nose and breathed in the scent, intoxicated by the iron aroma.

"Come now," Jekjarah said as he grasped at Zeriel's wrist, though his hands only passed through it. "Share it already."

A different set of hands grabbed the arm Zeriel used to hold down the dying man, the very real hands of his target who was able to rip his mouth free of the assassin's grip.

The dying man sucked air into his lungs and screamed, "Assassin! Guards! There's an—" He was cut off as he coughed blood all over himself. The knife had obviously missed his heart.

"Damn it," Zeriel said as he pulled the knife out of the man and rammed it back into his chest. He continued, not counting the number of times he struck. He just kept stabbing until there was no doubt the man's heart was shredded. Only once his target's eyes stared unblinkingly at the ceiling did Zeriel feel confident he'd accomplished his goal.

"Time to go," Jekjarah said, now standing next to the door.

"Obviously," Zeriel responded. He hurried to the door and stepped into the hallway in time to see guards appearing around corners from both directions, three on his left and four on his right.

"Assassin!" one of the guards yelled as he pointed at Zeriel. They sprinted toward him and cut off all routes of escape. He scanned the walls; the hallway had no windows. He steeled himself and pulled a second dagger from his belt, holding it point forward in his dominant hand while he held his second knife point backward in the other.

Jekjarah walked through the closed door to join him in the hallway. He noticed the guards who sprinted toward them. "You really messed up this time."

"I can see that just fine without your—" Zeriel was cut off by a pulling sensation at the base of his spine that unceremoniously ripped his consciousness from his body.

※

White flashed across Zeriel's vision. A few moments passed before he regained his sight and found himself sitting near the end of a long stone table. His eyes were fixed on the far side of the room, and he couldn't move his head when he tried. He stared past several tall beige pillars and out into a lush oasis with buildings that poked through tall palm trees. Beyond that was desert as far as the eye could see. Strangely, the sky was bright blue as if it were the middle of a light month.

"Are you listening Plaxes?" a man said, annoyance weaved through his tone.

Zeriel's body sighed involuntarily as his head turned to face the man. From his vantage he saw others sitting at the table—eleven total, including himself—and a single man at its head.

That man had bluish-gray hair that fell well past his shoulders and his eyes were a bright blue that gave off a slight inner glow.

"You want me to assassinate him," Zeriel said, but the unmistakably feminine voice that came from his mouth wasn't his. One of his hands moved to his face on its own and he rested his cheek against it lazily. Zeriel was shocked to see the skin on his hand was pitch black. Not the dark brown tone of the Allakhanians that bordered on black. No, the skin on his hand was blacker than anything he'd ever seen, darker than the night itself. "Assuming it's even possible to assassinate *him*," the feminine voice said through him.

"I agree," said a man from across the table. Zeriel's eyes shifted to regard him. He had shoulder-length blond hair and the strong features of a traditionally handsome man. He was adorned in gleaming silver plate armor with white and gold paint in the crevices of carvings that swirled as they traveled across its surfaces. "He brought every Keeper in—"

"Don't!" The man at the head of the table screamed as he shot to his feet. "Never use *that* title to describe us. We've grown beyond the servants he would make of us. Each one of us at this table cast that off long ago. *We* are the gods now."

The man raised his hands in surrender. "Must we always pick at that old scab, Nedon? Yes, we are gods, but we must still face facts. There may not be one of us at this table who has the strength—"

"I'll do it," Plaxes's voice said from his lips. She turned her head toward Nedon. "We may never get another opportunity."

Nedon smiled and returned to his chair. "I'm glad you see it as I do."

"When do—" The pulling sensation returned, interrupted Plaxes, and in a flash Zeriel was ripped from her body.

❖

White covered his vision a second time, and when he could see again, he watched in horror as the seven guards he'd completely forgotten about were moments away from slicing him limb from limb. He acted on pure instinct, dodging through their initial strikes, then rolling through a widened gap between the two on his left.

His effort wasn't enough. One blade sliced his left side and bounced off his ribs. Another sliced the outside of his right quadricep, and immense pain flashed through his leg when he put weight on it.

Terror threatened to freeze him where he stood and a sudden and powerful desire to disappear into the shadows overcame Zeriel. To his shock the shadows around him responded. They pulled from the cracks in the wall, the spaces under the shelves where the white vine lanterns cast their light, and even from the shadows of the men around him. Every shadow in a twenty-foot radius pulled toward him and exploded into a black mist.

Moving was agony, and he had no idea what had just happened, but an assassin doesn't miss a perfect opportunity when it presents itself. The moment Zeriel was back on his feet, he pushed the pain to the back of his awareness and exploded from the other side of the black fog, then ran as fast as he could.

He left the guards yelling and confused behind him. It seemed the seven of them were the only ones in the building, giving Zeriel the opportunity he needed to disappear into the darkness of the estate's grounds and make his escape.

By the time he arrived at the small copse of trees where he'd left his horse, he could barely walk. Mounting the beast took all the strength he had left. He flopped into the saddle and found himself lying across the animal, forced to grip its neck to keep from falling.

"It's a long ride to the nearest Whisper," Jekjarah said standing next to him. "The Veil doesn't reach this far from civilization."

"I know," Zeriel said through the pain.

Pathetic, a voice said in his mind. He recognized it, though just hours before he wouldn't have. It was the woman whose body he'd inhabited in the vision.

"Plaxes?"

Interesting. I wonder what you saw of my past that revealed my name to you.

Not once in the years since his affliction had a new voice appeared, and never had he descended into a vision so all-consuming as the one he'd just experienced.

"I don't—" A lance of pain shot through his chest and Zeriel growled through gritted teeth. His situation was dire, so he coaxed his horse to a trot, which was the most he could handle from the animal. "I don't have time for imaginary voices right now."

I'm not imaginary. Her tone had an element of annoyance in it.

"That's what they all say."

She let out the same sigh she had in the vision. *And when you used the shadows to escape certain death, was that imaginary?*

Zeriel paused at that. Plaxes had a point, but he had a hard time accepting what happened as anything *but* a hallucination? Then again, he couldn't see how he could have escaped without some magical black fog to cover him.

I was worried that after all these years someone would have found the sliver. Just creating the thing was distasteful enough. But to think, after all these millennia, I'd be saddled with someone like you. Zeriel caught a hint of contempt in her tone.

Exhaustion hit him and he felt suddenly very sleepy. That was not a good sign. "I don't think you have to worry. I'll probably die before I find a healer. When that happens, you can have your *sliver* back, whatever that is."

There was a long pause before Plaxes's voice entered his mind again. *This might be a good test, then. If you do survive, then perhaps I will make use of you.* Her presence left his mind before he could think to respond.

Zeriel was surprised at her sudden departure, then angry at her for cutting off their conversation. Though, what else could he expect from one of his voices.

Leaving the conversation behind, he emptied his mind of all thought as he rode. If he was going to die, he'd do it in silence. Unfortunately, his other voices wouldn't let him have such peace.

You deserve death.

Those guards are chasing you. Can't you hear the beating of hooves behind you? Surprisingly, he thought he could.

Slit your wrists and your pain will end.

No, cut your throat.

No, stab your heart.

On any other occasion he'd be able to distract himself from the voices, but injured and exhausted as he was, there was no defense against them. They spoke non-stop for hours, and a few times Zeriel almost obeyed them.

Despite his mind's antagonisms, and against all reason, Zeriel was alive and conscious when he entered the village of Bustan. It was a quaint hamlet nestled in the northern forests of Allakhan that bordered The Great Divide, a giant desert that separated the southern nations of the continent from the northern nation of Kloren. The forest that surrounded Bustan provided a pleasant green and blue glow as a backdrop to the spattering of small buildings. A creek snaked its way through the center of the village, separating farms from homes and shops. White vine lanterns hung on poles along the main road, exposing him in a way he'd been trained to avoid. Half-dead as he was, he didn't care. The Whisper saw him coming immediately.

This member of the Veil was also the local blacksmith, and despite the late hour, he was already outside his shop with a young man in tow hurrying to receive Zeriel. The Whispers were operatives of the Te Et Sha and part of a network spread across Eleshar they called the Veil. Whispers provided safety, rest, and even healers; whatever the Te Et Sha needed. The Veil was also the primary method the Te Et Sha used to pass messages to and from their assassins.

The Whisper grabbed the reins of Zeriel's horse and looked him over. "Go fetch Kulku," he said to the younger man. "And be quick about it. We don't have much time."

To the boy's credit, he obeyed quickly and without question or complaint.

The Whisper pulled the horse toward a small stable next to his smithy. It was barely large enough to hold two horses, though luckily one stall was empty. "Don't worry, you will soon be covered by the protection of The Veil."

Every muscle in Zeriel's body relaxed at the man's statement, so he was glad to let the Blacksmith help him off the horse and inside into a bed.

CHAPTER TWO

THREE MONTHS LATER

It took weeks before Zeriel accepted that his new powers were real. He'd spent the time learning how to use darkness to his advantage, but he'd had limited success. The most he'd been able to achieve was creating that same dark mist from his first use of the powers and cloaking himself in shadow. Though the latter was more of a natural progression of the former. For the time being, those two abilities gave him the edge he needed to make his missions as easy as he'd imagined they were for the rest of the Te Et Sha.

Plaxes hadn't spoken to him since the first night, which was just fine with him. It was hard enough handling the voices he already had. He wasn't sure he could handle a new voice he increasingly believed was attached to someone—or something—real. Just the thought of that brought a chill to his spine.

Zeriel's current assignment was to infiltrate the city of Shyal in the nation of Wylsh and assassinate someone there who called themselves the Slave King. It hadn't taken him long to sneak inside the city's outer wall. He just had to avoid the King's army that was besieging the city. Surprisingly, that wasn't a problem. The army had been camped outside the city long enough that the soldiers had grown complacent, giving Zeriel every opportunity he needed to sneak past them, especially shrouded in shadow.

The wall itself was huge on the inside. Large enough to house a barracks, kitchens, and weapons stores. And that was just the section Zeriel stalked through. An entire army could have been housed inside the structure of the entire wall and no one inside or outside the city might have noticed.

White vine lanterns lit the hallways inside the wall and moss grew in the joints between stones, its soft green glow difficult to see in the overpowering of the lanterns' brilliance.

A slave uprising had happened in the city months ago, and the very slaves who had cleaned the walls before now neglected that duty. Time in the heat and humidity of light months worked fast to foster the moss's growth.

From the intelligence he was able to gather in the towns along his way to the city, he'd discovered that a woman known as the Liberator had led the slaves' revolt. According to the stories, the Liberator had the power to control water, and used it to massacre anyone who owned a slave. Before he'd suddenly been able to command the very darkness around him, that would have sounded more legend than truth to Zeriel.

He stepped away from the corpse he'd made of a slave turned guard and navigated his way inward through the wall's hallways toward the city. The brightness of the lanterns hurt his eyes and cast a strong white haze over his vision. Since his powers appeared, his eyes had become more sensitive. So sensitive that during the light months he was forced to cover his eyes with a threadbare cloth just to reduce the glare of the sun enough to make out blurry shapes in the world around him. Tired of the effects of the lanterns on his vision, Zeriel paused to tie his blindfold over his eyes.

Despite the illumination in the halls, he'd found shadowed corners and alcoves to hide in throughout the corridor's stonework walls. In the months of experimentation, Zeriel had found his powers worked exceptionally well where darkness already fell. The effect made him practically invisible.

Zeriel drew on the shadows around him to cloak his presence once again, then stalked through the halls openly. If he moved in the light while cloaked, it was more likely someone would notice, though if he was careful, they might just attribute the movement to their own imagination.

Just as Zeriel rounded a corner he was stopped in his tracks by Jekjarah.

"Seems like a waste of these powers of yours, doesn't it?" he said. "It's not like there's anyone here."

Zeriel walked through the hallucination and continued down the hall. "There's a corpse back there that might prove otherwise." One more turn and a door to the city revealed itself against the wall at the end of another hallway.

Jekjarah appeared next to him. "But what if you have a limited supply of power? Once it's all used up, poof!" He flared out his hands in front of him, fingers outspread, in a mock explosion. "Gone."

"Plaxes never said anything about that." Zeriel stalked toward the door. "Seems like something she would have mentioned."

"She didn't say much of anything." Jekjarah said. "You can't trust her." The monotone way his voice flattened out at the last statement took on the inhuman tone of his other voices. It was jarring since the hallucination rarely spoke that way. "She's just another voice, after all."

"If she's just another voice, and I can't trust her, then maybe I can't trust you either," Zeriel said.

"Of course, you can trust me!" he exclaimed, his normal intonations returning. "I am the well-dressed exception to the rule." He stood taller and straightened his doublet.

Zeriel approached the door and grabbed the handle. He looked Jekjarah in his eyes, something he rarely did. "At least Plaxes doesn't torment me like the rest of you." He pulled the door open slowly until he could peer through the gap and into the city beyond. It was pitch black inside the city, so Zeriel removed his blindfold. With his sensitive eyes uncovered, the district looked well-lit from just the starlight above.

The Northern Gate District was just beyond the door, nestled in the northeast corner of the city where the wall met the enormous cliff to the north. The normally bustling district lay in ruins. Buildings were reduced to wooden frames charred to gnarled fingers that pointed toward the sky. The smoke-stained remains of walls formed a decayed webbing between those fingers.

Rubble was strewn through the streets, but looking further revealed more devastation in the distance. The usual presence of multichromatic, bioluminescent plants was gone, and no white vine lanterns were mounted on tall poles to chase out the darkness. The lingering scent of burned wood and silence that blanketed the air added to the sight and created an alien atmosphere that set Zeriel's teeth on edge. A haze of prismatic luminance rose in the distance as a beacon amidst the devastation.

You can't go there, whispered a voice in Zeriel's mind. *They'll be waiting for you.*

Those former slaves will know what you've come for, came another voice right on the heels of the other. *You should leave. Leave now!*

It doesn't matter if you leave or not, you're worthless either way. Just kill yourself, said yet another voice. *Then you'll be free of all these burdens.*

He shook his head as the voices increased in volume until they screamed their evils into his ears. "Shut up," Zeriel said through gritted teeth. Years of practice taught Zeriel to ignore the voices most of the time, but they were too loud inside his head now to shut out completely. Pushing forward was the only thing he could do now.

He opened the door the rest of the way and stepped out into the wasteland that was once the Northern Gate District. Covered in shadows as he was, no one would see him moving through the rubble. That allowed Zeriel to avoid his normal stealthiness and push on toward the lights in the distance.

Jekjarah appeared next to him and the voices quieted. "You think it's still there?"

"The Square of Virtues?" It was the major religious center of the southern half of the Western Continent and people traveled for hundreds, sometimes thousands of miles to visit. Even slaves who'd overthrown their masters would have the reverence to leave such a place unscathed. And the brightness of it indicated as much. "I think there's a good chance. If the church is standing, there's likely plenty of refugees there. It'll be a good place to get information."

"You always prolong these things. Gathering information, watching your targets for days on end, learning their routines, etcetera, etcetera." The hallucination waved his hands in a circle emphasizing his last words. "Wouldn't it be easier to just find them, kill them, and be done with it?"

Zeriel eyed Jekjarah. The hallucination walked with a casual gait, and the rhythmic click of his cane as it struck the ground was strangely soothing. For a moment, Zeriel wondered at how real the sound seemed in his ears. It echoed off the intact portions of walls around him. How did his mind create such nuanced and realistic sound?

He chose not to think too hard on it, so he didn't drive himself any more insane than he already was. "You know what I know, Jek. I was trained to be careful, thorough, and most importantly, undetected."

"True, but if I'm saying it, there's a part of your mind that's thinking about it." He made a show of poking Zeriel's head with his finger. "I'm a projection of what's in there, after all."

"Perhaps," Zeriel said as he swatted at the hallucination's hand.

Jekjarah moved on, abruptly changing topics. He started with the philosophical, moral, and psychological implications of talking to a self-aware hallucination. Zeriel often thought about that, but he never came to a satisfying answer. The hallucination continued onto other topics, but Zeriel let the man's voice turn to noise as he focused on his task.

The transition out of the ruins and into the District of Virtues was dramatic. Where the Norther Gate District was burned to ashes behind him, the District of Virtues was full of life and light ahead. On his right was the Square of Virtues with its huge gardens and massive church at the center. Even from his current distance, he could see the building's towers rising above the trees.

A garden called Ded's Flame stood in the southeast corner, its trees glowing with red and orange leaves. White vine plants were left to grow along the ground to illuminate the gardens from below, enhancing the fire-like hues. Red glowing hedges lined the garden's border, placed there to push visitors toward the main entrance further down the path.

On the south side of the district, living quarters for the priests who tended to the gardens and ministered to its visitors were nestled in the trees of an otherwise untouched forest. Those buildings were set in a circle of five structures that faced inward toward a communal fire pit. The life of these priests was a modest one. The beauty that surrounded them was enough to tempt Zeriel to join the church for the peace such a life promised, but he never could accept its foreign beliefs.

As he approached the Square's main entrance, Zeriel glimpsed The Ponds of Na on its western side. Its trees draped with vine-like branches that hung close to the ground. Blue glowing puffballs ran down the length of the branches. Bridges skipped over the ponds, extending the pathways that meandered through the garden. Like Ded's Flame with its spectrum of red and orange, the flora of The Ponds radiated its hues of emerald and blue.

The main gate led to a path that cut its way between the two gardens. Red light emanated from the garden on his right, and blue from the one on his left, created a purple equilibrium between them. The Church of Virtues stood on the path ahead, towering fifty feet high. Ornate carvings of the four deities of the Virtues adorned its outer walls framed by glowing vines—red for fire, blue for water, white for air, and green for earth. Behind the church was the white glow of Thaid's Spires, and the green glow of The Fields of Obe. The church stood in the center of all the gardens, a reminder that the four deities worked together to form the Church of Virtues.

Halted in his tracks by the sight, Zeriel took it in.

Shyal was one of the largest, and most influential cities in Eleshar, so Zeriel had killed many a person inside its walls. Each time he approached this building, though, he couldn't hold back his awe of its beauty.

"It never gets old," Jekjarah said.

"No, it doesn't," Zeriel said. He nodded to himself, then walked toward the main entrance. "We've got work to do, though."

CHAPTER THREE

As Zeriel approached the front of the church, a field of heavily disturbed earth on his right caught his eye. The remnants of a wooden fence that once surrounded the area lay in pieces around it. That was once the church garden, used to grow food for the priests who lived there and the poor of the city who couldn't feed themselves.

He shook his head and continued toward the doors to the church. They were made of thick vertical hardwood planks connected by long hinges that spread out into swirls at the edges that turned back on themselves. A large knocker in the shape of a snarling razorcat head warned those who came to do the church harm. As usual, he ignored such warnings. Zeriel grabbed the ring in its mouth and used it to rap on the door. The sound echoed through the hall behind it and left a heavy silence in its wake.

Several minutes passed before Zeriel reached for the knocker again, but the door cracked open and pulled away from his hand.

A man peered out and leveled a steady, if baggy-eyed, gaze at Zeriel. He was late in years and wore a red robe with a red sleeping cap that barely restrained his long, curly hair. The priest wore an irritated look on his face. "You took all the food already, what else could you—" He cut short when he finally let his eyes focus on Zeriel. "What can I do for you, son?"

"I need refuge for the night," Zeriel said. He softened his voice to appear as non-threatening as possible.

The man inspected him more closely. "Where have you been all this time?" he asked, leaning to the side to see past Zeriel.

"I've been hiding out in the Northern Gate District. I knew the slaves wouldn't look for me there, but eventually the rats realized I was the only food left."

The priest gave him a knowing look. "What are you, new at this?"

Jekjarah laughed behind him. "He saw through you in seconds. You really are a terrible assassin."

Zeriel stiffened at Jekjarah's comment. "I've never taken refuge at a church before, if that's what you're asking."

"I've met your kind before, passing through like a sudden gust of wind, leaving only the dead in your wake."

"If you know who I am," Zeriel said, "then you know what I'm here for."

The priest shook his head. "You won't find any information here."

Zeriel maintained eye contact and let the silence stretch.

The priest sighed and said, "Fine," then opened the door and stepped to the side. The inside of the church was lit dimly by a small number of white vine lanterns, their light diminished in the vast space. For Zeriel, those few lanterns were enough to light the inside as if the sun shone from the ceiling.

Past the door and beyond the entrance were the standard four rows of pews that formed the church's nave. To the left and right of the pews were sweeping arches that formed the nave arcade with depictions of the four natural elements carved into them.

More carvings of the deific elements covered the arches and above that the gods of virtues were depicted in the stained glass along the top of the walls.

At the head of the rows of pews stood four altars in the form of tables backed with a shelf that held carved renderings of the four gods. On the altars were various offerings piled high enough to obscure those depictions.

Despite the beauty of the architecture and pious displays, there was an emptiness to the place that emanated from the Northern Gate District, through the vibrancy of the Square's gardens, then finally to this church.

The priest stepped beside Zeriel as he took in the sight. "I'm the only one left. Most of the priests escaped during the riot. I thank Ded every day that the slaves, then the bandits that rose up in their wake, left this place mostly unmolested. In the beginning, that gave hope to the few of us priests who stayed behind. We should have known that hunger would eventually overpower respect, even for the gods themselves.

"They came for the garden a few weeks ago. The rest of the priests snuck out of the city a few days after that."

Zeriel looked at the man and saw a hint of sadness on his face. "Why did you stay?"

The priest met his eyes, tears welling up in them. "Some things in this world are worth risking our lives to preserve. If this isn't one of those things," he gestured around him, "then what is?"

This man seemed genuine. As misplaced as Zeriel thought his faith was, it was clear he cared deeply for this place. He wondered how it would feel to care that much about...well, anything. "I'm sorry for waking you," Zeriel said to the priest. He turned to leave.

"I wish I could have at least fed you," the priest said. "The Slave King rations the food now, handing it out each morning—to those still alive, that is."

Zeriel paused and looked back at the man. "Where does he do that?"

"City Hall. In the Guild District." The man's face was steady.

Zeriel nodded. He reached into the thin pack he had strapped to his back and pulled out a small bundle wrapped in cloth. He set it down before he turned to leave. "Thanks for the information."

"Wait," Jekjarah said as Zeriel stepped out the door and walked away from the church. "Did you just give that man all the food you had left?"

"He needs it more than I do."

The hallucination stepped in front of Zeriel. He walked backwards without any care for what was behind him. "Like hell he does. Aren't you about to execute another infiltration and assassination? Hunger pangs are going distract you and put the entire mission in jeopardy."

"My mark's not a real king and won't have trained bodyguards. Besides, I've gone without food before a kill many times. Not to mention, I've got powers now. How hard could it be to get through a few self-important slaves?"

Jekjarah shook his head and faded away as he said, "You're going to die."

Zeriel left behind the bright colors of the District of Virtues for the barren wasteland of the Northern Gate District. He wasn't always free of the voices in his head, but at that moment they chose to let him walk in peace. It was as euphoric as a temporary reprieve from chronic pain, or the sudden release of stress you didn't notice was there. The subtle white light of the Leif District became visible to the south, and Zeriel had to fight himself from finding the closest piece of rubble to sit on and never move again. Perhaps the silence would last forever if he didn't walk into that light.

The mission wouldn't wait for him though, so he continued until the rubble was replaced with affluent houses built one against another. Waist-high stone walls separated the small spaces in front of the homes. Turned over remains of house gardens sat with other detritus that had accumulated over time. The lanterns here glowed dimly from pots hung on the tall poles that framed the cobblestone street. Their vines reached almost to the ground, mostly dead and burned from neglect under the hot sun of the prior light month.

In a few of those gardens, Zeriel found discarded clothes, half-buried in the dirt. They were soiled and covered in holes, which was perfect for what he was planning. He collected items as he went until he accumulated a complete disguise perfect for the next phase of the mission. He slipped between the homes and out of sight where he could change into his new outfit: A thick, brown wool shirt over brown trousers held in place with a frayed rope for a belt. He went without shoes. Barefoot seemed to best tell the story of someone who'd struggled in the streets of Shyal over the last few months. A few handfuls of dirt rubbed in his face completed the look. Satisfied, he stuffed his assassin's leathers into his bag and headed toward City Hall.

By the time Zeriel exited the Leif District and entered the Guild District, he decided on the more nuanced parts of his disguise. He walked with a limp and tested out the accent of one of Shyal's street urchins. Some of them had managed to live to adulthood, never losing their unique speech pattern. Udulets, they were called, mostly to mock their childish verbiage. They were ruthless beyond measure. Made necessary by the nature of the streets that raised them. Even those in the underbelly of the city avoided them at all costs. It wasn't likely the slaves would dare approach him in such a disguise.

"Please, don't'a 'ave some food? I be big emp'y, sir," Zeriel said to get his mouth warmed up for the accent and slang. His tongue widened in his mouth and touched his molars, which is how he knew he was close to accurate.

Jekjarah winked into existence just ahead. "If only you were even the slightest bit convincing with that act."

"Egh! Q'it ya 'plainin. Time ta be big helpful, naw?" Whenever he took on a disguise like this one, Zeriel spoke to Jekjarah and his other voices in the open. His insanity lent a credence to the disguise that he couldn't have faked. Many times in the past it had covered mistakes that might have otherwise gotten him discovered.

"Right, right," Jekjarah said, waving a hand. "Tell me when we get there. I can't stand to watch you when you do this." He disappeared unceremoniously.

The Guild District was well-kept when compared to the last two districts. The lanterns were bright here, and the streets were cleared of soil and debris. At closer inspection, the district looked like someone doing the bare minimum to keep things functional. The cobblestone of the streets had water, mud, and other waste deep in its cracks. The larger pieces of dirt and debris were swept to the side to build up in the alleys and against the walls of the buildings.

The people huddling in the streets gave away the charade. Men without shirts to wear showed skeletons through their skin as they shuffled about. Women joined them with gaunt faces that hinted at a similar skeletal figure beneath their makeshift robes fashioned from bed curtains, sheets, and drapes. Some slept in the street, unconcerned about what might happen to them. Others groaned and cried in the night air, their mouths torn at the edges from the drug they hadn't taken in weeks. It all mixed together into an atmosphere of desperation, covered in a layer of despair. That put Zeriel on high alert. People were most dangerous when they had nothing to lose. Hopefully his disguise would hold and keep the residents at bay.

He arrived at the City Square, and while he expected this place to be crowded, he wasn't prepared for exactly how crowded it was. It seemed the majority of those left in the city had coalesced there. A blanket of humanity covered the square. They slept on top of each other on the cobblestone and inside the dried-out stone of the large fountain in the center. On top of the fountain stood the likeness of a woman made from mud, reinforced with shattered wood that protruded outward in all directions. Her outstretched arms bore shattered manacles on her wrists, and the words *The Liberator* were carved into mud at her feet.

Guards defended City Hall's doors. They were portly men who carried wide-bladed, curved swords and were surprisingly alert despite the early hour. They stood behind a wooden barrier, haphazardly assembled from the dilapidated wood of the buildings that surrounded the square. The priest had said the Slave King handed out food from City Hall. Knowing that, the scene made sense. As logical as it was, the palpable blanket of depression in the area, coupled with the odor of unwashed and decaying bodies, was almost too much to bear.

Zeriel stepped through the square, but finding a hidden spot clear of bodies in front of City Hall proved to be impossible. He eventually made do with the roof of a one-story building a little south along the main road.

"Why'd they even send you here?" Jekjarah said as he stared out at the square. "These people will all be dead in a matter of weeks."

"It doesn't matter. The job is the job."

Jekjarah scoffed at that and disappeared.

Zeriel settled into the quiet murmur of his voices and watched City Hall for the next few hours. The moon—which traveled the sky from south to north each day—rose over the southern wall of the city indicating morning had come. The bodies in front of the hall stirred at the moon's light. Some moved through those still asleep on the cobblestone. They stole anything of value from those not conscious or able to stop them. Scuffles broke out when someone would fight against their robber.

Others pressed against the barrier in front of City Hall. People awoke like the coming of rain—a few here and there at first, then increasingly more until they'd all awoken. As the crowd grew, they flooded toward the barrier and abandoned their squabbles and thievery to jockey for position as close to the barrier as possible.

The crowd evolved into a single organism. Chaotic movements unified into an undulating mass. Their cries melded into one desperate voice that didn't pause or take a breath. Seeing this, the guards drew their swords, which kept most of the crowd from rushing the barrier. One of the guards banged on the doors, his eyes locked on the crowd. The action excited the organism and caused waves of movement to gain speed through it. Its voice increased in pitch and volume.

The doors burst open, and thirty men flooded out. Each one dressed as a Shyal city guard. Some of the uniforms were too big for their wearers, others too small. They seemed to have chosen them at random, then refused to trade for a better fit.

Their display was clearly meant to impart awe and fear in the crowd, and for the most part, it did. To Zeriel, though, they just looked like children playing city guard.

The crowd organism settled into silence and subtle waves of

anticipation flowed through it. A man, taller than the other guards around him and dressed in a helmetless set of golden plate armor, stepped through the doors. The armor he wore had intricate patterns worked into it, and the edges of the plate flared out into elaborate wedged flourishes. Jewels were inlaid into the patterns of the plates which made it sparkle in the light of the white vine lanterns of the square. As impressive as it looked, there was little protection a ceremonial suit of armor like that could have provided.

The crowd cheered and pressed into the barrier further, requiring the guards to shore it up and drive them back. The man in the golden armor raised his hand and the square fell silent.

"Today is the eighty-sixth day since The Liberator helped us win our freedom." He pointed to the statue in the square and the crowd cheered. They fell silent again when he dropped his hand. "And it's the eighty-sixth day that I, King Mandias, ensure all among us can live full lives with our freedom! Now eat and be made full!"

Another cheer rose from the crowd. Then, as if on cue, another group exited the hall and parted around the Slave King as he walked back inside. Each new person carried a basket of a different kind of food. Zeriel watched as they threw the food at the crowd as one would throw food at a captive wild animal. The organism descended on it and roiled forward as it tried to taste a small piece of this man's scraps.

Within moments the food was consumed, the servers and guards had retreated into City Hall, and the crowd had devoured every crumb. The once congealed organism of humanity disintegrated, its remains spreading through the streets of the Guild District.

Zeriel climbed down from his perch and into a back alley. He stepped into the street to mix in with the other dispossessed masses. Forced to push against the flow of bodies, he made his way to the square. The aftermath of the chaos lay strewn on the cobblestone in the form of trampled scraps of vegetables and fruit. Some of the most pathetic of the city's residents picked at the leftovers and fingered them into their mouths.

A smashed bit of tomato caught Zeriel's eye, and it took a quick motion to grab it from the street before someone else snatched it up. The tomato was clearly rotten. The smell could have given it away on its own, but close inspection revealed the telltale black spots ringed with white mold.

"This might be the easiest assassination job you've ever accepted," Jekjarah said as he stared at the rotten scrap. "They don't have more than a few weeks before they starve themselves to death."

"My guess is King Heyman doesn't want to be seen as a cold-hearted tyrant," Zeriel said, "which is why he hasn't sent troops into the city." A few of the people near him who dug at the stones for the last specs of food looked at him warily and scuttled away.

"If he'd sent his troops in at the beginning, wouldn't he have avoided all this suffering?" Jekjarah asked.

Zeriel fixed his eyes on City Hall and walked north through the streets in a circle around it.

"What about all those soldiers who would have died in clashes with the city's defenses? What about those who would have died fighting a strong, well-fed force of slaves whose morale was bolstered by their recent victory?" The north wing of City Hall had no doors, but there were two floors of windows that could serve as entry points if nothing better presented itself.

"Look down that alley." Jekjarah pointed at something at the edge of Zeriel's vision.

He followed the hallucinations gesture and saw the pile of corpses hidden there. If his eyes hadn't become so sensitive to the light, he wouldn't have seen them, and the darkness of the alley would have only exuded its foreboding effusion. Instead, it portended things to come.

"How many more alleys do you think are piled high with bodies?" Jekjarah asked.

"Just a moment ago you argued to let these people starve to death and be done with it. Now it sounds like you want to help them." The hallucination was often contradictory. As a reflection of his own mind,

Zeriel knew it was the outward manifestation of his own conflicting thoughts and emotions.

Turning a corner to the south gave him a view of the back of City Hall. There were utility doors and servants' entrances across that part of the building. They were all boarded up but for the largest set of doors at the center of the building. The doors were guarded by two out-of-place boys who couldn't be past their seventeenth year. Their uniforms hung from their thin frames. Zeriel's eyes locked on them as he continued southward, watching them for their level of alertness.

One of them saw him as he drew closer and grabbed his sword. "Oi! Ya get'n taa close now." His accent gave him away as a street urchin, about to graduate to Udulet.

The other guard perked up, eyed Zeriel, and readied his sword as well. They both put on their most intimidating faces, but its effects on Zeriel were as weak as a kitten's high-pitched mewling.

"S'rry, sirs," Zeriel said, skittering away with his head bowed. "I mean naw danger."

"I mean danger if I sees ya 'gain."

"Yas sir." Zeriel said, then picked up his pace and continued southward until he made another left turn around the corner of the south wing of the building.

Jekjarah appeared in front of him. "Found your infiltration point, then?"

"Looks like it."

"What next? Wait for night fall?"

"Yes," Zeriel said as he turned his gaze southward. Masses meandered through the streets, but conspicuously avoided the one heading further to the south. Each person who walked by looked down that street, then nervously hurried past.

"You're not honestly thinking about going there, are you?" Jekjarah said.

He met Jekjarah's eyes. "Why is everyone avoiding that road?"

The hallucination looked at the road, then back to Zeriel. "While interesting, it doesn't have anything to do with your mission. And you don't *actually* want to know what's down that road. You're just looking for an excuse to see her."

"Can't it be both?" Zeriel said as he turned to make his way through the intersection and down the road no one else would travel.

"It can be both," Jekjarah said, "but it's not."

CHAPTER FOUR

The roadway extended south toward the Lower Market. Before the slave uprising, it had been the economic center of the poor and middle class. It was also home to many shops that sold items of less than legal status. Given the way the people avoided the road, Zeriel expected to find some atrocity there.

As he approached the market, corpses appeared, lining the streets and confirming his suspicions. Arrows riddled some of the bodies, while deep gashes carved through others. They were long dead, and the stench of their decay took root in his nose.

This is what awaits you if you keep going, one of his voices said. His anxiety dragged them back to the surface. With great effort, he returned them to the back of his mind. As he continued, he spotted bodies tied to balconies, hung by their necks. More followed, impaled on large wooden spears. The voices grew louder, more insistent at the sight of it all.

By the time he cleared his mind, he noticed a wooden structure in the road ahead. It was well-constructed, with thick spikes pointing outward in front. The heads of four men peered above the barrier, standing guard with far more diligence than had been displayed by the Slave King's cronies. Zeriel stopped, called on the shadows to cover him, then swept to the side, pressing against the shops there. Covered in a blanket of shadows, Zeriel pushed forward undetected.

"I have to admit," Jekjarah said next to him, "this is a handy trick."

As he got close to the barrier, Zeriel heard the guards talking. They were bored and engaged in the kind of vapid conversation meant to pass the time. They were more diligent than slaves, yes, but still not disciplined enough to keep Zeriel out. He found a gap at the edge of the barrier, no doubt there to make sure they didn't trap themselves inside while keeping everyone else out.

Zeriel slipped through the gap and continued, the guards never once aware of his presence. The Lower Market's shops and inns, usually run-down, looked loved and cared for compared to the other districts. Scorch marks on the walls of those buildings closest to the barrier were the only exceptions.

After he got some distance from the barrier, he noticed the stores here had been repurposed into housing, and large empty lots dotted the roadsides between the buildings. They'd traditionally been left to rot with the displaced and addicted but were now gardens and animal pens. Each one had workers tending to them, actual smiles on their faces. Bright white vine lanterns illuminated the streets, all trimmed perfectly. The tragedy of the slave riots seemed to have inspired the residents of the Lower Market to create a thriving community. One they probably would never have considered otherwise.

Deeper inside the district, Zeriel watched the locals moving about the streets with purpose. Their clothes had the worn and patched look common among the working class of the city, but each had the posture of nobles. They seemed happy, but more than that, they looked proud of what they'd built.

A quick turn into an alley allowed him to release the shadows and change out of his disguise. It would do him no good to look like one of the poor souls outside of the Lower Market. He moved to step out but paused when he noticed several people greeting each other. Warm smiles stretched across their faces, and they exchanged even warmer greetings. These residents were too closely knit to ignore an outsider's presence. He had to change his approach, so he turned and stalked back through the alleys, then over rooftops. Without his powers to assist him with his sneaking his limited skills became painfully obvious. Still, he managed to reach his destination, drop from a roof top, and land in a nearby alley. As he approached the front of the building that was his destination, he saw a sign hung above its entrance. It swung lazily in the slight breeze that moved through the streets. He'd seen the sign many times before. The words he'd scratched into the old wood years ago read *The Pick and Shovel.* The crude drawing of a pick and shovel crossing each other was carved next to those words. A light push on the door revealed that it was unlocked even at this early hour, so Zeriel stepped inside.

The interior appeared just as he expected. A bar stood on one side with bottles of drink and clean glasses on shelves behind it. Tables filled the rest of the room, and a fireplace sat in the far corner. Three people Zeriel knew all too well were inside. Aketen, a Donian man, worked his way through the tables, taking down chairs and setting them on the floor. The brown vest he wore over black trousers did nothing to cover the green hue of his skin. Faded coin-sized yellow circles dotted his cheeks, chest, and arms, and his deep purple hair was shaved into a short mohawk.

Behind the bar were two women. The first—her name was Pihua-nata—scrubbed the bar top. She was also a Donian, and Aketen's wife. She wore a long-sleeved blue dress with a rope holding a leather pouch tied around her waist. Her dark green skin had small yellow circles even more faded than her husband's and her light purple hair hung in dreadlocks to the small of her back. The high cheekbones of her face were sharp and accentuated the striking gold color of her eyes.

The other woman behind the bar was Lavel. She organized the items on the shelves behind the bar, and when she spun around to help Pihuanata, Zeriel's heart raced at the sight of her. The soft curves of her tan face, framed by her auburn hair, which fell just below her shoulders, were burned into Zeriel's memory.

As she reached out to wipe down the farthest edge of the bar, Zeriel remembered the first time he glimpsed her in her bed chambers, reaching out across her own four-poster bed to smooth out her sheets. The silk gown she wore then gave her an elegant air, and it was in that moment Zeriel fell in love with her.

Lavel noticed him standing there and spun toward the door with a smile. The expression made Zeriel's ears burn. When she recognized him, her mouth dropped into a deep frown. "I should have known *you'd* take the contract."

The Donians stopped their work and turned to see who Lavel had addressed. Aketen recognized him and stepped closer to Zeriel, but cautiously stayed out of reach.

"Why are you here?" Aketen asked.

Zeriel glared at him for a moment, then turned and addressed Lavel. "How did you know about my contract?"

"I asked you a question, Zeriel!" the man shouted.

Zeriel looked at him casually. "And I ignored you." He stepped all the way into the inn, grabbed a chair from on top of the closest table, spun it around to set it on the floor and sat.

Aketen snarled and clenched his fists.

"We paid for the contract," Lavel said, "that's how I knew."

"I was told King Heyman paid for it."

"Ha!" Lavel scoffed. "You think that self-righteous man would care about what happens inside these walls?" She threw her rag on the bar. "He's maintained the siege for months, just waiting for us to starve to death in here."

"You don't look like you're starving," Zeriel said. "In fact, it looks the Lower Market is thriving."

Pihuanata stepped next to Lavel. "We banded together after the riots broke out and kept most of the fighting on the outskirts of the district, but we weren't completely untouched."

Zeriel remembered the scorched buildings he saw on his way into the district.

"As things died down, we allowed a few families from the northern districts into the market, then we started to build the barriers. Mandias seized control of the rest of this city and organized the rioters in a matter of days. We had our barriers up by then and were forced to spend the rest of the month defending our territory. Then, the sun rose into the sky, and they had no more food to steal. They scavenged, stretched out into the rest of the city, and picked it clean. When there was nothing left to scavenge, Mandias took control of the food supply to keep them under his control."

"They can't have much food left," Lavel said. "And when what they have is gone, the Lower Market is the only place to turn. We weren't sure we could hold out against an assault from every hungry and desperate rioter left. So, I proposed hiring a Te Et Sha assassin to the council."

"The council?" Zeriel asked.

"We formed it in the early days. We knew we needed leadership, but didn't want power consolidated into a single person. The three of us, a few other business owners from the market, and several northern landowners who helped us plant our gardens, formed the council as a solution."

"And you told this council to hire the Te Et Sha to kill the Slave King?"

Aketen laughed. "Told you *Slave King* would catch on," he said to Pihuanata, who rolled her eyes while he selected a chair of his own and sat.

Zeriel remained focused on Lavel. "Don't you think ending the food distributions early would just cause the masses to descend on the market sooner?"

"Mandias used to distribute food three times a day. Now it's just once in the morning, and the rioters still won't come near us. Without their leader, we expect they'll surrender to the King's army."

"And if they don't?" Zeriel asked.

"Then we seize control and negotiate the city's surrender."

"That's not a bad plan," Jekjarah said from behind him. "You should just kill the Slave King and take her away from here, though. If you really love her, I mean. Things could get very dangerous if they don't go how she thinks."

Zeriel spoke the hallucination's words before thinking. "When I complete the mission, I want you to come with me for a while. At least until things settle down and the danger passes."

"Go with you?" Lavel said, her nose curling as if she smelled something rotten. "I wouldn't even be here if it weren't for you." She stepped out from around the bar and came closer to him. "I'm motherless. Fatherless. Stripped of my birthright and forced to hide away thousands of miles from my home." She paused, inches from his face. "You did that to me. So why would I *ever* go anywhere with you?"

Just as Zeriel opened his mouth to reply, the door to the inn opened and two men entered. The way Lavel's body stiffened at their appearance told Zeriel he should be ready for a fight.

CHAPTER FIVE

The men were taller than Zeriel, and more muscular by several degrees. They moved with the confidence of men who got what they wanted through violence. By the self-satisfied smirks they wore, they looked forward to the opportunity. One of them had his long brown hair in a tight ponytail and looked like the smarter of the two, though that was like comparing an ant to a slightly smarter ant. They shared the same soft jaw and round facial features, a stark contrast to their large physique.

Jekjarah appeared behind the two. "Oho!" he said. "Looks like we've got some excitement in our future."

Lavel turned to face them as Aketen stood next to Zeriel. "What are you two doing here?" she said. "I thought I told you to jump headfirst into a latrine?"

"Funny," said the one with the ponytail. "Your time's up. Are you going to leave peacefully, or are we going another way with this?"

"I hope we go the other way," the other man said.

"Get out, Dreth," Aketen said, "and take your idiot of a brother with you."

"Who are you calling an idiot!" the brother said, stepping forward, but was stopped with a hand to his chest from the other one.

"Now, now, Koth. Don't let these weaklings get to you." He dropped his hand and leveled gazes at Aketen and then Lavel. "This community you've built respects you, and that's the only reason I'm giving you the chance to walk away."

Jekjarah's face protruded from Dreth's chest, a maniacal grin stretched wide across his features. "*Slaughter* these two! How could she ignore you after she sees how powerful you've become?" He bounced his eyebrows in emphasis.

Zeriel gritted his teeth in response, his muscles aching from the strain of holding still.

"You know I can't do that," Lavel said, straightening her posture.

"Then it looks like we're going the other way," Koth said.

"Kill them!" Jekjarah said again, his face twisted unnaturally in frightening proportions.

The younger brother stepped forward with a grin of his own and reached out to grasp the innkeeper.

Aketen moved, but Zeriel was faster. He snatched the man's wrist, twisted and pulled, then rolled his body, bending the man's arm in a way it shouldn't. As he rolled the man over his shoulder, something popped. The thug screamed as his body slammed against the floor, cracking the wood around him. The impact knocked the wind out of the man and halted his screams.

"Yes!" Jekjarah screamed, sliding his head out of Dreth's chest and standing to the side. "Now *end* him!"

"You whore's bastard!" the criminal said. He lashed out, his large fist headed for Zeriel's face.

These two men thought they knew violence. They'd been using it to get what they wanted for years, obviously. But neither of them had met an assassin of the Te Et Sha. They couldn't be blamed for underestimating him because of his lean musculature. Neither had seen what those muscles could do. Memories of his friends who died painfully from the effects of the drug that had strengthened him flashed in his mind.

Ignorance would be the end of these brothers.

Zeriel dodged the punch, then delivered an elbow to the ridge of his nose where cartilage met bone. The man's face crunched under his strike and fluid exploded out of Dreth's nose. He fell back several steps as he tried to cry out but choked on his own blood instead.

"The beautiful gore!" Jekjarah yelled. He spun like a child in the rain as the droplets in the air passed through him. "Let me feel the warmth of its touch! Let me bask in the iron perfume in the air!"

The hallucination's glee ran through Zeriel like lightning, driving him to kill. In the blink of an eye he had daggers in both his hands.

"Stop!" Lavel cried.

Her voice froze him in place, the point of his dagger a hair's breadth from parting the skin of Dreth's neck. Simultaneously, Jekjarah winked out of existence and his voice cut short.

The innkeeper approached the thug, whose eyes were frozen to the knife still at his neck. "Get out. And take your worthless brother with you." Her voice was as hard as steel, drawing the man's eyes to her. "Come back again and I'll let my assassin finish the job."

The goon's expression filled with fear, and he nodded tersely. Zeriel stepped back and sheathed his daggers, then took up a casual posture. Dreth lifted his brother's unconscious body off the ground and stepped out the door.

Once the two were gone, Lavel turned to Zeriel, a strength and defiance in her face he recognized from years prior. "Now go do the job we're paying you for."

Pihuanata stepped close, eyes worried, and grabbed Lavel's arm to pull her away. "Maybe it's best to leave this one alone." She gave him the look so many others had given after they'd seen his bloodlust rise to the surface.

Lavel pulled her arm from the woman's grip and snapped her head toward the Donian woman. "You think he'll murder me?" She turned back around and slapped the assassin across the face as hard as she could.

"No!" Aketen yelled, rushing to her defense.

The innkeeper raised her hand at Aketen and he stopped short. Zeriel looked at her.

"See?" she said. "I'm the only job he'll never finish." The Donians stood in stunned silence as Lavel spun on her feet and walked into the storage room behind the bar.

Zeriel walked to the door and opened it partway, then paused. He turned his head around to address the Donians. "Thank you for looking out for her all these years," he said. "I know it was a lot to ask of you at the time. I'll do what I can to keep this place safe after the job's done." He stepped out of the *The Pick and Shovel*.

"I can't believe you let them live," Jekjarah said. He stood just to the right of the door, leaning against the outer wall of the inn and idly picking his teeth with a sliver of wood. Zeriel eyed him for a moment as he walked past him. The hallucination pushed himself off the wall and followed. "So, unsatisfying."

CHAPTER SIX

Mandias's cronies were inside the town hall, laughing and roughhousing so loudly that it seeped from the back door of City Hall and into the street. It had been going on for hours, and they'd left those boys outside to guard the doors and listen to the fun instead of inviting them in. The moon had set at least an hour ago, and the sounds were just then beginning to die down. That was Zeriel's cue.

"Me hatin' guard dooty," one of the boys said. He eyed the closed door longingly, taking in the sounds coming from it. "We miss da goo part."

"Quit your 'plaining," the other said. "Wotation better dan guard dooty all time."

"I know. Jus wish I drunk now."

They laughed and continued their complaints while Zeriel watched from ten feet away. He'd used his powers to blanket himself, crouched at the base of a tree near the exit. There was nowhere else to go after the events at *The Pick and Shovel*, so he'd sat by that tree since late morning. Without the dark mist around him, the white vine lanterns the boys had set up would have blazed like tiny suns.

He stood up and the familiar agony of stiff legs greeted him. He'd trained to manage the pain, and experience had taught him the best way to work out the stiffness without moving. Thanks to his powers, most of that training seemed obsolete. Zeriel brazenly shifted back and forth directly in front of the guards, slowly working out the stiffness.

His instincts screamed against the brazen movements, but with his powers for cover, they'd never notice.

"Dijya see that?" one of them said, pointing in Zeriel's direction.

Jekjarah appeared next to the boys. "I guess they did notice you." He glided in front of them as they inspected Zeriel's hiding spot. Each squinted as if they saw a hint of him there in the darkness. "He's right there, you morons!" Jekjarah pointed at Zeriel wildly, spinning in circles, then running to shove a finger in Zeriel's face. "Right here!" he said, then ran back and pretended to slap their faces. His hand passed through their heads. "Come on you cave slugs! He's right there!"

The sounds of the revelry inside the building died down, which was Zeriel's cue to move. He braced his foot on a stone in the ground, pushed off hard, then sped toward the boys. Jekjarah winked out of existence at his movement.

"What is—" one of them started to say, but Zeriel slid by, slashed his throat, then retreated into the darkness just outside the light of their lanterns.

"Dunno," the other one said. He didn't notice his dying comrade, instead frantically scanning the darkness around him. "I tawt I saw sumtin' moove 'round jus' now. Maybe moth crossin' da lanterns." He paused for a second, fixated at the spot by the tree where Zeriel had been. Eventually he gave up and faced the other guard. His expression turned confused when he saw the boy. "Ket?"

Ket grasped at his throat, struggling to speak. His face went pure white, as blood seeped through his fingers.

"Ket!" the guard said, as he caught the boy's corpse while it fell to the ground, dead.

Zeriel advanced again, silent as the wind, and this time made sure the boy he'd left alive saw him. "Where is Mandias?"

The boy tried to follow Zeriel's shadow as he clawed at the sword on his hip. "Who is yoo?"

Zeriel sped past, slicing his upper thigh. The boy cried out in pain. Zeriel spoke from the boy's other side to increase his confusion.

"Where is Mandias?"

The boy wore terror on his face—an expression as familiar to Zeriel as the clouds in the sky. "He be in'ide!"

He flashed past the boy again and sliced his upper arm.

The boy cried out again and abandoned his sword to hold up his arms as shields instead.

"Where inside?" Zeriel asked from yet another location.

"N—north wig. O—on two lebel." He cried as urine soaked his trousers.

Zeriel exited his black mists, letting them fall away behind him as he approached the boy, fully visible in the illumination of the white vine lanterns. "Thank you," he said as he took a position next to the terrified boy and slammed a dagger into the side of his head. He unceremoniously ripped the blade away. The boy's corpse fell on top of his friend's, and Zeriel wiped his weapon clean on the corpse's uniform, then returned it to its sheath.

Shadows pulled in around Zeriel again as he activated his powers and cracked open the door and peered inside.

The main hall was vast, longer than it was wide. Its walls had three-foot-high wooden molding at the bottom and wallpaper with painted flowers of every kind that covered the rest of it. White vine lanterns were mounted to wooden arches attached to the ceiling. Their bright luminance drove away the dark so completely that there was practically nothing for Zeriel to draw from.

A table covered in food stood in the center of the vast main hall. Various meats steamed among roasted vegetables, raw fruit, and steaming pies. Goblets sat on the tables as well, golden with jewels that glittered in the bright light. Some were knocked on their side, deep purple wine spilled out on the table before them. The men and women inside were either too drunk to notice him or passed out completely, their faces covered in grease and food particles, their stolen clothes stained with grease and wine. Those who weren't unconscious either ate alone or paired up and copulated in the open.

When he saw the state of the people surrounding this building, Zeriel thought they were weeks away from running out of food. Looking at the scene laid before him, he wondered how the food had lasted this long.

He entered the building, surprised by the brightness inside, so he dragged the darkness inside with him. The door cut it off as it closed. He'd seen his reflection when covered in mist, exposed by the light. Those inside would see a large black mass, leaking to the ground like mist from the side of a mountain.

Those in the hall aware enough to notice watched him lazily, rubbed their eyes, then shrugged their shoulders, and went back to their debauchery. Zeriel remembered a time in his life when a gathering like this would have been enticing. He'd been a boy then, and a decade of blood taught him to value other things.

With a glance, Zeriel saw that the north wing was down the hall to his left. He entered the hallway and felt boredom set in from the ease of the infiltration. His mind drifted and he imagined a farm nestled against the base of a hill with a forest on three sides. He tilled a field in this daydream as Lavel tended to the house with their son and daughter. They lived miles from anything and everyone, with nothing but their family and their animals for company.

"Quit your dreaming, assassin," Jekjarah said, walking backward in front of him. "You've got work to do."

The hallucination was right. White vines were tied into the corners where the walls met the ceiling. Zeriel didn't change his strategy, though. A dark mass moving through a hallway would be disorienting to anyone who might come across him. It would give him ample time to strike first.

The theory was proven right when he arrived at the stairway leading to the second floor and was stopped short by one of the guards on his way down the steps. This guard was a gray-haired man later in years but thick muscled. His uniform fit perfectly, but he appeared too uncomfortable in it to have worn one before. Even he stopped short at the sight of Zeriel's cloaked form which gave Zeriel all the time he needed to pull out a single poison needle from his belt and throw it. The needle sunk deep into the man's neck.

Surprise flashed onto the man's face as he touched his neck and the needle in it. Then his eyes rolled into the back of his head, and he dropped. Zeriel shifted to the side, caught the corpse, and found an alcove to hide it in.

He faced no other resistance as he glided up the steps and into the empty hallway of the north wing's second level. The stairs dropped him off a few feet from where the hallway turned right to follow the north wall of the building. Zeriel peered around the corner to find two men standing guard in front of one of the doors.

"Kill them," Jekjarah whispered from behind. "Let me bathe in their blood."

This time, Zeriel suppressed his euphoria and reached into one of the pouches on his belt. He pulled out a small round object, wrapped in glued paper with a single wick protruding from it. With his other hand he produced a small V-shaped metal tool with flint on one end and the other bent to point inward. A few quick squeezes of the tool sent sparks at the wick, setting it on fire.

Zeriel waited until the flame almost touched the paper then he rolled it on the floor toward the guards. As it advanced, the flame on the wick contacted the ball and it sprayed smoke with a hiss. The guards recoiled as it rolled close to them.

"What is that?" one guard said.

"I—" They both collapsed to the floor, unconscious.

Zeriel slid around the corner and toward the cloud without concern. His body—enhanced by training and the Te Et Sha's enhancements—could handle the smoke for several minutes without passing out. Stepping over the bodies he ignored the slight dizziness from inhaling the smoke and entered the room the men were guarding.

The room was dark except for a white vine lantern on a bedside table with a thick muting cloth that reduced the plant's illumination.

That dim glow was enough for Zeriel to see perfectly. What he saw was a neatly kept bedroom with a simple down mattress on a wooden frame on one wall, and a wardrobe on the other. Under the covers was Mandias, the Slave King, sleeping peacefully.

Not every job delivers their targets to him so easily, but when they did Zeriel never hesitated to receive that gift quickly and with great pleasure. This time was no different as he swiftly slipped a dagger from its sheath and dashed forward to plunge it into the form under the covers. He aimed for the part of his target's chest that housed the man's lungs.

When the blade entered his target, it didn't feel like it was piercing flesh. It felt like the wicker of the dummies he'd trained on as a young man learning to become an assassin. Zeriel ripped the covers off the bed to reveal a humanoid-shaped bundle of wicker.

The slightest shift in the air of the room set the hair on the back of Zeriel's neck on end. With all the strength and speed he could muster, Zeriel planted a hand on the bed and vaulted over it—but not before a line of fire ran up his right calf. Weapons were in his hands before he landed. He landed on the far side of the bed, rolling imperfectly to land on his feet. Mandias rounded the bed with a knife in his hand. A line of Zeriel's blood ran down the length of the Slave King's blade.

The pain in his calf flared at the sight of it and he inspected the cut. It ran vertically from just below the back of his knee to just above his ankle. Dark red rivulets ran down to the floor, and he left footprints behind at each step.

"So, my informant was right. Those bastards in the Lower Market hired an assassin."

"It was a waste of money," Zeriel said. "You'll starve to death soon anyway. They should have just let you die from your own incompetence."

"Ha! You think I wasn't ready to storm that place already?" Mandias advanced, holding his weapon at the ready. "What they have will be mine soon enough."

"Not if you're dead," Zeriel said.

Feet pounded in the hallway outside and shook the room. Mandias smiled. "Someday, but not tonight." The footsteps grew louder.

"Sorry if I cut our conversation short," Zeriel said, "but it sounds like the time for conversation is over."

Mandias's face settled into a hard expression. "Indeed," he said, seriously.

Zeriel draped himself in shadows. The action stopped Mandias in his tracks, giving Zeriel the opening he needed to rush the man and deliver a single blow to his chest, through the junction of his fourth and fifth ribs and into the apex of his heart. A quick twist of his dagger sliced into the right ventricle.

With the job done, Zeriel stepped back and let his power fall away. Mandias stared at him with shock on his face. Then the Slave King crumpled into a dead pile on the floor.

The door to the room burst open and guards flooded into the room. They attacked Zeriel without hesitation, but he called the darkness around him once more, creating an explosion of black mist that filled the room. The attackers hesitated, giving him an opening to speed through his foes.

"Yes! Bathe me in their blood!" Jekjarah cried out, appearing among the guards. He mimed the act of washing his body with arterial spray.

The euphoria took over, and as Jekjarah screamed in ecstasy around him, Zeriel let the emotion wash over him. Every minor vibration of the blade, as it passed through flesh, transferred through the hilt and into his hands, and the sensation made him giddy.

Jekjarah mirrored his emotions, releasing a murderous laugh in frenzied pitches. "A—hahaha!"

The hallucination's glee, combined with the rich scent of iron flooding the air, overwhelmed him with euphoria.

"He's dead, and he's dead, and *he's* dead!" Jekjarah said in a sing-song voice as he danced through the corpses on the floor.

The invisible flight of the enemy's souls as they left their bodies intoxicated Zeriel, and he lost himself in the drug of his own carnage.

In a matter of moments, Mandias and fifteen men and boys were corpses on the floor. A deep breath brought Zeriel back to himself. Jekjarah faded slowly and the shadows covering him melted away. Blood covered Zeriel from head to toe, dripping like macabre rain, softly pattering against the wood at his feet. A rectangle of light from the white vine lanterns in the hallway extended through the open door of the room, illuminating the aftermath of his work.

Zeriel paused at the door and turned around to survey the corpses. "Look on my works, and despair."

CHAPTER SEVEN

The way out of City Hall was unrestricted since Zeriel had just killed every guard inside the building. As he passed the now-sleeping revelers in the main hall, it became clear that Mandias had committed all his fighters to his defense.

On a whim, Zeriel wove his way through the sleeping bodies of the main hall and up to the doors at the front of the building. A strong kick sent the doors slamming open and crashing into the two guards just outside. A jolt of pain shot through Zeriel's leg where Mandias sliced him.

With a spin and flash of his daggers, Zeriel dropped both guards. They fell, leaving the building completely unguarded and unlocked. Most of the poor souls sleeping out in the square woke from the commotion and watched him fearfully.

"Your King Mandias is dead." Zeriel's voice echoed off the buildings. "All of his guards are dead." He paused to let his words sink in. "Surrender to King Heyman. You may be forced back into slavery, but you'll be alive." He turned around and limped back inside the building, leaving the doors open. Some of those unconscious inside woke and stared at him in awe.

"Do you really think that'll make them come to their senses?" Jekjarah asked, walking next to him.

"Probably not," he replied openly. "But on the slight chance that it did, we won't have to worry about Lavel's safety for long."

By the time Zeriel opened the rear door of the main hall, he heard shouting voices and the shattering of wood announcing the destruction of the barrier in front of the building. He stepped through the rear door and left it open as well. People huddling in the alleys watched him closely, and, after he was far enough from the door, they descended on City Hall.

Eastward was the Tailings River, Zeriel's goal. If he was lucky, these vagabonds wouldn't have polluted the river with waste.

"Where are you going?" Jekjarah asked.

"To clean up."

"Shouldn't you be leaving? You finished the job."

Zeriel glanced at the hallucination. "Yes, I should. But I have something else to do first."

Jekjarah threw his hands up. "You're staying for her?"

"Of course," Zeriel said, matter-of-factly. "I told them I'd make sure she was safe." But the weight of fatigue pulled on his eyelids as the adrenaline wore off. He fought through the weariness, not thinking to cover himself in shadows, nor change into his disguise. Instead, he walked through the streets of Shyal talking to himself and leaving a trail of blood in the dirt behind him. The streets cleared quickly at the sight.

"So what?" Jekjarah said. "It's not like you owe them anything. You paid them to take Lavel in and help her with the inn. It was a simple transaction that ended years ago."

"That's not the point, Jek."

"I don't think you *have* a point, Zeriel."

He stopped to look the hallucination in his eyes. "I love her."

Jekjarah stepped closer, a stern expression on his face. "You do not."

On reflex Zeriel tried to punch the hallucination, but his hand passed through his head harmlessly. His shoulders dropped and he turned to keep walking. "You don't know anything," he said.

"I know everything you do, which means somewhere inside that head of yours you know that what you feel isn't love."

"Liar," Zeriel whispered. Jekjarah vanished, leaving the assassin to his business.

The Tailings River was at least sixty-five feet wide. A nearby stone bridge with two arching gaps for the river to flow through connected the Guild District with the Color District on the other side. Moss and other plant life glowed shades of green and their shifting light emanated from the clear water. Even the slaves knew better than to desecrate the beauty of this river. Its banks were lined with grass and other bushes, left to add their orange and purple lights to contrast the green between them.

Zeriel wasted no time, shuffling awkwardly down the riverbank and into the water. Washing blood off was a slow, grueling task, forcing him to scrub it from the deep cracks in his skin. When he finished, he climbed back up the riverbank, sat at its edge, removed his pack, and set it in front of him. Reaching inside, he removed a salve, some bandages, a needle, and a length of silk thread.

Every mission ended this way, tending to the aftermath, confronting the consequences of his weaknesses. He fell into a trance, his hands moving purely from muscle memory, as he sewed up the cut on his thigh, then applied the salve and tied the cotton bandage around it. With that done, Zeriel limped his way down the riverbank and back toward the Lower Market. It didn't take long to find the barrier on the eastern edge of the district where it met the river. A tall fence had been built all the way to the riverbank. It turned from there to follow the river to the only bridge from the Lower Market into the color district. Four people stood guard at another spike barrier on the bridge.

Cloaking himself in shadows once again, Zeriel slipped past the barrier and the guards undetected. This time he pushed on with less caution, unconcerned if the residents of the district happened to see a shadow moving along the wall and at this late hour there were few people outside to see him. In minutes he was back in front of *The Pick and Shovel*, pushing open the door and stepping inside.

He expected to see those inside closing for the night. Instead, he saw a woman behind the bar, dressed in close fitting black leather armor, her arms tightly around Lavel's neck with a dagger held to her throat. The woman towered over the innkeeper, tall enough to rest her chin on top of the shorter woman's head. Her hair was cut to a few fingers in length, and her smile, coupled with the wide eyes she displayed, had a manic air. Her name was Lushame Ori, and she was one of the most skilled assassins in the Te Et Sha.

To the side of the bar, Zeriel saw feet protruding from behind it wearing thin leather shoes. The legs above those shoes had the dark green skin that Zeriel assumed belonged to Pihuanata.

Further inside the inn, near the fireplace, was another person he recognized. Denetek Ori, another top assassin, and Lushame's twin brother. Denetek wore a black leather outfit to match his sister and was standing over Aketen. The Donian man lay prone, propped up on his elbows, staring at the tip of the assassin's sword, leveled inches from his face.

The Ori twins, as they were called, were known to be ruthless and even more insane than Zeriel, which was saying something.

Finally, sitting casually at one of the tables, was Veshet, the top assassin in the Te Et Sha. He was heavily muscled for an assassin and even sitting, his posture communicated imminent violence.

Fear, rather than respect, was his tool of choice, which explained his desire to build his frame. All members of the Te Et Sha knew Veshet would become their leader one day, meaning few ever thought about crossing him.

Zeriel wondered why the future leader of his order was in *The Pick and Shovel* and why he needed the Ori twins for backup.

A half-eaten meat pie sat on the table in front of Veshet and he was in the process of spooning a bite into his mouth when Zeriel arrived. He stopped mid-bite and met Zeriel's eyes with a smile, then set his spoon back in his bowl. "You see, Denetek. I told you he'd come back here for her."

"Who would've thought he cared so much about this random wench?" Lushame said.

Jekjarah appeared in the center of the room, looking among the three newcomers. "This is bad, Zeriel. Just one of them could kill you in a one-on-one fight, even with your powers."

Working hard to control his emotions, Zeriel pushed aside Jekjarah's comment, as true as it was. "Let her go Lushame," Zeriel said, "or you die right here, right now."

The woman let out a wild laugh. "Big words from the Worst One."

"The Worst One," Veshet said as if tasting the words. He wiped his face with a napkin from his lap and tossed it on the table as he stood. "I wonder if that's still the case." He was taller than Zeriel, and the way Veshet looked down at him made him want to shy away. "He's Plaxes's champion, after all."

"Obe help you, Zeriel," Jekjarah said. "How does he know who Plaxes is?"

Zeriel couldn't keep the shock off his face, which only made Veshet smile more deeply.

"I don't care whose champion he is," Denetek said, "or what powers they've given him. Let's murder him now and be done with it." He made a move to approach Zeriel, but Veshet raised his hand, and the male twin froze.

"Interesting," Veshet said to Zeriel. "You look confused."

"What do you want from me?"

"To kill you," Veshet said. "I thought that was obvious. The only question is—" he gestured toward Lavel, "will I have to slaughter this pretty little thing and her friends, or will you surrender willingly."

"You can't execute me," Zeriel said. "Not without permission."

Veshet extended his hand, a small piece of wood sitting on his outstretched palm. It erupted into a small flame, burning the wood to charcoal and rising to hover above his palm. A small shiver rippled through Veshet's body as he said, "You think you're the only one who's changed, Zeriel? I don't need anyone else's permission to do what I want. Take what I want. *Build* what I want."

Shock jolted through Zeriel; somehow this man had powers too, and he saw murder in his eyes. It was clear that if he hesitated, he'd die. Zeriel pulled the shadows toward him. He stopped when he heard Lavel take a sharp breath. A line of blood from the shallow slice Lushame's knife made in her neck ran down her chest. He released his power and locked eyes with Lushame. His options were limited, and try as he might, he couldn't think of a way out of this.

"I'm Deavust's champion," Veshet said as he let the flame extinguish. He paused as if waiting for a reaction to his comment.

Zeriel finally broke eye contact with Lushame to look at Veshet. "So?" he said as he shrugged his shoulders.

"You really don't know what that means, do you? Plaxes has kept you in the dark." He laughed heartily. "I guess that's her specialty though, isn't it?"

Jekjarah planted his hands on his hips, sticking his nose in the air. "I told you she couldn't be trusted."

"Last chance, Worst One. Surrender, or everyone here dies with you."

His hand crept toward his poisoned needles, stopping just short of snatching one from its pouch on his belt.

"Only the strong survive," he heard Lushame whisper from across the room. He eyed her for a second, then met Lavel's gaze.

Until he met her, he'd never felt the urge to save anyone. Her beauty had captivated him, and he knew then that he'd die for her in an instant. It frightened him at first, but over the years he saw it as love. As he looked into her eyes, with all the anger and hatred burning behind them, he felt his resolve waver.

He turned his focus back to Veshet. Zeriel trained with him and the Ori twins as children. They were the top assassins in the Te Et Sha, and all three were sadists. This ruse to play on his feelings for Lavel was nothing more than a sick game. They were playing with their food.

Anger boiled up at that realization, solidifying something in Zeriel he hadn't felt before. He may be the Worst One, but he wouldn't—he couldn't—give these three the satisfaction they craved. If death was inevitable and he couldn't get out of this death trap, he'd go through it.

CHAPTER EIGHT

With a quick, smooth motion Zeriel snatched a poison needle from his belt and threw it at Lushame, aiming for her
right eye socket. The woman jerked her head at the last
moment, and the needle barely missed her face. She pushed Lavel away
and the two collapsed to the ground.

As he threw the needle, Zeriel summoned shadows with more force
than he'd exerted on his powers so far. They obeyed with a speed he
wasn't accustomed to and cloaked him as he dove to the floor. Veshet's
flames missed him by inches, but they were close enough to sear his
back.

Zeriel landed in a roll and kept moving, trying to disorient Veshet
with his shifting shadow. The assassin tracked his movements warily,
then reached out and shot columns of fire from his hands throughout
the inn. The flames' light exposed him. Veshet released his powers, his
breathing noticeably labored. He spotted Zeriel's cloak of shadows and
moved without hesitation.

As Zeriel dodged, he let his shadows evaporate—they were useless
in this environment. Veshet's speed was frightening, and before he
could react, a sharp pain cut across his right cheek. He hadn't even seen
when the assassin drew his blade.

Zeriel's lungs began to burn for air, feeding into a growing panic in
his gut. He didn't have time to think about it, though. Veshet was on
the attack, driving him back in a quick retreat. In his haste he didn't
notice the pincer attack Ori Twins had set up. They descended on him,

and he couldn't shift his momentum fast enough to avoid their strikes.

Just as he accepted defeat, two columns of flame shot toward him. He barely twisted his body in time and used his momentum to fall and roll out of the way. The right half of his body lit up with pain as he failed to avoid the blast completely.

The Ori Twins stopped mid-attack, but they couldn't avoid the flames either. Angry red burns covered their arms as they used them as shields against the heat.

"Damn it—Veshet!" Danetek screamed through heavy breathing. "You—almost killed—us!"

"Stay out of—the way you—idiots!" Veshet replied. "I can handle the—Worst One on my own."

Zeriel felt suffocated, understanding why his foes' breathing was labored. He struggled to fill his lungs with air, but no matter how much he managed to take in, it wasn't enough. Everyone in the burning building was doing nothing but fighting to catch their breath.

Denetek looked at his sister, communicated something silently between them, then spun toward Veshet. "We have—to leave! This— place is com—coming down!"

Smoke filled the inn now, and through that smoke Zeriel saw glimpses of the burning walls of the structure. He knew then that escape was impossible. He would die in that place.

Parts of the ceiling fell to the floor and sent slivers of burning wood in all directions. On instinct, Zeriel called on what few shadows existed around him, made even deeper by the stark light of the fire. They provided him with some strange sort of comfort he couldn't explain.

Without a reply from Veshet, the Ori twins abandoned the fight and stumbled toward the front door. Veshet held an intense, piercing gaze on Zeriel as he flailed his arms trying to call up more flames. Thankfully, none appeared. A frustrated expression grew across his face before he abandoned his power and lunged in a wild attack. Just then a huge beam covered in flames smashed into the floor between them. It crushed tables and chairs and sent flaming debris in all directions. Zeriel dove backward to avoid it, but another beam fell just as he did, slamming on top of him and pinning his left foot to the floor.

When Zeriel spotted Veshet again he was breathing frantically, clawing in Zeriel's direction while Denetek pulled him toward the exit. "You'll die—burning, Worst—One!" Veshet screamed as the twin dragged him out of the doomed building.

Movement to Zeriel's right caught his attention. He twisted and saw Aketen lifting Pihuanata's limp body over his shoulder as he hurried toward the storage room behind the bar. There was an exit to the alley that way, and Zeriel felt some relief seeing the two heading to safety. The Donian man stopped and spun around, eyeing Zeriel intensely. A mix of unreadable emotions played over the man's face. Several heart-beats passed before Aketen's posture changed and he headed toward the exit. A sudden terror overcame him when he realized he hadn't known if Lavel had escaped, and the Donian was her only hope.

He sucked in a painful breath and screamed at Aketen, "Lavel!" The smoke tore at his throat.

The Donian man spared only the barest glance at Zeriel, then at Lavel's still form behind the bar, before disappearing out the back. Quick as the expression was, Zeriel still recognized the deep sadness that overcame the man's features.

Real fear took root in Zeriel as he twisted to find the spot Aketen had focused on. Lavel lay motionless on the floor there, though whether unconscious or dead, Zeriel couldn't tell. Auburn hair fell around her head in a tangled mess and a thin pool of blood anointed the side of her face.

Zeriel's eyes welled with tears as the darkness crept at the edges of his vision. If she wasn't dead already, she would be soon. Just as he would.

As he accepted his fate, his body relaxed and his pain began to fade. There was peace to death. It promised a reprieve from the voices and all the pain and humiliation of his illness. He let his mind ruminate on that peace, and on that secluded farm of his dreams. He was out in the fields again, preparing them for planting. Lavel stepped out of their modest cabin, sipping from a wooden cup. Their two children rushed outside through her legs, the boy chasing the girl around the fields their cabin was nestled in.

The vision darkened and his children vanished, fading away into nothing. Then Lavel disappeared while waving at him with a loving smile on her face, her long red hair flowing in the wind. The cabin changed from lived in and well-maintained to a lifeless husk, its skeleton askew and ready to collapse to the ground. Then it disappeared and the darkness closed in further. Finally, the fields turned fallow, showing no sign of human intervention.

Then, fading into view among that field, Plaxes stood looking at Zeriel. She wore a dress of shadows that shifted in the wind like mist. "Fool," she said.

A huge crash brought Zeriel out of his vision. Behind him, a beam had fallen and destroyed a huge portion of the outer wall. A final glance at Jekjarah showed the man fading away, fiercely trying to communicate through silent screams. A strong, cool wind struck Zeriel just as the darkness took him.

CHAPTER NINE

The soft crackling of just-burned wood penetrated the darkness, waking Zeriel's mind. The agony of fresh burns across his body shocked his mind into clarity, while the sting of acrid smoke filled his nostrils, biting into his sinuses.

He blinked awake, surrounded by ash and blackened wood. Most of the structure had crumbled to ash, but some remained blackened, holding the shape of its unburned form while red embers glowed from within their deep cracks. Smoke curled into the air all around him.

His mind flashed back to the fight with Veshet and the Ori Twins. *How am I alive?*

Zeriel raised himself onto his elbows, battling through the searing pain of his burns. A charred beam lay across his legs. He gripped the beam and heaved it aside, pushing through the pain. Once free, he forced himself to his feet.

Jekjarah materialized in front of him. "I thought we were dead."

Zeriel winced, the slicing pain of his cracking burns making it difficult to stand. "So did I." He glanced around, taking in the carnage. *The Pick and Shovel* lay in a pile of wood and ash. Small fires dotted the floor around him. The shops next to the inn had caught fire, their frames still burning. Lines of people stretched out toward the river while buckets of water passed between them. A single man directed the work, shouting orders and encouragement. Luckily, Veshet and the Ori Twins were nowhere in sight.

"They must have assumed that you died in the fire," Jekjarah said.

Zeriel inspected the spot where he'd fallen unconscious. A perfect circle of mostly unburned wood surrounded it. "I should have."

Jekjarah wove through the remains to see the unburned section of the floor. "You think *she* could have—"

"You!" said the man leading the firefighting efforts. He fixed Zeriel with a hard stare. "What are you doing in there? We need every man on the buckets if we're going to save the market!"

"Coming!" Zeriel called back. He watched as the man turned away and continued directing the others. With the man's attention elsewhere, Zeriel swayed unsteadily on his feet as he exited through the back of the building. He sought out a place to regroup, and quickly found an alley with a dark corner to settle into.

Setting his pack down, he pulled out what supplies he had left. The pack itself had holes burned into it, and most of its contents were useless or missing completely, including what bandages he had remaining. All that remained were a handful of caltrops, the steel ball ends of his bola, and four backup throwing knives. Zeriel dropped the steel balls, then stowed his caltrops and the extra throwing knives in his belt pouches.

"What now?" Jekjarah asked, turning away from him and looking toward the corner of the alley he'd come down.

Zeriel leaned his back against the alley wall and relaxed. "We wait for them to put the fire out, then we go back."

Jekjarah arched an eyebrow at him. "Why go back? You have no allies there. And those injuries could get infected if you don't get help soon."

"Lavel's body is still there," he said, exhaustion forcing him to slide down the wall into a sitting position, "and the Donians can help with my wounds."

"No," Jekjarah said, turning to face him. "You can't expect them to help you."

"They took Lavel in when I first brought her here. They're good people."

"Better than you," Jekjarah said, nodding.

"That's why I think they'll help."

Jekjarah turned toward the quieting commotion of the recovery efforts they'd left behind. "From the sound of it, I think they're almost finished putting the fire out. Maybe you won't have to wait for long."

"That's good," Zeriel said. He drifted to sleep before he knew what happened.

❖

Zeriel woke up to pain. His body had stiffened up, and the awkward way he braced against the wall didn't help things. Green moss flattened beneath his hand as he pressed it on the wall to stand. The soft glow of the moss's bioluminescent fluid stuck to his palm as he got to his feet.

"Not very stealthy of you," Jekjarah said. He rested against the wall watching him.

"It doesn't matter right now, anyway." Zeriel ambled stiffly back down the alley toward the remains of *The Pick and Shovel.*

"Are you sure you want to do this? A lot can go wrong with this plan. It might be better to find a nearby healer."

"The closest Whisper is several days' ride from here, Jek. I can't wait that long." The trek back was painful. Falling asleep had caused his overworked muscles to stiffen and his burns to scab. By the time Zeriel made it to the inn, he staggered into the remains, exhausted and bleeding. Aketen and Pihuanata came into view. Aketen sifted through the remains, while Pihuanata stared at the spot where Lavel's body had lain. Tears fell from her eyes and onto a vaguely human shaped mound of ashes. Zeriel stumbled over the wreckage toward Pihuanata.

When she noticed him, she stumbled back in surprise. "Felle, help us!"

"I'm not here to fight." He stopped out of arm's reach, hoping to put her at ease.

"How dare you?" Aketen said, climbing over the rubble to get to Zeriel. "This is your fault."

"I never meant for any of this," Zeriel said, but he agreed with

Aketen and let his guilt do its work on his guts. If Zeriel had never come to *The Pick and Shovel* and simply done his job instead, Veshet wouldn't have found her. Aketen delivered a punch to his face that drove him to the ground. The Donian man seemed surprised that his punch connected, and he stepped back.

"I caused her so much suffering," Zeriel said as he struggled to stand back up. "Should I have killed her all those years ago and saved her from that suffering?" He looked at the Donians waiting for a response.

Their eyes fell to their feet in silence.

"I can't undo what I've done." Zeriel's legs gave out, and he dropped to his knees. The Donians shared a look. "I need your help. If someone doesn't tend to my wounds, I'll die."

"Then go ahead and die," Aketen said. "It's no less than you deserve."

He was right, but a small sliver of hope forced Zeriel to meet their eyes in turn. Aketen was resolute, but Pihuanata...

"We should help him," she said, not breaking eye contact.

"You can't be serious!" Aketen said.

She turned to her husband, her expression set in steel. "Lavel would have helped."

The Donian man's shoulders slumped as he let out a frustrated sigh. After a long pause he nodded and focused his eyes on Zeriel. "Follow us to our home, and if you don't die on the way, we'll save your miserable life."

CHAPTER TEN

In the weeks after the assassination of the Slave King, the council that Lavel had founded in the Lower Market surrendered to King Heyman. With Shyal back in the hands of the Wylsh monarchy, order returned quickly. The King's army executed every slave who had revolted for crimes against their masters and the crown, but the fires they set and the buildings they razed left scars on the city. With no one left but those who took refuge in the Lower District, a blanket of oppressive sadness fell on the city, its once lively streets lifeless, echoing with the memories of those who had fled or perished. Trade routes had been diverted for months, leaving the port empty. It would take months, if not years, to return Shyal to what it once was. The loss that hurt the kingdom of Wylsh the most was that of the Hisk family—owners of the largest platinum mines in all the eastern continent. Without their ore to sell, the country's exports were already suffering greatly.

To recover, King Heyman seized control and administered the city's recovery from City Hall. He'd seized the businesses, resources, and lands to reassert his royal control and had begun to auction them off. Merchants, families, and tradesmen traveled to Shyal to purchase a slice of the city's remains, all in hopes the King's efforts weren't in vain.

It took weeks for Zeriel to heal well enough to ride a horse again. He'd purchased one from a newly arrived merchant caravan just outside the city. He mounted his new horse, then observed the line of people waiting to enter the East Gate. Gaining access to Shyal was a slow process as each group was thoroughly vetted by the King's army-turned-city-guard. The line seemed unending, stretching to the eastern forest.

The cliff to the north drew Zeriel's attention and his eyes followed it back to the city wall. No one lined up at the North Gate since the King's men had sealed it off until the Northern Gate district could be rebuilt.

Just then, a crowd of people exited the city from the East Gate. The crowd was divided into several processions, each one of them bearing a coffin. Zeriel recognized them from the Lower Market.

Death had such a grip inside the walls that an untold number of bodies waited to be buried. Since the city's graveyard was outside its walls, the King had outlined a rotation of districts that were allowed to bury their dead. The Lower Market was at the bottom of his list, right before the Slums.

"She's not in any of those caskets," Jekjarah said, appearing next to the horse.

"I know," Zeriel whispered.

"Then why are you looking for them?"

"Because people need to bury something." Zeriel found the Donians in the crowd and caught Pihuanata's eyes, who held his gaze for a moment before turning back to the procession. "I don't think I'm wanted." The Donians helped him recover, but they never let themselves truly care for him, and Zeriel didn't blame them.

"But you still want to offer some sort of apology at her funeral."

"An empty gesture to an empty coffin," Zeriel said. Still, it hurt him to speak those words. Jekjarah was right. He needed to be there, to offer his apologies at the very least. A quick pull on the reins of his horse turned him toward the procession which he followed from a distance. It was a solemn march to the graveyard where Zeriel had to dismount to follow.

Built on a hill that butted up against the northern cliff, the cemetery spread out to the east until the hill cascaded into the forest in the distance. Cobblestone paths wound their way through the earthen charnel house, lighted by tall light poles with potted white vine lanterns hanging from their tops. The grass on the hill cast no light, amplifying the bright yellow, purple, and blue glow of the flowers that dotted the field.

To normal eyes, the cemetery would have been a sea of darkness, but to Zeriel's eyes, the moonlight was like sunlight from the sky's zenith. The bioluminescence of the plants was dull in his vision, except for the blinding light of the white vine lanterns.

The mourners separated and split down opposite turns on the cobblestone paths to different sections of the cemetery. Lavel's group consisted of the Donian couple—Aketen was acting as a pallbearer—and roughly ten other people. They stopped before a deep pit with a large mound of still-moist earth to its left. A tall tree stretched its canopy over the grave, covering it like a mother protecting their child while it cast its light as if to announce that an important person lay to rest there.

During the silent parade through the cemetery, Zeriel lagged behind the procession in the hope no one would notice him. The tactic succeeded for the most part—an easy feat for an assassin, even one as bad as he. Pihuanata had kept an eye on him from the moment she saw him at the city gates, though, and knew he had followed. Still, Zeriel found a pocket of deep shadow nearby and activated his powers to disappear more completely.

The pallbearers set the box carrying Lavel to the right of her grave. In a normal ceremony they would slide the casket open so everyone could see the body. As a child, Zeriel never understood why, even when his father explained that it was so those still alive could get the closure they needed and to make sure the person was actually dead. It had all felt pointless and unnecessary to him then. Lavel had died in the fire that consumed her inn, her body reduced to ashes, so the group left the lid closed.

As he stood and stared at the closed casket, Zeriel started to understand why people wanted to see. He couldn't confirm Lavel's death before he lost consciousness after the fight. When he woke, he was too disoriented to confirm her death before he was forced to escape the market's bucket brigade. They'd assumed she'd been reduced to ash with the rest of the inn, but something deep inside him, somewhere in his guts writhing and twisting, was the thought she could still be alive. The part of himself that knew better tried to convince his body, but it churned no matter what he told himself. His gut twisted with the gnawing feeling that she might still be out there somewhere, waiting to be saved. Pihuanata moved in front of the group just as the pallbearers stepped past her to join the rest.

"Thank you for coming today. We've not seen hardships in the Lower Market like what we've endured over the last few months—not in my lifetime. Yet somehow, we endured. We protected our lowly home and built something none of us thought possible." She paused and smiled to herself. An infectious expression that looked unconscious but cut through the sadness behind everyone's eyes. "We all knew it couldn't last forever, no matter how much we wanted to believe it could. I, for one, hoped we'd found something wonderful in the tragedy that cursed Liberator brought to us. Something that would last.

"Lavel believed more than any one of us that we would survive the Slave Uprising and come out the other side stronger." Pihuanata looked through the crowd with another, stronger smile on her face. "I happen to think that she was right. Though none of us could have known the shape that strength would take, or the true price we would pay for it.

"When Lavel first came to us, she was barely a woman, stolen from her home and deposited in our city by the very assassin who was meant to kill her." She glanced in Zeriel's direction, though he was sure she couldn't have seen him. "In the beginning, Aketen and I looked after her only because we'd been paid to do it. Over the years we got to know Lavel and we came to understand how special she was. She became like the daughter we never had, and she gave us the joy only a daughter could give." Tears formed in her eyes, and Pihuanata was forced to hold back the sobs that tried to cut her off. "Our souls will forever bear a dark void where Lavel once lived. Despite the pain of her loss, I know that her love and generosity will live on through us." She finally broke down and stepped into the crowd, into the arms of her husband who held her and shared in her tears.

Others in the crowd grieved along with Pihuanata, but for a long moment no one else stepped up to speak. In that time Zeriel wondered what it would have been like to be on the receiving end of Lavel's love and generosity. He'd only been given hate and contempt.

A man emerged to address the crowd. Young, close to Lavel's age, he was wearing the thick, dirt-stained clothes of a miner who didn't have the money to buy anything nicer.

"I was going to propose to her," he said. "Once the city was back to normal and I was back to work. We'd talked about it for a long time, and I'd saved the money to buy her a betrothal bracelet." He pulled a simple silver bracelet from his pocket. It was the width of a man's finger and polished smooth. The man stepped over to Lavel's casket and placed the bracelet on it, covering the jewelry with his palm for a moment before stepping back into the group.

A pang of jealousy struck Zeriel as he watched the man. It never once crossed his mind that Lavel might have found someone to love other than him. Somehow, he felt betrayed.

"I don't know why you're getting all worked up," Jekjarah said as he materialized next to Zeriel, eyes on the group ahead of them. "You saw her every other year. At most." The hallucination was right, of course, but that couldn't stop what he was feeling.

A young woman with a baby on her hip and a handsome young man in tow stepped in front of the group next. The edges of her mouth held old scars and deep horizontal crevices carved lines in her lips. "I was a grinner, living on the streets and doing everything and anything to put powder in my nose and let the world bleed away. Lavel pulled me from the streets and gave me a place to live and food to eat. After the sickness of the drug passed, she put me to work." She looked up at the man next to her and smiled.

"Imagine what it would be like to make someone else's life *better*," Jekjarah said. He looked over at Zeriel. "I bet you never once considered the idea of doing good for someone without asking anything in return. Not when it cost you something." Zeriel let those words sink in, and as much as he wanted to, he couldn't be angry. They were his thoughts, spoken as words through a hallucination created by his own broken mind.

"That's where I met Olien." When she turned her head back to the crowd, she had tears falling in rivulets down her cheeks. "I'd be dead by now if not for Lavel. Instead, I have a family. I pray to Thaid that he sends his winds to take her to the Halcyon City, and that I can have the strength to pass on a little piece of the lessons she taught me to my descendants." The woman tried to say more but couldn't. Instead, she leaned on her husband who took her in his arms as they walked back into the group.

"Lavel really did make a life for herself here. You didn't expect that, did you?"

"I put her here," Zeriel whispered, "like someone buries gold they want to save for the future. So no, I didn't."

"But she wasn't gold. She was worth so much more than that. A value so high it raised the value of those around her."

An old woman shuffled in front of the group next, but Zeriel had had enough. He'd looked at Lavel like his pathway to salvation. To a life without killing, where he could live in peace, with a family and a future. That fantasy had evaporated at the words of Lavel's loved ones. Such an honored station as a *loved one* would never have been bestowed to him, and for the first time since meeting her, Zeriel understood why. It was time he did something for Lavel that didn't cause her pain, even if she wouldn't know what he'd done. Even if it was too late.

The shadows melted away as he turned to leave, suddenly unconcerned with who might have seen him. A small figure stood behind him and stopped him in his tracks. It wasn't often a normal person could sneak up on him.

"We need to talk," Pihuanata said.

"How'd you know I was here?" Zeriel asked, concerned that he wasn't as invisible as he thought when using his powers.

"I saw how you fought those other assassins in the inn, calling up the shadows to your advantage. When I saw it was darker here than everywhere else, I knew it had to be you."

That, Zeriel thought, *is good information to have.* "I see," he said, keeping all emotion from his voice so Pihuanata wouldn't know how badly she'd caught him off guard. "What would you like to talk about?"

"Lavel filed a will with the town hall," she held out a scroll to him. "It bypassed the King's auctions and passed the inn directly to you."

Zeriel took the scroll and unrolled it to find an official Shyal city deed for the inn. It showed him as the owner of the property, granted to him as inheritance from Lavel and at King Heyman's discretion. With little way to prove exactly who "Zeriel" was, the document effectively granted ownership of the property to whoever held it.

"You just need to sign it," the woman said.

A frown settled on his face as he rolled up the deed. "I can't accept this." He tried to hand it back to her.

Pihuanata made no move to take it. "It was Lavel's wish that the inn went to you, though I can't fathom why she would want such a thing."

"I have no idea. I—" Zeriel turned to study the crowd around Lavel's grave. "I never really knew her." He turned back to the woman and met her eyes. "It's obvious to me now, seeing the impact she had, that Lavel was a force, more powerful than I could have ever understood." Zeriel shook his head.

The woman's face grew hard. "Lavel owned that inn, and she gave it to you. You want to refuse it and dishonor her wishes?" She shook her head. "Take the damned thing. It's nothing but a burned husk anyway."

An invisible weight like a massive stone settled on Zeriel's shoulders as he stared at the deed. "My entire life I've had trouble fitting in. My father wanted me to be a farmer, but I dreamed of fighting. The Te Et Sha expected me to be an assassin, but I could barely do the job. I'm a failure at everything I try, so what would I do with the ashen remains of an inn?"

"Rebuild it." Pihuanata stepped closer to him. "You fail because you expect to. Leave that life behind and keep Lavel's memory alive."

Zeriel thought about it; really thought hard. It was close to the escape he'd always wanted, and a piece of him pushed to do exactly as the Donian woman suggested. But after a moment of contemplation, Zeriel shook his head. There was only one way he could be sure if he was truly free. "I can't. Not right now." He stepped closer and the woman recoiled. He ignored her fear, holding the deed out to her again. "I accept her wishes, but I need you to keep this safe for the time being. Can you do that for me?"

She took the scroll reluctantly and nodded. Zeriel walked away, a surety of purpose stronger than any he'd had before. "What are you going to do?" she called to his back.

Zeriel turned to look at her, then looked to Lavel's memorial, then back to Pihuanata again. Rage at himself for what he'd brought down on Lavel, at Veshet for what he took, and at the Ori twins for their part in it all, brought clarity to his purpose. "I'm going to get revenge."

CHAPTER ELEVEN

In the months since El's return, her life at the southern edge of the Yawdaw archipelago had changed so drastically that she hardly recognized it anymore. To remind her of just how true that was, she entered a room in the Ocean's Blessing that Healer Zo had converted into a classroom, now full of her numerous students. Lines of desks filled one end of the room, all pointing toward a small podium to the side of a giant chalkboard. All twenty desks were filled with women from various villages throughout the Yawdaw islands.

Interest in her healing knowledge grew quickly after a merchant from Neltel—the largest and northernmost of their villages—collapsed while negotiating for some Uklak meat. He was lucky El was there when it happened and that she could heal him on the spot. The man proclaimed it a miracle to every person he encountered along his voyage home. He had suffered from heat sickness, something a seasoned healer like Zo could have handled in her sleep. If El had left it at that, perhaps nothing would have happened, but she made the mistake of fixing some of the aging man's aches while she was at it. After that, villages sent women to learn her secrets.

She didn't like the idea of keeping such important knowledge to herself, so she happily taught them. That was until the flood of women never stopped. Healer Zo pushed her to formalize their training—much like what the healer had experienced in the university in the Kloren capital of Ferrix. She was reluctant at first, but it turned out to be the right choice. They'd decided to allow twenty students a year, giving them daily instruction and as much hands-on experience as possible.

Her students' heads turned toward her. Their faces—lit by the several white vine lanterns in the room—were a blend of early morning energy and groggy disinterest. A strange mix for a group of women who chose to be there. Each one had the brown skin typical of Yawdawians and wore the single-wrap dress covered with different patterns of palm leaves, flowers, and ferns plentiful across the islands. Where the women differed most was in the vast spectrum of their ages, ranging from girls barely more than seventeen, to women whose backs were bent from the weight of time, bearing the deep wrinkles of years working long hours.

Unlike her students, El wore skintight linen trousers and a blue, long-sleeved linen dress that fell just above her knees. "Sorry I'm late," she said, closing the door behind her, then making her way to the podium.

"Late night with Reon?" a young woman in the back corner asked. The room snickered at her comment.

"Very funny, Luti," El responded, a smirk across her face. It took her some time, but she eventually accustomed herself to the long names of the northern villages. "I suppose studying the effects of prolonged eshenroot powder use is what keeps *you* up at night, then?"

"Of course, Healer El!" she said, sitting at attention and stifling a smile. "I eat, sleep, and drink the healing arts."

The room laughed, and El joined them.

"Alright, let's get serious." She snatched a piece of chalk from the podium and approached the blackboard. "Yesterday we had a patient with breath fever, so I thought we could use that opportunity to talk about the lungs." As she drew a crude picture of the organs, El settled into her explanation of their inner workings.

Without the insights she gained from tending to the patient, she couldn't have given this lecture. Using her power for healing forced her to focus closely on the man's lungs. As it tended to do, the power guided her as if it had a mind of its own, flooding her mind with the knowledge that even the healers in Ferrix didn't know.

In some ways she felt like a fraud, teaching things that she only recently discovered herself. And while she had gained generations of knowledge about the functions of the human body in a few short months, only a portion of that knowledge would be useful to these women. To help bridge that gap, she used her powers to monitor the workings of Healer Zo's medicines inside the patients, helping the healer improve on traditional methods while building her own knowledge.

Still, the old healer's skill humbled El, reminding her just how little she knew, despite the education her powers gave her. Several weeks ago, she'd become so discouraged that she almost walked away from her students, sure that Healer Zo could do infinitely better than her. Luckily Reon had helped her see the value of her insights, and she'd resolved to push on regardless of her shortcomings.

Time evaporated as she steered her lecture toward the way breath fever attacked the air sacs inside the lungs, effectively drowning the patients in their own fluids. The women in the classroom were surprisingly attentive, asking questions as she went, dutifully noting her answers. El wondered what she might have learned had she paid as much attention to her childhood studies as these women did to her.

Just as El was about to wrap up, the door to the classroom opened and Ki stepped in, holding a stack of papers to her chest. Her friend was a bit shorter than her and wore the same dress as the students. Her black hair flowed freely over her shoulders and a smile stretched across her angular face. Since returning, El had finally established her trading company, but when its growth was too much for her to handle on her own, she'd reached out for her friend's help. The work had given Ki a confidence she'd never had before and she stood straighter and carried a presence of authority. It looked good on her. "You're late again."

"I am?" She regarded her students, who looked eager to leave. "Well, we've covered all the important parts. You're dismissed. Make sure you get your duties for the day from Healer Zo."

The women packed up their things and began filing out of the room.

"Maybe you should bring an hourglass next time," Ki said as she approached El.

"I have one sitting on a shelf at home," El said. "I just keep forgetting to grab it on the way out."

"You're spreading yourself too thin. I know your—" she looked around to make sure no one was close enough to hear, "your powers make you feel like you have this a duty to the village, but even with them, you're only one woman."

El stepped past her friend, heading toward the door. "I'm fine. I just need to manage my time better." She looked back as she walked out the door, startling her friend as if the woman hadn't seen her leaving. "So, how's trade going?"

Ki hurried to catch up as the two strolled down the hallway. "Income continues to improve. The villages are starting to rely on the goods we're providing, which keeps them buying from us, but we're making enemies of the merchant fleets."

"I'm not worried about them," El said with a dismissive gesture, "either they adapt, or they don't."

"The new ship is ready to set sail as early as tomorrow."

El perked up at that. "That's great news! And the crew is prepared?"

"Yes. And a bit eager, I would say."

"Then let's get them sailing. I'm sure I can be ready by tomorrow morning." El turned right at the main hallway, heading out of the Ocean's Blessing.

"Right, except there is one problem."

El sighed as she stepped outside. "There's always a problem." Stars twinkled in the sky above, and the village below shone brightly with lantern light. In less than two weeks the next dark month would start to set in. She'd hoped to get her new ship to port in Shyal before then, though the opportunity for that had probably past several days ago.

Looking down from atop the hill where the Ocean's Blessing stood, El could see across the entirety of Baharkar village. On the terraces to her right, modern huts were more tightly packed than they had ever been. The farms between those homes and the port had expanded their fields, busy with people harvesting the crops planted the month prior. The port itself, ringed with shops and inns that now stretched farther south than even the harbor, bustled with activity. She caught sight of her new double masted caravel, docked at port with men—small pinpricks from this distance—moving across the deck to prepare for its maiden voyage.

Taking in those sights, it was impossible to avoid how much Baharkar had grown. While she supposed it was inevitable, given what she'd accomplished, she wasn't completely sure how she felt about it. Sure, she felt proud of what she'd accomplished. Throughout her youth, she dreamed of contributing to the village's prosperity, and now she was the main cause of it. The work she did teaching the other healers was unexpected but allowed her to uplift the rest of Yawdaw with more than just her goods.

Yes, there was pride. But also, a feeling of profound loss. The village in her memory—the one she grew up in—was slowly fading. As the village grew and expanded, she lost something. The small pool east of their home, nestled in the woods and filled up by a wispy waterfall, had been her secret for years. Just a week ago she found a group of visiting ship crewmen swimming in it and drinking on its shores. Deep down she knew she didn't own that pool, but she also recognized that something had been lost.

"It is incredible, isn't it?" Ki said, looking out at the village and shaking El out of her contemplations.

"What is?" she asked as she glanced at her friend.

"The things you've achieved, and in such a short time."

Nodding, she regarded the village again. "This is what I dreamed of as a child. I should be happy, shouldn't I?"

"You're not?" Ki turned to face her.

"I guess I am. But also, I'm not. I didn't expect to feel so much grief over the changes."

"I think I know what you mean. The village isn't what it was even a year ago, and the power behind those changes won't stop, no matter how much you want it to."

A smile stretched across El's face. She felt lighter knowing she wasn't the only one feeling that way. "I guess that's the price of progress, isn't it?"

"It's your fault, you know."

"Ha! I suppose it is." El gestured to Ki's papers. "So, what's that problem we have?"

"We're short on Uklak carapace. The inventory we had was the only thing making the trip profitable."

"Really?" El said, taking the document from her friend. "How short are we?" She inspected the figures written on it. "Half? Where did it all go?"

"An order came in from Neltel a few days ago."

"Of course it did." She surveyed the cove, looking for the Uklak that the hunters had brought back several weeks ago, before the dark month had set in. The lights of Tet Nadad's workers were nowhere to be seen, leaving only the inky black of the cove's shifting waves. A clear sign that there was nothing left of the creature.

"Oh! That reminds me." Ki shuffled through her stack, pulling a sheet from the middle of the bundle and handing it to her. "The hunters looked over the information you gave them."

El reviewed the paper. It was a map with Kekkek Island in the center, and ocean surrounding it. A grid of squares covered the map, and several areas in the southern part of the map showed clusters of dots with dates next to them. Arrows flowed through the dots, ending with one leading further to the south, and one returning to form a loop. On the back, the hunters had provided their conclusions.

We already knew about most of these locations, though some are new. With the meticulously tracked dates, we think we found a migratory pattern.

The pattern matched what we already expected, except for an anomaly in the dates that make us think we're missing a cluster further to the south. If the Chief agrees, we'll send out an expedition as soon as the light month begins.

After the last hunt, El noticed there had been a sharp decline in the population of Uklak. Worried that the increased efficiency she brought to the hunt was driving them close to extinction, she sent the hunters this map that Reon had been updating over the months.

"This is good." Her eyes left the map, focusing on the Velels in the harbor, and plans formed in her head.

Her friend took the map and set it on the top of her stack, then followed El's gaze. "You know how much your father hates it when you go off hunting on your own."

El huffed. "That's not what I was thinking."

"That expression of yours was saying otherwise."

"Actually," El said, eyeing her friend, "I was just reminding myself that the light month is only a few weeks away. I can wait until then."

CHAPTER TWELVE

The sky was in transition for a few days at the end of each month. Stars twinkled on the dark side, and a pale purple gradient stretched from east to west as it traveled across the sky. The plants' glow began to fade or grow, and the animals would wake or settle in for their month-long sleep.

With a craned neck, Zeriel peered through the pine canopy of northeastern Wylsh at just such a sky. The months were transitioning from dark to light as Zeriel rode northeast, approaching the northern border between Wylsh and Allakhan. The distant sounds of Eletenynbrah's bustling village mixed with the bubbling of the river close by to become a single melody that weaved through the trees to touch his ears.

Jekjarah winked into existence walking next to him. "You're *really* going back to the stronghold? Aren't you afraid they'll kill you on sight?"

"There is that danger, yes. We'll know more once we've talked to the Whisper here."

"And if the Elders really did sign off on your assassination?"

"We kill the Whisper before they can report my survival to the rest of The Veil."

Jekjarah stepped to the side and looked out into the passing forest. His feet slid strangely across the ground as he walked on his own invisible platform. "I think you're overestimating your abilities." He turned his head to look at Zeriel. "Even with your new power."

"Perhaps, but what choice do I have?"

"Walk away."

Zeriel pondered the hallucination's response. Did a part of him really want to walk away? His resolve had been strong when he left Shyal, and until that moment he never questioned it.

A simple sign at a fork in the road caught Zeriel's attention—a rough plank of wood nailed to a post. On the plank was scratched the word, *Eletenynbrah*, with an arrow pointing to the left. This wasn't the first time Zeriel had passed through the village, so he knew that travelers might get the wrong impression of it if they based their expectations on that sign alone.

He made the turn and broke through the tree line. The terrain opened into a field at the base of a set of rolling hills. Ahead was the main village, a line of homes and shops strategically placed to encourage visitors to spend their coin. An inn stood as the last building in the line. It was twice as tall as all the other buildings and far more expertly crafted. Smoke rose from chimneys, blanketing the area with the smell of wood fires and morning meals as they cooked.

Past the main village was a large orchard, the leaves of the trees casting green light in well-orchestrated lines. Shadowed dots stippled the green leaves where the fruit grew. On the hillside to his right were fields and pastures. Because all bioluminescent plants were poisonous—except for most trees—farmlands were always covered in darkness. These fields were no exceptions, so the area surrounding the hilltop where the city lord's manor stood was a black landscape. The only light came from the manor itself, a beacon on the hill.

Without the trees of the forest casting their shadows over him, Zeriel found that even the pale light of the rising sun created a white haze over his vision and pricked his eyes like tiny needles. He pulled a threadbare cloth from his pack and tied it over his eyes like a blindfold. The cloth helped him see in the light, but when the sun was high, it only afforded him a few feet of vision. Something was better than nothing though, so he made do with what the cloth gave him. When the sky was in transition, like it was at that moment, it allowed him to see much farther.

The villagers, who were already familiar with a variety of travelers, recognized Zeriel as a dangerous man, and so kept their distance. It wasn't anything new, border villages like this always had folks knowledgeable about who to stay away from and who to welcome. How these villagers reacted to Zeriel was different, though. The sounds of the village faded as they noticed him. Villagers hurried away, their heads down, though they tracked his every move from the corners of their eyes. Children were rushed indoors, and men with farming tools that doubled as weapons stood watch as he passed.

They know, said one of his female voices. He tried to name them once, but there were too many to count, and he lost track of the names. Somehow those names made the voices stronger, more insistent, so he'd abandoned the practice hoping to keep hold on what little sanity he had left.

They're going to kill you, came another voice. *You should kill them first. Yes! Kill them!*

Jekjarah materialized on his left and the voices quieted. "Think it's the blindfold?" he said as he watched the villagers. "I'd take it personally if I were you." He turned his head to Zeriel, a maniacal grin on his face. "Maybe you *should* kill them."

"Shut up," Zeriel whispered. Jekjarah disappeared at that, and a woman who'd been passing by broke into a run. With a shake of his head and a sigh, Zeriel got control of himself and steered his horse toward the village's apothecary. The shop was a cover for The Veil, of course. Despite that, Zeriel had found it one of the more useful ones. As quickly as he could, he dismounted and took off his blindfold as he entered the shop.

He'd been there many times, so the union of smells from the various herbs, roots, and other unknown *things* were familiar. This time the melody of scents was infused with the thick smell of iron and topped with a hint of decay to finish it off.

A body was draped over the counter in the back of the room, its blood flowing down the front and forming a pool on the floor. Other than the dead man, nothing else in the room had been disturbed. In fact, Zeriel could see a tiny glint off some silver coins that had fallen from the man's grip to drown in the pool of his blood on the floor.

Jekjarah appeared on his knees rubbing his hands slowly back and forth through the pool of blood. "How terribly unexpected."

Zeriel thought back to something Veshet had said to him at *The Pick and Shovel.*

I don't need anyone else's permission to do what I want. Take what I want. Build *what I want.*

He quickly pulled the list of ingredients he needed out of a pocket, and started grabbing them off the shelves, then shoving them into his pack.

"What could he possibly be building by going after The Veil?" Jekjarah asked.

"I don't know. But we need to hurry." A pit formed in his stomach.

As he passed a mirror on the wall, something in his reflection caught his attention. Upon closer inspection, Zeriel saw that there *was* something strange. It was in his eyes. His pupils had grown so large that very little of his iris was visible. The normal light brown color of his eyes had been replaced with black. "What's happening to me?"

Jekjarah stepped behind him. "A side effect of your new powers, no doubt."

Pluck them out! A voice said, then was joined by a chorus of other voices offering different ways for him to remove his eyes from his skull.

Zeriel growled at their volume and tried to forcibly shove them to the back of his consciousness with sheer willpower. As always, his efforts had failed. Once the voices quieted, he finished getting the rest of his supplies, then left, Jekjarah on his heels. He reapplied his blindfold and got back on his horse.

"You think it's something other than those powers that's having that effect on you?" the hallucination asked.

Zeriel followed the main road out of the village and toward the northern border, waiting until they were alone to answer. "No, you're right. It must be something to do with these powers Plaxes gave me. Now I understand why I can't see when there's a strong source of light around."

"You're cursed!" Jekjarah said. "I knew it!"

"I'm not cursed!" Zeriel shouted to interrupt him. "It's like you said: Consequences of using the powers."

Jekjarah shook his head and huffed in annoyance. "Sounds like a curse to me." Then he disappeared.

Fortunately, the voices disappeared when Jekjarah did, leaving Zeriel alone for the rest of the day. Unfortunately, this gave him time to wonder if his power was a curse like the hallucination said. Hours of thought didn't bring him closer to a decision, but as the moon began to set on the northern horizon, he found a copse of trees growing at the connection of the base of two hills. Taking a short detour off the path brought him to those trees and a stream running through them, the water so clear he could see to the bottom.

The trees provided Zeriel enough shade that he didn't need his blindfold. He spent the next few hours going to work, collecting clay from nearby, and using the materials he collected to start making new bombs. The ones he used in Shyal's City Hall were sleep bombs, and a typical tool of the Te Et Sha. The bombs he made now were anything but typical.

A design of his own making, Zeriel had dubbed them stunners. Unlike all the other assassins, he'd found himself escaping a chase at the end of most missions. He assumed he'd eventually get caught in the back by an arrow, so he spent years devising a bomb that would stop a pursuer in their tracks.

His stunners exploded and let out a bright flash of light along with a loud noise when thrown on the ground. It'd left him blind with his ears ringing on more than one occasion. The process to make them took time and some specialized materials. Jythim, the dead Whisper he left behind, always had what Zeriel needed to make more.

A few hours later he'd done the first part of his work and eaten the rest of his jerky. There wasn't anything left but to sleep, so he laid down for the night.

In the morning, Zeriel did some fishing in the stream, finished making his stunners, and set off toward his goal once again. The implications of the dead Whisper swirled in his mind, and he found himself reconsidering what Jekjarah had said back in Eletenynbrah. About walking away. He could, of course. It would be easier to abandon this path, to settle down in a place where no one could find him. No king, no lord, and certainly not the Te Et Sha to control him.

Except...

The Te Et Sha—if they wanted him dead—*would* find him no matter where he hid. So as tempting as it was to flee, he was committed. He had to get to the Stronghold and find out if Veshet and his cronies were acting alone, or if the Elders truly wanted him dead.

CHAPTER THIRTEEN

El stood on the docks of the village's port, watching as hunters hurried to finish their preparations. Ten Velels, the single-masted vessels built specifically to hunt the Uklak, lined the spaces between docked merchant ships. The sun peeked halfway over the eastern horizon, providing the light they needed for the hunt.

A powerful drive to move pushed El to jump down into her own Velel and double-check her provisions. Unlike the others, she brought a barrel full of drinking water. She couldn't be without something to drink when there was a chance she'd have to use her powers while on deck, completely dry.

"You're sure you can leave your students for the day?" her father's voice sounded from the docks. Even while shifting his feet nervously, he cut an imposing figure with his thick frame and commanding presence.

El looked up at the man and smiled by habit at the sight of him. "I'll be fine," she said as she tied down a few bundles of rations for the trip. "I sailed across the ocean to rescue *you*. I think I can handle a day trip to investigate some Uklak."

"Right." A hint of uncertainty laced his voice. He surveyed the preparations and said, "Dok knows what to do."

She couldn't tell if he was worried about her, the men, or both. He'd become chief in the time since they returned, and Dok Betet had taken his place as the hunters' leader. Her father was still adjusting to the changes, finding it hard to let go of what he once was.

Movement on the beach in the center of the cove caught El's eye. A small group returned from Nedon's Seat after giving last-minute prayers for everyone's safety. A tight knot formed in her stomach at the thought of anyone worshipping that god. Though she could lay waste to that shrine of his, she'd decided it wasn't her place to make such a decision for the rest of the village. Still, she refused to set foot even on the Aelel Plains that surrounded the Seat. Nedon's presence hadn't returned to her mind since the fall of Shyal, and she avoided even the barest thought of him as if it would invite the god's return.

Turning away, she focused back on her father. "The men will be fine too. Really, father, you worry too much. With me along, they're more likely to die of boredom than to get hurt hunting."

He nodded, eyes locked on the hunters. "Just don't take any risks." After a pause, he met her eyes with an intense look. "And remember what we agreed about your powers."

El sighed. "Any other instructions you'd like to give before we go on this incredibly safe hunt?"

Her father snorted at that and turned to step away. "I guess you have it all under control then." Despite his fussing, she smiled at him as he stalked away.

Dok approached, waving at her. "We should be ready to set sail in a few minutes. You have everything you need?"

She touched the pocket of her trousers, feeling the rolled-up map inside. "Yep. I thought we'd start with the usual spots for this time of year. Once we grab one, I'll leave with the expeditionary force."

The lead hunter shook his head. "This isn't your trading company, El. I'm the one who makes the plans on the hunt."

"Oh! Of course," she said, heat building in her cheeks. "Sorry about that. Everything I've been doing lately, it's just—I'm used to being in charge. What's your plan?" She meant it to sound genuine but cringed when even she heard the tiniest bit of condescension in her tone.

The man hissed through his teeth and shook his head. "I'll make sure the men we selected know to go with you after we've secured the

Uklak." He walked away without another word. El could tell she'd have work ahead of her to make up for that exchange.

❖

Something about this excursion reminded El of her first disastrous voyage out into the ocean alone. She sought comfort at the sight of everyone sailing in their Velels. She wasn't alone on this time, and even after her conversation with Dok, she knew the hunters would be there for her—especially after everything that happened in Shyal.

Since those events, she'd expanded her skill with her water sense and could now plot her location on the ocean based on the landscape of the seafloor. She'd never find herself lost on the water again.

So, what was this feeling, then? Was it simply nostalgia for a time that had a profound impact on her life, terrible as that time had been? She felt the map in her pocket again and smiled, realization coming to her. She was on a mission of discovery, much like she was then. Only this time, she hunted for knowledge and opportunity instead of family and friends.

Dok's Velel swerved toward her coming close until she could make him out, facing her with one of his feet on the rail. "We should be close."

El signaled her acknowledgment and locked her lines in place, then reached over the rail, calling water to her hand. A column rose from the surface and engulfed her arm up to the elbow. Closing her eyes, she activated her water sense, and that now-familiar flood of awareness crashed into her mind. She directed her focus into the depths, searching for the sea floor and finding it a league below the surface. A wrecked caravel sat at the bottom, and she could almost feel the grain of the wood hull as the water flowed around it.

Releasing her power and pulling her arm from the water, she opened her eyes and called to Dok, "Another mile southeast."

He waved to let her know he understood, and the fleet continued. As they sailed, she found her mind wandering to thoughts of Nedon. She wanted to believe he was gone for good. That this life she was building would last forever, but each time she remembered his final words, that hope was crushed.

Get stronger El, but rest assured that when we meet again, I won't be alone.

There was too much unspoken beneath the statement for El to guess at all of its meanings. The one thing she was sure of, though, was he wasn't done with her. The question of when he would surface again fueled an anxiety that tore at her insides. Even now, she found it difficult to see the future with her in it. As she watched the hunters, she wondered if they'd go back to their old ways once she was gone.

Once I'm gone... Do I really see it as a foregone conclusion? She wasn't surprised to find that she did. She'd have to face Nedon, he'd all but guaranteed it, and that would certainly pull her away from Baharkar. The best she could hope to do was prepare for that inevitability, and if she never returned, they'd be better for her efforts.

The men slowed and started dropping anchors, tearing her attention away from her contemplations. Dok looked to her and nodded, signaling that it was time to do her part.

El stood, dropped her own anchor, wrapped a white vine around her wrist for light, then unceremoniously stepped off the side of her Velel, and plunged into the ocean. In the vast waters of the ocean, El didn't have to worry about accidentally dehydrating herself while using her powers. There was plenty of water to fuel them here. The moment she was fully submerged—and with her powers unrestrained—she spun the water above her head until it created a vortex that crept from the surface to touch her lips. It expanded into a pocket of air around her nose and mouth, giving her fresh air to breathe, and allowing her to sink to the ocean floor without worry of drowning. Through her water sense she knew what she'd find before she got there, but she wanted to see it for herself.

Her feet touched down on the rocky floor. There wasn't an Uklak in sight. It was a bad sign considering they'd had a full month to reproduce. That should have given them enough time for a few hatchlings to become juveniles.

Concerned, El surfaced and conferred with Dok. They agreed to move to the next closest location, hoping that maybe their smaller numbers shifted their migratory patterns. That assumption was perfectly logical.

It was wrong.

El found nothing in the next spot. And nothing in the one after that. No sign of a new predator driving them away, and no remnants of recently hatched egg clutches. Just—nothing. They kept going, though, but all in vain. The only glimmer of hope she found was a tiny Uklak, barely the size of El, using its side fins to hunt a school of minnows.

"Anything?" Dok asked her the moment she surfaced. The hunters had pulled their ships into a circle as they waited for her. Every one of them leaned toward her, faces expectant.

"A single baby. It looks like they abandoned it here." Groans sounded around her, and many of their shoulders slumped.

Dok eyed the moon. It was well past midday. "We don't have time to sweep unknown waters hoping to find them. But..."

"...We can still investigate the new location," she said, finishing his thought. "If there's a cast of them there, we might be out of trouble."

"If," Dok said softly.

El skidded across the surface to her ship. The hunters had seen what she could do back in Shyal, so there was no need to be bashful. A water column lifted her up, allowing her to step lightly onto the deck. She grabbed the map from a compartment at the helm and studied it. The area they were going was farther south than El had ever been, and probably farther than the others had visited, as well.

After a quick discussion with Dok, they had their bearing, and El had a helmsman so she could use her water sense as they sailed. It would be several hours before they arrived, though, so she manned the helm.

The two were silent as they sailed, neither wanting to accidentally say anything that might jinx them. El thought to herself how silly that was, knowing full well nothing they said would change the reality that awaited them. But just in case...

Time passed slowly, but they eventually arrived. She handed off helming duties and made her way across the water to Dok again. She shivered the moment her feet sunk into the ocean. The cool waters this far south were an unwelcome surprise, adding an alien feel to this part of the ocean. Goosebumps that had nothing to do with the cold crawled across her arms cold. Unfortunately, she had to maintain contact with the water to use her powers, and they had to find the Uklak, so there was nothing to do but grin and bear it.

"Can you sense anything from here?" Dok asked the moment she arrived.

El used her water sense to *see* into the ocean. At first, she couldn't believe what she felt below them, but as she continued to probe, she was shocked to find *nothing* below them. When she'd first discovered this power, the vastness of the ocean had overwhelmed her, and it had taken months to accustom herself to the sensation. This new reality, of oceans so deep even her senses couldn't find the bottom, terrified her.

"No," she whispered.

"So, they're not here either?"

"It's not that. There's no *bottom*, Dok. It's too deep."

"*Empty waters.* If even *you* can't find the bottom..." A hush fell over Dok's ship.

"I'll dive as far as I can," El said, testing the tightness of the vine wrapped around her wrist, "and see if I can find the bottom. We can't return empty-handed."

The men nodded, and Dok said, "I met a Nuuian not too long ago at The Hero's Cove missing his left arm. Claimed he'd gotten lost in a snowstorm and the cold had taken it." The lead hunter eyed the water ominously. "I don't know what kind of cold could do such a thing, but it's best not to tempt fate, I think."

She became suddenly aware of frigid temperatures of the water stabbing into her feet. "Right. I won't be long." She'd never had to endure the cold, so she wasn't sure she'd last long enough to do any real damage. And with that thought in her mind, she dove into the water. The shock of it almost made her suck water straight into her lungs, but she managed to contain the urge. When her air mask was in place, she took a large gulp of air.

Unwilling to linger, she wasted no time and dove as fast as she could, reaching with her senses into that endless void below. El counted fifteen seconds, and still there was nothing below her. Fear crept into her chest as she felt the weight of the water above. It pressed in on her chest, making it difficult to breathe, forcing her to focus a piece of her power on pushing back against the water. With the air mask, her water sense, and her efforts to keep the ocean from crushing her, El was stretching herself to her limit. Still, she continued.

The fear took root, speaking to her about a horrid death, crushed from all sides by the unfamiliar waters of the southern ocean. Soon, even the lights of the white vine lanterns on the ships above faded to darkness. All she could see were tiny particles illuminated by the white vine on her wrist. Still there was nothing below.

Her feet grew numb, and her fear sprouted. Images flooded her mind of herself, limbless and miserable, unable to do anything but lie in a bed being tended to by her family. Surely even Reon would abandon her in that state.

The fear turned to panic and El fought against the sudden, unrelenting need to turn around and surface. Thoughts entered her mind, reminding her that whatever time she spent diving, that's how long it would take her to surface. Then, just as needles of pain stabbed at her ankles and her body began shivering uncontrollably, just as she was about to turn around, they appeared to her senses.

Uklak, lumbering around on the sooty floor of those depths. They were four times larger than any specimen they'd ever hunted, and there were *thousands* of them. As soon as she'd sensed the big ones, the others came to her awareness. Uklak of all sizes in a massive cast that covered what parts of the seafloor she could sense, all traveling east.

A bit of her fear retreated, but not all. There were too many dangers to become complacent, and she had precious little time to act before the cold would claim her. She wasn't sure she could manage what she was about to do, and as she gathered the will to achieve it, she could feel her concentration slipping. Still, she managed to reach out her hand in the direction of one of the larger creatures, and as she made a quick fist, the water around it froze solid. The Uklak she'd trapped shot upward, racing past her and spinning her around in its wake.

El righted herself and followed, shooting upward as fast as she dared, hoping she'd get out of the water before she lost any limbs.

CHAPTER FOURTEEN

It has been said that the greatest inventions were born from the most desperate of circumstances. At least, that's what the foreman at the mine in Zeriel's home village told him as a child. He'd been mesmerized by the intricate system of pulleys used to suspend tools and workers down the deep fissure they mined. The gems and precious metals they pulled from that chasm built their Clan. The necessity to mine deeper into that fissure had forced them to design that system.

Zeriel's desperation wasn't so grand, though, to him it felt that way. As the week passed, the sun rose higher into the sky as he came closer and closer to the Te Et Sha stronghold. The higher the sun rose, the brighter the world became and the more it blinded him. This was only his fourth month with his power, and only his second light month. He remembered the first one where, in a desperate attempt to ease the pain in his eyes, he'd wrapped a used cheesecloth around them. It was the first of many different cloth variations he'd tried until he settled on his current blindfold.

The snow that accumulated on the mountain pass during the dark month reflected the sunlight and penetrated his blindfold, so even that wasn't enough anymore. He was unable to sleep through the first night due to the brilliance of the snow's reflection, and his desperation for relief from the luminous onslaught peaked. He'd retreated into his thoughts—a normally dangerous activity—contemplating the brightness of Veshet's fire, and how it was the brightest thing he'd ever experienced, until he traveled that snow-covered pass, that is. Then he remembered how that fire had dimmed when he'd cloaked himself in his power. Its brightness had become bearable, and he'd been able to see well enough to fight.

Without an idea in his mind, Zeriel pulled on what little darkness existed around him, cloaking himself once again. The brightness receded immediately, easing the strain in his eyes and causing an unconscious tension in his body to relax. He wanted more, so he pressed at the limits of his power and called on shadows at distances he'd never called on before. It was a struggle, like trying to lift a heavy stone just outside your ability. Nothing happened and Zeriel almost gave up. Then he felt a snap—like a barrier giving way—and those distant shadows came to him.

With the help of his power, he managed to sleep that night. With clearer vision in the morning, the rest of the trek through the pass went smoothly. Other than encountering the occasional traveler and being forced to release his power, that is. The blindfold alone was strange—though there was nothing he could do about it if he wanted any sort of vision—but it was far less strange than a black mist riding a horse over a snowy mountain pass. It would be best if he didn't encourage would-be heroes from hunting him down as some sort of ghost rider.

Once he made it down from the pass it was a single day to the Te Et Sha stronghold. Its location was in the thickest part of the Be Bek Ki forest, in the domain of the Central Clans of Fei En Ar. They built it there knowing that only the lost or foolish might find it. The compound was triangular and lined with a deep trench for defense. The only way to pass through the inner wall was to enter the trench and find one of the heavily guarded entrances. The inner wall and the trench were built out of earth and stone to look like natural terrain features, further deterrence from would-be intruders.

The elegant defensive structure had kept the assassins hidden for centuries. Those who stumbled on them would be pressed into service as either slaves or Whispers.

Only once, a hundred years ago, had anyone tried to attack the stronghold. It was a short fight, and the Te Et Sha's response was swift and terrible. The Central Clans only speak of it in hushed tones. As the story went, Clan Eten had angered a great monster that killed half the Clan. The other clans scoff at the story, saying it was just a metaphor for an illness that swept through their village, but the Te Et Sha know differently. They have the skulls of Clan Eten displayed in the stronghold as a reminder of their own strength.

Zeriel had no illusions about that strength. As a precaution against it, he cloaked himself in his power as he dropped into the stronghold's trench. The canopy of trees around him rebuffed the sun enough that there were plenty of shadows around to use and hide in. This use of his powers was becoming second nature to him after all those months, so he moved confidently through the southern trench and toward the main entrance.

What he expected to see as he approached the entrance was the slave guards high on the inner wall. Those too weak to become assassins, but useful enough to die in an assault. Instead, he saw—nothing. The stronghold was never unguarded, and the sight of empty posts put Zeriel on edge. He slowed his approach and found the entrance's stone doors destroyed, strewn across the ground in large sections. The tunnel behind the door was dark, empty of the white vine lanterns that normally lined its walls. Zeriel's eyes could make out the inside as if it were fully lighted and saw nothing there. He entered the tunnel carefully.

Nothing happened as he stalked forward. No hidden traps, no ambushes. Just an empty tunnel. He slowed at the other end but again found nothing, so he stepped carefully into the compound.

The view inside struck him like he was seeing it for the first time. The inner wall was at least a hundred feet tall and curved into a continuous circle that stretched out into the distance. It was a wonder the place had never been discovered. Stone buildings lined the wall and faced inward to look over the field at the center. Farmland, orchards, and pastures stood near a wide river that passed through the western side of the stronghold. The eastern side held a large training field with obstacles, mock fortifications, and everything else needed to train the assassins inside. A barracks stood in the center of the training field where the fledglings would live until they passed their final tests. The scale of the compound overwhelmed him.

At first glance, nothing seemed amiss, but something *was* wrong. The wrongness was so stark that daggers appeared in his hands by reflex.

"Where is everyone?" Jekjarah said, stepping past Zeriel and surveying the stronghold.

A quick glance at the moon told him it was just past midday. The place should be busy with people. "That's a good question," he said.

"Maybe they knew you were coming," Jekjarah said, "and set some sort of trap."

Zeriel gave him a flat expression. "If they knew I was coming they'd have sprung the trap in the trenches, or the entrance tunnel."

"Then why are you holding your daggers?" Jekjarah said.

"Because I could be wrong, obviously." Zeriel stayed close to the inner wall, using the shadows of the buildings to keep from exposing himself. As he passed one of the buildings, he noticed something through an open door. Peering inside he saw the bodies of a man and woman, both lying in pools of wet blood. They wore the burlap clothes of slaves, and both of their throats were slashed.

"Clean," Jekjarah said. "Looks like assassin's work."

It didn't make sense. There were no signs of the prolonged battle that would have ensued from an invading force. A close inspection of the surrounding buildings showed more corpses, all killed with the same precise strikes. He didn't need to see more to know that the Te Et Sha had turned on their own. But the question he couldn't answer was, why?

Anxiety gave speed to his feet as Zeriel hurried to his goal, visible from anywhere in the compound. It was the tallest building there, close to the southern entrance and cut into concentric half-circles that rose to the full height of the wall it sat against. Towers three stories tall and topped with parapets lined the bottom level. Of all the sights in Eleshar, this building—the Fortress of Adversaries—had a unique way of making Zeriel feel small each time he approached it. He had to crane his neck awkwardly just to take in its full majesty.

The building held the Elders' council chambers, where he'd planned on getting answers. It should have been the most heavily guarded location in the stronghold, but as Zeriel approached he saw that even here there was no sign of activity. Not a single archer on the towers.

"I told you it was a trap," Jekjarah said, floating off to the side.

"You don't know that." Zeriel approached the side of the lowest ring and quickly scrambled through an open window.

"You seem to be pretty sure of it, though."

The hallucination was right. A small piece of Zeriel's mind—the one Jekjarah was latching onto—felt like there was a noose closing around his neck. As usual, though, he overstated Zeriel's true thoughts. Why kill so many people who were necessary for the workings of the stronghold just to set a trap for *him*?

Zeriel found a window far from the main entrance of the Fortress and slipped inside. The room he entered was one of the many small bedrooms meant for attendants of the tower. Like the rest of the compound, it was currently empty. Quickly shifting to the door, Zeriel opened it to peer into the hallway. It too was empty. As he moved into the hall, he noticed it wasn't just empty of attendants, but the stagnant air was empty even of sound. The stillness pressed in on him from all sides. Since Zeriel had arrived at the stronghold, he hadn't released the shadows that cloaked him. But as he stalked the halls of the tower, he let them fall. The inside was dark enough that his blindfold was sufficient for sight, and holding his power was like tensing a muscle. If he held it for too long, it drained his stamina, and the powers became increasingly difficult to maintain.

After passing a few doorways, Zeriel came across an open archway with a staircase heading down into a basement room. He paused for a moment, then quickly took the stairs.

"Where are you going?" Jekjarah asked, as he followed behind.

"Just a hunch I need to check on," Zeriel whispered.

"It would be the end of the Te Et Sha if they destroyed it all."

Zeriel nodded in response, not willing to speak even a whisper as the bottom of the stairs came closer. There was another open archway to the chamber below. The chances of someone with malicious intent making it this far were miniscule to the point that no one even considered locking up what was inside.

The stairs deposited him into a circular chamber. At the center was a station with various glass tubes and bottles all arranged purposefully. Burns marked the bottom of the bottles and dried gray reside caked the inside. A distinct sour odor had taken root in every inch of the chamber's floor and walls and Zeriel quickly banished the painful memory it brought up.

Along the walls of the chamber were tall shelves, all lined with bottles full of an aggressively reddish purple colored liquid with swirls of black throughout.

Eleshar's Curse. There would be no Te Et Sha without the abominable concoction.

The chamber was completely undisturbed.

Jekjarah walked up to a set of shelves and inspected the bottles there. "I guess they didn't want to *completely* destroy the organization."

"Or maybe they plan to come back for it later?"

"Maybe." Jekjarah turned to Zeriel. "Satisfied? Isn't there something more pressing you should be worrying about?"

The hallucination was right. While this did answer one of his questions, there were many more answers he needed, all more important than this one.

Zeriel made his way back to the hallway and circled the tower toward the main entrance. Not a soul was in sight, and that continued to be true when Zeriel found the main steps that led to the upper floors.

He turned to take the stairs. They lead straight to the top of the Fortress where the council chamber sat.

What he saw on those stairs stopped him in his tracks.

Blood dripped down the steps in macabre, slow-moving waterfalls. Bodies lay strewn across the staircase, lost weapons rested near slack hands, their skin ghost white. With careful steps Zeriel navigated through the gore, taking in the sight of it all. The corpses were wearing the grey clothes of fledglings.

Jekjarah appeared at the top of the staircase, his eyes opened wide, and the edges of his mouth hinted at a grin. "I can't believe we missed this," he said breathing heavily. "*We* could have bathed in this carnage!"

Zeriel ignored Jekjarah's comment. It was best not to unnecessarily feed into it. "We can rule out a trap," he whispered.

"Looks like it." Jekjarah went down on one knee as Zeriel reached the top of the steps. He pressed his ghostly hand into the pool of blood. "But if it's not a trap, then what happened?"

"I'm not sure," Zeriel said as he turned and looked up at the steps heading to the next floor. More bodies littered the staircase ahead. "I have a feeling we're about to find out."

As he continued his climb the corpses began to transition from the fledglings to those of full assassins. He'd happened to catch the face of one of the assassins and it made him pause. Zeriel had been given the name The Worst One. A pejorative title given to the least skilled among them, and it was the excuse the other assassins used to persecute him. The face he stared at was that of Otelema, the closest thing to a friend he'd made in the organization, and the only one who ever stood up for him.

A memory flashed through his mind at the sight of the woman. A group of fellow fledglings had tied him up and dragged him outside of the barracks where no one could see. They meant to kill him that night. Zeriel tried to fight back, but there were too many of them, and they'd caught him by surprise.

Otelema saved him, rushing in and beating them to within an inch of their lives. The masters had whipped her for it, but they'd executed the ones who'd jumped him. Their trainer, Elilta, had laid out the rules at the start of their training: Any fighting would be severely punished, but those who tried or succeeded to murder one of their own—without the express approval of the Elders, that is—would die for the privilege.

In a quick motion Zeriel pulled his gaze away from Otelema and continued up the stairs. He needed to make it to the council chambers if he was going to find answers. He ignored the rest of the bodies and gained speed as the stairs exited the building and exposed him to the open sky for the last two levels. A white haze covered his vision, but the steps cleared of all obstacles from this point, easing the burden of his obscured vision.

The large doors to the council chambers were finally in sight. They were wide open—something Zeriel had never seen before. He increased his speed, bursting through the doorway. The haze lifted from his vision in time for him to clearly see ten elders sitting around their stone table, throats slit. On the far end of the table was the Eleventh, his head being held up to expose his neck. The elder bled from his nose, terror spreading across his face. He tried to cry out when he saw Zeriel, but he didn't have a chance before the man standing being him slit his throat to match the rest.

The assassin wiped the blood off his dagger on the elder's clothes as a woman stepped up next to him with her eyes on Zeriel.

"Look who's just darkened our doorway, brother," the woman said, resting her arm on the man's shoulder. The excited look on her face sent a chill down Zeriel's spine.

The assassin looked in Zeriel's direction and smiled. "The Worst One? I thought he died in that fire."

"I guess not," Lushame said.

"Looks like being the cleanup crew paid off this time."

Without a word of warning, the Ori twins attacked.

CHAPTER FIFTEEN

Zeriel could never properly describe the experience of being at the bottom of the most elite group of assassins in the world. It meant finding a limited few in the world who could match his skills, let alone best him. Though the extraordinary strength he gained from Eleshar's Curse played a large part, the combination of the potion with the extreme training of the Te Et Sha elevated him to a level few could match.

When he returned to the stronghold and sparred with the others, he failed to match their skill. He secretly hoped his new power might elevate him in the ranks of his peers. But even if it did, it wasn't enough to put him on the same level as of one of the Ori twins, let alone both of them at the same time.

That's why he slammed one of his stunners on the ground the moment he saw them advancing, then turned and ran. This wasn't the time to get heroic. Likely he wouldn't survive this encounter.

"Arg!" Denetek yelled as the stunner went off.

"Ded burn it!" Lushame screamed to the foreign god of the Virtues. Her voice rose to the pitch of a terrifying screech that propelled Zeriel forward.

Partially blinded and deafened by his stunner, he took the stairs behind him two, sometimes three, at a time.

Jekjarah appeared at the entryway where the stairs entered the lower levels. "Faster!" he said, waving him forward. "That'll only slow them down."

"I know!" Zeriel yelled, focused on his footing.

"Insane worm! I'll kill you!" Lushame screamed from close behind.

The bright sunlight on the stone stairs created a sharp contrast to the black mist that surrounded him. Instead of hiding him, his powers made him as obvious as a bright light in the dark. At the same time, he couldn't release his power, or he'd be blinded. He *needed* to get inside before they caught him.

A throwing knife hit one of the stone steps to his left. He zigzagged to avoid future projectiles. It would slow him down but giving up a little speed to save his life seemed like a good trade.

"What are you doing, you fool?" Jekjarah said. "They're going to catch you!"

The hallucination was right, they'd already slowed him down, the other one could easily catch up and land a killing blow. He pivoted and sped in a direct line toward the entrance, now a handful of steps away from him.

As if on cue, he heard a sword clang against the stone just behind him. "Damn slippery bastard!" Denetek shouted.

Zeriel dove down the final group of steps, entering the building at an angle to land in a roll on the floor. He came up on his feet just out of the direct line of the doorway. Darkness touched him and he pulled on it to deepen his cover, then he found the darkest location and slipped into it. With the blazing sun in the sky, he wouldn't be completely invisible, but he'd have enough cover to make a good escape attempt.

He waited several heartbeats, but they didn't pursue him. Not willing to let them plan his death without taking action, he continued through the most shadowed areas inside the tower, pushing farther away from the stairs.

"Where'd he go?" came Lushame's voice from behind him.

"There!" Denetek said. "I saw something move around that corner."

Jekjarah appeared to Zeriel's right, floating alongside him. "What's your plan now?"

An open door showing a dark room caught his attention. Mid-run, he slid his foot into the corner of the outer wall and the floor and launched himself into the room. He slipped into the darkest corner of the room and knelt while he fought to control the pace and volume of his breathing.

"Zeriel," Jekjarah whispered, his lips almost touching Zeriel's ear. "I just remembered—"

He swatted the hallucination away like a pestering bug, and caught the Ori twins speeding past the door, barely making a sound. He'd bought himself some time, but he harbored no illusions of safety. Memories of countless chases at the end of his missions reminded him of the tenacity of a motivated pursuer.

There were many paths to the lower levels, he just needed to find *one*. Preferably in the opposite direction of the Ori twins. After a short pause to let the Ori twins get further down the hall, he moved for the door.

"Zeriel," Jekjarah said from behind him. "You really need to hear me out."

He didn't respond.

"Just stop for one damned second!"

Stepping out into the hall, he turned to face the way he'd come.

"Arg! Gold crush me," Jekjarah said, as if through gritted teeth. "Zeriel!"

The hallucination's persistence was strange, but he didn't have time to dwell on it. A dark spot in the ceiling caught his eye. He looked up just in time to dodge out of the way of Denetek as the man dropped from the ceiling, daggers slicing out at him.

"Zeriel!" Jekjarah said. "Listen! Remember—"

"Shut up!"

Distracted, he didn't see Denetek's attack. A hard kick into his stomach launched him toward the outer window. The man's enhanced strength defenestrated Zeriel, sending him into the open air.

Glass shards sliced his back open. Twisting in the air, he looked down and saw the rough shapes of the tower below through the haze of blinding sunlight. Hovering a hundred feet above them made one thing frighteningly clear: He was about to die.

The adrenaline in his system kept him painfully lucid as he began to fall. His stomach lurched into his throat as the naked pull of gravity took hold. With his eyes closed, waiting for his inevitable death.

"Think about the inn," said Jekjarah's disembodied voice. "Remember what you were feeling as you passed out among the fire."

He did remember. He felt now as he had then. Desperate, staring down the inevitable. Yet he'd escaped. The image of a circle of unburned wood flooring underneath him flashed into his mind.

"That's it!" Jekjarah exclaimed.

Zeriel's eyes shot open. He had seconds to act. He focused on the emotions Jekjarah pointed out. Thinking back, he remembered his need to survive. He pressed all his will into his powers, commanding them to do...*something!*

Nothing happened.

He focused on the roof of the first level of the Fortress as it rushed toward him and released his grip on the darkness around him. At least his miserable life would finally be over.

Instead of dissipating, the shadows moved of their own accord, coalescing into a ball around him and solidifying. As he passed the second levels' outer walls, dark tendrils reached out from the ball and dug into the stone, slowing his descent and swinging him toward the wall.

Then he hit the roof.

❖

His eyes crept open to the sound of a beating drum. Someone slammed against the inside of his head in time to the beat. The sunlight shot red hot daggers into the back of his eye sockets.

"Thank Obe," Jekjarah said standing over him. "I thought we were dead for sure."

Zeriel dragged his body to the corner where the wall of the second level met the roof of the first, then painfully sat up and leaned his back against the wall. Pain throbbed throughout his bones. "What happened just before I hit?"

"Looked to me like you used the shadows to protect you and cushion the fall."

"I didn't do that," Zeriel said as he noticed his blindfold had fallen around his neck. He put it back over his eyes, dulling the pain.

"Well, you're not a pile of gore, so does it matter?"

Zeriel looked up at the wall. Two deep grooves were gouged into it, like the giant claws of some monster had run down its length.

Voices sounded from the open windows of the wall he'd slid down.

"How do you know you killed him?" Lushame asked. "You didn't watch him fall to make sure."

"I saw him fly out that window and fall half the height of the Fortress," Denetek said with a thread of annoyance weaved into his tone. "No one could survive that."

"No one can survive four hours inside a burning building either, but he did."

Lushame was right, of course. They were trained to visually confirm their kills. Luck must have caused Veshet's arrogance to leave him in those flames without finishing the job.

Completely exposed, he knew they would find him. He painfully repositioned his body and played dead. In a bittersweet stroke of something like luck, he'd bled enough already that blood pooled around him.

"You're not going to let this go, are you?" Denetek asked.

"No," she said flatly. "I'm not going to report this to Veshet only for that rat to show up alive again because we were sloppy. Do you know what he'd do to us?"

"Fine. He should have fallen near here."

Zeriel heard the shutters of one of the windows on the wall squeal open and he held his breath.

"Look at that," Denetek said, "one dead weakling."

"Good. Not so hard, was it?"

"Let's just go. I'd like to be part of the raid on Clan Ra. They spawned this one, after all."

"You just can't let things go, can you brother?"

Their voices grew muffled as the two left. Hearing Denetek say, "You know I can't," was the last thing he could make out.

He sat back against the wall, dug his emergency medical kit from his pocket, and got to work. The deep cuts in his back had caused the pool of blood he lay in, so he focused on that. He removed his shirt and awkwardly wrapped his last bandage around his body, pulling it tight to keep as much pressure on the wounds as possible.

After a more thorough examination, he concluded he hadn't broken any bones, a small miracle he didn't expect. He reached in his backpack and removed the small amount of eshenroot powder he carried with him—it had incredible pain-relieving properties. The powder was difficult to swallow without water, but he managed it.

Roughly an hour later the wounds on his back stopped bleeding and the powder reduced his pain to a dull ache. When he tried to stand, his muscles were weak, and it took considerable effort to get on his feet. Once up, he spotted a door in the second level's wall and moved toward it.

Jekjarah appeared next to him. "What now?"

"You heard them. They're going after my Clan."

"So what? Didn't you run away from that place and vow never to return."

Zeriel opened the door, then paused to look at Jekjarah. "It's not about the Clan," he said, memories of his childhood swirling in his head. "With any luck, Veshet will be there."

Jekjarah shook his head. "You don't even know why they're headed there."

"Does it matter if I find and kill them?"

"You're making a lot of assumptions."

"I'm following the information."

Jekjarah threw his hands in the air. "And now you're the worst assassin *and* the worst Whisper."

Zeriel stepped inside the second level. "I'm the worst at *everything*."

CHAPTER SIXTEEN

Before leaving, Zeriel took his time to scavenge supplies from the Fortress, moving from the kitchen and the armory to the supply closets. With a pack filled with food, several skins of water, two new daggers, and a bastard sword he'd slung across his back, he left the stronghold.

The eshenroot dulled the pain, allowing him to travel the several miles to the west where he'd left his horse. It was still there, munching on the grass by a stream. The horse glanced at him as he approached and snorted. Not exactly the greeting he had hoped for, but he never let himself get too attached to the animals, being in the habit of abandoning them when it suited him. Or use one as a decoy or eat one in a pinch. There were many uses for horses that became more difficult if you named them.

A glance at the moon through the tree canopy told Zeriel it was late afternoon. Considering the events of the day, the time had come to camp and rest. After about an hour, he built a fire and had fish cooking. Soon enough, the eshenroot started wearing off and the pain returned.

"Jek," he said. It wasn't often that he called upon the hallucination, but there are times when one needs someone to bounce their thoughts off. Without companions to rely on, he often turned to the hallucination.

Jekjarah appeared suddenly, sitting on a rock across from his fire. "When you get to the Clan and Veshet isn't there, what will you do?"

"I'll follow him wherever he went from there. But that's not what I wanted to talk about."

The hallucination plastered a fake look of interest on his face. "Oh? What *did* you want to talk about?"

"Mostly how you knew to remind me about what happened in the fire."

"I don't know," Jekjarah said, letting the disdain for that comment show on his face. "I know what you know, and you know that."

Zeriel sighed heavily and rubbed his forehead. "So, you don't know how I did...whatever it was I did to save myself."

"No clue."

Intrigue mixed with fear spiraled through him. If he didn't know how he controlled his powers like that, and Jekjarah didn't know, then what *had* happened? On a whim he decided to reach out to Plaxes and called out to her. Silence was her only response.

"She seemed kind of busy the last time you saw her," Jekjarah said. "You must not be very important to her."

"Maybe I should just—"

"Try to do what you did at the tower?" Jekjarah interrupted. "What could it hurt?"

Trees cast shadows all around him, making this the perfect place to try. He pulled on the darkness around him and drew them close. That part was familiar, but the next steps—if there were any—were a mystery. Combing through his memory of the event, he searched for an out of place sensation or emotion, but there was nothing. Then he searched through his thoughts, and again found nothing. Focused his awareness on his body—nothing. There were no answers.

Difficult things took time and effort for Zeriel, more so than for others, so he pressed on. Instead of waiting for his power to direct him, he focused his will toward directing the power. Stretching out his hand, palm up, he set his mind on coalescing the shadows into a layer over his hand. To his surprise, they moved at his command, coalescing over it like a glove of misty darkness. As he moved his fingers, he could feel a slight resistance as if a thin mucus covered his hand.

"Well, well," Jekjarah said. "You did it."

"It seemed to need a very explicit intent. But this isn't quite the same as that bubble, or the tendrils that carved into the stone, is it?"

"No, I guess not."

Zeriel pressed his mind against the shadows again and told them to rise above his hand. Again, they obeyed and rose in an undulating mass that floated in the air over his palm. Progress was enough to motivate him, so he tried hardening them.

Nothing happened.

"Try harder," Jekjarah urged.

Things of the mind were where he struggled the most, so he did the only thing he knew how. Muscles tightened all over his body as he physically strained to harden his will. The misty black ball began to coalesce further into the consistency of slime, dripping from the ball then vanished into back smoke as it fell. A weariness spread through his muscles and forced him to drop his hands and release the shadows, leaving them to evaporate into nothingness.

"I can't believe you never thought to do that until now."

"I *am* the Worst One, after all." The weariness turned to tiredness that practically drove him to the ground. "I'll need some practice to make any use of that."

Jekjarah began to fade away. "Knowing you, it'll be a lot of practice," he said then disappeared completely.

As sleep took him, his eyes fixed on the sword that lay next to him. A bastard sword wasn't the typical assassin's weapon, and he wasn't quite sure why he'd even grabbed it. The light of the sun that flashed through the swaying tree canopy touched the silver of the weapon's hilt and flashed white across his vision. A memory, blurry and amorphous, touched at the edges of his mind. Imaginary silhouettes danced clumsily around each other and the trees, striking out in unpracticed motions. The memory, hazy like a dream lost in the hours after waking or buried by illness—sharpened in his mind.

❖

Laluk darted around a tree and tagged Zeriel on the left shoulder with his wooden sword.

"Ow!" Zeriel dropped his own wooden sword and rubbed at the pain.

"Oh, come on," Laluk protested, "I barely touched you."

The two were around ten years old and had been playing in the woods on the northern section of Zeriel's family's land all day.

"I can't block anything you do, let alone get a hit on you."

"You just need more practice. You'll get it eventually."

"I'll never be as good as you."

"I've been training with my father since I was five, Zeriel. You've been farming. Of course, I'm better." Laluk meant it to be comforting, as if pointing out the insurmountable difference in their skill, and the futility of his efforts would make him feel better. It didn't.

He didn't want to be a farmer. He never did. It was why he'd been forcing Laluk to spend entire days sparring with him in the woods whenever he got the chance. His friend was right, though. As hard as he tried, and no matter how many hours he trained, he could never match Laluk's skill.

Pushing through the frustration he said, "Let's go again."

❖

"Shouldn't you be sleeping?" Jekjarah said, pulling him out of the memory. The hallucination's legs were crossed as he sat on the log with a bored look on his face.

"I was just replaying a memory in my head. I hadn't thought about it in a long time." He closed his eyes.

"You should worry more about Veshet than some village you abandoned a decade ago."

"You're probably right." His thoughts turned to the use of his powers. Now that he'd discovered there was more to them than cloaking himself in shadow, his excitement grew. The ride to Clan Ra was a long one, giving him plenty of time to practice.

It was with that thought in his mind, and the burden of the Te Et

Sha lifted, that Zeriel drifted into the best sleep he'd had in years.

CHAPTER SEVENTEEN

A small globe of condensed shadow hovered over Zeriel's hand as he rode southward toward Clan Ra. He moved his fingers, shifting the ball of shadows through different shapes. Without warning it exploded in a puff of mist. He leaned back in frustration and exhaustion, eyes resting on the sky through the tree canopy. The sun's light was diffused and darkened through a layer of clouds as it started its slow trek down the western sky. In the last few days of his journey, he'd been working with this new aspect of his power, making painfully slow progress.

When the sun was obscured, as it was today, his control of the shadows was stronger. Even with that assistance, the effort was exhausting, both physically and mentally. It made him wonder how Veshet used his powers with such ease.

"He's the best of the best. Why wouldn't it be easy for him?"

Zeriel snapped his head to the side to see Jekjarah floating over the ground alongside him with his arms crossed. "I guess you're right," he said, turning his focus back on the road. It led him through the bottom of a deep valley following the banks of a large river. The river's water flowed slowly through the valley and brought with it a cool breeze and a crisp scent.

The mix of deciduous trees on each side of the road were in the process of shedding their bright red, pink, and purple leaves to prepare for the cold of the dark month that would come in a few weeks. Those leaves joined with the river to fill the air with their aroma of fresh earth and flowers. Thin grey smoke— perhaps from a distant forest fire—hung in the air and added the oddly sweet aroma of burned wood to the redolence of the valley. The soft glow from the trees scattered through the smoke and added an otherworldly aura to the forest around him.

"We're almost there now," Jekjarah said.

"It's a strange feeling to come home after all these years."

"Except this isn't your home," Jekjarah said.

"True. It hasn't been for years, but with the Te Et Sha gone..."

"You can't possibly mean—"

"Shh!" Zeriel said with a sharp gesture. The road turned a corner and gave Zeriel his first view of Clan Ra in the distance.

Dark columns of smoke rose into the sky beyond where the path exited the forest. The glowing lights of the trees felt like a message, now. A silent rebuke for thinking the haze foretold their destruction. In truth, he'd arrive too late. Zeriel coaxed his horse into a canter and quickly broke through the tree line.

When he thought of Clan Ra, he remembered a vibrant mining town with well-kept roads and modern, almost out of place buildings for such a small village. Precious metals and gems of all kinds, priceless anywhere else in the world, were on display as mere ornaments on the town's buildings and signs. The townspeople would wear them as casual jewelry. The mine in the south of town was so rich that, for centuries, they'd practically given its riches away to the foreigners who visited. One entrepreneurial king tried to lay siege to the town long ago. He didn't know enough about the people of Fei En Ar, so Clan Ra made sure to educate him properly. That arrogant king and his army never returned home, though Clan Ra made sure to send his head back to his family. Out of respect to his title, of course.

The village Zeriel saw before him now looked nothing like that strong, vibrant home he remembered. He'd entered from the north where most of the peoples' homes had stood. They were burned husks now. Wisps of smoke rose from piles of ash and wood. The slight crackling of still-hot embers could be heard in all directions. In the distance was more of the same. While some buildings looked untouched, the destruction was significant.

In the distance a large pillar of smoke rose from the main square, filling the village with the nauseatingly sweet yet putrid stench of burning flesh. Zeriel recognized it now that he was close, though he'd caught a hint of it on the road earlier.

As he crossed the bridge over the river where it bent across his path, he looked down to see the burned and trampled remains of the banners that carried Clan Ra's Stripes. He stared at the cloth that bore three black stripes on top of a field of rust, one stripe larger than the others in the center with the two next to it leaning inward at the top. The condition of those banners reflected the destruction awaiting him. The roads were empty except for burning coal, the debris of destroyed buildings, and blood. No one worked in the rubble, salvaging what they could of their belongings. The lingering shadows where lights once shined told a story of ruin.

"Clan Ra is dead," Jekjarah said, floating at his side and giving voice to his thoughts.

Zeriel ignored the hallucination and pressed on. His first instinct was to explore the village, find more information, and devise a plan from there. Those impulses were remnants of his assassin's intuition, and he almost followed their urgings. Then he came across an intersection where a road branched off to his right and over the river as it bent its way south again.

On his left were the remnants of a building he remembered well. The old widow Hesh had lived there during his childhood. He'd spent countless hours playing pranks on the poor woman. It was a favorite pastime of his best friend, Laluk, and his. Though she'd likely died years ago, he felt a pang of sadness as he looked upon her ruined home. Sadness turned to regret as he remembered the torment they'd put the poor woman through.

He pulled his eyes away from the memory and toward the bridge on his right. A mill stood on the other side of the bridge against the bank of the river, its water wheel still turning from the drive of the river's current. Zeriel had spent most days of his adolescence working in that mill. A small act of defiance against his father for—

Movement in the buildings up ahead caught his eye.

Someone sneaked through the rubble toward him. From the person's movements, they weren't a skilled stalker. Unconcerned, he let his focus push beyond the mill to a large home in the distance. It was his childhood home, or what may still be left of it. It looked intact from that distance, though he was too far to see if any damage had been done.

The devastation around him was a stark reminder of just how much Veshet and the Ori twins had upended his life. He was no longer an assassin, the woman he thought he'd loved had died, and his childhood home had been reduced to ashes. A strange wave of relief washed over him. By sheer chance he'd found that, for the first time in his life, he was free.

A vision of Lavel's body lying on the floor of a burning inn came to him.

Guilt and grief mixed with his relief. Guilt, for the sudden desire to abandon his quest for vengeance, and grief for what he'd lost. But those emotions were brief. For the first time in his life, he was free, truly free. There was nothing in his past weighing him down, and no one in his present to whom he owed loyalty. He could go anywhere, and do anything, just like he'd dreamed. Without realizing it, Zeriel was already coaxing his horse down the road to his family home.

"Where are you going?" Jekjarah asked.

"I need to see what's become of them."

"Hopefully they're dead."

"Enough of that," he said tersely.

Jekjarah disappeared.

A quick shuffling sounded from behind. He ignored it, taking several deep breaths to calm himself and pressed forward. As he passed the mill he was hit with a wave of nostalgia from the rhythm of the water as it dripped from the blades of the water wheel. The longing he felt after that emotion surprised him. Those distant memories, once alien, now offered a ray of hope for a new beginning.

With the mill behind him, the valley flattened out on his right and turned into farmland; his family's farmland. To his left was a hill that hid more farms to the south. A large windmill stood in the distance there, nestled in the seat of a saddle between the hill Zeriel was passing and another one to its south.

Memories threatened to distract him again, but he pushed those aside. The road forked and he took the right path toward his family's home, remaining focused on his goal. As he approached the home, he could see remnants of a fire. Oddly, it failed to consume the entire structure. The building wasn't completely unscathed, but it was mostly intact. He stopped in front of his former home for a moment, taking in the sights and trying to ignore the memories that threatened to flood his mind.

Jekjarah appeared in front of him, staring at the building. "What is it you were hoping to see here?" he asked.

"I still don't know, Jek. Stop pestering me."

Jekjarah turned his head to look at Zeriel. "You're pestering yourself. The question you might want to ask is why you have so many reservations about the thoughts forming in your mind."

Zeriel dismounted his horse and headed toward the door. "I don't know what you're talking about."

"Of course you don't," Jekjarah said, then winked out of existence.

Zeriel stepped up to the door that was cracked open and slowly pushed it the rest of the way. The scent of extinguished fire stabbed his nose and brought tears to his eyes. Stepping inside, he was met with a sight he'd seen a thousand times before. The door opened to the ransacked remnants of a living area that consisted of a small sitting area just inside the door and a dining table and chairs on the far-right side of the room. The table had been knocked on its side and the chairs were tossed throughout the room with a sense of callous indifference. Beyond the table was a cooking area against the far wall, equally thrashed with its various accoutrements scattered everywhere.

On his left was an open door. The family's shared sleeping space could be seen on the other side. Zeriel saw the western mountainside through a hole in the outer wall created by a wagon that crashed through it. Between the home and the mountains was a large field. A well stood at the center of four crop fields, three of which had obviously been harvested recently while the fourth stood fallow.

Wisps of smoke escaped from the top of the bedroom doorway, which caught his attention enough to bring him into the room. Someone ransacked the space, piled the furniture in the center of the room, and set it on fire. Black smoke rose from the pile, collecting against the ceiling, then escaping mostly through the hole in the outer wall.

As he stepped up to the hole Zeriel saw why the blaze hadn't fully consumed the house. Two bodies lay face down on the floor, their hands still clutching buckets. Blood stains encircled them. Upon inspection he confirmed what he already knew. The two men were his brothers.

It looked like they'd used the wagon to break through the wall to make a quick path from the well to the fire and had almost extinguished it before Veshet's forces cut them down. Looking at their bodies, Zeriel felt a strange numbness. There was grief in there somewhere, but also anger. After a decade of attempts to put his family ties—and the drama that came with them—behind him, it seemed he'd failed. There was a bond with his brothers he could never shake, no matter how hard he tried. They'd been forced to band together back then, or—

Footsteps pounded on the floor behind him and Zeriel spun to see a figure charging him. He pulled the shadows close, doing his best to fade away against the blackened pile of furniture. Almost instinctively he managed to bring up a waist high wall of solidified darkness between them. The figure bounced off the wall and fell away. Zeriel's powers gave out a second later and exhaustion drove him to his knees.

He breathed heavily from the exertion of his powers when he locked eyes with his attacker. Surprise and fear showed on the man's face as the last remnants of his powers dissipated, but what surprised Zeriel was he recognized the man.

"Laluk?"

His old friend's face shifted to confusion. "How do you know my name?"

"It's me. Zeri—"

He felt a sudden impact to the back of his head, and unconsciousness took him.

CHAPTER EIGHTEEN

Zeriel woke with a pounding headache and a deep ache on the back of his head where he'd been struck. He tried to move but found himself bound to a chair with his arms tied behind his back. Opening his eyes, the brightness of the room practically blinded him. As his awareness sharpened, he realized someone had removed his blindfold.

"Zeriel," came a familiar voice. The man's tone was more confident than Zeriel remembered.

"It's been a long time, Laluk."

Through the haze across his vision, he barely made out the silhouette of his old friend looming nearby. The man's arms were crossed and his posture hostile. He was stocky as ever, but more muscular than he was as a child. He wore a thick leather vest and brown trousers with a sword strapped to his waist. Obscured as he was, Laluk commanded the space with just his presence. He grabbed a chair and placed it in front of Zeriel, then sat facing him. "We thought you were dead."

"I probably should be, if I'm honest."

"No, I mean your father told us you died. Gored by a wild boar in the woods on your property. We buried you in the village graveyard."

"I don't know what you buried, but it wasn't me."

"Clearly," Laluk said. "Where have you been all this time?"

Something was off. This wasn't the temperament of the friend he remembered. He decided to test the man. "Why do you have me tied up?" he asked as he got to work on the knots tying his hands.

Laluk leaned back in his chair. "I'm not sure I can trust you."

"Why not?"

A slight movement in his face seemed to indicate a raised eyebrow. "A dead man shows up alive in the same outfit as a group of people that practically wiped out our entire village. I'm not even sure you are who you say you are."

"You've got a good point," he said, then finished freeing his hands. Leaning forward, he tossed the rope to Laluk. "Put like that, I probably wouldn't trust me either. But rest assured, if I wanted to hurt you, I'd have done it by now."

Laluk looked at the rope, the shock obvious in his face even through Zeriel's partially obscured vision. "That was my best knot."

"It could use some work."

His friend didn't react visibly, he just dropped the rope on the ground and leaned forward. "You're not how I remember. If it really is you."

Zeriel sighed, settled back in his chair, and crossed his legs casually. "We were eleven and just starting to like girls. It was the middle of a light month, and we had the idea to collect as much cow manure as we could and rig to drop on widow Hesh's head when she opened her front door in the morning. That night we'd snuck out and met up by the mill, but to my dismay you'd brought...what was her name again?"

"Andelei," Laluk said flatly.

"Right, Andelei. You thought she'd be so impressed by our cleverness, even though she thought you'd snuck her out for something more romantic." Zeriel chuckled to himself. "I remember the look on her face when we showed her the pile of manure we'd gathered. She ran off and told the Chief that very night."

Laluk shook his head, and his shoulders dropped. "Where—"

Laluk was cut off by the voices in Zeriel's head. They came out of nowhere, frantic and explosive in his mind.

He doesn't believe you! He's going to kill you!

Kill him first! It's the only way!

Zeriel shook his head trying to silence the voices as they stacked one top of the other.

No! Kill yourself! It's the only way out!

"Shut up!" he screamed. Blessedly, the voices obeyed.

Laluk's silhouette didn't move. "Wow, it really is you, isn't it?"

"It is. So, what now?"

"We wait. I sent Vinedesh to fetch the new Chief. She'll decide what to do with you."

"And if I don't agree with her decision?"

Laluk lifted a sack and shook it. It jingled.

Zeriel searched for his daggers and tools. They were gone.

"I'm not sure you have much of a choice."

"I don't need those to overpower you."

Laluk laughed. "You can't bluff me, Zeriel. I remember how hopeless you were with a sword." He dropped the bag which let out a cacophony of metallic clanging as it hit the floor. "And it wasn't very hard to catch you just now, either. I'm guessing you stole the outfit off a corpse and wear it to scare off anyone who'd otherwise use your insanity to take advantage of you."

"I didn't know you thought so little of me." Zeriel learned not to take it personally over the years. He *was* insane. However, this was an opportunity to gather information, and he was glad to play the hurt friend if it got him what he wanted.

"Not this again," Laluk said as he stood up and started pacing. "We were friends for a long time. That never changed, even after you got sick. But that also means I know you."

"You *knew* me, but I've changed quite a lot since then."

Laluk shook his head and sighed heavily. "Somehow I doubt that."

Before Zeriel could respond, someone with a thin frame burst through the door. A woman followed close on his heels, if her silhouette was anything to go by. The boy was tall and scrawny, his clothes seeming to hang from what was mostly likely a skeletal frame. His movements communicated the anxiety he felt about the situation.

The woman behind him was everything the boy wasn't. Her mostly gray hair was obvious even through the haze in his vision, but she had a strong posture and confident gait that would stop anyone from calling her elderly. She wore a modest gray dress with a belt that held a bag on her hip. As she came into view, Laluk stepped back, giving her space to command the situation, almost by reflex.

He knew who she was the second he saw her obscured form move through the room. She was the wife of Clan Ra's chief. Though, if what Laluk said was any indication, she was Chief now.

"Hello Leksha," Zeriel said.

She stopped in her tracks at his statement, and eyed him, then turned to Laluk. "Why isn't he tied up?"

"Slipped my knot. But he's not one of them, Chief. It's Zeriel."

She looked back at him and the barest shift in her expression was noticeable through Zeriel's hazy vision. "You're sure?" she asked Laluk.

"I am. He knew about our past, and he had an episode while we were talking."

Chief Leksha nodded, then turned to face Zeriel. "You're supposed to be dead."

"I'm aware. My father didn't want to admit that I ran away, it seems. Faking my death seems a bit drastic though, don't you think?"

"Renniel wasn't known for being a liar."

"There was a lot of things he was in truth, yet not known for," Zeriel said. There was an unspoken weight underneath his statement. A truth they all knew, but none acknowledged.

The Chief turned her head away for a moment, then recovered quickly and said, "Why'd you come back now, and wearing those clothes nonetheless?"

"It's a long story."

"Assuming your life depends on it, would you tell us anyway?"

Zeriel huffed at the threat. The woman was everything he remembered—a stone that had barely been worn down by life, time, or circumstance. Solid, dependable, and willing to do whatever was necessary. The Clan was lucky she'd survived.

Initially he was going to lie. He hesitated, though. Something warm grew in his gut at the situation. A feeling he wasn't familiar with, but one that had no desire for secrets. So, he decided he'd tell his story, in its entirety. Why he ran away from the Clan, about joining the Te En Sha, and about failing Lavel. Even the mysterious powers that appeared with Plaxes's voice in his head.

"You might want to take a seat," he said to them. "This is going to take a while."

❖

It took several hours to tell his story in full, and there was something cathartic about getting it out. Since leaving home he'd never had anyone to confide in, so releasing it all felt like he'd dropped a thousand stones off his back.

"He's lying," Laluk said from a chair next to Chief Leksha. "If he really was one of them, Vinedesh would never have been able to sneak up behind him." He gestured to the boy sitting next to him.

"Maybe his madness is causing him to believe this delusion," Chief Leksha said.

Zeriel sighed and held his palm toward them.

They fell silent and stared. It seemed their doubt didn't fully snuff out their desire to believe his story. Or maybe it was just morbid curiosity that just maybe he was telling the truth.

With an effort, he called the shadows to him, enveloping his entire body.

Vinedesh shot out of his chair and scrambled backward. "He's a Sha Te!" The boy invoked the name of a popular monster created in the imaginations of parents to scare their children into behaving.

Focusing as he had practiced over the last week, Zeriel brought the shadows into a ball floating above his palm. The Chief and Laluk were transfixed, staring at the shadows, waiting for what he might make them do next. Without warning, the ball of shadow puffed into a dark mist and fell toward the floor, dissipating in the air moments later. He leaned back in his chair, breathing heavily.

"I can't believe I'm saying this," Laluk said, "but is that all you can do?"

"That isn't enough?" The Chief responded.

"I understand, but it doesn't seem like a very useful power to have."

Zeriel caught his breath and said, "For an assassin it's incredibly powerful." Then he called on the shadows again, this time letting them envelop him completely. He shifted in the darkness, watching their shocked expressions as he vanished. "You'd never see me coming." They looked in his direction, searching for any sign of his presence.

A small amount of satisfaction washed over Zeriel to see Laluk dumbfounded at his display. When enough time had passed to get his point across Zeriel released the shadows and walked back toward his chair.

"Eleshar protect us," the Chief muttered.

"So, what, you *let* us capture you?" Laluk sounded perturbed.

"No, you really did catch me. I'm new to these powers and when I created a wall of shadows between us it surprised and exhausted me. Vinedesh jumped me before I could recover."

Everyone turned toward Vinedesh who was sitting in a corner hugging his knees to his chest. The sudden attention caused him to startle.

Chief Leksha sighed and shook her head. "What do you want then, Zeriel?"

"I came looking for Veshet."

"You're too late for that."

"Did you come only hoping to get revenge, then?" Laluk asked. "For...what was her name again?"

"Lavel. And yes. Though I doubt I have the skill to get that revenge. I realize that now, with my powers as they are."

"What then?" the Chief asked. "You move on? Stay on Veshet's trail and hope to catch him by surprise?"

Zeriel pondered those questions. The easy answer was yes, but as he considered it more, there were other questions he hadn't allowed himself to ask. Could he keep up the chase? What was different about his current skills that would give his mission even the smallest chance to succeed? Would he be sprinting toward a pointless death? Ruminating over those questions, the answer felt obvious when it finally came to him. "I should take time to train. It might be the only way I have a chance to defeat Veshet and the Ori twins."

Chief Leksha eyed Zeriel, then turned to Laluk. "Take Vinedesh home and tell no one about this."

"I won't leave you with him." Laluk gave Zeriel a wary glance.

"I'll be fine. If he meant to do us harm, I'm sure he could have done it by now."

"That's what I told him," Zeriel said.

The Chief snapped her head toward him, surely giving him a reproachful glare though he couldn't make out her expression. She turned back to Laluk and said, "Now go."

Laluk nodded tersely, scooped up Vinedesh, and the two left, leaving Zeriel alone with Chief Leksha. He suddenly felt like a child again, in trouble after she'd caught him misbehaving.

"Take a walk with me, Zeriel," she said, then turned to step out the door.

CHAPTER NINETEEN

On his way out the door Zeriel picked through his sack. He stashed his tools in his belt pouches, then replaced his blindfold. When he stepped outside the Chief gave him a puzzled look.

"Why the blindfold?" she said, gesturing to her own eyes.

"The powers make my eyes sensitive to light. The more I use them, the worse it gets."

"I see. You use the blindfold as one might to avoid snow blindness." It was an apt comparison. Being a mountain tribe, they knew how to deal with the snowy months of winter in Eleshar.

"Yes. It seems these powers come with some downsides."

Leksha nodded. "Power usually does." She spun around and walked toward the main road. Once Zeriel caught up she said, "The story of your death *did* seem strange."

"How so?"

"The way your father told the story felt...rehearsed. He told it the same way, with the same words, every time."

"And I assume no one saw a body."

"Just a closed casket. Renniel said your body was so mangled that you were unrecognizable." She turned right on the main road, away from the Village proper and toward the other, smaller farms on the outskirts of the village.

"He wasn't a clever man, my father."

"No, he wasn't. But you were in those woods all the time as a youth, so no one questioned him."

"They were my only refuge," Zeriel said, more to himself than the Chief. The thought stole his focus, and a memory flashed through his mind, so vivid it was like he lived it again.

❖

Beams of sunlight sliced through the shadows of trees and touched the ground. In the forest on his family's property a twelve-year-old Zeriel rushed Laluk with a squeaky war cry, his wooden sword held high over his head. Laluk smirked at the outburst, barely lifting his own wooden sword in defense.

As Zeriel swung, Laluk casually stepped to the side and swatted the boy's sword away. Zeriel stumbled and fell face-first in the dirt, eliciting a laugh from his friend.

He bounced to his feet and rubbed his dirt-covered nose. "Shut up," he said, unable to keep the embarrassment out in his voice.

"How long have we been out here, and you still won't listen to me. You're letting the sword control you. You have to let it become part of your body; an extension of your arm."

"I don't understand what that even means," Zeriel complained as he wiped the rest of the dirt from his face. "It's just a sword."

"That's where you're wrong."

This isn't how I recall things. I thought I'd gotten a few good hits on him back then.

He shook his head at his friend, wondering when he would stop talking to him in riddles and teach him to fight like he promised. Laluk had trained with his father for five years so he could join the village watch when he was of age. Zeriel saw it as the perfect opportunity to learn to fight. This was their fifth lesson and he was starting to get tired of the miniscule progress he was making.

He sighed heavily and looked up through the tree canopy. The last time he spotted the moon, it was high above his head. Now, he couldn't see it at all. "I'm late!" he exclaimed, taking off toward his house. He tossed Laluk his wooden sword as he ran past, his friend juggling it before finally making the catch.

The anxiety I felt was so strong, but I can't remember where it came from.

"Same time next week," Laluk called after him.

Zeriel didn't look back or break his stride. By the time he exited the tree line he was out of breath and had to slow to a fast walk. The remainder of the walk through the freshly tilled fields between his house and the forest was agony. A sharp knit had set itself in his side and refused to loosen its grip.

The savory aroma of his mother's cooking hit his nose before he even stepped through the door. A loud growl released from his stomach at the scent, and his mother and two brothers stared at him.

"Gone all day when work needs to be done, but home in time for food," said his oldest. "If only the rest of us lived such a charmed life."

"Stop that, Odenel," Zeriel's mother chided, then focused on Zeriel. "I hope you have a good excuse."

"I was training in the woods with Laluk and lost track of time."

The middle brother scoffed. "You're still trying to join the village watch?"

"What if I am?" Zeriel responded as heat built up in his ears. He entered the rest of the way and closed the front door.

"Then you're even more of an idiot than we thought."

"Kledini!" his mother scolded. "That's no way to talk to your brother."

His brother let out a huff and sat back in his chair, arms folded.

Zeriel's mother pointed at him. "Get yourself cleaned up for dinner. I don't want your father to come home seeing you in that condition."

"Yes, mother," Zeriel said, stepping toward their shared bedroom.

Just then the front door slammed open, a formless silhouette standing under the frame.

Who is that, and why do I feel so much fear?

"Where—"

❖

You're sick!

Death is coming for you.
Everyone knows you're lying to them.
They hate you!
They're lying to you.
Kill them!
Bathe in their blood.

His voices rose in volume and their speech quickened until it was undecipherable noise.

"Enough!" Zeriel screamed. The sudden and deafening rise of the voices brought him out of his reminiscence. "Leave me alone."

The voices quieted—though not completely—leaving Zeriel sweating and breathing heavily. When he finally composed himself, he looked up to see Leksha wearing a strange expression.

"You haven't...changed much," she said.

"I guess not."

The two walked in silence for a time, and Zeriel was thankful for it.

As they passed the farmhouse closest to his family's land, Leksha finally broke the silence. "I remember when you started hearing those voices. You were sixteen at the time, working in the mines."

"Those old miners were lowing me into the deepest part of the cleft. We were opening a new tunnel, hoping to find a new gem deposit. None of those cowards would go, so I volunteered. Half-way down a rope snapped, and I fell."

"You fell through a crack no one knew existed, sending you deeper into the mines than anyone had ever been."

"I was lucky. The cavern I fell into had green moss covering the walls, and that green light kept me out of the dark. The memory of what I saw down there feels like it happened just yesterday."

Leksha perked up. "Why didn't you tell anyone? You'd told us that it was dark and you couldn't see anything."

"There *was* something down there. A crystal I'd never seen before with black smoke pouring out. It melted into my skin when I touched it."

"By the Spirit of Eleshar!" Leksha exclaimed.

Zeriel stopped walking.

Leksha took a few more steps before she stopped to wait for him.

"I didn't think anyone would believe me, so I lied and told them I'd been trapped in the dark."

She took time to formulate her response. "Do you think that's where your powers came from?"

"I don't know. If they did, why did they take so long to manifest? Though I do remember feeling drawn to the darkness after the incident, like it was calling to me. It's what drove me to the Te Et Sha. I thought I would make a good assassin."

"But you didn't?"

"They call me the Worst One for a reason."

The two continued, silence covering them as they walked. They stopped near the windmill and watched its vanes spin.

"So, you're going to train with those powers of yours, then?"

"I am."

"Then rebuild your family's home and train here. We could use the extra hands to help rebuild the Village."

Something strange lodged itself in Zeriel's chest at her offer. A sense of rightness that radiated through his body, relaxing muscles he hadn't realized were tight. An unfamiliar emotion tightened his throat and caused tears to well up in his eyes. All he could manage was a nod in response.

"Start with your home," she said. "When you've settled in, we can talk about how you can be useful to the Clan."

"Thank you." Zeriel managed. He turned and headed back as tears fell down his face.

"While you're here," Leksha called to his back. "Maybe you should show Laluk some of what you learned in the last ten years."

Zeriel blinked tears from his eyes and turned back. He gave her a smirk and responded, "Sure."

The Chief nodded at him and left for the village square.

Once she was out of sight, Jekjarah materialized in front of him. "You can't trust them, you know."

He stepped through the hallucination without breaking stride. "We'll see, won't we?"

CHAPTER TWENTY

It wasn't long before Zeriel's leather armor started to feel uncomfortable and inappropriate. He'd found some of his brothers' old clothes early in his cleanup efforts, and after donning a loose shirt with a circular emblem of the Clan's Stripes on the left breast, and simple brown trousers, he realized how long it had been since he'd worn something other than leather that wasn't part of a disguise.

Restoring his old home was harder than he anticipated. Other than the obvious hole in the western wall, he found scorched wood in the hidden corners of the home. When he thought he'd fixed the last section of charred wood, he found another. He was in the process of completing work on a burned floorboard when a knock came at his door.

After setting his tools down, Zeriel grabbed a cloth to wipe his hands off as he went to answer. He opened the door to reveal Laluk on the other side. His friend immediately tossed a wooden sword at Zeriel, which he caught easily.

"Nice catch. Weren't you the *worst* assassin? I thought I'd get you with that one."

"I was still one of them," Zeriel replied. He spun the practice weapon in his hand and pointed it at his friend. "Are you challenging me to a duel, then?"

"Something like that." Laluk revealed his own practice blade from behind his back. "I wanted to see how I faired against you after all that fancy training." He leaned in conspiratorially and whispered, "Even if you are the Worst One."

Zeriel laughed. "You might not like the result."

"I'll take my chances."

"Alright, but don't say I didn't warn you."

The two stepped outside. It was roughly a week until the next dark month was fully upon them. The sun sat near the western horizon, which put it well below the mountain peak, leaving the entire village draped in twilight shadows. It was dark enough that Zeriel didn't need to wear his blindfold. The chill of the air hit Zeriel as they squared up in front of the house.

"Ready?" Laluk asked, getting into a fighting stance.

"Are you?"

His friend moved in and tried Zeriel with a quick strike. It was easy enough to block and gave Zeriel an opening to reach out with a probe of his own. Laluk blocked his attack with ease.

Laluk shifted back, putting distance between them after the exchange. "Your repairs look good. It's easier work than the rest of us are dealing with, though." He charged in, this time with more speed and power.

Zeriel blocked his strikes. He let his body relax to emphasize to his friend that he wasn't taking the match seriously.

"In most cases we're rebuilding homes from the ground up," his friend said while they continued their exchange.

"It doesn't feel easy, but you're right." Zeriel shifted from defense to offense, putting Laluk on his heels. "I've seen the state of those buildings. Their construction is going to push into the dark month while I'll be done in the next few days."

"Exactly." Laluk managed a skillful parry and went on the attack, again increasing his speed and strength.

Zeriel dodged and swept his friend's weapon to the side. He decided to stop the charade and advanced on Laluk in earnest. His strength and speed overcame his friend and left him disarmed in mere seconds.

Laluk watched in shock as his sword fell among some rocks, its clattering marking a change between them. "I never thought you'd do that to me."

"A lot has changed since we were kids," Zeriel said. He bobbed his eyebrows up and down for emphasis. A deep satisfaction took root in his gut, and he'd be lying to himself if he didn't admit that he'd dreamed of this moment for the last ten years.

Laluk relaxed, their sparring apparently over. "I could feel the difference in your strength and speed. It feels like cheating."

"There's no cheating in contests of life and death." Zeriel said.

Laluk raised an eyebrow. "Is that what this is?"

"No. But you must practice for the fight."

Laluk laughed and the sound of it felt like old times. He regarded the fields in the distance and shifted the hilt of his blade in his hands, remembering a time when he held a much different tool. The sudden nostalgia pulled his mind into another memory.

❖

Zeriel was seventeen and it was one of the few days he let his father talk him into helping on the farm. Most of the time he outright refused, no matter what his father did to him. *What did he do to me? Why am I remembering it this way?*

It was late in a light month, and he drove a horse-drawn plow through the fields to prepare them for planting before the sun dropped below the mountain tops.

"Not like that, you demented idiot," his father said from the next field over, driving his own plow. "Let the horse do more of the work."

"I'm trying," Zeriel replied.

His father threw a rock at him which he barely managed to dodge. "If you ever helped the family that feeds you and puts a roof over your head, maybe you'd know how to do it right."

Heat rose to his cheeks, but Zeriel decided to ignore his father and keep going. The faster he finished the chore the sooner he'd be back to his real training.

Jekjarah appeared, facing the horse. "You should kill that man."

"And how would I do that?" Zeriel asked as he lightly tapped his horse with his whip to coax it along.

"A dagger through the heart sounds good."

"Stop it, Jek. You know I couldn't."

"But you should," the hallucination said before fading away.

"Maybe," Zeriel said.

His father stopped and stalked toward him. "What did you say to me?"

Worried about what his father might have heard, he grabbed his water skin and held it up. "That I'm getting a drink of water."

With a quick motion, his father smacked the water skin out of his hand. "I won't be out here late because of your laziness—"

❖

Stop!

I'll kill you!

His voices burst at once in his head, bringing him out of the vision. Laluk stood opposite him, a concerned look on his face.

"Are you alright?" Laluk asked.

Zeriel rubbed his forehead. It took several breaths to calm the voices and slow the beating of his heart. "I'll be fine."

"The voices again?"

"They've been increasingly oppressive lately."

"You think being here is triggering them?"

"Probably. I'm having memories pop up every now and then. Things that I'd forgotten until now. The voices don't seem to like them."

"Maybe they're trying to protect you."

"I'd be shocked," Zeriel replied.

"I did have one question that's been nagging at me, if I can ask."

Zeriel nodded, glad to change the subject.

"Why'd you leave without telling me all those years ago?" There was a lot behind that question. They'd been best friends; shared everything and did everything with each other. Something in his friend's voice conveyed that he'd taken it personally.

"I'd taken the test for the village guard that morning."

Laluk's eyes widened. "Why didn't you tell me? How'd you do?"

"I failed miserably. Itekel said I was the worst fighter he'd ever seen. He told me to go back to farming where I belonged."

"You never were very good with a sword—when we were children, that is."

"I wasn't. He was right to reject me, but I let my pride blind me, so I blamed him for being biased."

"Itekel was blunt, but never biased."

Zeriel nodded. "He told my father later that night in the pub. When he got home, we fought."

"That makes sense. Your father could be...overbearing."

"Anyway, I left that night, sure that I didn't want to be a farmer and more certain that ever that I needed to leave."

"And you chose to become an assassin? How'd you pull that off?"

"As kids, we'd all heard stories of the Te Et Sha from passing merchants or other travelers. Phantoms in the night that prey on those who misbehave. In the first few days after I left, I ran into a merchant who was so convinced they were real he had me believing him. The man said that if you found their hideout, they'd assess you and if you were strong enough, they'd let you join.

"I thought if the village wouldn't have me, maybe they would. I trained myself on the road for a year before I found them. I went through their trial and barely passed. That's when I found out if you didn't pass the trial, you died."

"They really killed you for that?"

"Not exactly. They made us drink a potion called Eleshar's Curse, though they didn't tell us it was deadly, and only a very few could survive its effects. If you lived, it granted incredibly magnified strength and speed. Of the thirty of us who drank it, twenty-two died."

Laluk stepped over to the wood cutting log in front of the house and sat. "Sounds like you went through hell."

"It was my choice."

"Yet you came back." Laluk looked at the repaired home. "To be what, a farmer?"

Zeriel laughed. "Hardly. I'm only visiting so I can train up for this quest that's probably going to kill me."

Laluk stood up and cracked his neck. "Then we better get to your training." He went into a fighting stance, his wooden sword pointed at Zeriel, and started bouncing on the balls of his feet. "We wouldn't want you to go to battle unprepared."

His thoughts turned to Veshet and the promise he made to Lavel's spirit. The inevitability of the battle ahead loomed over him as he raised his practice blade. "No, we wouldn't."

CHAPTER TWENTY-ONE

The village square was, ironically, a large circle paved in cobblestone. The shops that lined the edge of the square, normally vibrant and busy, were now nothing more than cremated remains.

Thick poles were driven into the ground at the center of the square. Thinner poles jutted out of the thick ones in all directions, with smaller ones coming from those, giving the entire structure the appearance of a large tree. The thick poles were painted the rust color of Clan Ra's stripes, while the branches were painted black. Normally a memorial such as this would be small, and its poles would carry the clothing items of the deceased. This much larger one was heavily draped with so many clothing items, from so many people, that it almost completely obscured the poles. The cobblestone under the structure was scorched black. Veshet and his forces had piled bodies there and set them ablaze. Perhaps it was the image those scorch marks conjured, but Zeriel couldn't expel the lingering odor of death from his nose as he studied the structure.

As he predicted, he'd completed the repairs to his home before the start of the dark month. Since then, he'd been working with the villagers to help restore their homes to a livable condition. He was currently in the town square working with Laluk and several other men to complete the repairs on the pub. He walked across the cobblestones of the square carrying freshly milled lumber.

"Zeriel!" Chief Leksha said from behind. "There you are. I need to ask something of you."

Zeriel turned and Leksha stopped in her tracks, seeming to only then notice the wood on his shoulder.

"Oh—I'm sorry. Are you busy?"

"I'm on my way to the pub with these beams."

"Sure, sure." She nodded absently and her tone made him think she didn't hear what he had said. "In the last few days some of the new members of the village watch have been setting up traps in the forest, in case of another attack. I'd like you to check them."

"You want me to make sure they're armed correctly?"

"I think this is the first time many of them have thought to use them as defense. I'd feel better if you examined them, just in case."

He nodded. "Do you know where they are?"

The Chief removed a small scroll from her pouch and handed it to him. "I've marked their location for you."

He set the planks down and accepted the scroll. Unrolling it he saw a crudely drawn map of the town with locations marked on the northern and southern borders. "Sure, let me drop this lumber off at the pub first, and I'll make my way out there."

The Chief grunted. "Let me know when you're done. I'll be helping with homes south of the square today."

Zeriel stowed the scroll in his pocket, then shouldered the wood. "Shouldn't take me too long."

❖

Stars flickered around the moon, its position indicating that it was shortly past midday. The red, pink, and purple glow of the forest was enough to keep Zeriel from tripping over roots and branches. Chief Leksha's map was surprisingly accurate and guided him well. The first trap was placed over an ant trail and covered in leaves. He kneeled to inspect the device.

Jekjarah's legs appeared in front of him. "What are we doing here?"

"We're helping with the Clan's defense."

"You know that's not what I mean. Why aren't we hunting Veshet or the Ori twins."

Satisfied with the set of the first trap, he stood and used the map to navigate to the next one. "They need my help here, and I need time to train."

"Because you've done so much training already."

A stab of guilt penetrated his sternum at the hallucination's sarcasm. He hadn't thought to train since he'd arrived.

"The villagers don't trust you," Jekjarah said. "It's obvious you're using them. Trying to relive the past."

"What if I am?" He glanced up at a large boulder up ahead, then checked the map to verify he'd found the correct one. "I don't answer to anyone. Not anymore. Is it such a bad thing if I take some time for myself?"

"What about Lavel? Don't you have a duty to her?"

Nestled between the boulder and the ground was a box of small darts. A tripwire extended from the box to a nearby tree. "And I'll fulfill my duty to her. In time."

"In time?" Jekjarah said. "It's like you don't care about her anymore."

Zeriel stood and locked eyes with Jekjarah. "I never knew her, Jek. Not really. I owe her the same duty I owe the dead here." A quick look at the map gave him the next location and he continued toward it. "If I went after Veshet now it'd be a suicide mission." He spotted plant light glinting off the exposed metal teeth of the next trap. He shook his head at the carelessness.

"This place is clouding your judgment. You can't trust the people here."

"You say that about everyone." This one was rigged well enough, though it needed better concealment, so he covered it with nearby leaves and sticks.

"Because *no one* is trustworthy! Haven't you learned that by now?"

Zeriel paused and released a heavy sigh. "For the first time since I can remember, I feel like I belong somewhere, like I have a community and a purpose greater than blind killing."

"But you don't belong here. That's what I've been trying to tell you." The hallucination peered into the surrounding forest as if he heard something. "This distraction is going to kill you." Jekjarah winked out of existence, replaced by the barest whisper of feet running through the trees.

Zeriel's instincts took over immediately at the sound. He tossed the trap into the air, then dove to the side. The trigger mechanism clicked and clamped its jaws around something.

"Ah!" exclaimed whoever he'd caught in the trap.

In seconds, Zeriel had daggers in his hands and crouched to lunge at his attacker. Before he could, something heavy slammed into his skull. Stars burst to life across his vision as he crumped to the ground. Pain flared in his head as his heart thumped in his ears.

"You idiot," a voice said from behind with the high-pitched tenor of a man barely out of adolescence. "He may be the Worst One, but he's still Te Et Sha. You shouldn't have attacked so brazenly."

"Shut up and help me get this off." This other voice sounded younger, barely old enough to join the order.

Zeriel didn't recognize either one.

"You got yourself into that mess, you get yourself out. *Only the strong survive.*"

"*Only the strong survive.*"

They chanted the words like an oft repeated incantation.

The one behind Zeriel put a knee in his back and bound his hands with the clumsy movements of an amateur. "We'll get a huge reward from Veshet when we bring this one back."

Zeriel heard the click of the trap releasing, followed by a harsh clang as the young one dropped it on the ground. "It's a good thing we decided to follow up on that lead. Who knew this idiot would come back here."

"Weakness breeds stupidity."

Zeriel felt a sharp poke on the side of his neck and the world spun downward, drawing into unconsciousness.

CHAPTER TWENTY-TWO

Zeriel recognized the effects of the poison that coated the tip of the needle that pierced his neck. That familiarity prepared him for the headache that greeted him as he returned to consciousness. A red light flooded his vision, even with his eyes closed. When he risked opening them a bit he was completely blinded by white light. He fought the urge to flinch, managing to avoid giving his captors any indication he'd woken.

He reached out for the shadows next. If he could call even a small bit of darkness, maybe he could shape it into a knife and free himself, though he'd never accomplished something so ambitious up to this point. He activated his powers, but nothing happened. Straining, he tried to push his power further than the white light that blinded him. Still nothing.

Giving up on that, his final test focused on escaping the ropes around his wrists, but after employing every technique he knew, they wouldn't budge. These assassins clearly knew their knots.

With nothing else to do except lie still, Zeriel focused on their voices, content to listen until his circumstances changed.

"I honestly don't understand how he survived a direct assault from Veshet," said the voice belonging to the older of the two. Zeriel silently gave him the name One.

"He survived for the last ten years," the younger one said. It must have been this boy whom he'd caught in the trap. He named him Two.

"How good could he be if everyone calls him Worst One?" Two said.

"He's still a fully trained Te Et Sha," One countered.

"I guess you're right."

These boys' whispering reminded him of childhood nights when sniggering with his brothers at their dirty jokes kept them awake. The vivid memory unlocked into a vision that engulfed him.

❖

Zeriel was sixteen and he and his brothers lay in bed, stifling their laughing at the latest joke Odenel whispered to them. Their sniggering escalated to laughter, abandoning all attempts to avoid waking their mother in the bed on the other side of the room. It was late, and their father still hadn't returned from his nightly visits to the pub in the village square.

This was one of the few times I remember having fun with my brothers.

"Shh!" their mother chided.

They gave each other knowing smirks before snorting a final laugh and turning over to go to sleep. But Zeriel's mind was never quiet—not anymore. So, despite his best efforts to quiet them, the voices screamed in his mind, clawing at the veil of his sanity. They'd come a few months earlier, their threats of pain and death a constant attack for which he had little defense. The Clan's healer said the voices weren't real, but knowing that didn't stop their torment.

Zeriel endured the torment for hours before the sound of the front door banging open shook his bed.

"Vuteli!" His father's slurred voice sounded throughout the house. "I'm coming. I hope you're ready."

"What? What's going on?" Zeriel's mother asked after being woken by the racket.

His father entered the sleeping room smelling of booze and something else Zeriel couldn't place. It reminded him of those nights when his parents would kick him and his brothers out of the bedroom. He carried the same odor as the room did when they were let back in.

I recognize that smell now. My father wasn't at the pub—he was with another woman.

Heavy, unsteady steps traveled from the door to his parents' bed.

"Take that off," his father said.

"No, Renniel, not with the children here."

"Forget them. I want you. Here and now."

"Stop!"

The unmistakable crack of a hard slap reverberated through the room. Zeriel sat up reflexively, a strong protective urge surging through him.

❖

Jekjarah's voice, roaring into his ear, crashed through the memory and yanked him to the present. "Why are you thinking about that right now, Zeriel? You need to free yourself!"

Despite being suddenly pulled from his memory, Zeriel managed to keep still. He could hear his captors talking, but luckily not of anything interesting. It was difficult to recover from the emotions of the memory and the sudden way he was ripped from it. He kept his breathing steady and cleared his mind, using a technique he learned in his training.

An hour later he'd finally calmed down and had the clarity to notice One and Two were talking about Veshet.

"Do you really think he can do it?" Two asked.

"You mean successfully execute a coup against the Ai Jels?"

It was quite the question indeed. The Ai Jels didn't come to rule the nation through politicking alone. They were known for their ruthlessness, and with an army of their own at their disposal, overthrowing them wouldn't be an easy task.

"He took over the Te Et Sha, didn't he?" One's voice was steady and resolute. "If he can do that, the Ai Jels won't be a problem."

"I guess so," Two said.

After a period of silence, they changed subjects to something uninteresting again, but the little bit that they did give away was enough. Veshet's goals were starting to become clear, and now he had an idea why the man tried to kill him back in Shyal. Zeriel spent the rest of the night mulling over his memory and the new information his captors leaked about Veshet.

⋄

The group spent the next morning in silence as if they were playing a game where the first to speak lost. He'd finally discovered that the light that blinded him came from several white vine lanterns they'd placed around him. Apparently, word of his powers spread through Veshet's forces, and they had developed a plan to counter them.

After some time, they untied Zeriel from the tree, hung the white vine lanterns from his shoulders, and continued through the forest. Two tied a rope around Zeriel's waist and dragged him along while One led the way. The light of the white vine lanterns, even hung on his as they were, continued to leave him nearly blind. Luckily, he could still get a decent glimpse at the moon in the sky when it finally appeared through the trees. With a way of telling time, and a careful count of his steps, he had an idea of their distance and direction. They were heading north, and at a decent speed considering the mountainous terrain.

The weight of the silence was too much for Two. He turned around and said, "I don't get how you could have survived two encounters with the Generals, let alone one with Veshet."

The Generals? Interesting.

"Utenash!" One said.

Two spun to address him. "What? It's not like he can do anything tied up like that."

One simply huffed and turned back around.

Two turned back to Zeriel again. "*We* could have killed you easily. How could you have escaped Veshet and the Generals? It doesn't make sense."

"Mostly luck, but their own hubris helped."

"Luck. Right."

It didn't matter much to Zeriel if Two believed him or not. He was too focused on keeping track of their progress to hold much of a conversation.

Silence fell among the group again, and a few hours later One directed them eastward toward the southern plains of Fei En Ar. Zeriel estimated they'd find the edge of the forest before the day was out.

❖

The group made camp near the edge of the forest. Two tied him to a nearby tree, but Zeriel didn't argue or struggle. Frustration at his helplessness gnawed at him, but he swallowed its bitterness. He had no choice but to bide his time and wait for an opening that had yet to come.

Once Two was satisfied the ropes were properly secured, he and One set up camp. The crackling of the fire and the rich aroma of cooked meat filled the air. For a time, it seemed the pair ate in silence, but once again Two was compelled to fill the empty space.

"What do you think they'll do with him?" Two asked.

"I'm sure Veshet wants to make an example out of him. Probably some sort of public execution."

"Makes sense. With how fast the stories spread, it's only a matter of time before the clans hear them. I bet they'd fight harder if they thought there was someone out there who survived a fight with Veshet."

"Right, but there's more to it than that. The stronger the Clan, the more likely they are to fight when given a symbol to rally around. We're trying to cull the weak, not the strong."

"*Only the strong survive,*" Two chanted.

"*Only the strong survive,*" One repeated. "But it doesn't matter to us what they do with him once we've handed him over. What matters is the reward."

"What do you think they'll give us?" A hint of anticipation laced Two's voice.

"Coin, for one. Probably an increase in rank."

"I like the sound of that. Maybe we'll command our own unit during the raid on Clan Gor."

"Hush!" One exclaimed.

"Stop being so paranoid Hueled, he's a dead man walking. What's he going to do?"

"We don't know the extent of that power he has. Maybe he can send messengers through the shadows or something."

That would be handy.

"If he could do that, don't you think he'd have done it already?'

"Maybe you're right," One said, deferring to Two for the first time since capturing Zeriel. "Better to be cautious, anyway."

"I guess."

Jekjarah snapped into existence in front of Zeriel, his form eerily unaffected by the brightness of the white vine lanterns. "This wouldn't be happening if you hadn't stopped to play villager."

"I know," Zeriel said.

"What was that?' One called out. Footsteps crunched on twigs and leaves signaling his approach.

"You know?" Jekjarah's face contorted into an exaggerated sneer. "That's all you have to say? We're going to die because you let your own selfishness get in the way and all you can say is, 'I know?'" The hallucination spat.

"Did you say something?" One said, close enough that his silhouette came into view next to Jekjarah.

"You don't know what you're talking about, Jek," Zeriel said.

"Really?" One said. "Then educate me."

Jekjarah came closer. "I'm you Zeriel, and if you're too blind to know that you're trying to tell yourself something important, then we really are dead."

Zeriel met Jekjarah's gaze, a sudden flare of hate for the hallucination grew like a fire from his chest. Resentment for all the years of torment his illness inflicted on him fanned the flames of that hate until he couldn't contain the pressure of it anymore. "Kill yourself." It was the first time he fed the words back to one of his voices, and it felt better than he ever imagined.

Jekjarah's face screwed up into something unnaturally proportioned and evil, and his arm reared back.

"Kill myself?" One asked. "I don't think so. Maybe I'll kill you instead." His silhouette twisted as he hurled a punch.

Jekjarah's fist sped toward Zeriel's face and connected at the same moment that One's did. Pain exploded in his jaw as the twin punches landed, sending him reeling. The world spun as he collapsed to the ground, blood filling his mouth, the taste bitter and metallic against his loosened teeth.

One's face came close to his. "Say something like that again and I'll forego handing you over alive for the pleasure of killing you myself."

Zeriel blinked against the lingering haze, his mind refocusing on the world around him. One's silhouette had vanished, along with Jekjarah's ghostly form. They left him with the echoes of their blows manifesting through the throbbing pain in his jaw. As he propped himself against the tree again, the voices returned, more vicious and terrible than ever.

CHAPTER TWENTY-THREE

It took the entirety of the next day to travel to the camp Veshet's forces had set up. Having spent several days without using his powers, Zeriel's eyes were beginning to adjust to their normal function. The white vine lanterns hung on him were reduced to a haze that he could now see through.

One had taken them north again along the edge of the forest until a large wall crudely built from fresh logs appeared. Abatis encircled the wall, threatening to impale would-be attackers but for a small area where a crude gate was placed.

It stood outside the forest where rolling hills filled with tall grass extended out to the horizon. Reeds popped up through the blades of grass and shone bright yellow dots that swayed from the breeze. The edge of the forest nearby had been pulled back, reduced to nothing but stumps.

Smoke from fires inside the camp rose into the air, wafting through the forest. The scent of those fires was accompanied by the tight clang of blacksmith hammers at work. As they approached, the aroma of unwashed bodies and cooking meat joined that of the fires, creating a unique bouquet one only found in a camp such as this.

One stopped them in front of the gate. "Hey! It's Hueled and Utenash. We've captured Zeriel."

A head popped up over the wall. "Wait. The one Lord Veshet's been after?"

"That's the one."

"We thought you ran off. Where'd you find him."

"We'll tell you once you let us in."

"Fine, but you'll answer to the commander first. She's already called for your heads for desertion."

"I'm sure our cargo here will quell everyone's worries."

"If you say so," the guard said as his head disappeared from above the wall.

The three of them stood waiting for a time, and Two began shuffling his feet nervously. "Do you think she really wants us dead?"

"Of course not," One said. "He was exaggerating."

One and Two jumped when the sound of straining rope signaled the gate was opening. A woman, flanked by young men on both sides, exited the camp. She was the tallest in the group, and though her frame was slight, she carried an air of danger. Her raven-black hair was striped with silver and tied into a tight ponytail, and she wore the black leather armor of the Te Et Sha. Zeriel remembered the first time he met Elilta when she presented herself as the instructor of his group of trainees. Fear had filled him then, as it did to see her now.

The men around her, though they also wore the black dress of the Te Et Sha, all but cowered in her presence. They were young, barely into their twenties, and Zeriel didn't recognize a single one. Veshet, it seemed, had given her charge of the trainees who survived his culling.

One stepped up, mustering his courage to speak. "We brought Zeriel, commander."

She looked him over, then eyed Zeriel for a moment, a slight smirk growing on her face. "So you have. Is this why you abandoned your post?"

"Yes—I mean—no commander. I made sure my duties were covered. We'd," He turned around to point to Two, "Utenash and me—we heard that someone saw a man at Clan Ra. We thought—"

"You thought?"

"Well, yes commander. We—"

"You see Hueled, that's your problem. You thought." She waved her hand forward and a young man stepped up, holding a sheathed sword out for her.

"We thought if we brought Zeriel—"

"Yes, yes," Elilta said as she slowly drew the sword from the scabbard, "you thought you'd claim fame, glory, and riches."

One's shoulders slumped forward, and he fell silent.

"Isn't it too bad that your ambition got you killed." Elilta swiped her weapon across One's body so fast Zeriel barely saw the motion.

One's head hit the ground and rolled to a stop, revealing a stunned expression.

"It was Hueled's idea commander. I swear!"

Elilta fixed her gaze on Two. "You poor little sheep. Couldn't make a decision of your own?"

"No, it's not—" The boy's head was spinning through the air before he could finish his sentence.

Elilta wiped her blade on One's corpse. "Children these days, Zeriel. Always looking for the easy way to get ahead. No one's willing to put in the hard work anymore." Her head snapped up and they locked eyes. "Not like you."

Zeriel shivered as he remembered why she frightened him so. "I had to work hard, you know that. It was pass or die."

"It was, wasn't it." Elilta slid her sword back in the sheath in the young man's hands, then stepped toward Zeriel. Her motions were more sensual than they were threatening now. "But you worked hard, didn't you? You trained morning and night. Even when you thought no one was watching. Even when you missed meals"

"I wanted to be a Te Et Sha, and I wanted to live."

Elilta walked around him like a predator stalking its prey. "I've never had a trainee with such perseverance." She ran her hand across his shoulder blades as past behind him. "Not before you, and not after." Finishing her circuit, she stepped in front of him and placed her hand on his chest. "Do you remember the fun we used to have?"

That whore!

She must die.

She'll tell everyone what she did to you.

Zeriel shook his head to rid himself of the voices. "I'd rather not, Elilta."

The commander took a step back and gave him a sour look. "Such a pity. I might have tried to save you from your fate." With a shrug of her shoulders her expression went blank, and she waved at the young men behind her once more. "Put him in his own cage." She looked down at the lanterns that hung on his shoulders. "Bring those with you, in case the rumors about his power are true."

Two of the young men hurried to Zeriel and dragged him toward the gate.

"Put these corpses on spikes outside the camp as a reminder for what awaits deserters. Everyone else, finish the preparations. We leave for Clan Gor in the morning."

The inside of the camp was haphazardly organized. Tents were erected without thought to pathways, hierarchy, or function. The ground was trampled into mud and white vine lanterns seemed randomly posted through it all. The only good news was the amount of shadow it afforded to Zeriel, if he could find a way to break free.

In the very back of the camp were four poorly constructed cages made from leftover cuts of lumber bound together with rope. Mud-covered men, women, and children sat inside; their eyes locked on the ground. Only a few looked up at Zeriel as they approached.

A single young man stood guard in front of the cages. "This the one everyone's making such a fuss about?"

"Seems like it," the guard on his left said. "Though I don't know why. He doesn't look that intimidating."

"You've got those lanterns on him. From what I hear he'd be a heap of trouble without those."

"Ha!" The guard on his right exclaimed. "You believe that stuff?"

The guard pointed at the lanterns. "Seems like whoever caught him did. And since the commander didn't tell you to remove them, seems like she does too."

"Whatever," said Left Guard. "We have put him in the empty one with the lanterns all around."

"Sure."

His two escorts walked him to the far-right cage which stood empty. They took the time to set up white vine lanterns in every spot necessary to eliminate the shadows in and around the cage. This took them almost a full hour and forced them to use lanterns from other parts of the camp.

Zeriel approved of their attention to detail, though he made no indication to them of that fact. He'd never been treated like such a threat by the Te Et Sha. They were new to the organization though, so they didn't know how completely useless he really was.

Once they were satisfied there weren't any shadows for him to use they tossed him into the cage with his hands still tied to his back. Once they chained the door Zeriel was left alone.

Jekjarah appeared outside the cage looking in at him. "This is what you were waiting for, wasn't it?"

"I was hoping they'd be less careful about the lights." He looked around through the white haze. "Those kids did a good job."

"Who cares! How are you going to get out of there, Zeriel?"

"I don't know, honestly. I guess I'll have to think of something."

Jekjarah threw his hands in the air and began pacing. "Well, take your time then. It's not like your life depends on it."

The echo of footsteps crunching on the rocky ground approached Zeriel's cage. He fell silent and faced his visitor.

"I can see why you survived all these years as The Worst One. You're harder to kill than a gleam roach." Zeriel recognized Veshet's voice and the very sound of it sent him into a rage. He dashed toward it with teeth bared and no concern for his bound hands. He slammed into the wooden bars of his cage and pain exploded across his face as he fell back to the ground.

Veshet laughed. "You've fostered quite the grudge, I see."

Zeriel spat and looked toward the assassin's voice though the man himself wasn't visible through the white haze blocking his vision. "I'm going to kill you."

"Then come do it." Veshet's invitation was laced with arrogance and mockery and all Zeriel could do was growl back in frustration. "Deep down you know it doesn't matter what powers you attain, or what sort of moral precipice you stand on, you are and always will be The Worst One. You have no hope of challenging me."

"You took everything from me. So Worst One or not, and even if I have to rise from the grave itself, I swear to you I'm going to repay that favor."

Veshet chuckled. "I like your resolve, Zeriel." The assassin's voice moved as he began pacing. "I really do. It's difficult not to root for the puppy nipping at the feet of a razor cat. I almost want you to succeed, but in the end you can't." His voice stopped moving and quieted slightly, becoming more intimate. "Do you know why I took your woman from you? Why I decimated the Te Et Sha and built my army from its remains? Why I slaughtered your Clan and didn't take any prisoners? Because I could. Because I'm stronger than any before me, and because *only the strong survive.*"

Veshet's footsteps crunched on the ground again as he walked away. "Don't worry though, I'll keep you alive long enough to watch as I conquer Fei En Ar, then march my armies across the rest of the southern continent. Before I'm done everything south of the Great Divide will be mine."

Zeriel stepped up to the bars of his cage again, this time feeling for them before pressing his face into one of the gaps. "I'm going to get out of this Veshet!" He screamed. "I'll bring destruction upon your armies! Your generals will die by my hands! And the last thing you'll see before you die will be my face staring back at you!"

A full-throated laugh rang out in the distance. "Let's see you try!"

CHAPTER TWENTY-FOUR

The camp came alive in the morning, and the bustle of their pre-battle preparations woke Zeriel. Young men gathered in groups, each at different stages of preparedness. An assertive youth barked orders at stragglers as they hurried through the camp. Morning fires were lit, and soon the scent of breakfast filled the air. Zeriel's stomach roiled at the aroma, but no one thought to feed him.

He hauled himself up against the wooden planks of his enclosure and into a sitting position. The voices tormented him, doubting he'd ever escape, driving him—as they always did—to end it all. His predicament weighed heavy on his mind and allowed the gloom of those voices to blanket him. The film of light over his vision had cleared overnight, though. A small blessing that was enough to keep him from completely giving up.

He twisted his head and spotted people in the cell farthest from his, their clothes covered in mud and filth. Most were still asleep. Those who weren't hung their gaunt, stoic faces toward the ground.

Zeriel's attention was drawn to an older man with a well-groomed ring of gray hair encircling his bald head. His muscled physique belied his age, suggesting he wasn't someone to cross lightly. Deep wrinkles carved lines through his face, but a spark of clarity and intelligence shone behind his eyes. He wore the Stripes of Clan Din on a deep blue waist cloth, longer on the left side than the right with four gold stripes down the left side. The man observed the camp's activity with a surprising alertness. He eventually met Zeriel's gaze across their enclosures, and after a pause, said, "They sure made a fuss over you last night, though you don't look like much, if I'm honest."

Zeriel huffed. "I'm not."

An awkward silence passed between them as the man tried to find a way to respond. Eventually, he decided to change the subject. "Didn't think anyone from Clan Ra survived."

Taken aback that the man would know what clan he was from, Zeriel noticed his clothes again for the first time since he'd been captured. He forgot he had changed out of his leathers weeks ago, and the emblem with Clan Ra's Stripes was clearly visible on the left breast of his shirt. "A few of us. What about Clan Din?"

"We're all that's left, I'm afraid. The attack came at night. Half the Clan was dead before anyone knew what was happening. They killed most, only taking those of us who put up a good fight. Then they burned the village to the ground."

"Hey!" cried the guard posted nearby. "Shut it you two!" The old man put his head down and turned away.

Zeriel turned his attention back to the camp. After wrapping up their final preparations, the trainees attempted to line up in formation. The way they jockeyed for position and shoved their way into unsteady lines made it clear they had no idea what they were doing. It was almost laughable to watch these men try to mimic something they'd seen real soldiers do as if they were comparable.

Even as a group, Te Et Sha never marched in formation, nor did they attack in the open. That was for soldiers with codes and morals. Assassins were only concerned with the kill, and whatever it took to achieve it. Something deep within Zeriel balked at the sight of the trainees shedding their training and playing soldier.

Elilta emerged beyond the assembling youth. She was dressed in her assassin's leathers and weaved through the formation toward Zeriel. The act was unnerving, like a snake weaving through the grass toward its prey. A twisted smirk played across her face as she stopped in front of him.

Zeriel recognized that smirk, and it made his skin crawl. The condescending expression foretelling the seduction that was coming. He only knew because he'd been fooled by her games before.

"Hello Worst One. I hope your stay has been enjoyable so far."

"Oh, fantastic. Though the food leaves something to be desired."

Elilta laughed. It was like the call of the Uoiga from Donian legend, clear, beautiful, and intoxicatingly pleasing, but if you let it draw you in, all that waited for you was death. "I do love that sarcasm of yours." She drew nearer, her voice becoming soothing as she trailed a finger along the wooden bars of his prison. "You could still join us, you know. I'm sure if you did well in our assault on Clan Gor, I could persuade Veshet that you'd be useful to the cause." Her smirk turned into a wide smile. "Useful to me, anyway."

Zeriel felt suddenly tired. Tired of the constant struggle against those determined to use or abuse him. "I'll die before I put myself under your power again."

She drew back, hand to her breast as if offended. "Come now, was our time together really that bad? I know you enjoyed it just as much as I did."

Zeriel blinked and Jekjarah was there standing next to Elilta, revulsion twisting his features. "She hasn't changed at all, has she?"

Zeriel glanced at Jekjarah. "No, she hasn't."

"What?" Elilta turned to the side to see whatever Zeriel was looking at, saw nothing, then shot Zeriel a perturbed glare. "What are you playing at?"

He met her gaze. "Oh, you mean you never noticed? I'm insane. I was talking to Jekjarah, the disgraced merchant who's been following me around since I was sixteen."

"Hey," Jekjarah said. "I'm not disgraced. I just had to flee from some customers who objected to the *small* handling fee I added to our transactions. It wasn't my fault they didn't technically know I charged them the fee until a week later. They should have read the fine print."

Elilta narrowed her eyes. "You use that illness of yours and that smart mouth as a crutch far too often."

"If only I cared what you thought of me."

Elilta's features turned to blank stone. "You've made your choice, then. Fine. It's better this way, really. After I get back from our raid on Clan Gor, you'll be mine for the entirety of our journey to Ki Al Tesh." She spun around and strode away. "I'll get what I want, Zeriel. Whether by choice, or by force."

"You'd better find a way out of there, and fast," Jekjarah said. "You don't want to find out what she has planned for you." The hallucination was right. Ki Al Tesh—capital of Fei En Ar—stood far to the north. The journey would give Elilta ample time to inflict whatever tortures she had in mind. And despite how enticing she made it sound, it *would* be torture.

He had gained something, though. Elilta had inadvertently revealed Veshet's plan: Finish wiping out the Southern Clans, then continue his rampage north. Crush the Central Clans on his way to the capital, killing the Ai Jel who rule there, and take control of Fei En Ar.

It was clear now that he'd made a mistake staying at Clan Ra for the last month. Regret set in and drove up his anxiety as he watched Elilta's trainees march out of camp. A small group was left behind. Those that remained had sour expressions on their faces, clearly upset they weren't allowed to join in the fight. Knowing Elilta, these were the least capable of her trainees; the ones she didn't fully trust. It was the exact opportunity Zeriel had been waiting for.

To his right was a guard he hadn't seen yet, the angry red marks of adolescence still visible across his cheeks. The boy settled into a cross-legged seat on the ground, his sword lying next to him in the dirt. He idly carved shapes into the loose earth in front of him.

Watching the boy, an idea started to formulate in his mind. By the time it coalesced into something feasible, another youth approached. This newcomer was of the same age as his counterpart, but with clear skin and an optimistic look on his face.

Finalizing things in his mind, Zeriel's frustration built. His plan was terrible. On any other day, he wouldn't have entertained it. But in the mental state he was in, he didn't care.

"Fetufa," the newcomer said, "you shouldn't sit like that. What if one of them escapes?"

"Bah! Look at them, Veltuzu. They're starved and their spirits crushed. No one's escaping."

Veltuzu eyed Zeriel. "What about that one. Isn't he the one with the powers everyone's been talking about?"

Fetufa glanced over and shook his head. "He's tied up in there. Even if he got loose, he'd still be locked inside."

"You've got it all figured out then, don't you." Veltuzu took a seat alongside Fetufa.

"You worry too much."

Several minutes passed before Fetufa got bored with his drawing and threw his stick over the wall. "Don't you ever get tired of being left behind?"

"Sometimes, I suppose. But there's nothing we can do about it. The commander gives her orders, and we follow them."

"I guess so. I just hate that we survived everything they put us through only to be stuck in the rear with the most pointless assignment in the camp."

"You'll get used to it," Zeriel said, finding an opportunity to put his plan in motion.

The boys spun toward him in unison.

"Shut up Worst One," Fetufa said.

"Not that long ago, I would have been the one assigned here, guarding the tied up outcast and the half-dead Clansmen? They put the most important missions in the hands of the most capable. Which means—" Zeriel put his finger to his mouth as if thinking. "You must be dead weight."

Fetufa shot to his feet. "Keep talking and I'll show you what dead weight can do."

Veltuzu reached up to grab his wrist. "Calm down. He's just trying to provoke you."

"You're okay with him talking to us like that? We may not be the best, but we're better than that scum!" He pulled his wrist out of Veltuza's grip.

"It's not all that bad being on the bottom," Zeriel said. "No one expects much out of you. If you fail, it's because of your own incompetence, and you barely get punished."

"I said shut up!" Fetufa screamed. "If Lord Veshet didn't want you alive, I'd kill you right now."

"Ah yes, *Lord* Veshet. We wouldn't want to let him down, now, would we?"

Veltuzu stood up at that. "Careful what you say about Lord Veshet."

"You mean that sadistic narcissist? The overconfident, insecure, white slug who surrounds himself with weak sycophants to make himself feel strong? He'd be the first to slit your throat if you lost your usefulness. I'd be more careful who you swear loyalty to."

"*Only the strong survive,*" Veltuzu chanted.

"*Only the strong survive,*" Fetufa responded. He stepped up to unchain the gate to Zeriel's cell, Veltuzu close behind him.

Jekjarah appeared standing next to him. "You succeeded. Congratulations. I hope this works."

"Me too," Zeriel responded.

The boys entered, the steadfast assurance from youthful decision-making written across their faces.

"You're going to regret those words," Veltuzu said.

Zeriel had taken beatings before, and while he doubted that these boys' onslaught would rival those of his past, he prepared himself mentally, nonetheless.

Fetufa attacked first, raining punches into his face. Veltuzu followed, planting kicks into his side. Zeriel visualized the pain forming a ball in his mind. Then he imagined that ball shrinking smaller and smaller, until it fit into the darkest corner of his subconscious. He'd learned this trick years ago, whenever someone in the Te Et Sha thought beating him would prove their own strength.

It was a short, but effective, beating, the boys tiring themselves out faster than Zeriel anticipated.

Weak and undisciplined. It's no wonder Elilta left them behind.

Fetufa slammed the door behind them, then chained it. The boy didn't notice that his outburst shifted one of the lanterns around Zeriel's enclosure, letting a small sliver of darkness creep a few feet inside the cell.

Jekjarah appeared next to the dagger-shaped shadow. He kneeled, inspecting it. "You lucky bastard." He turned his head toward Zeriel. "I can't believe that worked."

He wanted to reply, but the beating was worse than he'd expected. His mind was focused on his pain blocking technique, which left barely enough mental capacity to process a rational thought. But a small piece of his mind still found comfort that his idea, as terrible as it was, had *actually* worked. And when he could take advantage of the darkness that crept toward him, he would.

Until then, Zeriel shuffled painfully back to his original spot. After settling in and letting some time pass until he could think clearly again, he noticed the members of Clan Din watching him. There was a day that he might have felt shame at so many people witnessing one of his beatings. He was a child then, though, so he ignored them while he waited for his pain to fully subside.

"Are you alright, son?" the old man asked. "I can't imagine why you provoked them like you did."

"It was all part—" Zeriel grunted in pain, then paused by what he saw. Previously, the old man had been sitting, so he didn't notice anything amiss. But now, as he stood upright and leaning against the side of his cage, Zeriel saw him balancing on a single leg, his *only* leg. The sight of the old man's missing leg wrenched a memory from the deep recesses of his mind. The trauma of the memory squeezed every emotion out of him and dragged him into a vision of it.

CHAPTER TWENTY-FIVE

As the vision pulled him in, the world shifted until he was no longer in the present. When everything settled, he found himself in his family's field, driving a plow behind their horse Lumo.

His father looked at him angrily as he said, "I won't be stuck out here all night because of your laziness. Get your drink of water if you must, but be quick about it." The man stomped away into the southern fields.

Zeriel hurried to their well, got his drink, and filled his waterskin. After returning he urged Lumo forward through the northern fields. He understood his father's urgency. The peak of the light month had passed, and the cool air warned of the fast-approaching darkness. If they didn't prepare the fields this week, they'd be late for planting and might not get a harvest in the dark month that followed.

I remember that day now, and why I'd spent the years after trying to forget it.

Sweat poured down Zeriel's forehead as he let the discontent over being forced to do the chore increase his anxiety. He'd avoided farm work his entire life, even worked in the mines for the last year to just get out of it. Since falling into the deepest part of the mine, his father forced him back on the farm. For a time, Zeriel thought it was a rare display of love, but in the last few months he realized it was for the extra pair of hands. The thought worsened his mood, causing him to miss a boulder in the ground. A loud metallic shriek carried over the fields and the plow stopped short. Lumo reared up at the sudden resistance and let out a scream. Zeriel's eyes shot to his father who threw down the reins of his own plow and yelled, "What now?"

If I wasn't consumed with the ruminations of my own discomfort, maybe I would have noticed that boulder. I wonder what would have happened then. Or what wouldn't *have happened.*

"Whoa there," Zeriel said. He walked up to Lumo and patted her neck. "Sorry about that girl." Turning back, he investigated the damage. The tip of the plow was cracked and mangled. His heart raced as the implications became clear. This alone could cut their crops in half, which would cut the money they made from those crops in half. It would destroy their family, who was already in debt because of his father's drinking and gambling habit. Terror pumped through his veins as he realized it would be moments before his father saw what he'd done.

"You should run." Zeriel turned around to find Jekjarah standing next to Lumo, pretending to pet her.

"Why won't you leave me alone?"

"Would if I could, but I'm stuck with you as much as you are with me."

"You're not even real," Zeriel said, returning to inspect the plow.

Jekjarah stepped up and regarded the broken tool for himself. "Oh my! That'll take a week for the blacksmith to fix." The hallucination watched his father as he approached. "He'll probably kill you this time."

Zeriel puffed up his chest. "No, he won't." The year he worked in the mines had strengthened his muscles. The voices came to undermine that confidence and remind him how weak he was. He squeezed his eyes shut at the onslaught and shook his head. "Shut up! Get out of my head!"

The voices grew louder, and the sheer volume drove him to his knees.

"What are you doing you lazy bastard!" His father's voice carried across the fields and brought with it the anger that so often flooded out of him.

Adrenaline shot through Zeriel's veins, and in response the voices quieted to whispers of impending death. It allowed him to stand and meet his father, and prepare for the confrontation.

Zeriel was accustomed to his father's anger, and the violence that would inevitably follow. Maybe it was his new strength, or maybe his father had hurt his family one too many times, but as the man approached, the smallest amount of courage coalesced inside of Zeriel.

His father's voice raised in pitch as he regarded the broken plow. "What's this?"

Zeriel raised his hands into what he thought was a fighting position and realized he was ready, and willing, to hurt the man. His hands trembled uncontrollably, and the most obvious realization dawned on him: He'd never once been in a fight. He had wrestled with his brothers in the past, yes, but that never truly came to blows.

"You're going to fight me now?" his father asked as he closed the distance, raising his own hands.

Doubt caused Zeriel to freeze for a moment, giving the older man an opening. His father attacked, easily slipping past the shaky defenses and threw all his weight behind a punch that smashed into Zeriel's nose. The resulting crunch was sickening, but it was quickly overshadowed by the flare of searing heat that exploded across his face.

"You've doomed us you good for nothing—" His father's words turned to a deep growl and then an animalistic cry as he planted his boot into Zeriel's stomach. It was his father's signature final blow.

It knocked the wind out of Zeriel, and he vomited. He struggled to breathe only to take the liquid into his lungs. Several panicked seconds passed before he coughed his throat and lungs clear and sucked in a deep breath of clean air.

When he finally composed himself, Zeriel got to his feet to see his father cursing to himself as he inspected the damage. Zeriel had spent months telling himself he'd never let this man, *Renniel*, lay a hand on him again. He was furious at himself after watching what Renniel had done to his mother the night before. So he finally gathered up the courage to fight back, and with all that built up animosity and intent, somehow, he still ended up humiliated on the ground. The indignity of it all heated his fury into a rolling boil.

I—I'm remembering now.

Jekjarah appeared next to his father, his expression twisted into something primal yet wholly unnatural. "End him Zeriel!"

For once Zeriel agreed with the hallucination. He rushed forward, fists held high, ready to pounce on the man and repay the years of torment he'd inflicted on his family. Renniel barely had time to see through his own rage to react to Zeriel's attack. Pain lanced through his knuckles as his fist connected with Renniel's head, but he ignored it and brought down more strikes. As fast and as hard as he possibly could, Zeriel unleashed violence on the man with more savagery than he thought he was capable of. It broke something in his mind. The snap bathed Zeriel in the cold water of pure pleasure at his violence. All other emotions drained from him, and his attack became something more calculated, colder.

Justice. Retribution for what Renniel did to my family.

"Yes Zeriel! Shed his blood! Let me bathe in it!" Jekjarah tried to scoop blood from the ground and wipe it over his own face.

A sense of dark exultation surged through Zeriel as the hallucination mirrored his own unspoken desire. It gave voice and action to emotions he couldn't understand or explain.

Somehow, Renniel had gotten his feet underneath Zeriel and launched him into the air. The action was so sudden Zeriel was still throwing punches as he flew. His back slammed into Lumo, knocking the wind out of him again and sending him to the ground next to the horse. Lumo reared up and cried, then took off.

The plow dislodged from the ground, but as twisted as it was it caught Renniel's leg and dragged him along with it. He howled in agony as the plow pulled him through the fields and toward the forest beyond.

Zeriel watched in stunned disbelief, barely noticing his own struggle to catch his breath. He caught something odd at the edge of the field. It was Renniel's leg, severed by the plow and left behind as Lumo dragged him into the forest. A surge of triumph, like he'd never felt before, overcame him, caused his mouth to twist into an uncontrollably smile. He stood up and cheered, screaming at the spot Renniel had disappeared to in the woods.

"Yes!" Jekjarah cheered. "Finish him! Quickly while he's injured!"

I didn't finish him. The satisfaction of seeing him completely beaten, knowing he'd never hurt me, my brothers, or my mother again, had been enough.

That thought brought back memories of all the times Renniel had hurt them. One time stood out.

❖

The visions transitioned and Zeriel found himself standing in his family home. His mother had just chided the youngest of his older brothers, Kledini.

She turned to him. "Get yourself cleaned up for dinner. I don't want your father to come home seeing you in that condition."

Why this memory again?

"Fine," Zeriel said, then stepped toward their shared bedroom.

Just then the door slammed open to reveal Renniel, wavering from the effort. He steadied himself on the doorframe. Looking at his face Zeriel saw his flushed cheeks and heavy eyelids. He was drunk again, which was becoming more and more common.

I was afraid of what he'd do to me.

"Where'sh tha goo fur nothin' pile uh cow dung?"

No one answered him. They just watched as he scanned their faces.

Zeriel stayed silent, too afraid that anything he said would set the man off. Each second of silence stretched into agonizing infinity until finally his unsteady gaze landed on Zeriel.

"You!" he said, then stepped forward and reared back for a wild punch.

The attack moved in slow motion compared to what Laluk had been throwing at him all day. He slipped Renniel's drunken punch easily.

A shocked look overcame the man as his momentum sent him spinning off balance. He collapsed to the floor.

"Are you okay?" His mother rushed to Renniel's side and helped him to his feet.

He shoved the woman hard. "Get off me, ya hag!"

She spun and caught herself on the still-hot cooking stove. The sizzle of burning skin mixed with his mother's screams, echoing through the room.

"Don't you hurt her!" Zeriel's eldest brother, Odenel, screamed. He climbed on the table and dove at Renniel.

The man, drunk as he was, managed to dodge out of the way of Odenel's feeble attack. The boy landed on the floor with a dull thud. Renniel capitalized on the mistake and planted a boot into Odenel's stomach.

The man stuck his finger in his brother's face. "Don' ya try ma boy." With his focus on the eldest brother, Renniel didn't see the middle one, Kledini coming up from behind.

Kledini brought a pan down on Renniel's head, knocking him to the floor unconscious. Then he helped Odenel to a sitting position. They both regarded Zeriel, hate set deep behind their eyes.

Zeriel looked between them and his mother who was weeping and clutching her hands to her chest. She, too, managed to look up at the scene and glare at Zeriel, though her expression was mixed with emotions he couldn't place.

Odenel caught his breath and stuck a finger at Zeriel. "You did this!"

"We'd all be better off without you," Kledini said.

Tears welled up in Zeriel's eyes and his chest tightened. He looked back at his mother, but she looked away in silence, an angry expression on her features.

I was used to hate and rejection from Renniel. Even my brothers at times. But that evening, my mother's condemnation shook me to my core. It was a betrayal I'd never expected. That night was the first time I ever felt truly alone.

A new memory teased him at the edges of his consciousness, something dark he barely recognized. Before he could focus on it, that darkness approached.

❖

A black shroud covered his vision as he found himself pulled into a new memory. At first, he was glad to leave that one behind, but then he realized what was coming. Renniel's voice was muffled at first, and Zeriel fought the clarity as it came. He knew now how hard he'd tried to bury this, and he wanted with everything in him for it to stay buried even now. But it was too late. It clawed its way back to the surface.

He'd been trying to sleep but something was going on in his parents' bed.

"Stop!" his mother yelled.

The echo of Renniel slapping her reverberated through the room. Zeriel sat up and snapped his head toward his parents. Renniel was on top of his mother, breathing heavily. Her head was turned toward Zeriel and he could see the tears streaming down her face while an angry red mark grew across her right cheek. "What did you do to her?"

"Shut up and go back to sleep," Renniel said as he shuffled under the covers.

"It's okay dear," his mother said through her tears. Her expression was stoic, and voice calm, but somehow Zeriel knew she was holding back for his sake. "Go back to sleep now."

I don't want to remember this.

Fully understanding the horror of what was happening, he did as his mother instructed and turned away from the scene, then closed his eyes. Even with his fingers in his ears he couldn't block out the mixture of Renniel's grunts with his mother's sobbing.

This was the moment I knew the evil that consumed Renniel. I fell asleep wanting him dead. Hate and anger toward Renniel, and shame at my inability to act, created a melody that became my lullaby that night. Renniel lost his leg the next day.

Now I know why I left that place.

CHAPTER TWENTY-SIX

The memories faded away into utter darkness, and Zeriel found himself standing in an endless black void. A soft white light lit his body, though he couldn't find its source.

"Where am I?" His voice didn't echo through that void. Instead, it faded to nothing, and the sensation created an unnerving pressure in his ears.

"We tried to keep you from this place."

Zeriel spun around to find Jekjarah standing nearby. His normally aloof posture was gone, replaced by a defiant stance and crossed arms. The look on his face was stern and unmoving.

Shadows undulated at the corner of Zeriel's eyes. He spun to catch a glimpse of them, but they moved too fast.

You're broken.

Never should have come.

—tried to save you.

It will kill you.

—failed.

Jekjarah stepped forward and caught his attention. "Why didn't you just leave that cursed village and go after Veshet like I told you?"

"You know why," Zeriel responded.

Jekjarah dropped his arms to his side and shook his head. "And now you're here, trapped in utter darkness because what? You wanted a friend?" Anger twisted the hallucination's face.

"I wanted to belong!"

"Now you'll die!" The outburst lasted only a moment before Jekjarah's emotions deflated, and he let out a sigh. "Destroyed by your own mind."

"What do you mean my own mind?"

"He means," Plaxes's voice said, "that this place is in your mind, and unless you can escape from here, you'll die." Her voice echoed strangely through the void. It was odd how quickly he recognized the sound.

Zeriel spun frantically but couldn't see her. "Where are you?" An area of the darkness caught his attention as it shifted, like someone pushing a tapestry from the other side. Eventually it resolved into the form of a woman, then snapped back as if she'd torn a piece of it off to manifest herself.

She approached him, moving with a supernatural grace that made her look as if she was floating. Her skin was jet black, which accentuated the sclera of her eyes. Her black hair shone slightly from the ethereal light. A soft black mist fell from her skin and trailed behind her as she approached. Her black pants and a tight-fitting black shirt looked gray against her skin and gave off the soft swish of cloth rubbing together as she walked. Twin daggers rattled in the sheaths tied to her thighs. "I'm right here, my champion."

This was the first time he'd seen a voice take physical form, other than Jekjarah, but there was something different about Plaxes. The void recoiled from her, rejecting her very presence in that place. Oddly, the shadows underneath her, Jekjarah, and Zeriel, cast by the soft white light, reached for her. They stretched longingly, like she was their mother, and they wanted nothing more than her presence.

It took Zeriel a moment to compose himself before he could speak again. "What do you want?"

She smiled and ignored his question. "This place," she paused and turned a full circle, taking in her surroundings, "it isn't what I expected."

Jekjarah stepped up. "What would you know about it?" He drew the sword from his cane.

Plaxes raised an eyebrow and met Zeriel's eyes. "Touchy, aren't you?"

"Only when I'm being mocked," Zeriel replied.

"Oh, I wasn't mocking you. I've never seen a mind as at one with darkness as yours." She looked around again, a smile stretching across her face. "It's rather wonderful, really."

"What do you know about my mind?"

When she finished her admiration of the void, she made a motion with her hand that called the darkness toward her and coalesced it into a chair. She sat smoothly and crossed one leg over the other. She motioned to the darkness around them and said, "when I felt your mental barrier snap, I brought you to this void. It's a place inside your mind, created from the cross section of your personality, memories, passions, and fears."

Zeriel's eyes widened. "This is where my memories are?"

"Among other things."

He looked out into the void and thought he saw something there. A sound accompanied the sight, resembling his mother crying quietly into the night once more. He pulled his focus, the memory too fresh since it came back. He looked to Jekjarah, who was avoiding eye contact. "You kept me from here?"

"You didn't want to remember." Some strength set into his expression, and he met Zeriel's eyes. "You practically begged me."

"I never knew this place existed!"

Jekjarah faced Zeriel squarely. "You've always known. You broke away the part of you that knew and shoved it in here."

A version of Zeriel appeared next to Jekjarah. He was dressed in ratty clothes bearing the Stripes of Clan Ra. His frame was small and frail, and he was balled up in the fetal position. Soft whimpers escaped his lips.

"That's not me, not anymore."

"No, because you rejected him." Jekjarah knelt and cradled Zeriel's doppelganger. The hallucination met Zeriel's eyes again, a hint of fury on his face. "I've cared for him all these years."

Zeriel couldn't bear the sight of Jekjarah cradling the weak version of himself and turned his head away. "That's not me," he whispered. The whimpers stopped, and when Zeriel looked back both Jekjarah and the weak version of himself were gone.

Plaxes sighed and stood. "You're more broken than I thought." She started walking out into the void.

"Wait!" Zeriel called.

She stopped and looked back at him.

"Why did you bring me here?"

"I need something from you, and you must do it of your own free will." She shook her head. "But I don't think you'll be much use to me like this."

"I've never been much use to anyone. Surely, if you've been in my head, you know that much."

She turned to face him. "Do you truly want revenge for Lavel's death?"

"Yes," he replied without hesitation.

Plaxes smiled at him. "You're more than you give yourself credit for Zeriel. That conviction—I might be able to work with that, if cultivated properly." She walked up to him and met his eyes. "I can help you exact your revenge."

"I'm not looking for another master."

"You'd rather wake into your body, be taken to Veshet the way you are, and die as a message to those who would defy him?"

"That's how this was going to end anyway." Zeriel surprised himself at how strongly he believed what he'd just said.

"It doesn't have to. I can teach you to use my power in ways you never thought possible. You'd become unstoppable. With the fullness of my power at your command, you could get your revenge *and* save your country."

"I don't care about my country."

"Ah, but haven't you delayed pursuing Veshet for the acceptance of a handful of people you barely know?"

"I know them."

She put up a finger. "You *knew* them."

Anger surged within him. "I know them better than I knew Lavel!"

"True, though not for the reason you think. The point, Zeriel, is that you don't want revenge. You knew that before you walked into that dead whisper's shop in Eletenynbrah. You want the thing you've always wanted since you were a boy. The thing your father and brothers refused to give you, that your mother took from you: Acceptance, belonging."

He knew she was right, and he hated the smug look on her face as she watched him accept the truth for himself. He'd been avoiding it, but it was impossible to ignore it now. He'd never believed he'd get justice for Lavel, so he'd defaulted to the thing he always reached for, but never found.

What she offered him seemed too good to be true, but if it was true—if he could somehow find a way to kill Veshet, he would get his revenge *and* save his country. She was his only hope to achieve those goals.

She'd forced him into a corner, but even if she hadn't, he knew there was only one choice he could make. Nothing is ever free, especially not power. "And what do you want in exchange for this gift?"

CHAPTER TWENTY-SEVEN

In the void, Plaxes's training was an unrelenting nightmare. There was no sleep, no physical exhaustion, just a constant mental strain.

"Your mind is the weakness holding you back," Plaxes had told him when he asked why she had to train him there.

But Zeriel knew that. He had life experience to draw from, after all. Memories of when he almost died from the onslaught of mental noise that gave his enemies an opening or drove him to act irrationally. The fear of new, temporary hallucinations that would draw him into deadly encounters forced him to make the kind of mistakes that could get him killed. The mental weakness that plagued him was written in the scars on his body and the recollections of his mind.

He quickly discovered that time flowed differently in the void. For what felt like a month, Plaxes had him continuously drawing and releasing the shadows. When the voices grew louder, she'd intensify the training. By the time he'd done enough to satisfy her, the noise of his auditory hallucinations blended with Plaxes's corrections to become nothing but distant and muffled whispers. His being was consumed with manipulating the darkness, which he did by reflex at that point. It became as natural as breathing.

The next several months were focused on creating objects. It started with small spheres but ended with enormous and complex shapes that he'd make move and undulate through the void. He'd thought he knew what mental exhaustion was after spending years dealing with his illness. By the end of this phase of his instruction, he realized how naive he'd been, like a child crying over a splinter. There were no breaks. No time to rest, reflect, or process his failures. Just non-stop, unrelenting work.

Once the next phase started, he knew true mental agony. The kind that reaches into your body, crushes organs, and sheers at your joints. This last phase was the longest and most brutal. Months and months of sparring with the Goddess of Darkness herself. They fought with weapons made from their power, but no matter what he tried, he was no match for her. She flayed his skin, pierced his body, and removed cognitive limbs. Though there was no physical damage, he felt the mental anguish of it all.

During his time in the void, Plaxes never showed anger or malice. She was cruel, but nothing more. She didn't punish his failures, she let their consequences punish him. There was only the purpose of action that someone sharpening their knife might have shown. And he *was* sharpened. Distractions were ground away. His only goal in that void was to get sharper.

❖

Finally—and blessedly—Zeriel opened his eyes to the physical again and the black void was traded for white. The use of his powers in his mind manifested in his body as the white vine lanterns blinded him once more. The pain from his beating returned immediately, multiplied by the loss of adrenaline in his system, the stiffness of bound limbs, and a body left unmoving for several hours. It was nothing compared to the torture he'd just endured, so he pushed it aside for the moment. Stowing it away in the recesses of his consciousness was easy. His training had given him new tools and focused him on his purpose. The darkness at the far edges of the light of the white vine lanterns around his cage waited for his command.

A small effort of will drew it in easily, and a soft black mist exuded from his skin, falling toward the ground and dissipating shortly thereafter. He formed the shadows into a curved blade in his hand he used to cut through his restraints. A smirk flashed across his face as he mused over the fruits of his labor. Free from the ties that bound him, Zeriel stood, stretching stiff muscles, and rolling lubrication into his joints. It felt good to move freely after the several days he'd spent tied hand and foot. He hopped on the balls of his feet, warming up for what was coming.

"How'd you get loose?" came the voice of his guard.

Wood creaked against rope as the young man hastily opened the gate to his cell. That was Zeriel's cue. He drew in more darkness and let it explode through the cage like a mist. The light of the white vine lanterns withdrew to pinpricks and allowed Zeriel's eyes the cover they needed to see clearly again.

The guard scrambled away, letting out a cry of panic. He fell on his back and put his hands up as he tried to defend himself from a threat he couldn't see.

"This isn't personal," Zeriel said as he circled the boy.

His head whipped toward Zeriel's voice. "Please. I'm—sorry."

"The Te Et Sha do not beg."

"I know. I'm pathetic. Not worth the effort."

Zeriel knelt next to the boy who was trembling now, still trying to see through the black mist. "Do not fear. I will show you mercy."

The boy's body relaxed. "Thank you." Those were his last words. Zeriel shaped a dagger from the mist and drew its edge across his throat. The blood-covered corpse went limp and Zeriel was struck by how easily he overpowered the trainee. A spike of anxiety shot through his body, forcing him to spin around, expecting a trap. But there was nothing and no one. Just a cell covered in his power. The anxiety was replaced with a thrill at this sharper, more ruthless version of himself.

Good, came Plaxes's voice in his head. *Now get your revenge, but don't forget what you owe me.*

"Of course," Zeriel responded. He stood and looked out at the mostly empty camp. The trainees all milled through the tents with heads hung low. To the side he noted the other prisoners in their cage. They were openly gawking at the dark mist that surrounded him. All except the old man who was pulling a shard of broken wood from the neck of a guard next to their cage. Zeriel smirked as his assessment of the man improved by several degrees.

The prisoners were safe for the moment, so Zeriel went to work on the rest of the camp. He felt invisible currents in the darkness and manipulated them to carry him along. This ability allowed him to move at incredible speeds and cover a hundred yards in the blink of an eye, the shadow mist clinging to him as he went. A piece of him was surprised when he moved as fast in the physical as he had in his mind. He pressed himself against the rear wall of a tent, melting into the darkness.

"This is handy," Jekjarah said, looking around the side of the tent as if watching for assassins. He turned his head and that crazed look he got before the killing started twisted his features. "What are you waiting for?"

He'd spent his entire life being the worst among his peers. Even the distance between his skill and those of a well-trained fighter was marginal. Though he'd lived through what felt like a year of grueling training with these new powers, now that he was back in the physical, doubt tried to weasel its way back into his mind.

Jekjarah's face returned to normal. "Stop thinking so much." He pointed behind himself. "Those children don't stand a chance against you. Not anymore."

You're still weak. Too weak.

Go forward and die!

It wasn't often that Jekjarah and the voices spoke in such dichotomy. Just hours ago, he'd have had a difficult time dealing with it, but after the void, he could feel the strength in his mind to resist. He pushed the voices to the back of his consciousness and met Jejarah's eyes. Excitement for the upcoming massacre energized Zeriel's muscles and the hallucination's expression distorted again to mirror his emotions.

Zeriel sprang into action. He moved with incredible speed through the camp. When the white vine lanterns provided too much light, he tore off the shadows from their progenitors and surrounded himself with a black mist. Young assassins fell one after the other.

His first few kills happened with the flash of his shadow daggers, using the muscle memory of his assassin's training. As he continued, he found himself testing the limits of his powers, silently thanking Plaxes for molding him into the weapon he now was. He shot through the entrance of a tent, created needles in his hands and flung them at the three trainees inside. The needles, made from his power, stayed under his control while in flight. The result was perfectly placed throws and quickly falling corpses.

As he made progress, his killing spree accelerated with reckless abandon. He no longer had to physically touch the shadows, the weapons simply formed around him and flew toward their targets. His defense was similarly impressive. The dark mist that fell from his skin solidified and deflected projectiles with ease.

A few of the assassins had grouped together and were mustering up an attack. They didn't fully understand the folly of their efforts until they closed in. Zeriel sent forth dark tendrils from the mist, parrying their blades, and spearing them. In just a few short minutes, he'd managed to kill every assassin in the camp.

Zeriel paused for a moment to watch Jekjarah in his usual worship of the slaughter. Seeing the hallucination like that usually caused his own bloodlust to rise, but this time he was too consumed with his goal. He glanced to the southeast toward Clan Gor. Veshet, Elilta, and, perhaps, even the Ori twins were there. If he was fast, and a little lucky, he'd end everything before the moon set.

Out of the corner of his eye, he saw Jekjarah pause and look toward him. "You don't actually think you'd be that lucky, do you?"

Zeriel glanced at the hallucination, then back toward the cages. "I won't know until I try. But there's something I need to do first."

❖

He reached out and grabbed a dagger as he crafted it in the air. The survivors of Clan Din cowered away as he sliced the rope hinges of their door. It fell away awkwardly, held by the lock that still attached it to the cage.

Zeriel stepped aside. "Everyone in the camp is dead. You're free."

The old man hopped forward. "Thank you, but what are we supposed to do? Our homes have been burned to the ground. Our friends and families killed..."

Zeriel understood the man's sentiment, he'd felt similarly when he first arrived at his Clan. "If you can't find it in you to rebuild, then come to Clan Ra. We can find a path forward, together."

The old man gestured to his missing leg. "I don't think I'd be much use to your Clan."

Zeriel nodded his head toward the huddled group behind the man. "What about them?"

He glanced at them for a moment, then turned back to Zeriel. "I doubt they'd want to become part of another clan." He shook his head. "Feels like turning your back on your ancestors."

"I understand. If you change your mind," Zeriel said as he gathered his power, "you know where to find me." Once he fully wrapped himself in a dark mist, he was taken aback by the looks of awe on Clan Din's faces. That and...was that hope? No one had looked at him like that before, and the impact of those expressions forced tears into his eyes. They saw him as someone they could rely on, and Zeriel felt a sudden and powerful need to sacrifice everything for them.

Before his emotions could overwhelm him, he found the flow of the shadows and let them pull him along, navigating his way south toward Clan Gor, toward Veshet, the Ori twins, and Elilta. His resolve solidified as he wiped the tears from his eyes. This time, he wouldn't be late.

CHAPTER TWENTY-EIGHT

The light of Eleshar's moon was bright enough for a normal person to see during the dark months, though many in the cities had forgotten how reliant they'd once been on the moon, leaning on white vine lanterns to chase away the darkness, instead. An assassin, even one as bad as Zeriel, could never forget. He was reminded of the moonlight's strength as he worked to avoid its rays while speeding through the shadows of the southern Fei En Ar forest. It felt strange to use the power for an extended period. The darkness cradled him and pulled him along, his feet barely touching the underbrush below as he went. In the void he'd only boosted his speed while sparring with Plaxes. This was on an entirely different level.

If he'd estimated properly, Clan Gor was half a day's journey on foot to the southeast of the camp. With luck he'd arrive before Elilta and Denetek's forces, and with enough time to warn the Clan and set up proper defenses. They'd need his help to face an army of assassins. The Te Et Sha wouldn't attack head on. They'd attack from hidden positions, even en masse.

Anxiety at the thought drove him to strain his abilities and push through the shadows faster. His feet swung behind him as he increased his speed. The only thing that slowed him was weaving through the trees.

Jekjarah appeared next to him. He followed along, leaning on his cane as if he were standing on solid ground. "Do you even know if you're going the right way?"

"I'm headed south. What other way is there?"

"Maybe you should check your location before you speed past them."

Zeriel wanted to jab back at the hallucination, but he had a point. The only way to know for sure was to find higher ground. He looked at the ground as it passed under and had a thought. With an effort of will he commanded the shadows to draw him higher, and, to his surprise, they obeyed. The ground pulled away and became streaks of bioluminescent colors underneath, mixing into a single, glowing color unlike any he'd ever seen before.

Slowly, Zeriel continued to rise until the branches formed into a roof and forced him to punch his way through the canopy. Dark tendrils reached up through the trees and kept him afloat. The unrestricted space of the open air allowed him to speed up further, subjecting him to the power of the wind. The flapping of his clothes and the tears the wind brought to his eyes gave him an idea of the frightening speed at which he was travelling.

That fright was overshadowed by the sight he'd been given. On his right were the Ut Fesh Ta mountains, home of Clan Ra to the south and Clan Din to the north. To his left were the Southern Flatlands. An expanse of gently rolling fields of mostly grass and farmland. In the far distance of the flatlands, Zeriel could see the lanterns of Clan Gor, their unwavering glow a beacon on the horizon. Jekjarah was right, if he hadn't found a way above the trees, he would have flown past it.

A quick turn to his left pointed him in the right direction, but the sudden change in motion pulled painfully on his body—a fact he would have to remember for the future. In moments he cleared the forest and found himself over the grassy fields. He felt himself losing altitude as the strands of shadow from the forest stretched to their limit until they finally disintegrated. Gravity pulled him to the ground, and he barely managed to find new shadows underneath the grass below. They stretched weakly upward, barely keeping him afloat once they connected. While this left him just a few feet above the ground, it didn't slow him. He left a wake in the grass as he sped forward.

The green, orange, and blue glow of the grass below rippled and left a wave of color on the wake behind him and for a moment, he was lost in its beauty. Ahead, lines of those soft colors rolled across the modest hills in the breeze, and euphoria washed over him. He found himself weaving through the curves of the flatlands, caressing the grass as he went. He let himself get carried away, spinning and flipping in the air.

"You're about to go into battle against an unknown number of the Te Et Sha. I'd think you would take this more seriously."

Zeriel looked to the side where Jekjarah glided along with him, smoothly mirroring his movements. "It's likely I'm going to die today."

"I didn't say—"

"I know what you said, but it's still true. Just let me have this. It might be the last morsel of joy I'll ever experience."

Jekjarah studied him for a moment and simply nodded, a stern look on his face. Zeriel looked away from the hallucination and felt him disappear. For a time, he watched as the lights of Clan Gor filled his vision. It forced him to tear his shirt into a makeshift blindfold and tie it over his eyes, allowing him to see the Clan's walls. Two silver banners hung from the walls, one on either side of the main entrance, carrying the Clan's Stipes: Two white vertical stripes with a smaller dark blue stripe crossing over them diagonally. He let himself get distracted by the rhythmic way they flapped slowly in the breeze.

Movement stole his attention away from the banners. He'd been distracted for too long and had flown right into the middle of Elilta's forces. Unfortunately for him, they *were* paying attention, and several knives flew from the grass at once, forcing Zeriel to launch himself sideways and higher into the air.

"Blinding light!" he shouted reflexively. The meager tethers of shadow the grass provided snapped as he did, leaving him floating dangerously. Zeriel struggled to draw the darkness further toward him but could only watch as they stretched to their limit several feet out of reach.

Dark forms exploded from the grass below to take advantage of the opportunity. Their blades glinted in the moonlight to foretell the doom that approached. All Zeriel could do was watch and pray he could touch the shadows before those blades connected.

Gravity seemed to allow him to float rather than fall as he crept toward the shadow tendrils. Two of the assassins reached him first, carving lines of fire across his arm and chest. That snapped him back to the fight and he managed to coalesce the shadows that still surrounded him into a shield. The remaining assassins' blades bounced off his defenses and gave him the time he needed to reconnect with the shadows below.

He felt, rather than saw, the shadows reconnect, then immediately exploded them into dark mist around him. Cries of surprise erupted all around. Awareness of everything that touched the mist flooded his consciousness, telling Zeriel exactly where the nine Te Et Sha were. They were moving erratically, trying to get their bearings in the pitch-black of his smoke screen.

He reached into the mist and formed daggers as he began his attack. With the force of the shadows pressing him forward, Zeriel moved among the assassins with blinding speed. In a single snaking motion, Zeriel weaved through them. He severed Achilles tendons, then opened critical arteries. One by one, bodies fell to the ground until he struck his final blow and let his dark mist dissipate.

The grass crackled around him as the men he'd just killed writhed on the ground, breathing their final breaths.

Jekjarah stepped through the grass and approached Zeriel. He shook his head as if he'd made a show of surveying Zeriel's work. "I guess there was something to Plaxes's training."

An explosion sounded, followed closely by a shockwave that collided with Zeriel's body and sent him back a step. The injuries he'd received from the morning's beating lit up at the impact and drew his attention to the blood soaking into his clothing.

"The attack started," Jekjarah said. "You better hurry."

Zeriel found his nearest victim, already unconscious from blood loss. He tore pieces of the man's clothing off to use as bandages, then called on the shadows to bring him into the air again.

A bell ran loudly from inside the Clan as dark forms moved through the grass toward the explosion. They flooded into the opening the explosion made in the wall. Arrows rained down from the top of the wall in hopes of slowing the attack, though they did little to stop the mass of assassins. Their enhanced bodies and elite training gave them everything they needed to knock arrows out of the sky with their daggers. Thrown weapons left the hands of the attackers and felled the archers one by one.

Despite the frightening speed at which the assassins moved into the Clan, there was still a chance to slow them down. Zeriel caught the shadows' current again and went to work. He flashed through the battlefield and killed with abandon. Jekjarah cried in excitement as they went, which drove Zeriel to push harder.

It didn't take long for the Te Et Sha to realize what was happening. They threw daggers and poisoned needles at the cloud of shadows around him. They all missed. Someone nearby had seen what was happening and tried to take control, forming those around him into lines meant to funnel him into something of an ambush. What they failed to realize was, unlike them, the moonlight lit up his surroundings like the sun for Zeriel's eyes. The darkness revealed its mysteries to him. Things it hid from everyone else, even from the eyes of the Te Et Sha.

With another effort of will, he commanded the shadows to toss him high in the air. They obeyed, and just as he slowed to a stop in the air, he looked down to see the assassins below, lined up in defensive positions. Zeriel grinned as he stretched out his arms and physically pulled the shadows from the ground under them. How he knew to do that, he wasn't sure. He simply executed the move by instinct.

Dark spikes erupted from below as he went, piercing the men below and lifting bodies into the air. Those ahead of him who saw what was happening scattered, but they couldn't outrun him.

Zeriel landed in front of the man who'd led the ambush attempt.

The screams of the assassins the man had so recently commanded echoed in the darkness as they died on spikes of shadow. Another look at the man showed Zeriel he wasn't as old as he first thought, clearly of Elilta's trainees. He stepped back, shock frozen across his face.

"It wasn't a terrible plan. How could you have known you were so outmatched?"

Shock turned to rage. "I'll show you outmatched, *Worst One*." The boy let out a battle cry that cracked in his throat, then he attacked.

The boy was skilled, and Elilta had trained him well, but she'd trained Zeriel as well. The young assassin sidestepped, dug his dagger into the ground and sent dirt at Zeriel's face. He knew the move was coming and blocked it with minimal effort. The boy continued to the next part of the attack, but it only worked if you successfully blinded your opponent. As it was, Zeriel sidestepped with his powers to enhance him to level far above any Te Et Sha, avoiding the trainees circular dash and his quick motion to stab at Zeriel's side. He zipped behind the boy in the blink of an eye, opening a deep cut in his throat on the way.

Jekjarah cried out in victory, but Zeriel knew he couldn't let his guard down, not with more enemies surrounding him. As if on cue, a group leaped from the grass around him, catching him in a pincer attack.

He launched himself on shadows into the air, avoiding their attack. The battle cries rang in Zeriel's ear as he cleared the top of the grass again. It dawned on him in that moment that someone was sending these children to die at Zeriel's hand. Were they simply a distraction to keep him from stopping their forces inside the city? It sounded like a plan Elilta would have come up with.

Zeriel gritted his bared teeth reflexively as he let out a deep growl of frustration. He had to move fast if he was going to be of any use to Clan Gor. This time he readied himself for the force the sudden shift in momentum put on his body as he commanded the shadows to pull him toward the gap in the village's wall. Even prepared for it, he barely managed to fight the darkness that closed around the edges of his vision.

The grass sped by under him once again as he focused on the jagged gap in the wall. Throwing daggers came for him from below as arrows flew at him from above. It seemed the archers of Clan Gor couldn't recognize that he was on their side. He didn't blame them, given the circumstances. This time he hadn't neglected his defenses though, but with so much of his efforts on staying in the air, the best he could manage was to redirect the projectiles. A few managed to open shallow cuts as they sped past.

With a final push through a thick volley of arrows, he flew through the opening and landed just on the other side. Zeriel spun toward the opening in time to see several Te Et Sha dashing inside after him.

Suddenly, the world spun, and he lost his balance. A strong fatigue washed over his body, and the combination of the two forced him to his knees.

Plaxes's training had acquainted him with this side effect of prolonged use of his powers. Though in the void of his mind it took much longer for them to kick in, several days in fact. He'd only used them for a few hours in the physical world and he was already close to his limit.

The assassins who'd entered the village behind him pressed their advantage and attacked. Without his new skills, those boys would have killed him in an instant. Now that his mind wasn't focused on keeping him in the air, he devoted his entire focus to defense.

The relentless nature of Plaxes's training forced him to find reprieve. Necessity led to the creation of an impenetrable bubble, a shield against all forms of attack. He held that shield now, though he wouldn't be able to maintain it for long.

After all their attacks bounced off his bubble, the assassins tried a last-ditch lunge with their daggers. Their weapons collided with solid shadow and were turned away once more, but Zeriel's control slipped a second later. The shield exploded into a black mist that quickly evaporated into the darkness.

He'd bought himself the time he needed, though, and struck while the assassins were still on their heels, managing to drop all four. The exhaustion was building which forced Zeriel to find a dark corner to hide in. When he peered back at the opening in the wall, a large form stood there, surveying the scene.

Denetek had just entered the city.

CHAPTER TWENTY-NINE

With significant effort, Zeriel controlled his breathing. He'd been winded before, but never had a breath of air felt so empty. No matter how fast or how deeply he drew his breath, the burning in his lungs only grew. Suffocation began to feel like a real possibility.

Rubble crunched beneath Denetek's feet as he stepped into the village, a testament to the level of arrogance necessary for an assassin to abandon a decade's worth of training and experience. He dragged the tip of a straight-bladed sword along the ground behind him, the scraping sound echoing off the buildings. "I know you're in here Worst One. I saw you fly through the wall."

Zeriel turned his eyes to watch Denetek as he scanned the shadows. The gap in the wall opened into a wide street, the stucco buildings on either side showing brick underneath damaged walls. Denetek was the only one standing in the street. The sounds of fighting deeper in the village pulsated past them like the waves of a turbulent ocean.

"Do you hear that?" Denetek asked, gesturing deeper into the village. "It won't be much longer before we have this village and its Clan. Give up now and I'll make your death quick."

Jekjarah appeared in front of Zeriel. "Get ahold of yourself. Are you so weak that you can't manage a few hours of using your powers? Or was all that training for nothing?"

The hallucination was right. Zeriel had let unfamiliar emotions get the better of him. Fighting through pain and exhaustion was something he had years of experience doing. He pushed aside the fear and nerves to empty his mind, then he pushed his pain to the dark recesses of his mind and, with an effort of will, ignored it. With that done, he focused his mind solely on his mission.

Echoes of clashing metal and the cries of the dying rolled through the street, distracting Zeriel from the revenge stalking past him.

"What are you waiting for?" Jekjarah said, as his face distorted in a mixture of anger and the anticipation of violence. "Now's your chance to end him!"

Zeriel looked to Denetek as the man looked for him. He tried to block out the distant noise but couldn't. Jekjarah was voicing his desire to kill the man and end things now. But something about that noise nagged at him. In the end, he couldn't ignore it. "No," he said, finally.

"What do you mean, *no?*"

Zeriel shifted further down the alley, remaining hidden as he turned at the nearest intersection toward the battle raging deeper in the village. "Part of the reason I came here was to help Clan Gor. Denetek can wait." He picked up speed as he drew on his power, though it strained like muscles nearing failure. Zeriel drew from his newfound mental resolve and pushed forward.

Jekjarah floated alongside him as he zipped through the streets. "What good is saving this Clan going to do?"

"It achieves both goals of getting revenge *and* saving the clans. That's what."

"And after you save the clans? Then what? You think they'll appoint you their leader? Zeriel, the new Ai Jel!"

"No, Jek. I'm no leader—"

"Exactly! You're an assassin. So why don't you start acting like one?"

Zeriel shook his head. Jekjarah gave voice to his thoughts, but he'd made his choice, and nothing was going to stop him now. After turning a corner, several Te Et Sha caught his attention. They stood over a woman cradling a wailing baby. With a swipe of his hand the darkness around him coalesced into spikes and shot toward the assassins. Each one hit their target perfectly, dropping them before their daggers fell. He wavered on his feet at the effort, then leaned his shoulder on the wall next to him.

The woman cried out in shock and scrambled back. Zeriel shoved himself off the wall and approached her. Terror stretched across her features as she watched him.

"I'm not with them," he said, gesturing toward the bodies.

The woman looked at the bodies, then back to him.

"Are you hurt?"

She shook her head. "N—no." Her baby's cries finally drew her attention, and she focused on comforting it as though they hadn't almost been killed.

"Find someplace to hide. This isn't over yet."

She nodded absently, stood, and hurried away from the sounds of battle.

With an effort of will he drew the shadows around him again and sped through the streets once more. The main fight was further into the village, and the noise of the battle had been going on for several tense minutes. An eternity on a battlefield. He could only hope he'd make it in time.

Along the way he caught several of the invaders terrorizing the clansmen. Zeriel didn't miss a step as he threw shadow spikes into the backs of their necks. Each one dropped and left their victims wondering what had saved them. A spike of joy flashed through him as he saw the confusion on the faces of those he saved when they couldn't find their savior. Usually, he left only death in his wake. He did that still, but now there was something...more.

A quick turn around a corner brought Zeriel out of his thoughts. The road opened into a large common area. A tall fountain stood in the center made of bowls stacked haphazardly one on top of the other. Water poured from one bowl to the next, reflecting the starlight above and the soft glow of the trees and flowers around it. Bushes glowing blue and green created a sort of barrier from the outer edge and the fountain within. Trees stood at the corners of the square created by the bushes. White vine lanterns hung from the trees' branches, lighting the area.

Men and women of Clan Gor filled the square, each one fighting as best they could against the stronger, faster assassins. Swords clashed, gore sailed through the air, and people died. A tall figure caught Zeriel's eye amidst the fighting. A man towered above even the other Fei En Ar around him and fought like nothing Zeriel had ever seen. He had an unbelievably broad build, and a claymore as tall as he was, brandished in both hands. Despite all that bulk he managed to move with the grace and agility of a dancer. And most amazing of all, he was holding his own, creating a barrier between the assassins and his clansmen.

For a moment, Zeriel thought he didn't need to come to their rescue. That this man's strength alone was enough to save the Clan. A quick look around reminded him that one man can't fight off an army. The Te Et Sha who weren't piling on the giant in the center of the square were fighting smaller groups nearby, and they were winning. Soon enough, the man would be overwhelmed by sheer numbers.

A wave of exhaustion threatened to roll across Zeriel's body, but he moved before it could stop him from doing his duty. He rode the shadows, sweeping through the square and cutting down assassins as he went. He slashed throats, opened bellies, and pierced hearts. Crimson rain filled the air around him, and the familiar scent of iron entered his nostrils.

Jekjarah lost himself in the carnage in his usual way, and Zeriel let the hallucination's glee wash over him and drive him forward. He hadn't lost himself in the killing like this since Mandias, and the familiarity of it felt good. Before he knew what had happened, every assassin in the square was dead. He found Jekjarah on the ground trying to scoop handfuls of blood from the cobblestone and onto his face.

"Surrender now, and I may still let you live." The voice boomed through the courtyard and over the cries of the dying.

Zeriel froze. He was suddenly on his knees, his hand stopped halfway to his face. Jekjarah wasn't the one bathing in gore—he was.

He looked in the direction of the voice. It was the large man with a group of clansmen standing behind him. Somehow, he was holding his enormous weapon straight out with one hand, its point aimed at Zeriel. The man's eyes widened at what he saw, and he took a step back, the tip of his sword clanging on the cobblestone.

"End him! He must have *so much BLOOOD!*" Jekjarah appeared on his knees next to the man, clawing uselessly at his exposed skin.

Panic coursed through him, worried that they thought he was with the Te Et Sha. Despite his clothing being different from the assassins', it would be a logical assumption, considering how he fought. His bloodlust pushed him past the panic to continue the carnage, so he stood, ready to use his new power to carve through every person there. Something deep in his mind told him to stop. The thought, logical and commanding, told him these people weren't his enemies. He struggled to grab onto that, fighting to regain control of himself, and took an unsteady step forward.

The group behind the man stepped back reflexively. A crash sounded from a road behind them, causing the group to flinch and turn their backs to him. The large man watched Zeriel, unfazed by the sound. He lifted his claymore and said, "So, it's death then."

Zeriel readied his power, drawing dark tendrils of deadly shadow from the cracks in the stone under his feet.

The clang of metal on metal echoed from that road at the edge of the square, louder than even the crash from earlier. Something was coming.

He tried to release the dark coils, but couldn't. Sweat poured down his forehead, drawing lines in the deep red mask of dried blood on his face.

"Zeriel!" Boomed a voice from the road.

The cry broke Zeriel's bloodlust, and his power slipped, causing the shadow tendrils to dissipate. He breathed heavily in relief and looked toward the road to see Denetek entering the square, his eyes fixed on

Zeriel. "This is the last time you meddle in our plans, *Worst One!*" He bent down and snatched two falchions from dead hands on the ground. The clansmen around them went into action as one and attacked Denetek with a ferocity Zeriel didn't expect.

The large man from Clan Gor turned to face Denetek and eyed Zeriel. "It seems we have a common enemy for the time being."

Zeriel paused, unsure if he could trust this man who had just witnessed him smearing gore on his face. Luckily, it seemed he didn't think Zeriel was with the Te Et Sha. "We do," he said, carefully.

The man turned to face Denetek. "Then I say we postpone our disagreement and fight him together." He got in a fighting stance, his blade held in both hands. "I am Ketik, Chief of Clan Gor."

The battle wasn't going to wait for Zeriel to decide if he trusted the Chief. For now, it seemed, he had no choice but to join forces with the man. "Zeriel, former assassin, member of Clan Ra." He drew up the darkness again and formed it into two falchions that he snatched out of the air. "There's more where he came from."

"Then we'll finish them too."

Zeriel nodded.

Jekjarah appeared next to Ketik. "On second thought, you'd better let him live a while longer. He seems useful."

"Perhaps."

Ketik looked back. "What?"

Zeriel ignored the man and cloaked himself in darkness.

CHAPTER THIRTY

Denetek had entered the square from the corner furthest from Ketik and Zeriel, so when the chief's men—five of them in total—attacked, they had the entire length of the square to cover. It gave Denetek plenty of time to sprint along the edge of the square, putting the fountain between him and Zeriel. Several quick motions of his arm sent throwing daggers at the chief's men, dropping the front two.

Ketik glanced at Zeriel. "Flank right," he ordered, pointing, then sprinted left to join his men.

Instinct guided Zeriel as he fell in line under the chief's leadership. His confidence combined with the expertise he'd shown in battle made trusting his commands easy. But what was most shocking was Zeriel *wanted* to follow him. But he couldn't dwell on that now.

Zeriel sprinted, his legs heavy, and his exhaustion drove him to the limits. This wasn't the time for weakness, though. Zeriel pushed on despite his weakening muscles and called upon the shadows to lift him up and over the fountain. They came slowly, lifting him upward just in time to see Denetek on the other side.

Surprise flashed across the assassin's face at the sight of Zeriel vaulting over the fountain. The satisfaction he felt at the man's reaction was short-lived. His power faltered just as he crossed the top of the fountain, and his foot caught on the edge of the top bowl. Pain shot through his foot and up into his leg as the shift in momentum sent him flailing to the ground.

Zeriel landed in an awkward roll that, when he popped up, left him stumbling on one foot as he struggled to regain his balance. Denetek watched with the clear focus of a predator and a smirk that let his arrogance slip through.

The assassin glanced at Ketik and his men, turning away from Zeriel to face them. The statement was clear: He wasn't a threat.

But Denetek was right. The chief had taken command of his men who were now flanking him. Zeriel tried to attack, but his limbs were too heavy to catch the assassin when he disengaged.

He was faster than the clansmen, but not Ketik who shot in with a thrust that left them trading a flurry of strikes. It was a gambit to give his men time to attack, and it worked.

Zeriel struggled to move, to join the battle, but his body was too slow to respond. He watched as the chief's men beat him to the fight. Denetek noticed them and reared back with a powerful kick, sending Ketik flying onto his back. With a deft spin, he quickly cut down the two men with precise, lethal slashes.

Ketik's face twisted in pain as he staggered to his feet. "You and all your men will die here tonight."

Zeriel couldn't see the look on Denetek's face since the man was looking away from him, but he was familiar with that gleeful expression that was surely plastered there. The man's arrogance, and that moment of distraction was exactly what Zeriel needed to finally close the distance. He struck, slashing two deep cuts in the assassin's back.

Denetek cried out in surprise and spun, dropping one of his swords and letting several throwing knives fly as he did. Zeriel dodged the projectiles, the motion throwing him off balance. The assassin pressed his attack with the sword in his other hand, and for a time he and Zeriel traded blows.

Amazingly, Zeriel was holding his own, but his muscles were close to giving out, and his abilities were weakening. He was reminded of his time as a trainee, sparring with more skilled opponents. This was no sparring match, though, and Denetek would eventually crush him.

"Give it up *Worst One*. Accept your death with the honor of a Te Et Sha."

Zeriel gritted his teeth and bolstered his attacks, forcing Denetek back a step. "The Te Et Sha are dead."

"Ha! You would think that." The man recovered and went on the attack, gaining the upper hand again. "We've simply evolved."

But then the man shifted, and in an instant, he saw it. An opening, clear as the sunlight at the height of a light month, one the assassin couldn't avoid. A chance had come, one Zeriel had experienced only once before.

Without hesitation he thrust his sword at the opening and watched as the point of his blade contacted Denetek's chest. His eyes went wide with shock and fear.

Then Zeriel's blade, constructed from will and shadow, popped into a black mist and out of existence.

The assassin reacted faster, thrusting his own blade at Zeriel. He torqued his upper body, putting every bit of energy he had left into a dodge, but it wasn't enough. Denetek's blade caught him in the shoulder and drove him to the ground.

"Ha!" The man said as he stood over him. "Even with the darkness at your command, you're as weak as ever." He pulled the sword from Zeriel's shoulder, raising it for the final blow. "Now die."

Just as he was about to finish Zeriel, something large slammed into him, sending him flying into the wall of a nearby building. Zeriel twisted his head to see Ketik standing between him and the assassin lying crumpled on the cobblestone.

The man was breathing hard and favoring his right leg, yet he managed to look imposing despite the injuries. "Are you okay?"

"I'll live," Zeriel said, as he tried to get up. The wound in his left shoulder made it nearly impossible to carry weight with his left arm, and his right was on the edge of failure. His right hand slipped on the bloody cobblestone beneath him and sent him lying on the floor again. "I'm not sure how much more help I can be."

"You've done your part. I'll handle him from here."

"His body has been enhanced. Even injured he's stronger and faster than you."

Ketik turned to Zeriel and smiled. "A challenge then?" He turned back to watch as Denetek struggled back to his feet. "Just the way I like it!" The chief leaped into action, his large sword held straight up and by his side while his battle cry echoed through the square. Even against a Te Et Sha, Zeriel pitied any man Ketik faced with that level of killing intent.

The assassin steadied himself just in time to defend a powerful overhand swing. The impact almost knocked him back to the ground, but he kept his footing, pushing the blow back and responding with several strikes of his own. Ketik parried each one, but only just. Against one of the top three Te Et Sha, it was a feat of pure skill and determination that Zeriel had never seen.

The chief saw an opening and responded to Denetek's attack with one of his own. The difference in their styles became apparent as Zeriel watched the chief wielding his large sword. He moved it with speed despite its size, using it to force his opponent into unfavorable positions as he tried to go on the attack.

Jekjarah appeared next to Ketik. "Look at him, Zeriel. Have you ever seen anything so beautiful?"

He twisted and glided the blade in ways Zeriel didn't know were possible, but perfectly positioned it for an attack or a parry, and for a moment it looked like Ketik would get the upper hand.

A sudden rush of speed from Denetek changed that. His enhancements came into play and were more than Ketik could overcome.

The chief took a shoulder that drove him back and set him on his heels. He defended most of the assassin's quick strikes, but some were making their way through the chief's defenses. Zeriel watched as slices appeared across his armor that let blood seep through. They weren't deep cuts, but they were starting to pile up.

He knew he had to act, but he could barely move, so he reached for his powers instead. There was—nothing. The shadows didn't respond.

Ketik was slowing, and the outcome was clear. The assassin drove a kick into his chest. The chief shot through the air and slammed against a wall. He crumbled to the ground, somehow managing to stay on his knees by planting his sword point first in the ground. He coughed blood onto the cobblestone before raising his eyes defiantly at his opponent, then forced himself to his feet.

Denetek paused for a moment. *"Only the strong survive."*

"What?" Ketik said.

"You've proven your strength. Swear loyalty to Veshet, and I will let you live."

Ketik raised an eyebrow. "I don't know who this *Veshet* is, but I sure as hell wouldn't swear loyalty to him even if I did. My duty is to Clan Gor." His strength gave out for a split second, but he caught himself and got back into his fighting stance.

"A pity." To Zeriel's surprise, Denetek sounded like he meant it. "Are you ready to die?"

"Come and find out."

Zeriel stared at him in shock. He'd never known someone willing to sacrifice so much, even for his Clan. Sure, he'd heard of men who had such convictions, but he'd never seen one in the flesh. Time and time again, as he went on missions across the world, he'd watch as people sacrificed others to save their own lives. Even the chief of his own village stood by as his family lived under Renniel's tyranny.

Yet there Ketik was, knowing full well he was going to die, defying Denetek, never wavering. The expression on the chief's face didn't show a hint of fear. Instead, all Zeriel thought he saw there was determination. In that moment he understood why so many followed this man; why he'd followed him by reflex.

The assassin moved and Zeriel felt a spear of panic shoot through his gut. He had to stop this, had to preserve whatever this man represented. He called on the shadows, drawing from every reservoir of strength he possessed. They didn't come, fanning the flames of Zeriel's desperation at each one of Denetek's steps. He dug deeper than he ever had, tried to find the last drop of power he could muster.

The assassin leaped into the air, his swords ready to strike and kill Ketik.

Zeriel strained, then screamed as pain flared through him. Then he found it, at the very core of his essence. Touching it was painful, but he did it anyway and used that last bit of what Plaxes gave him to attack.

A line of shadow, as thin as a piece of thread, shot out from the cobblestone and pierced Denetek through the heart. The assassin's momentum carried him into Ketik and the two collapsed to the ground.

A tense moment passed before Denetek's corpse shifted. Ketik used his sword as a lever to lift the assassin off him. The chief regarded the corpse with clear confusion on his face, then touched its chest. He glanced at Zeriel with wide eyes.

Zeriel responded with a nod.

A soft crunch came from the rooftop behind Zeriel. He snapped his head toward the sound to find the silhouette of Elilta standing on the nearest building. "Shit," he cursed. After all that, they were still going to die.

A few moments earlier, he would have accepted his fate and lain still so his death would be quick. But he'd just watched Ketik prove that men could be more than he ever knew.

He fought through the pain and managed to move his limbs. It took a long time, but he eventually got to his feet. Then his legs gave out. To his own surprise he began again, and though it took longer, he fought his way to his feet.

His strength left him, and he collapsed once more.

It took longer still the third time, but when his legs failed him again, this time he didn't fall. Instead Ketik was there to catch him.

"Thanks."

"A lot of good it will do us." The chief spun around and when Zeriel followed his gaze he finally saw the crowd of Te Et Sha that surrounded them.

Zeriel glared at Elilta, his fury burning. "What are you waiting for? Give the order to kill us already!"

"*Only the strong survive.*" She let the statement sit in the square, its weight falling on every person there.

"*Only the strong survive,*" said one of the assassins.

Then another one repeated it, and another, until it became a murmur that cascaded through the group.

"You've earned your life today, Zeriel, and with it the lives of everyone left in this Clan, for now."

"Veshet isn't here, is he? He's marching toward Ki Al Tesh while he left you and Dentek to take this Clan."

Elilta eyed him for a moment. "If you know all that, then surely you know you're struggling against the inevitable. He will rule Fei En Ar."

"Not after I've killed him."

"Still the same fool you were when I trained you." Elilta put her fingers in her mouth and let out a whistle in a distinct staccato, then disappeared.

The Te Et Sha in the square vanished with her as they repeated the whistle, creating an eerie echo that faded as they left the village.

When the whistle fell to silence, Zeriel relaxed and slipped through Ketik's grip. Unconsciousness took him before he hit the ground.

CHAPTER THIRTY-ONE

Baharkar Village bustled with activity in the early morning. Villagers and merchants weaved their ways through town by the light of white vine lanterns mounted on poles along the streets. El stood on the southern tip of the cove in the heart of the port, ignoring them and staring at the enormous shell of the Uklak she'd caught the last light month. It was nearly half the size of the cove itself, its shell a darker brown than the smaller specimens they were used to catching, and the spikes across its body protruded at least three times as far.

The creature's carapace was barely half-harvested, partially due to the sheer amount there was to extract, but it was also several times stronger than any Master Tet had worked with. It took the man a week before he discovered the adjustments necessary to cut through the material. In some ways it was good news, as they'd produced weapons, armor, and raw material far stronger and more valuable than anything they'd had before. In other ways it hurt them. The longer processing and crafting times meant longer waits for new stock, and the higher costs meant alienating a large group of their normal customers. It had also pushed back her own expansion plans, taking more time to restock, and costing more than she initially planned.

El watched Master Tet and his team working by the light of their lanterns, wondering if she made the right choice bringing the beast back. Though she didn't have much time for decision making in those cold depths, she wished she'd chosen one of the smaller Uklak, more of the size and quality to which they were accustomed. But regrets weren't going to solve her problems, so with a sigh of acceptance, El spun around and headed south, toward the building she'd commissioned the month prior after realizing the delay she'd forced on herself.

The smell of fresh meat buns wafted to her, attacking her stomach through her nose. It growled to her in response. She obeyed, making her way to the small stand and waiting in the long line. She bought three buns, then continued to her destination.

Her new building was at the southern edge of the trade district, which had grown far enough to the south that they had cut back the forest to make room. The large structure, built to include several offices and plenty of storage for her goods, faced south, overlooking the Jurjur blowholes. Steady, white lantern light flooded out of the windows, illuminating the street in front of it.

A sign hung above the door that read Baharkar Trading Company, written in Yawdawian with a Kloren translation underneath. With the influx of new merchants, practically everything in the village had to be written in both languages. El smiled at the sign, a comforting satisfaction radiating through her body, then stepped inside.

The door opened into a small waiting area with a desk in the far corner. Two hallways branched out from the room, one to the left leading to the main warehouse, and one to the right to offices, and meeting rooms. Reon leaned against the desk reading something on a piece of paper. He cut the same striking figure he always had, the one she remembered when she first saw him what felt like a lifetime ago, when she was chained and waiting to be sold into slavery. A shiver crept up her spine as she banished the memory.

He looked up as she closed the door behind her and gave her a smile of his own. "There you are." Practically tossing the paper on the desk, he hurried to her, swept her into his arms, and kissed her. She'd never get tired of that.

They broke off the kiss and El gently pushed him away, looking around. "Is Ki here?"

Reon sighed, his body deflating a bit, and looked down at the meat buns in her hands. "You brought breakfast, I see."

El huffed and handed him one, which he took greedily. "Is she in the main room?"

"Yrrp," he said through a bite of his food.

Straightening her clothes and patting him on the chest she said, "Come on then," and breezed past him toward the left hallway. She turned into the first door to her right. It was the largest meeting room, containing a table that could seat at least ten people. Windows on the far wall overlooked the blowholes and the ocean beyond, though the outside was a mask of darkness against the harsh light of the white vine Lanterns inside.

Ki sat in a chair near the middle of the table, reviewing papers and making notes with a pencil. "You realize I can hear everything from here?" she said without looking up. "You two should really get married if you're going to keep acting like that in public."

El blushed fiercely at her friend's reprimand, set the woman's food in front of her, and took a seat across the table from her. "I wasn't thinking about who might hear."

"You don't need to apologize," Reon said as he took a seat next to her. "Just because everyone else in this village is reserved to the point of prudishness doesn't mean you have to be." He shoved the last bite of his food in his mouth.

She smiled at him and patted his shoulder. "Thanks." He meant well, but he didn't understand the weight of the expectations put on her. Not just from her family, but from the entire village. Leaders weren't just strong, decisive, and caring, they were the living embodiments of their culture and traditions. *But they can't keep looking at me like a leader. I'll be gone soon enough.* The thought was involuntary and quick, and it took some effort to force it from her mind. She would *not* worry about that right now. It was a problem for the future.

Ki set her pencil down and picked up the bun in front of her. "Starting with some good news, we're close to fully stocked on everything we need for the voyage." Her friend said, then took a huge bite of her food.

"When I took inventory last we had everything we needed. What are we waiting for?"

Ki swallowed, then thumped her chest to help the oversized bite go down. "The funds for everyone's slave debt."

When she heard that the King of Wylsh himself was overseeing the rebuilding of Shyal, she'd decided to pay her and all the hunter's slave debts as soon as she could save the funds. The higher priced Uklak goods had forced her to dig into those savings, adding to their delay. "Will we be ready in time to sail in the sunlight?" El's stomach rumbled softly, forcing her to take a bite of her own bun.

"Should be," she replied, "though you may have the sun on your backs instead of over your heads."

"That's fine, I'd just prefer not to make the journey in the darkness if I could." Ships sailed during the dark months all the time, navigating by the position of the moon and stars. In fact, it was easier in the dark with a map in the sky and no danger of sun sickness. But it wasn't the dark she wanted to avoid as much as it was the frigid waters that came with it. By nature of her powers, she found herself wet more often than not.

"I still can't believe you're going to waste our money on a debt no one expects paid," Reon said, his annoyance at the thought thick in his tone.

"*Our* money?" El asked, raising an eyebrow.

Reon met her eyes, a stubbornness there she hadn't seen in him during their time in Shyal. After a moment he huffed and waved a hand in front of his face. "Fine, *your* money."

"I won't have the blood of Finders on my hands after they come here trying to take me and the hunters back to that *ocean's forsaken* city."

"I know," he said, pursing his lips and saying nothing more. She could tell he had further objections but held them in, letting her win the exchange anyway. That made her more angry than if he had just said them out loud.

"Regardless," Ki interjected. "Everything is on track, barring some unforeseen crisis." As if to mock her, a loud banging sounded from the front door of the building. The three shared a look before hurrying to the door.

El opened the door to find no one was on the other side. She poked her head outside, looked both ways, and again saw no one. Looking down as she turned to reenter, she noticed a small package on the ground in front of the door. It was box-shaped and wrapped in a thin burlap cloth tied tightly with some simple twine. The corner of a slip of paper with a symbol stamped on it— a large circle, surrounded by an oval of twelve smaller circles with lines connecting them to the center—was secured under the twine. Two words were written under the symbol in flowy Kloren script that read, *Nedon's Champion*.

"What is it?" Ki asked, peeking around her.

El stepped back inside, closed the door, and showed the package to them. "It says it's for Nedon's Champion."

Reon brushed past her and barreled out the door. Ki stepped closer, inspecting the package. "An ominous note for such a simple looking package," she said, stepping back and placing a hand to her chin. "What do you think it could be?"

"Not a clue." She went to the small desk in the corner, placed the package on it, then began unwrapping it.

"Are you sure you should do that?" Ki asked. "What if it's some sort of assassination attempt."

El flashed a smirk back at her friend. "Who would want to assassinate me, Ki?"

Her cheeks flushed. "Someone from one of the other merchant fleets?"

"They wouldn't know to address it to Nedon's Champion. Stop worrying so much." Removing the cloth, she found a wooden box underneath with the same symbol branded on each of the sides. The top of the box slid open easily, revealing a folded note on top of a crystal bracelet unlike anything El had ever seen. One side was hinged, the other side latched closed with a simple iron clasp. It was fashioned from an opaque sky-blue crystal that was perfectly, almost supernaturally smooth, and it had short spikes on the inside face that were long enough to pierce the skin when closed around the wrist.

Ki picked up the jewelry and inspected it. "Why would someone put these spikes here?"

El looked at the note that came with it. The outside had more of the same looping handwriting that read, *Only if you're alone.* Somehow, she knew it didn't mean being alone physically. After a pause to confirm she couldn't detect Nedon's presence in her mind, she unfolded it.

Hello El,

Your appearance has confirmed that the Keepers have recovered their powers. The moment our order has feared for millennia has come. We can only hope Azerez hasn't abandoned us.

We've sent this bracelet to you after much deliberation and disagreement. Most of our leaders still believe the risk was too great. But the resistance must start somewhere, and our informants don't believe you've sided with Nedon. I hope that is true.

Put on the bracelet and come to Ferrix. We will find you once you've arrived.

The Wardens

The front door opened and Reon entered. "Nothing. Whoever left that package is gone."

"This was inside," Ki said, handing the bracelet to Reon.

He inspected it with a furrowed brow. "I've never seen anything like this. Who would wear such a thing?"

A sudden and powerful desire to keep the note hidden caused El to tuck it in her pocket. She'd always been completely transparent with Reon and Ki. They were her closest friends, after all. Reon more than that. But the note represented something she wasn't ready to face. And though she'd felt this moment approaching, now that it was here, she found she wasn't ready to face it. There was still so she had to finish. Baharkar Trading Company needed to establish stronger trade routes.

The healers she trained had so much more to learn. And they hadn't discovered the cause of the Uklak's change in behavior. She couldn't leave, not now. "None of us will be wearing that," she said, snatching the item from Reon a bit more aggressively than she intended. "We have more important things to worry about."

"More important than a giftwrapped bracelet addressed to you using Nedon's name?"

El turned to walk to her office down the right-side hallway, pausing before exiting the room. "Reon, I need you to arrange a meeting with the hunters to discuss the plan for the next hunt. I don't think we can reasonably expect to rely on those larger specimens moving forward."

He shook his head and spun on his heels. "Right," he said, frustration dominating his tone.

El turned to Ki and said, "Come up with some contingency plans, just in case that crisis you mentioned does come and we have to pivot."

Ki eyed the bracelet. "Sure." Something in her friend's tone conveyed what El was thinking. *That crisis may have already come.*

El nodded curtly and continued down the hall. These Wardens had just grabbed the helm of her life and tried to wrench it toward their purpose. She wasn't about to let that happen. While she'd accepted that she would be forced to leave Baharkar eventually, she wouldn't let anyone, god or man, determine when that would happen.

Fate would have to be postponed.

For now.

CHAPTER THIRTY-TWO

Muffled voices coaxed Zeriel out of a dreamless sleep. The speech seemed far away, barely at the edges of his perception, and try as he might, he couldn't make out the words.

Soft fabric cradled his body, and a comforting weight pressed down on him. His aches and pains were diminished by the body heat trapped under that weight. For a few blessed seconds the voices withdrew further as he breathed deeply, enjoying the moment for as long as he could. Inevitably, reality asserted its control once again and pulled him from the peace of sleep.

The muffled voices coalesced into discernable speech. "—can't believe you brought him here." The voice was aged but rang a clear, deep baritone.

"I'm not sure our Clan would be here without him," Ketik's familiar voice responded.

"Did our Clan's efforts count for nothing, then?"

"Every single person's effort counts. You know that."

"Then it was a shared victory." The old man's tone was resolute, like that of an argument settled.

"You weren't there. We'd been beaten, surrounded by the enemy—"

Zeriel shifted his attention from the conversation and opened his eyes to find himself in a bed, covered with layers of blankets. Each blanket was the same patternless, sterile white. The room matched the blankets with its absence of decoration. A bed, table, and cabinet with a wash station on top were the only pieces of furniture. A rag hung over the edge of the wash station's bowl, lightly bloodied from presumably being rinsed and rung out after its last use.

The man talking to Ketik was older than even his voice gave away. The top of his bald head reflected the light of the single white vine lantern in the corner. A half-crown of long gray hair hung from the sides of his head no higher than the top of his ears. Liver spots dotted the man's skin, adding additional texture to the deep wrinkles around his ears and at the corner of his eyes. The scowl on his face as he argued with Ketik looked like an artifact from a life of dealing with the sick. His flat tone matched the scowl that seemed to be his face's natural state. Zeriel was surprised by how much this man reminded him of his father, except for the lack of anger in his voice.

Most surprising was that they'd tended to his injuries. While yes, he did help them push back the invaders, he hadn't done enough to prove himself as their ally. And they'd seen the full measure of his bloodlust, and how he nearly attacked them because of it. There was little chance they trusted him, and he feared bringing up the subject might just make things worse.

Despite all that, he hoped that if they were willing to give him aid, there might still be a chance he could make allies of them. He continued to watch the two men argue, waiting for an opening to interrupt them. When he found it, he said, "Are you two going to stop bickering long enough to tell me where I am?"

They abruptly cut off their conversation and looked at him, the old man's eyes narrowing. "What do you want here?" The abruptness of the statement took Zeriel aback.

Jekjarah appeared next to the man, inspecting his face at a distance that would have made him uncomfortable if the man could see the hallucination. "He doesn't seem to trust you, Zeriel." Jekjarah turned to Zeriel with his eyebrows raised. "Better come up with a good story, or you may not make it out of here."

"I came for revenge."

Jekjarah rolled his eyes and let out a melodramatic sigh. "We're dead," he said, before disappearing.

Ketik stepped toward him. "The way you fought. It was just like them. Are you a deserter, or something?"

"More like an unsightly blemish they cut away."

Ketik paused in thought, then asked, "And the man we killed, is he the one you wanted revenge on?"

Zeriel sat up and took in a sharp breath as pain sliced through his shoulder at the effort. His hand went to the pain by reflex, felt the bandage there and came away wet with blood. His other bruises from the previous morning's beating ached, and he grimaced when he spun his legs over the side of the bed. "One of them, yes."

"Seems like you could have killed him and taken off," the old man said. "No one would have known. So why didn't you?" His tone was stern, and speech clipped at the ends.

Zeriel met the old man's gaze, then with a glance at Ketik said, "I doubt I could have killed him on my own." He turned back to the old man. "Helping your Clan was more of a...mutually beneficial accident."

Ketik raised an eyebrow at that.

"I'm sure." The old man's words were laced with skepticism. He turned to leave, speaking with his back to them as he walked out of the room. "You should send him back where he came from, chief. He's trouble." The man opened the door to leave but paused and twisted to look at Zeriel. "Thank you for your help," he said, without a hint of malice, then disappeared behind the door.

Ketik's eyes lingered on the door for a moment. "Odenuk's a good man. It's just that—with everything that's happened—" Ketik turned to Zeriel. "He's warier of outsiders than usual."

"Smart man." Doing his best not to jostle his shoulder or use his injured arm, he pushed himself to his feet.

"Maybe you should rest a while longer."

Zeriel regarded Ketik. The man looked genuinely concerned. Zeriel almost let the edge of his mouth twist into a scant smirk. Almost. "I wish I could," he said, "but when word gets to Lushame that I had a hand in killing her brother, she'll abandon everything and come for me."

"What about Clan Gor? I still don't understand why they attacked in the first place, let alone why they left so abruptly."

"Veshet, their leader, used to seek only to lead the Te Et Sha—the group of assassins we belonged to. He ended up destroying them instead, and now seems bent on world domination, starting with the clans of Fei En Ar. To justify his actions, he claims that weakness must be eradicated, and strength preserved."

"*Only the strong survive.*" Ketik walked to a window in thought. "That *was* strange."

"Since I've known Veshet he was obsessed with building his strength. He'd use it as proof of his own superiority and dominate those weaker than him. Several recruits died in our group, and though no one could prove who the murder was, everyone knew it was Veshet. And when you're training to be an assassin, killing without getting caught only increases one's reputation."

"So, he wants to exterminate the weak, then conscript the rest into an army he'll use to take over the clans?"

"That's the first stage of his plan, yes."

Ketik seemed to decide something. "Take a walk with me," he said, without waiting for an answer, and stepped toward the door. Once again Zeriel followed the chief on instinct and the two exited the room onto a street.

The buildings were made of the same stone, wood, and plaster construction as those in Clan Ra. The damage left behind by the Te Et Sha was nothing compared to what his Clan experienced, though. Arrows protruded from the outer walls next to deep cuts from blades of all sizes, blood marring it all.

Clan members were busy cleaning up the gruesome mess, and as Ketik lead him through the streets, Zeriel caught a glimpse of someone pushing a cart full of bodies. The grief was thick in the air, and for the first time in his life, he felt remorse for the dead. He saw assassins' bodies laid on top of clan members'. They'd fought each other, both believing their cause was just, yet both were just as dead. As all things would eventually be. It evoked a feeling of uselessness and confusion, and for a moment Zeriel questioned whether he was any different from Veshet. They both fought for what they believed, and both left bodies in their wake.

Ketik rounded a corner into the square where they had killed Denetek. White vine lanterns were brought in to light the area, and though the bodies were removed, the evidence of the massacre remained. Dried blood covered almost every inch of the ground, wet only in the small indents between the cobblestones. Clan members worked throughout the square, some carting off bodies, others repairing damage to buildings, and still others mopping the blood from the ground. The bottom inch of everyone's shoes were stained red from walking through it.

Jekjarah appeared next to Zeriel and took a deep breath as if savoring the scent of iron that still hung in the air. He let out a contented sigh. "Good memories."

Zeriel looked at the hallucination. *Is that how I feel about this?* The hallucination using spoke his own thoughts back to him, but this time was different. There was no sense of fulfillment from this. The sight just made him feel...empty.

Ketik approached a group of three women cleaning the bloodied cobblestone, grabbed a mop, and joined them. "Thanks for your work here Enesa, Alditi, Odenai. This isn't easy work."

Enesa gave him a smile that didn't touch her eyes. "No, not easy. But necessary."

"Are your husbands—" he cut off the words, not willing, or able to finish the thought.

Alditi dropped her gaze and the other two moved quickly to comfort her.

Enesa looked up at Ketik. "They haven't found Alditi's husband yet."

Ketik set his mop back against the wall and moved to take the woman's hands in his. He met her eyes. "We'll find Shutek. I'll make sure of it."

Alditi answered with a sniff and series of quick nods. "Thank you."

Ketik gave the women a reassuring smile and moved on, scanning the square before finding someone and walking in their direction. Zeriel followed closely.

"Patitet," Ketik said, as he waved at the man he'd spied.

The man had been having a conversation but paused to look at whoever had called his name. When he saw it was Ketik, he quickly dismissed the man he was talking to and hurried over. "Good morning, Chief."

"Who's in charge of collecting the dead?"

"That would be Ulete. He's just outside the western gate."

Ketik put a hand on the man's shoulder. "Good work here. Keep them focused. It will help dull the grief."

"Yes Chief." The man's expression seemed to show a grief of his own, though he never voiced it.

"Good man." Ketik said, then made his way out of the square.

Zeriel followed, struck by the care Ketik showed the members of his Clan. It was clear they cared for him too. To see the effects of the deaths on these people made him reflect on all the times he left similar scenes behind. In that way, he was the same as Veshet, though that didn't feel completely right. He remembered the woman with her child that he'd saved in the street during the assault. In this fight, his efforts saved lives that would have otherwise been lost. As selfish as his motives were, it wasn't his decisions that killed people.

Jekjarah appeared on the other side of the square. "You're nothing like him," he whispered, his voice sounding near despite the distance. For once, Zeriel let the hallucination convince him.

Ketik looked back at Zeriel and said, "Have you seen the aftermath of a battle before?"

"I've never stuck around long enough."

"Right. You were an assassin after all."

They walked in silence the rest of the way to the gate which stood open as carts full of bodies were brought out of the village. As they passed the gate, they saw a single man in simple wool clothing directing the cart pushers where to place the bodies. Others would inspect them and move the remains to one of two locations. On one side was a pile of corpses unceremoniously piled up in a ditch. On the other lay several neat lines of at least a hundred bodies, each carefully wrapped in white cloth with a name written on them.

Zeriel couldn't take his eyes off those dead clan members. Though his mind knew those corpses weren't his doing, his lingering connection to Veshet brought him a stab of guilt. He couldn't call himself a member of the Te Et Sha anymore, and he certainly didn't have the strength to stop an entire army on his own, but he couldn't shake the feeling that if he'd been just a little stronger, none of this would have happened.

"Ulete," Ketik called out as they approached.

The man turned toward them and nodded seriously. "Chief. What can I do for you?"

"I ran into Alditi a moment ago and she said we hadn't found her husband yet. Have you seen his body turn up?"

"I'm sorry to say, I wouldn't know. There have been too many to remember them all." He turned to wave over a young man who was writing on a piece of paper backed with a shoddy wooden board.

The boy ran toward them and stopped suddenly, his back too straight, and eyes staring at nothing. "Yes, sir."

With a sigh, Ulete held out his hand. "Relax, boy. Let me see your list."

The boy's cheeks flushed as his back slouched a bit and he held out his paper.

Ulete took the paper and looked at Ketik. "What is Alditi's husband's name again?"

"Shutek."

"That's right." He scanned the paper carefully, and just as Zeriel was sure he would come up empty, Ulete tapped a spot at the bottom. "Here he is. Took an arrow to the stomach, I'm sorry to say."

"I see," Ketik said. "Can you send someone to the square and let her know? I promised we would notify her right away."

"Of course."

With a word of thanks, Ketik led Zeriel to the lines of bodies. They walked through them as Ketik inspected each one. "What useless slaughter."

"How could he say that?" Jekjarah said as he stood among the corpses. "This is art. A beauty found nowhere else in all of creation!"

Anger filled Zeriel at the hallucination's words. Those were thoughts he'd had before, when the only thing he'd known in life was bloodshed.

"What will you do now?" Ketik said.

He paused as he brought himself back to reality. Then he glanced at the rolling hills between him and the mountains in the distance, lit gently by the light of the rising sun. At that moment, he realized that, while Ketik had cared for his people along the way, he'd subtly led Zeriel out of the village. A pang of disappointment shot through him. But he recognized that saving the clans was secondary to his real goal. "I'll kill Lushame, then Veshet."

"Still can't shake the assassin's nature, then?"

"What do you mean?"

"As we walked you seemed contemplative, like you'd discovered something important."

"Well yes—" Zeriel paused, trying to reconcile the emotions he'd been forced to confront. "But it doesn't change what I must do. They killed someone I loved."

A moment of surprise flashed over Ketik's face. "You had a lover then?"

"No, not quite. It's—" Was he ready to tell this man everything? No. He couldn't trust a stranger with that. "It's hard to explain. But I swore

I would avenge her death, and now that accomplishing that goal also helps the clans, it seems like things are aligning."

Ketik smiled and nodded. "I think I understand. Well, good luck to you Zeriel."

He hesitated. It had dawned on him in the fight with Denetek that he was no match for Veshet alone. He needed help. Before he knew what he was doing, he said, "You could join me."

"What?"

"I can't fight an army on my own. I need help, no matter how much power I've attained."

"True, but Clan Gor has been broken. We need time to heal."

"Bring them to Clan Ra. As far as Veshet's concerned, no one in my Clan survived their assault, but some did, and we're rebuilding. The survivors from Clan Din are on their way, too." He felt a sting of regret at the exaggeration, though he did hope they would come. "We can join what's left of our clans and give Veshet a real fight."

To the chief's credit, he paused to contemplate Zeriel's proposal. "I do agree that this new threat concerns us all..." he said, pondering the decision. "We would need more than three wounded clans..."

Zeriel let himself hope as Ketik spoke. But when the chief seemed to make up his mind, he shook his head as he said, "No, we just can't. It'll take time for us to recover enough to put up a real fight. I'm sorry."

Zeriel deflated. His decision made sense. The man wouldn't want to put the wellbeing of his people in jeopardy.

But something made Zeriel push. "They'll be back, you know. And with a bigger army than before. What will you do then?"

"We'll fight, whatever happens. But I can't ask the Clan to uproot themselves and prepare for war when we're still picking up the pieces of the last fight."

Zeriel nodded his head. Ketik had made up his mind, and he knew better than to keep pushing. Then, he did something he'd never done. Something that left him vulnerable in a way he swore he would never allow. He held out his hand, a gesture that left him open to attack. Even though he trusted the man before him, a spike of anxiety settled in his guts at the offer.

Ketik accepted Zeriel's hand, and they shared a firm grip, which said more between them than Zeriel ever thought a simple touch could.

"If you change your mind, you know where to find me."

"I do," Ketik said with a smile. "Good luck."

They released the handshake and Zeriel wrapped himself in shadows and flew eastward toward Clan Ra.

CHAPTER THIRTY-THREE

After a few minutes, the rolling hills of the Southern Flatlands gave way to the Het Je Ra Forest. Zeriel collected the abundant shadows of the forest to push himself above its canopy. The height put him in line with the light of the rising sun, and it radiated its heat on his back. The light caught the treetops and lit them up like a thousand blinding beacons that cast a white haze over his sensitive eyes. He hadn't noticed his missing blindfold until then. Odenuk obviously hadn't known why he'd worn a torn piece of his shirt over his eyes and must have discarded it. Zeriel hadn't thought to ask since he could see in the relative darkness of the newly rising sun.

He was fine now, but the light would increasingly blind as the days continued. He needed a solution. Thinking back to his training and the battle afterward, he thought of the many things he'd created from shadow, and the solution practically smacked him in the face.

Pulling from the shadows holding him aloft, Zeriel manifested a dark mist in front of his eyes. It worked far better than the threadbare blindfold he'd been relying on. The sunlight receded immediately and the world became perfectly clear. He sighed in relief and satisfaction.

Jekjarah appeared next to him, nodding his head in approval. "You've really gotten the hang of that."

"A year's worth of training will do that for a person."

"You were only there for a few hours at most."

"Yet I gained a year's worth of experience."

Jekjarah huffed and paced in a circle in the air around him, taking in the sights of the forest canopy. After a few laps, he stopped in front of Zeriel. "Are you sure we should go back?"

"We need their help."

"There's no one left there that can help, Zeriel."

"You don't know that."

Jekjarah let out an exaggerated sigh. "I *do* know that. Because I can see what you can't."

Zeriel shook his head. "You can *only* see what I can, Jek."

"Not when you've blinded yourself to the truth, even when it's staring you in the face." He let himself float closer to Zeriel, his arms crossed. "You won't achieve your goal without Clan Gor, but this obsession with Clan Ra will only cause you more suffering."

Heat rose in Zeriel's cheeks at the hallucination's words. "You have no idea what you're talking about."

Jekjarah threw his hands in the air, gliding backward. "This is a distraction, Zeriel. You need to go back to Clan Gor and get them on your side. Whatever it takes."

Zeriel felt his anger boil, and he sped up, zipping around the hallucination, leaving him behind rather than confronting his objections. He didn't want to admit that Jekjarah was right, but the doubts were ultimately his own and they needled at his mind.

He'd come close to turning back when he spotted Clan Ra ahead. Smoke rose from chimneys, and as he closed the distance, he could see clan members moving around the village as they rebuilt.

He had approached from the south, which gave him a full view of the cleft where Clan Ra's mine was located. Surprisingly, the light of white vine lanterns glowed from below its surface, and the sounds of picks and hammers hitting stone echoed from within.

"You see, Jek, Clan Ra isn't useless. At the very least they'll provide the minerals we need for weapons and armor." There was no reply. "Fine, ignore me if you want. But you know I'm right." He turned and flew over the square, which was still the hub of the village's rebuilding efforts. Jekjarah's words still lingered, turning into doubt. Would the

Clan really help? Would they want to? Recalling his previous discussions with Chief Leksha did little to help him gain confidence that he was on the right path.

The chief came into view, stepping from underneath the main tent to direct the recovery efforts. Doubts or not, he was here now, and there was only one way to know what Chief Leksha was going to do.

With a simple force of will, he shifted his momentum and let the shadows drop him. As he fell, he coalesced them under his feet as he dropped like a meteorite from the sky. He landed in an explosion of dark clouds and dirt. Cries of surprise reverberated through the square. When the dust settled, a crowd surrounded him, many of them with swords drawn.

"This isn't exactly the welcome I expected," he said.

"Zeriel?" Leksha said, pushing through the crowd. Their swords lowered as the crowd recognized him.

"Sorry about my disappearance. I was ambushed while checking on those traps of yours."

Leksha ignored him and eyed the spot where he'd landed. "Do you know how long it's going to take to repair that? We're stretched thin as it is."

Zeriel looked down and saw a spider web of cracks in the cobblestone around him. "Oh." He rubbed his neck, expecting Jekjarah to tease him, but the hallucination stayed silent. "Sorry about that," he said.

Leksha sighed and waved a hand. "There's nothing to do about it now. Just be more careful next time."

Zeriel nodded his head, and everyone stood awkwardly silent, not sure what to do.

"What are you all gawking for?" she asked the crowd. "Get back to work." They obeyed as if they'd been waiting for just such a command. She waved for Zeriel to follow as she turned back to the tent. "Come on, then. I'm sure you have an explanation for yourself."

❖

Leksha didn't interrupt Zeriel's recounting of the last few days, but her face was scrunched up the entire time. "You invited people from Clan Din *and* Clan Gor to come here?"

"Banding together is the only hope we have of stopping Veshset."

"I don't care about stopping Veshet. Look around you, Zeriel," she said, gesturing around them. "What do you see?"

He spun in a slow circle and saw clan members hard at work. The buildings around them were a mixture of fully rebuilt, in the process of being rebuilt, and burned to the ground. "An example of what can be achieved when a group of people work toward a common goal."

Leksha scoffed loudly. "*I* see people struggling to recover what life they can from the ashes of their destroyed homes and families. What I don't see is an opportunity to build an army for your personal vendetta."

"Sure, it's personal for me, but it should just as personal for everyone else, too. Veshet's army did this to you. Don't you want revenge for the clan members he's killed?"

"Fool," she said. "Revenge only extends the cycle of death, corrupting those seeking it."

That statement confused Zeriel, and was perhaps the most ridiculous thing he'd ever heard. Revenge was the death of those who deserved it. A balancing of the scales; a natural force as unquestionable as the rain.

Chief Leksha eyed him for a moment then shook her head. "You don't understand a word I'm saying."

He didn't respond, but his silence was enough.

"Fine. Assemble your army here, if you must. But when you go, don't take anyone from our Clan with you."

It wasn't an outright rejection, but it hit harder than he expected. He hadn't realized just how much he was counting on Clan Ra's help, and he was convinced Leksha would be as driven as he was to seek revenge. Childhood emotions returned, and he felt the familiar sting of apathy and rejection. He remembered how the Clan had let Renniel terrorize his family. Not once did they step in to help, instead pretending that nothing was happening. Zeriel grit his teeth as he came to realize he'd never convince her. This was yet another betrayal in a long line of them endured over his childhood, and it felt like one too many. "That will have to do," he said trying to keep his growing anger from his voice.

Leksha nodded and went about studying the papers on her table. "You should head home and get some rest," she said as she casually motioned to his shoulder. "You're no good to us if you can't use both of your arms."

"You'd be surprised," he said.

Leksha looked at him and arched an eyebrow.

"Okay, okay," he said, raising the hand of his good arm defensively. "You know where to find me."

She made a shooing gesture and went back to her work.

Zeriel decided to walk home, thinking he may have overdone his entrance and didn't want to alienate himself more with further displays of his power. The clan members he encountered along the way gave him a wide berth, whispering to each other as he passed. The suspicion they had grated on his nerves. Relief came when he finally arrived home, glad not to endure their scrutiny any longer.

A sudden and deep exhaustion came over him as he opened the door. Once inside Jekjarah's voice came from behind. "They still don't trust you completely."

Zeriel sighed and moved toward the bedroom. "So now you want to talk to me?"

"I've been trying to talk to you. Talk some sense into you!"

He eyed the hallucination skeptically as he made his way to the straw bed he'd built himself from the rubble.

Jekjarah followed him. "They don't want to help you or even talk to you, and the longer you stay here the more danger you're putting yourself in."

Zeriel shook the dust off his blanket, grunting from the pain in his shoulder, and got into the bed. "What are you talking about?"

"Once Lushame finds out you killed her brother, this will be the first place she looks for you."

Zeriel hadn't thought of that, or maybe he had since it was Jekjarah saying it to him. As he considered the possibility, he decided it wasn't something to worry about. "She wasn't at Clan Gor during the attack, so we have no idea if or when she might find out. And even when she does, it's more likely that she goes to Clan Gor first. It's the last place any of the Te Et Sha saw me."

"Then you'd abandoned Clan Gor to another attack?"

Zeriel sighed, turning over in the bed to look away from Jekjarah, closing his eyes. "They didn't want me there, Jek. I can't force them to let me stay. Now leave me alone."

Jekjarah let out a frustrated huff and his voice went silent, but his words lingered. What if Lushame searched the Clan for him? What if Clan Din didn't show? There was too much unresolved, and as exhaustion drove him to sleep, he felt his plans slipping away, bit by bit.

❖

A knock at the door woke Zeriel, bringing immediate irritation. "I'm coming!" He threw off the blanket and got out of bed, the stiffness in his muscles slowing his movements. It took a few steps to work his muscles loose, but the pain of his injuries, and the swelling in his shoulder remained.

He opened the door, and his vision washed out from the sunlight that streamed inside. With an effort of will he pulled on the nearby shadows and created a mask, his vision clearing immediately. His childhood friend Laluk stood on the other side of the door. The apologetic look on his face forced Zeriel to stile the snippy comment he was about to make.

"Sorry," Laluk said. "I thought you'd be awake by now."

"What time is it?"

"Almost midday."

"Really? Feels like I slept longer than that." Zeriel stepped back into the house, leaving the door open for Laluk to enter.

His friend stayed where he was, talking through the doorway. "Well, you got back yesterday. You've been sleeping for an entire day."

Zeriel raised his eyebrows in surprise. He knew he had needed sleep, but he didn't realize just how much.

"But that's not why I'm here."

"Why then?"

"Clan Gor's chief is here, and he asked for you personally."

Energy shot through Zeriel's muscles, and he quickly made for the front door, then stepped past Laluk on his way out. "Where is he?"

His friend hurried to catch up. "He's in the square now, talking with Leksha."

Zeriel picked up his pace. Hope grew as he closed in on the square. He tried not to expect good news, in case Ketik had some other motive, but he couldn't help but feel optimistic. If Clan Gor joined his cause, he still has a chance. Once they made it to the square, Zeriel found the two chiefs in conversation under Leksha's tent.

"Have you changed your mind, then?" Zeriel asked as he approached, unable to keep his excitement at bay.

Ketik looked at him and smirked. "Something like that. I told my advisors about your proposal, and much to my dismay, they agreed with you. They sent me to see if Clan Ra survived the attack as you said."

"Of course we did," Leksha said indignantly. "We're not so easily brought to ruin."

"Of course you aren't," Ketik said with a placating smile. He turned back to Zeriel. "You told the truth, it seems."

"Well, we're still waiting for the survivors from Clan Din."

"I see," Ketik said. "They are coming, though?"

Zeriel's head dropped. "Well, I may have exaggerated a bit. I invited them, but they never committed to come."

A surprised look came over Ketik's face, and his nervousness grew.

"And I never asked them to join the fight."

Ketik grunted, and Zeriel didn't need to guess if it was a good or bad sign. The chief glanced at Leksha. "I guess you haven't agreed to join him either?"

She scoffed. "I have not."

Ketik raised an eyebrow at Zeriel.

"I never explicitly said Clan Ra would fight with us."

"You inferred it."

"Would you have come if I hadn't?"

"Chief Leksha," Ketik said turning to her, "it was great to catch up, but it appears I was brought here under false pretense." As he turned to leave, he leveled a hard stare at Zeriel.

The bottom dropped out of his stomach, and regret settled in. If Ketik lost trust in him, he'd lose the support of Clan Gor. Without them, and without Clan Ra, his plans would completely unravel. Desperation drove him to step forward and make one final plea. "Wait!" he called out.

Ketik paused. "I don't suffer being lied to, Zeriel. How could I trust you in battle if I can't trust you with the words you use?"

The Chief had a point, but Zeriel hadn't lied. Not outright. Gaining the help of Clan Ra was always part of his plan, he just hadn't figured out how to persuade them yet. "I give you my word I wasn't trying to deceive you. It's true Clan Ra doesn't want to fight, but we have more than just bodies for fighting."

Ketik's eyes narrowed. "The mine?"

"That, and our blacksmith survived the attack. With the right help, we can build all the weapons and armor we'll need."

That was enough to get Ketik thinking. "And you'd agree to that?" he asked Leksha.

She looked between the two, and after a moment of consideration, let out a deep sigh. "We barely have enough people to work the mines as it is, but if you can provide more workers, we can commit Altid to adding some of his time and his skill to your effort."

"I'll need to talk to Altid before I commit to anything." He leveled a steady gaze at Zeriel. "But no more exaggerations. These aren't games we're playing, though it may feel that way to an assassin."

Zeriel found himself taking offense to the statement. "Trust me, *chief*, this is no game to me."

The two held each other's eyes for a time, and Zeriel's doubts crept back in. When he had heard Ketik had arrived, he knew his initial hopes were fleeting. But this moment—waiting on this man's singular decision—was where his plans lived or died.

Finally, Ketik nodded. "Very well. Let's go talk to your blacksmith."

CHAPTER THIRTY-FOUR

The cleft holding Clan Ra's mines cut deep into the space between the eastern mountainside and the southern hills. The din of the skeleton crew working there echoed through the small valley that the features created, audible to Ketik and Zeriel as they stepped onto the main road.

Ketik paused and looked toward the hills for a moment. "When I was young, my father always said he hated relying on your Clan for ore." He glanced at Zeriel. "More than once, he tried to convince the council to send our soldiers to conquer you."

"They didn't agree with him?"

"They weren't convinced that our Clan of mostly farmers could work the mines." Ketik started walking again, turning south. "I believed what he said back then, and vowed that, when I was the chief, I'd ignore the council and do what he couldn't."

"What changed your mind?"

Ketik eyed Zeriel and said, "At first, my new duties consumed all my time and attention. Over time, the wellbeing of my people became more important than risking lives in the pursuit of power and wealth."

"But you *would* have made your Clan very rich. If not for the current generation, for future ones."

"True."

They walked in silence for a moment as a pensive cloud covered them both. For Zeriel's part, he considered what Ketik said. If he'd followed his initial plans, he would have fulfilled his father's dreams and secured a stable future for his Clan. Put like that, he started to wonder if the chief would have gone through with his plan if the right opportunity had presented itself. The position Clan Ra was in, he worried he might have just handed them over to Clan Gor.

They turned off the main road and onto the central bridge over the river. As they approached the other side, he decided that being taken over by Clan Gor might not be the worst thing for either Clan.

Ketik broke the silence. "The truth is, I wasn't just weighing the lives of our clan members against what we might gain. I'd come to genuinely care for each of them and couldn't allow myself to bring them harm."

Zeriel studied Ketik's face and saw something there he wasn't saying. He opened his mouth to question the chief but decided against it at the last moment and let them continue in silence.

On the other side of the bridge a dirt road led onward toward the many farms nestled against the western mountainsides. To their left were a group of buildings between the river and two large hills. This segregated space held the Clan's artisans.

Most of the buildings there were reduced to rubble and ash. One of those still standing was the windmill. Its vanes spun calmly in the wind while the creaking of its innerworkings bled from the open door.

Past the mill and nestled against the far hill was where Altid's forge provided the only other sign of life. Smoke rose from the building, accompanied by the rhythmic hammering of a master smith.

Zeriel stopped short and looked at his feet. "I've never put much value in human life." He thought of Lavel, smiling at him from behind the bar of *The Pick and Shovel*. The image shifted to that of her lifeless body lying in a pool of her own blood with fire and smoke closing in. Zeriel grimaced at the visions. "I'd thought I cared for someone once. It took her death for me to realize I only cared about what she could give me." He managed to meet Ketik's eyes. "The fact that you put your own needs aside for the sake of others is something I can't even comprehend. I watched you put that into practice in the aftermath of the attack on your Clan, and how your people responded to you." Zeriel huffed at himself. "All I saw was a person who knew how to get what he wanted."

Ketik placed a hand on Zeriel's shoulder. "The fact that you recognize that is a sign you're headed in the right direction."

A warmth grew in his chest at the gesture. "You think so?"

Ketik smiled warmly. "Absolutely."

Zeriel stood a little straighter at the encouragement. "Thanks. Now, we have a blacksmith to see."

"We do," Ketik agreed, then the two continued.

When they arrived at the forge, Altid was working iron into long nails to assist in the rebuilding efforts. The man was in his early twenties, and his body carried the unnaturally slim frame only provided to the young. The thick muscles of his arms—a natural outcome of his work—looked out of place on his frame. His face was marred with ash and had the soft features women tended to find attractive—though Zeriel could never understand why. His dark brown hair was cut short and disheveled.

"Altid," Ketik called out, "it's been quite a while!"

The blacksmith paused his hammering and looked up with surprise. "Chief Ketik? What are you doing here?" He set his hammer down and rubbed his hands on the leather apron he wore. When he held his hand out to Ketik it was clear the gesture did little to nothing to clean the man's hands.

Ketik took Altid's hand and flashed a large smile. "Things at Clan Gor have been busy." He let go of the handshake and inspected the nails the blacksmith was forging. "Fighting for our lives, much like you have been."

"They came for you, then."

"They did. If it weren't for Zeriel here, we might have been completely wiped off the map."

Altid faced Zeriel and said, "We thought you'd ran off and gotten yourself killed."

"I was captured," Zeriel said flatly, letting a silence stretch between them.

Ketik took a step deeper in the forge. He scanned the inside and broke the silence, asking, "Where's Urigel?"

A shadow fell across the smith's face. "He didn't survive the attack."

"I'm sorry, Altid. May Eleshar birth him into peace and happiness in his next life."

"As Eleshar wills," Altid responded.

They let a moment of silence pass. "It looks like you're doing well since taking up Urigel's hammer."

"More than well!" A spark of excitement flashed across his face. "I've been working on alloys to strengthen the nails for longevity. Let me show you." He turned back to the forge, hurrying to a pile of ore set up near his anvil.

Ketik smiled and followed the smith without question or complaint.

Zeriel watched the interaction closely. He was still skeptical of the regard Ketik showed others. How could this man genuinely summon so much interest in people? The thought of focusing so much on another person felt exhausting. What he couldn't ignore was how people responded to the man. He decided to try and learn his methods, joining the two and listening closely to what Altid was saying.

Zeriel's frustrations grew as he listened while the young blacksmith droned on about the details of different metals and alloys. Despite his best effort, he could grasp the nuances of metallurgy. He forced an interested expression on his face and managed to ask a question when he thought he started to grasp some of the concepts. When Altid wrapped up, Zeriel realized he hadn't retained a single thing.

"You've got a lot of great ideas," Ketik said. "But before you get too far in your experiments, I have a favor to ask you."

Altid's face lit up again. "Of course. What do you need?"

"Zeriel and I are planning to launch a counterattack on the Te Et Sha, but we're going to need weapons and armor."

"How many people are we talking about?"

"At least a few hundred, to start."

Altid's shoulders dropped. "I'll do what I can, but I could work all day and night for an entire year and not be able to outfit that many people."

"I don't expect you to do it on your own. I'll bring smiths from Clan Gor to help."

The blacksmith's expression lightened. "That could work." He looked around his workspace. "We'll need to build several more forges to support additional smiths."

"Excellent," Ketik said. "I'll leave it to you. It'll take me a few days to bring help, so you've got some time."

Altid smiled broadly at the chief. "I'll be ready."

Zeriel followed Ketik as he left the forge, finding himself in a bit of a daze from the interaction. When they were out of earshot, he spoke up. "How did you do that?"

"Huh? Do what?"

"Altid didn't just do what you wanted, but he seemed genuinely excited to do it. You barely had to ask, and he was solving problems we hadn't even considered yet."

"We both share a sort of passion for the nuances of working metal, which grew into a close friendship, and friends help each other."

"So, you *were* interested in what he was rambling on about."

"Immensely! Well-crafted metal can be the difference between life and death."

A weight lifted from Zeriel a bit, knowing that Ketik had a genuine relationship with Altid and wasn't simply manipulating the man. That weight returned when he realized he'd have to learn how to make friends. That thought led to another, and he said, "If you have a friendship with him, that means you've spent time at Clan Ra."

"Often, yes. As chief it's important that I maintain good relationships with surrounding clans. It fosters strong trade lines and keeps us from constant infighting."

"But there was more to it than that. You were setting up an ambush to catch Clan Ra off-guard and take control of the mine, weren't you."

"At first, but I didn't expect to make friends—"

The door of one of the nearby buildings flew open, interrupting him. A woman with a mix of happiness and anger plastered across her face stood in the doorway. "Chief Ketik! I hope for your sake you just arrived and were in a hurry to see me."

CHAPTER THIRTY-FIVE

Zeriel recognized the woman as Shemua, the town's master tailor. She let her straight, light brown hair fall to her lower back where it framed her brown dress. From top to bottom, the dress was a patchwork of stains in every color. Her hands were similarly stained, except her fingers which wore weathered bandages.

She exuded passion in everything she did, but often channeled that energy chaotically. It was all currently directed at Ketik.

"Hello Shemua," Ketik called out to her. "I was just coming to see you in fact."

She smiled broadly and practically skipped toward them.

"Let me guess," Zeriel said as he planted an elbow into Ketik's ribs, "another *friend?*"

Ketik pulled back and rubbed his side. "It's nothing like that."

"Sure, sure." Zeriel found it humorous how the usually in-control chief squirmed in her presence. It tugged at the edges of his mouth, threatening to put a smile on his face.

Shemua stepped up to them, glancing at the forge as she did. The woman deflated slightly. "You came to see Altid, didn't you?"

Ketik blushed. "We needed his help to make weapons and armor. Zeriel and I are working together to stop the people who attacked our clans."

Shemua eyed Zeriel in a way that said she hadn't even noticed he was there, which left him feeling particularly unwelcome. "I thought the assassins killed you."

"Nice to see you too, Shemua."

She spun to Ketik's side and took his arm in hers. "You brought Ketik back with you at least." Zeriel disappeared from her consciousness again as she looked up at the chief. "It's been so long since we've seen each other."

"I've been busy," Ketik said, trying not to meet her eyes.

Shemua leaned back in mock offense at his blunt response. "Don't tell me you've found some other woman, and you've started a family."

"We've been over this, Shem—"

She spun toward the river and dragged him by his arms to the water's edge. "Do you remember those nights we would spend sitting on the riverbank, talking until the moon came up?"

"You refused to let me leave, if I remember correctly."

"I suppose I did." The tailor giggled girlishly and gave him an adoring look.

Ketik stifled a smile but couldn't hold it in and turned away as he gave in to the expression. "I suppose I did enjoy those evenings."

"Of course you did," she said. "Now do whatever important thing it is you're doing, but don't you forget about me." She squeezed his arm, then released the chief and walked up to Zeriel. "If you let anything bad happen to that man, I'll make sure it's visited back on you tenfold."

"What?" Zeriel exclaimed. "I'm not part of whatever you two have going on."

"Well, you are now." The tailor gave him a wink as she walked past him.

Zeriel fell silent, baffled by the woman as he watched her return to her shop.

Ketik joined him at his side and said, "I've tried so many times to tell her it would never work between us, but she refuses to hear it."

"Maybe it's because she knows you're lying."

The chief tensed up. "I would never."

"Not to her—" Zeriel shook his head and started walking toward the central bridge. "Forget it. Let's get back to Leksha and let her know

Altid agreed to help."

"Right," Ketik said. He hurried after Zeriel, his head twisted and eyes on Shemua who had stopped at her doorway, watching them as they left.

"Come by tonight for dinner Chief Ketik," she called. "I promise you won't be disappointed." A quick spin caused the bottom of her dress to flare as she stepped inside the shop.

"I know she's a bit forward," Zeriel said, "but you could do a lot worse."

"As Chief I need more stability in my family than she can provide. As much as I wish things were different, we just aren't a good fit."

They came to the central bridge and Zeriel paused. He met Ketik's eyes and saw a hint of regret on the man's face. "You know," he said, "sometimes two people can have dinner together, and it doesn't have to mean anything more than that."

Ketik glanced up at him then looked at Shemua's shop. "Yet some of us are bound by duty."

"You bind yourself Ketik. I may not fully understand the responsibilities you feel for the people in your Clan, but I can't imagine they'd want you to sacrifice *everything* for them. Would it really be such a betrayal for two people who enjoy each other's company to spend an evening together?"

The chief's gaze lingered on Shemua's shop. He leaned forward as if to go back to her. The heel of his back foot parted from the ground for just a moment. Then he sighed heavily and straightened his posture. "Even so, it wouldn't be fair to her."

Zeriel shrugged. "Have it your way," he said, then continued across the bridge.

CHAPTER THIRTY-SIX

K etik left the next day to bring blacksmiths and warriors from Clan Gor. Leksha had to practically hold Shemua down to keep the woman from following him.

In the days that followed, Zeriel put himself to work on the Clan's rebuilding efforts again. He found something peaceful and fulfilling in the work that quieted the voices in his head, somehow. Even Jekjarah had left him alone which was simultaneously a relief and point of anxiety. He hadn't been free of Jekjarah for more than a few hours at a time since the day he appeared. A nagging fear told him the hallucination's absence was a sign of a larger problem. Normally the voices would relentlessly repeat such fears to him. Their unnerving absence only served to heighten his anxiety.

A full week passed before Ketik returned with practically half of Clan Gor. As promised, a group of blacksmiths went to work at the forge while the others helped in the mines. Things moved smoothly after that, and it wasn't long before the two clans were eating, working, and laughing together. Zeriel even caught Ketik heading toward Shemua's shop one evening. It all felt—normal. He hadn't felt that since he was very young, and it almost made Zeriel forget about Veshet and the threat his Te Et Sha posed.

The third day after Clan Gor arrived, a knock came at Zeriel's door that woke him from a deep sleep. "Coming," he called out groggily as he climbed out of bed and rubbed the sleep from his eyes. The knocking persisted as he approached the door. "I'm coming already!"

The moment Zeriel opened the door his vision washed out from the light that flooded through the doorway. "Ack!" he exclaimed as he instinctually called nearby shadows to form a blindfold around his eyes. The world came into view, which revealed Ketik on the other side of the door, taking a step back.

"Would it be too much to ask that you don't do that while I'm around?" Ketik asked.

"Sorry, I need it to see in the light. You wouldn't want me to walk around completely blind, would you?"

"I suppose not," Ketik said as he pulled a wooden sword from behind his back and tossed it at Zeriel, which he caught easily. "Everyone's hard at work outfitting our warriors. I thought you could show me how the Te Et Sha fight."

"You sure you're not just trying to get out of the hard work?"

Ketik smirked. "You don't think this will be hard work?"

Zeriel exploded forward, striking with his wooden sword. Ketik barely responded in time. Out of habit, the chief had dropped his practice weapon, drawing his blade to block the surprise attack.

Zeriel looked where the swords met. Ketik's metal blade was buried nearly halfway into the wood of his practice weapon. "The first thing you need to learn is the Te Et Sha don't care about honor or etiquette. The mission is all that matters, and they'll do *anything* to complete the mission. You must be ready for the unexpected."

Ketik looked at the sword in his hand, only then noticing he was wielding steel against wood. He stepped back quickly and sheathed his sword. "I see what you mean." He picked up his wooden sword and took up a fighting stance. "See, hard work."

"Ready?" Zeriel asked. Ketik nodded and Zeriel lunged forward again, this time digging his sword in the ground to fling dirt in Ketik's face. The chief spat the soil from his mouth and frantically rubbed his eyes clear.

Zeriel sidestepped to strike out at his ribs, but Ketik spun suddenly, barely managing to deflect the blow. It was Zeriel's turn to be surprised.

Ketik moved quickly and thrust his sword at Zeriel's head. A new set of instincts kicked in, and Zeriel called on his own shadow to rise from the ground and grab the wooden sword. He managed to stop it only inches from his face.

Ketik let his sword fall to his side. "Now *that's* cheating."

"There's no cheating to the Te Et Sha. Only winners and the dead."

The chief barked out a laugh. "A touch dramatic, don't you think?"

"It helps drive home the mindset of the people we're going up against."

"Then that's probably all the drama I can handle for one day." Ketik held out his hand.

Zeriel handed over his wooden sword. "Good idea. It wouldn't be good for a chief to lose to a lowly assassin."

"See, and everyone else keeps telling me how incompetent you are."

"Then I'm in good company I suppose." The chief laughed at the gibe and warmth radiated through Zeriel.

"Actually, the sparring was just a bit of fun. I need to check on the smiths at the forge and thought you'd like to join me."

"Sounds better than letting Chief Leksha bully me into more manual labor."

The two took the road that passed through the various farms of Clan Ra, most of them still blackened from fires lit by the Te Et Sha. A few surviving farmers tended to their fields, holding the drying stalks of plants that had been harvested several days earlier to avoid the burn of the mid-month sun.

He caught a glimpse of Ketik staring at the fields as they passed, what looked like concern on his face. "We'll do everything we can to keep this from happening to the other clans, Zeriel."

"What if we're too late? It's been some time since the attack on Clan Gor."

"You're right. Which is why we need the weapons and armor as soon as possible. Our goal isn't to save the life of everyone in Fei En

Ar. That's impossible. Though we will save who we can."

"Then we can't stop at the Southern Clans."

"Of course not."

Zeriel stopped at a fork in the path. The turning left would take them to the central bridge and the artisan district beyond, while going right would lead to the southern farms set against the mountainside. "Then the plan doesn't change. We gather as many warriors as we can from what's left of the Southern Clans as we march north to Ki Al Tesh."

"Right, but don't lose sight of the people, Zeriel. While the goal of defending Fei En Ar aligns with your personal vendetta, we can't lead them into a bloodbath, sacrificing their lives for the sake of your revenge."

The blunt statement caught Zeriel off guard. The chief rarely spoke with such harsh criticism, but it forced Zeriel to consider how his plans affected the ones helping him. Until now, he'd only considered how he could use them. The chief forced him to confront his selfishness. "I know that," he said as he turned onto the left-hand path.

They walked the rest of the way in silence, neither of the two ready to acknowledge the truths buried in their statements. Zeriel had been mission-first since becoming an assassin. And this *was* a mission-first moment. Even as he considered that point, he doubted his approach.

Though the truth was that they weren't managing the well-being of a Clan, trying to improve lives and create long-term prosperity. They were about to fight a war.

How to get Ketik on board, though. That was the question he couldn't find an answer for. Zeriel felt Jekjarah's absence more than ever. He'd relied on bouncing his thoughts off the hallucination for everything, so not having that opportunity made him feel alone in a way he never had before.

He was forced to push those feelings aside as they finally arrived at Altid's forge. They'd expanded it to accommodate the additional smiths, who were all hard at work hammering steel into weapons and armor. Wooden stands were set up around the building to store their creations.

As they approached the forge, Ketik called out to Altid. "Hey there Master Smith! I hope I brought enough people for you."

The blacksmith set his hammer down and met them in front of the forge, a smile plastered across his sweaty, soot-stained face. "More than enough. We should be done in a few weeks."

"Excellent! And you have everything you need?"

"We do. The additional workers you provided for the mines are supplying plenty of ore."

Ketik clapped the blacksmith on the shoulder. "Great work. Make sure to let us know the moment you need anything."

"Yes, sir!" Altid hurried back to his hammer a bit lighter on his feet than before.

"We should tell Chief Leksha the news," Zeriel said.

Ketik nodded his agreement and the two started toward the village square. A curtain pulled back in one of Shemua's shop windows, revealing the tailor who smiled and waved at Ketik as he walked past. The chief smiled and waved back. Zeriel was happy he'd finally given in to his feelings while he could. They were weeks away from an extended military campaign, and there were no guarantees any of them would make it back.

They left the tailor's shop behind and Ketik said, "I couldn't help but notice no one from Clan Din has arrived like you hoped they would."

The thought had occurred to Zeriel more than once, but Ketik's mention of it made him grimace. "I'm starting to feel foolish for thinking they'd come. When my life was thrown into chaos, my first instinct was to settle in my childhood home and rebuild. It makes sense they'd do the same."

Ketik stepped forward and spun around to face Zeriel as they stepped onto the central bridge. "Well, you heard Altid. It'll be several weeks before they're done. We could make the trip to Clan Din and ask them in person."

"You're saying we go, together?"

"Why not? What better way to convince them to join us than to show Clan Gor's support?"

It was a strong argument, and the more Zeriel thought about it, the more he agreed. A strong example of the momentum they were gaining would be hard for them to ignore. Supernatural powers were great, but nothing showed the value of your cause like the ability to rally others behind it. "When would we go?"

Ketik smirked. "I'll need a few days to organize things among my people." He watched Zeriel carefully as they exited the bridge and turned left toward the square.

"That should work. There's some chores I'll need to finish before I leave, otherwise I'll never hear the end of it from Chief Leksha."

❖

The square was busier than usual as the members of Clan Gor and Clan Ra worked together. The two peoples melded together well, and it became difficult to tell who was from what Clan without the display of their Clan's Stripes on their clothes.

Chief Leksha stood under her canopy tent and scowled at Zeriel and Ketik after having listened to their plan. "You two basically forced me to accept all these people here and now you're going to leave me to manage them all myself?"

"I'll have leaders from my Clan help with organization, so it won't be an additional burden on you."

The chief shook her head and turned her focus to the papers on her table. "They take orders from me while you're gone."

"I'll make sure they don't make any decisions without your blessing."

She eyed Ketik. "See that you do." Ketik and Zeriel moved to leave but were stopped when Chief Leksha asked, "Zeriel, can I have a minute?"

"Sure," he responded, sharing a look with Ketik.

"I'll start preparing things and come find you later," Ketik said to him.

Zeriel nodded and the chief of Clan Gor left with the brisk walk of a man with too much to do and not enough time to do it.

The stoic woman put her quill down and turned her eyes toward the people moving through the square. "It's only been a few months, but the attack feels like so long ago. Seeing all these people in the village is already making me nostalgic." She released a long sigh and for the briefest of moments, Zeriel saw real exhaustion in her features. "It's not lost on me that what you're doing with Clan Gor is for the good of all the clans. But the needs of Clan Ra are my priority. It's new homes and new shops. It's the clarity of purpose and the focus of meaningful labor that drives them toward healing, and preserves the future of this Clan."

"Even if it means burying your head in the sand?"

Anger crept across the creases of her brow. "Does it look like my head is buried? Zeriel, you're the only one of us able to confront a crisis of this magnitude. The rest of us would be fodder."

He felt a mix of pride and foolishness for having challenged her.

"Clan Gor's help has energized our people, no doubt. But that novelty will wear off quickly, and all that Clan Ra will see when they look at them is a reminder that another attack isn't just possible, but likely."

He'd never known the Chief to be so verbose. It made him wonder if it was anxiety that caused her to open up. Hoping to get to the core of the issue, he asked, "What are you trying to tell me?"

"When Altid's finished with the weapons and armor, Clan Ra's assistance will end. Take Clan Gor and go destroy the Te Et Sha and get your revenge. Hopefully you'll come back to tell us that we'll never have to fear them again."

"And if I don't come back?"

Leksha locked eyes with Zeriel, letting the moment linger before picking up her quill and turning back to the papers on her table. "Then Eleshar help us all..."

CHAPTER THIRTY-SEVEN

Sunlight beamed into the windows of the meeting room where El and Ki reviewed the Trading Company's financials. Ki's voice morphed into a single muffled noise as El struggled to stay awake. She hadn't been getting much sleep in the last few weeks, too worried about Nedon and the Wardens for her mind to calm down long enough to let her rest. She yawned deeply.

"Did you hear anything I just said?" Ki asked.

"The last thing I heard was we'd be ready to set sail for Shyal at the beginning of next week." That was three days away, and much sooner than they'd initially planned. Her friend had worked hard to make that happen. "I'm sorry, Ki. I think I need a break."

"You need a good night's sleep." She closed the ledger in front of her and stood up, disappointment on her face. "I know you've got a lot on your plate. Nedon knows—"

El cut her off with a sharp glare.

"Sorry. Habit. *I* know how much everyone on this island leans on you. But you need to take care of yourself first, or you're no good to anyone."

"You're right. I'm worried about the future, that's all."

"There won't be a future if you don't catch up on the sleep you've missed. We can pick this up when you get back."

El stood up and felt the exhaustion in her bones. "Thanks, Ki. You sure you can handle everything here?"

Her friend winked at her and said, "What do you think I've been doing this whole time?" then stepped into the hallway.

El smiled and followed, pausing to watch Ki as she headed toward the desk in the front waiting area. She *did* need sleep, and planned to go home to get some, but there was one task she'd been putting off all morning that had to be done today.

Turning right, she headed deeper into the hallway to her office. Inside the room was a large cabinet built into the back wall. Bookshelves filled the remaining wall space on either side of it. Papers laid strewn across a desk in the center of the room, and the chair behind it was pulled back and askew from the last time she hurried out to some business or another. She wasn't usually messy, she'd just been too busy to keep up with it all. These days it felt like if she slowed down for even a moment, everything around her would collapse.

She settled into her chair, letting her muscles relax until she could feel the grip of sleep pulling on her. Straightening up, she scooted her chair up to the desk, cleared a spot, and opened a drawer to retrieve a fresh piece of paper. The crystal bracelet sat atop the paper she was after, its blue color so vibrant, even as opaque as it was, it almost seemed to glow. El stared at the object for a long moment, wondering—for what felt like the hundredth time—what would happen if she put the thing on. Those spikes would surely stab into her wrist if she did, but that posed no real threat to her. The more intriguing question was why some organization she'd never heard of would send her such a thing with instructions to wear it.

Just like every other time she'd pondered the question, no answers came to her, so she pulled a slip of paper from under it and closed the drawer. She'd had a conversation with a merchant from Ferrix yesterday, asking if he knew anything about the Wardens. He didn't, but he had mentioned a different organization, seemingly just as secret, that might be able to find the information she sought. After some convincing, the man agreed to take a request to his contact, for a sizeable fee, of course.

Grabbing the pen at her desk, El started writing.

Dear Whisper,

I hope this letter finds you well. I certainly paid Thim enough to get it to you—

Her pen froze, hovering above the paper as she felt Nedon enter her mind. It had been so long she thought she wouldn't notice his appearance. But the absence had made his arrival even more pronounced.

Hello again, my Champion, Nedon's voice said in her mind.

"All this time, telling myself you'd return, somehow I'm still surprised by it."

His laugh rang in her head. *Of course I would return. I told you that I would.*

El set down her pen and leaned back in her chair. "What do you want? I'm a little busy."

Careful, his voice warned, a hint of anger creeping into his tone, *I'll not suffer insolence.*

"I don't really care what you'll—" sudden, white-hot agony flashed across her body as her every muscle tensed. She felt the frighteningly unnatural way it bent her limbs and shifted the organs inside of her body. If she could, she would have screamed from the pain, but since she couldn't breathe, no sound escaped her lips.

The pain pushed El to the edge of unconsciousness, but then it disappeared as fast as it came. She fell forward, knocking over the inkwell and leaving her arms strewn across the desk. The black liquid spilled across the letter she'd been writing. El sucked in a breath, not realizing that the event had also been suffocating her.

I gave you freedom in Shyal because it was what my plan needed. But that has ended. It's time for my champion to do her job.

"How?" El asked, still dazed from the shock. "I thought you couldn't hurt humans."

Oh child, I lied. I thought you'd have deduced that by now. Everything that happened from the moment we met that morning was planned. The disappearance of the hunters. You, lost at sea and sold into slavery—none of it was chance. I orchestrated it all.

"But, you didn't have your powers, how could you have done all that?"

Even before you gained the powers you have now, don't you remember benefiting from even the smallest portion of them?

She thought back, all the way to when the hurricane first hit. She'd known instinctively how to move in the currents of that tidal wave and had healed faster than was normal. Not sure why she hadn't realized until that moment, she understood what Nedon was saying. She'd had access to her powers since the moment that crystal melted into her body. Another, more frightening realization came to her. If her powers came from him, and she had some small amount from the start, then he—

Yes, you see now, don't you? I had use of the barest portion of my powers as well. And what is the barest portion of the power to shape the very oceans of this world? Perhaps it's manipulating a current to send a fleet of hunters to the edge of a hurricane, then dragging their remnants towards a roaming slave ship. Perhaps, I did the same to the foolish daughter who chased after them.

It was too much to comprehend. Had he truly manipulated her from the start? Was he manipulating her, even now? There was no way to tell. No way to know if he was even telling the truth. He was trying to shake her to her core, and despite the uncertainty of his claims, he succeeded. Desperate to find something solid to hold on to, her mind raced through the facts of his claim. The only thing she found; the one thing she knew for certain was that he could hurt her, more than she ever thought possible. The torment he inflicted on her just then was more intense than even the lashings she took at the hands of the Hisks.

No response? Well, I trust it's because the reality of your situation has finally sunk in. You're mine, El, and I will be obeyed. Nedon's voice paused for a moment, but his presence in her mind remained. She couldn't trust herself to respond, lest he unleash his ire on her once more. *Honestly, I didn't intend to teach you a lesson today,* he continued, *but you forced my hand, and I need an obedient Champion for what's next. You will go to Ferrix immediately and wait for me there. We have much work to do.*

"Okay," she forced through gritted teeth. The reality of her situation was sinking in quickly, and it felt like a knife slipping into her guts and twisting endlessly. The ordeal was too much for her to absorb, so her mind detached from reality. Her eyes fell on the letter she'd been writing, covered in spilled ink. A detached part of her mind told her she needed to re-write the note, so she righted the inkwell and slid the paper to the side. "What's in Ferrix?" she asked as she opened the drawer to get another piece of paper.

That doesn't concern you. All you need to—Nedon cut off as soon the bracelet inside the drawer entered her vision. *What is* that! His voice changed, deeper, colder than she'd heard before, and replete with power. *PUT IN ON THE DESK.* He said, and El's body obeyed.

She placed the bracelet on the desk before she could even think to tell her body what to do.

How did you get that? TELL ME.

"A l—letter," she said, though she fought the words. "A—package— Wardens." She felt the grip of his power release and breathed heavily from the effort of resisting.

He remained in her mind, silent and smoldering. *DESTROY IT*, his voice came, practically audible in her mind.

Her powers activated on their own, ripping water out of her body, creating an ice hammer in her hand. Her mouth went immediately dry, a powerful thirst overcame her, and her stomach muscles started cramping. Calling on every ounce of her will, El strained against his control.

Suddenly it didn't matter who sent her the bracelet, it only mattered that Nedon wanted it destroyed. His normally condescending tone and air of superiority has disappeared, leaving a powerful and immediate, almost desperate, need to destroy that bracelet.

Her arm slammed the mallet into the desk. Straining with everything she had, she barely managed to divert the strike. The struggle wasn't over, though, as her arm moved up to deliver another blow. The best El could muster was to veer the hammering, and for a short time it was working, but she felt each impact creep closer to the bracelet. She was certain now that if Nedon wanted that thing destroyed, she'd do everything in her power to put it on before he succeeded.

Hoping Nedon wouldn't notice, she inched her other arm toward the bracelet. One of her strikes nicked the clasping mechanism, flipping it in the air. Loosening her will on the swinging arm, El instead reached for the bracelet with her other hand. Miraculously, her gambit worked, and she managed to slam her wrist down against the inside of the bracelet.

NO! Nedon's voice rang in her head, and his control became more powerful than before, pulling on her wrist to wrench it away, but it was too late.

The spikes of the bracelet pierced her skin, and it snapped closed as though some external force had clamped it shut. Nedon's presence disappeared from her mind immediately. The pain of those spikes remained, shooting up her entire arm and into her shoulder, but she didn't dare remove the thing. Instead, she made sure to close the outer latch to secure it in place.

Ki threw her door open and rushed to her. "Are you okay? I heard banging. What happened?" Her eyes scanned the room. She eyed the ice mallet on the desk, then her gaze fell on the bracelet around El's bloodied wrist. "Why'd you put that on?"

"I'll tell you in a minute, but I need some water right now." Her struggle with Nedon must have activated her powers without her knowing.

"Got it." Ki left quickly, and El was thankful for her friend's willingness to help without question.

Suddenly afraid she'd lost her powers when Nedon left, El glanced at the ice mallet she'd dropped on the table and commanded it to liquify. In the blink of an eye, it melted into a puddle. Relief filled her, even as she felt her organs shutting down. She'd need a lot of water to recover from this.

She fell back into her chair, head facing the ceiling, as she wondered if she'd just escaped one enemy only to fall into the hands of another. Did the bracelet give the Wardens the same control over her that Nedon had? Curious, she tried to reach out with her mind to see if there was someone there, hiding in the shadows of her thoughts, waiting to reveal themselves. She searched until Ki returned with several water skins, but didn't detect anyone.

She guzzled the water, using it to rehydrate herself and heal her body at the same time. As she recovered, she thought about the fact that some strange group had seemingly freed her from Nedon, and somehow, both had directed her to the same place. Ferrix, the capital of Kloren and the financial center of Eleshar.

That big 'fate of the world' responsibility she'd been dreading had just collapsed on her shoulders, and the weight of it was as crushing as she had feared. But surprisingly, an anxiety she hadn't recognized until now dissolved. She'd been tense, unsure when this moment would come, or in what form it would arrive. Now that it had come and gone, she found that knowing what was next strengthened her.

Once she sated her thirst, she looked at her friend with a smile. "Thank you." She stood up and headed toward the door. "Let's find Reon. We need to make some changes to our plans."

"Wait," Ki said as she hurried to catch up. "What happened in there?" She looked back at El's office as they stalked down the hallway.

I found the strength to fight a god.

CHAPTER THIRTY-EIGHT

The sun hung at the top of the sky on the morning Zeriel stepped out of his home to leave with Ketik for Clan Din. The light was so bright it even cut through his shadow blindfold, forcing him to squint in the intense illumination. He looked to the peaks of the southern mountains high overhead, knowing that somewhere on the other side of those peaks was the rising moon.

Zeriel had dawned his Te Et Sha leathers and filled them with his usual loadout of throwing knives, a variety of his custom bombs, a few caltrops, and four daggers strapped across his body. Wearing the assassin's outfit again felt familiar, but not comfortable. The leather felt like the skin of the man he was, the one who'd died in *The Pick and Shovel*, lying among the ashes of his own mistakes. Anxiety tightened the muscles of his chest as he realized he wasn't that man anymore, but had no idea who he was becoming.

No, he wasn't an assassin anymore, but if not, then what was he? Contemplating it, he found his identity difficult to define, but clear in form: He was a tool. A dangerous one that could just as easily destroy as it could build.

He was a weapon.

People of both clans went about their mornings as Zeriel headed for the Northern Bridge. They nodded to him politely as he passed, but he couldn't help but notice the nervous posture they held, and the almost imperceptible way they hurried by. The difference between those terse nods and how they treated Ketik made Zeriel wonder if he'd ever bridge that chasm.

As he approached the north edge of town, he noticed a single figure waiting there, holding the reins of two horses. The figure reached up and waved at him, a gesture his childhood friend made often. "It's about time you made it out of bed." Laluk wore a set of new leather armor. Ketik's armorers had made several sets for Clan Ra's guards as a gesture of thanks for their help. A sword hung in its sheath on his belt, balanced by a water skin on the other side.

The uncertainty Zeriel felt before washed away. "I didn't know you were coming with us."

"Go with you? Sorry to disappoint, but I've got too much to do around here." Laluk tied the horses to a post as Zeriel approached.

They shook hands, and Zeriel said, "That's a shame. I could have used an easy sparring partner."

"Ha! You wish. While you've been galivanting around the southern clans and dining with chieftains, I've been training."

"Have you now?" Zeriel made a quick motion, and daggers appeared in his grip. "Let's see what you've learned then."

Laluk drew his blade with a smile. "None of your magic shadow business."

"I wouldn't dream of it," Zeriel said, then attacked, catching Laluk off guard.

To his friend's credit, the man managed to deflect his strike, even flatfooted. A small line of blood appeared on his cheek. He touched it and inspected the blood on his fingers. "Do you even know what a fair fight is?"

Zeriel took several steps away from the road and into a grassy field between it and the river. "There's no such thing."

Laluk followed and shook his head. "Those assassins really did mess with your head, didn't they?"

"Don't make excuses, just—"

Laluk twisted the steel of his weapon, flashing sunlight into Zeriel's face, blinding him even through his blindfold. It sent daggers of pain into his eyes, forcing Zeriel to raise his hands as a shield. The sound of feet crunching on grass in quick succession reached his ears and Zeriel moved on instinct. He sidestepped quickly as the footsteps got close and took several steps backward to create distance. He reached out for the shadows around him to deepen the cover of his blindfold.

Small morsels of darkness tucked under the blades of grass at his feet obeyed and gave him sight again in time to catch Laluk advancing on him. Zeriel crouched with blades outstretched then launched himself in the air, flipping and twisting over his friend. The man's sword swiped through the air, missing him completely.

The surprise on Laluk's face as he watched Zeriel soar over his head and out of reach brought him satisfaction. The momentum of his strike carried him forward, and he twisted his body trying to adjust his attack, instead tripping over himself and landing on his back in the grass.

The moment Zeriel's feet touched the ground he shot forward, settling on top of Laluk with his knife to his throat. "You've gotten better."

"You said you weren't going to use your shadow magic."

"Not to attack. We never said I couldn't use it to see." Zeriel stood up and helped his friend to his feet. "The whole point of blinding you was so you couldn't see."

"And it wouldn't have worked so well if I didn't have my powers, so it all balances out."

Laluk looked at him skeptically. "If you say so."

Zeriel stepped up to the horses, smoothly returning his daggers to their sheaths. "Did you bring these for me and Ketik?"

"I was going to have someone else do it, but Laluk offered," Ketik said from behind them.

Zeriel spun to face him. "You're stealthier than you look. I didn't even hear you coming."

Ketik laughed. "You were kind of busy."

"Busy cheating," Laluk said, lightly punching Zeriel's shoulder.

"It was a good match, for sure. Don't be too hard on yourself Laluk.

Even without his powers, he's a former Te Et Sha, after all. No normal man could have vaulted over someone's head like that."

"See?" Laluk said, glaring at Zeriel. "Cheating."

"When we get back, I'll give you a few pointers to even the scales." Ketik approached the horses and inspected them, eventually grunting his approval. "I see they're loaded up with everything I asked for."

"Someone else prepped them," Laluk said. "I just brought them here."

"Thank them for us," Ketik said as he mounted his horse.

Footsteps crunched on the road behind them and everyone looked to find Leksha approaching.

"You didn't have to come see us off, Chief," Ketik said.

"I wanted to remind the two of you not to take your time. You're not going there for pleasure, and I expect you back before those smiths of yours finish their task."

Zeriel mounted his horse and pivoted to face the Chief. "We're just checking on them. It shouldn't take more than five or six days."

"Good." She paused for a moment before digging into the pouch strapped to her belt. She held out two items to Ketik who took one and gave the other to Zeriel. They were wooden pendants on a string. On it was the carving of a woman standing atop a circle, her hands outstretched and touching a ring encircling the entire image.

It had been a long time since Zeriel had seen this image. The woman was the personification of Eleshar itself, standing atop the world and sending out her power. It was a protection charm often gifted to family members when they went on a journey to ensure a safe return home. He knew the significance of what she'd just given them. He regarded Chief Leksha, who struggled to look back. "Why?" he asked.

"You don't have anyone else to give you one, and I didn't think it was right for you to leave without it."

A tightness seized Zeriel's throat, like someone was choking him. Tears came to his eyes, something that hadn't happened to him since he was a child. He quickly turned his horse to avoid the others.

"Thank you," Ketik said.

Zeriel steadied himself and said, "Yes, thank—thank you."

"Just come back safe."

Zeriel managed to look behind him and nodded.

Then Leksha leveled Ketik with a hard stare and said, "Don't forget what we talked about."

The Chief of Clan Gor nodded. "I won't."

Leksha nodded back curtly, then spun on her feet and walked away.

Laluk stepped up to Zeriel with a grin on his face. "Better put that on."

"Right." Zeriel put it around his neck and tucked it under his leathers.

"Let's get going, then," Ketik said. "You heard the Chief, this isn't a holiday." He swiveled his horse to face Laluk. "Be diligent while we're gone, there's no telling if the Te Et Sha will return, but you'll be the last line of defense if they do."

Laluk straightened his back and lifted his chin. "You've got nothing to worry about."

Ketik smiled and said, "Good man," then swiveled his horse northward on the road and coaxed it forward.

"We'll be back soon," Zeriel said, then trotted his horse to catch up to Ketik.

"Just be ready to get your ass kicked when you get back!" Laluk yelled.

"We'll see about that," Zeriel responded without looking back.

The two men rode in silence for several minutes before Zeriel broke the silence. "What did Leksha mean when she told you to remember what you two talked about?"

Ketik glanced at Zeriel out of the corner of his eye. "We agreed that you were the most important resource we had to fight the Te Et Sha, and to make sure I brought you back."

He wanted to believe that she'd said that because she cared about him. The familiar numbness of Zeriel's emotions settled in as he wondered why she would. "That makes sense," he said, not knowing how else to respond. He thought of memories of his childhood and found nothing there that pointed to an affection she might have had for him. Even after his return, she'd been aloof. *Resource*—that's the word Ketik had used when repeating what she'd said. It suddenly made sense. She didn't care about what happened to him, only what the Clan lost without him.

Ketik watched him thoughtfully, then focused back to the road and said, "She told me how you grew up without any support. Not from family, and not from the Clan. She wanted to change that and made me swear to bring you back, saying something about never leaving you out in the world alone ever again."

Zeriel didn't know how to respond. He couldn't, really, because he was choking up again. *Maybe I'm the one who sees myself as nothing more than a weapon, and that's why I can't fathom why anyone else would see something different.*

Jekjarah's absence left his thoughts echoing into the void of his mind. It created an almost physical pain in his gut that longed for the hallucination's company, if only to help him process what was happening. But the man never appeared, leaving Zeriel to ruminate, yet again, alone.

CHAPTER THIRTY-NINE

Hours passed as the two rode silently north through the Het Ja Ra Forest. Usually, Zeriel would have enjoyed having the time to let his mind settle. Now he found it racing over the events of the last month. His life had changed in the blink of an eye, and just as quickly he'd found a new purpose, and perhaps somewhere where he might finally find acceptance.

For the first time in his life, he wished Jekjaerah would return. How could he navigate this new life without someone to talk to, about everything that had happened? He'd even welcome the voices at this point. Anything to stop his mind from spiraling through events, his emotions, or the weight of his most recent decisions. *Is this how people go through life, bearing the burden of it all alone?*

"You've been quiet since we left," Ketik said, finally breaking the silence.

Zeriel was glad to have the chance for a conversation. This was the opportunity he needed. There was so much he wanted to talk about; where did he start? Did he trust Ketik with the secret of his illness so he could talk about the weight of its current silence? Did he talk about his uncertainty about life now that he wasn't an assassin? He wasn't quite sure, but before he came to a decision, he found himself asking the question he wanted to ask the chief most, "How do you spend all that energy pretending to care about everyone? It seems so…exhausting."

"*Pretending?*" He seemed almost offended. "I'm not pretending.

Zeriel. I'm genuinely interested."

"How could you be *that* interested? And in everyone you meet?"

"Do you think I like you?"

That gave Zeriel pause. He did assume the Chief respected him, and that they had the same goals. Had Zeriel fallen for his manipulations like everyone else? He decided not to say that out loud, instead replying, "We're on the same mission."

"Wiping the Te Et Sha off the face of Eleshar?"

"Yes. I honestly don't expect you to care about me personally. It's enough that we're working toward that goal, together."

"That's the first step."

"Toward what?" Zeriel asked, confused.

"Caring. First, you find common ground, or in our case, a common goal. Then you build a connection from there; eventually, you sacrifice things for each other. Small things at first, but as the trust builds, those things become larger."

Zeriel sighed. "That seems like so much *work*. When I watched you lead your people, not through fear and intimidation, but through respect, I saw something I wanted. I could never lead by fear and intimidation, anyway. I'm too weak for that. But respect, you made that seem so attainable."

Ketik straightened in his saddle and the two continued on. "You don't need to mimic me to be a leader. Some people, like Clan Chieftains, lead hearts and minds. But other stronger, more influential leaders carry the hopes and dreams of the people. Executing their will. Change cannot come but for those who act. Leaders like that—the ones who act—they're the ones who move nations. They're the ones with the power to change the world."

"That's a great speech, but those people aren't the ones who make the big decisions—they die carrying out other people's vision."

"Do you really want to make big decisions?"

Zeriel looked away. "No. I'm not the kind of person people *want* deciding important things."

"But you can still show them what it looks like to act. To face violence for the sake of those who cannot face it themselves. Not for your own sake, but for the sake of the people. You seem capable of that kind of leadership."

Zeriel wasn't sure. The kind of person he described didn't seem like a leader. People who put aside everything they want for the sake of other people sounded more like a myth. Heroes like that only existed in stories. Those kinds of people followed others, died, then were forgotten for weaker men who sat on thrones, unable and unwilling to do the work themselves. "I understand what you're saying, I do—"

"You just don't believe those leaders have real power."

"They don't, no."

"Is that what you're looking for? Power?"

"I...I don't know," Zeriel said.

"Maybe that's something you should figure out."

Zeriel clenched the reins tighter as he wrestled with those words. Ketik's question about power weighed on him, but as he considered it, a realization set in that it wasn't power over people he was after. Yet he couldn't put words to what he was reaching for, and the more he tried, the further it seemed to be.

For the rest of the day, silence filled the space between the two men and left Zeriel to face his racing thoughts once again. He tried to pass the time by emptying his mind, but when that didn't work, he turned to the forest. Its heightened activity in the middle of the light month turned out to be the perfect distraction.

⋄⋄

The moon was just setting below the northern horizon when Ketik and Zeriel stopped to make camp. Zeriel had gone to gather firewood, hoping to be alone for a time.

He was bending over to pick up some fallen branches when Jekjarah's voice came from behind. "You've got to stop this, Zeriel."

A flood of both relief and anger covered him. He'd felt anxious without the hallucination around, but now that he'd returned, he was angry at his absence. Anger would do no good, though, so he let it go and sighed, then stood and faced the hallucination. "And what would that be, exactly?"

"How about this long-lost-son-come-home game you're playing with these people you assume are your friends."

"They *are* my friends. You just don't like that I have someone other than you to rely on."

A shadow crept across Jekjarah's face. "I can assure you, I don't care who you rely on."

Zeriel shook his head as he continued gathering. "Then what's your problem, Jek?"

The hallucination blinked into existence in front of Zeriel. "My problem is you forgot what you're supposed to be doing." He pointed toward the place Ketik was setting up camp. "You're out here with *that*. Doing what? Checking on some people you saved on a whim?"

Zeriel stood to face Jekjarah. "You know as well as I do, that we need him."

"You do not need him. You're an assassin—"

Zeriel slammed his bundle on the forest floor. "Not anymore!"

The outburst shocked Jekjarah, and forced the hallucination to take several steps back. "What are you, then?"

"I'm..." Zeriel turned in the direction of camp, looking through the trees of the forest. "I don't know what I am."

Jekjarah composed himself, absently straightening his doublet. There was compassion in his expression for the first time Zeriel had ever seen. "I know you're struggling. But there's something you'll always be, and it's what Lavel needs from you right now."

Zeriel's chin dropped to his chest. "I know. She needs a weapon. Everyone does, it seems."

Jekjarah disappeared but his voice still reached Zeriel's ears. "It's not as bad as you're making it out to be. And besides, if you survive, you can be whatever you want." Considering what he'd promised Plaxes, that wasn't strictly true.

Zeriel bent down to pick up his firewood when he heard a branch snap in the distance. He looked up to see a deer among the trees that had yet to notice him. He set the wood down slowly, forming a shadow sword in his hand. In that moment, he became a weapon once more.

❖

With the firewood in his hands and his shadows dragging the deer behind, Zeriel entered camp, dropping it all near the fire pit Ketik had dug.

"I guess we don't have to worry about dinner."

Zeriel went over to the creek next to the camp and cleaned the blood from his hands. "The animal stumbled across me. I didn't want to let the opportunity go to waste."

Ketik stood up. "I'll get it strung up." He went to his saddlebags and pulled out a length of rope.

While Ketik did that, Zeriel built a fire. With the fire raging, he helped the chief clean the deer, and the two made quick work of it. In no time, they had venison cooking on sticks over the open flame. They settled in near the fire as they waited for the meat to finish.

Ketik looked at Zeriel for a bit longer than was comfortable before he said, "I've been suppressing my interest in these things you're capable of, because we've had other things to worry about. But now that we're here, I've got some questions."

"Go ahead," Zeriel responded. He'd wondered when the chief would have this conversation with him.

"I'm curious how you got your powers."

"I'm not completely sure how it happened. All I know is that someone—something—named Plaxes began speaking in my head several months back. She was profoundly unpleasant, and these powers came along with her."

"Interesting. Do you think she's not human?"

"Your guess is as good as mine, honestly. I'm still not sure if she's real."

Ketik stood up and checked the meat, sliced off two portions, handed one to Zeriel, then sat down. "If she's not real then it would stand to reason you were born with these abilities, they just didn't manifest until recently."

His logic was sound, but something about that didn't feel right to Zeriel. "No, the difference between before they manifested and after was unquestionably distinct. *Something* happened to me, which made me lean toward her being a real entity. Whether Plaxes caused it, or something else; that's the real question. Though the more time that passes, the less I'm sure it matters."

"Quite the mystery, that's for sure. Once we've defeated the Te Et Sha, will you look for answers?"

"In a way, yes."

"Good. For now though, we have the Te Et Sha to worry about."

"We do," Zeriel said as he stood up. "Now get some sleep. I'll handle the rest of the meat and take first watch."

"Thanks," Ketik said. He lay on his bedroll then looked up at Zeriel. "See. Little sacrifices." He flashed Zeriel a quick smile then settled in and closed his eyes.

CHAPTER FORTY

Z eriel was in and out of his dreams, never quite asleep but never fully awake. When he did dream, they were harsh things that left ragged emotions instead of memories. Time dragged on and sped up, until a scream shocked him fully awake.

"Zeriel! An ambush!"

There was no time to think, so Zeriel let his instincts take over. Daggers appeared in his hands as he launched himself to his feet at the same instant his eyes shot open. There were only seconds to assess his surroundings, but when he did, he saw four assassins mere feet from driving their daggers into the space where he had been sleeping.

The light of the sun overhead washed out Zeriel's vision. If the attack had happened the light month prior, they would have killed him easily. As it was, Plaxes's training changed that.

Weak as they were, Zeriel was able to call every shadow to him in a hundred-foot radius. The result was a dense fog of darkness that burst into life around him and his four attackers. Luckily, the sun's rays penetrated the dark fog enough that Zeriel's sensitive eyes could see, where the assassins couldn't.

He hadn't created the fog fast enough to stop their attack though, and one of the assassins' daggers bit into his collar bone. He suppressed a growl of pain as he fell back to keep the dagger from penetrating too deep.

A sudden effort of will shot Zeriel through the current of shadows in the fog at incredible speeds, spinning around his attackers and stepping behind them in fractions of a moment.

They collided with each other and let out several frustrated grunts.

"What the hell?" one of them exclaimed.

"I can't see a thing," said another. "Where'd he go?"

"Get ahold of yourselves. This is one of his unholy abilities."

Zeriel smiled at their confusion. "You almost had me." He shifted to the side just as one of the attackers swiped at the sound of his voice. Zeriel flashed next to them and slipped his dagger in the assassin's heart. "Gotcha," he said quietly in the man's ear.

"What did you say Kikatek?"

Zeriel moved toward the speaker, this time opening their throat. "Just one left."

The last assassin stepped away from his voice. "Stay away!" The voice was feminine despite her attempts to deepen her tone.

Zeriel watched as she held up her daggers in a defensive posture, facing away from where he currently stood. He shifted behind the woman and rammed his dagger through her back and into her lungs.

She drew in a sharp breath instinctively. It sounded wet as she exhaled.

"Zeriel! They have me!" Ketik cried out in the distance.

He dropped the shadow fog and turned in the direction of the Chief's voice. Movement in the distance caught his eye and he left the woman to drown in her own blood as he took off at a sprint to give chase.

The white haze of the sun's light covered his vision even through his blindfold and made it hard to see details at a distance. He pulled on shadows as he ran, adding to the depth of the darkness over his eyes. It barely helped.

The assassins who had Ketik were fast and maintained enough distance that Zeriel saw glimpses of them through the trees. Desperate, he reached out to the extent of his ability and called shade from as far as possible. It worked and gave him enough to cover himself. He shot dark ropes to connect with trees and drag him along faster than he could run. The effort stretched the limits of Zeriel's concentration, and he found himself wishing this had happened in a dark month.

Despite his efforts, the assassins maintained the distance. Zeriel growled in frustration, straining for his powers to carry him ever faster. It didn't matter. He couldn't catch up to them this way.

Finally, he let the shadows lift him from the ground, increasing his speed even further. Even that was no use, and Zeriel started to think he wasn't chasing normal assassins. He was travelling several times faster than a horse. How could they stay ahead of him like that? Frustration boiled inside him, and he finally used his power to propel him into the air and over the treetops.

The sun immediately burned out the darkness around him and he found himself in free fall. The light—now exposed to the naked sun— whited out his vision and sent pain through his eyes.

Branches whipped him as he fell beneath the trees, and he barely managed to call the darkness in time to break his fall and land safely on the forest floor. The exertion of using his powers to that degree against the light of the sun finally caught up to him, causing Zeriel to gasp for air. His chest burned and his desperate need for air pulled him to his knees.

"What are you doing, Zeriel?" Ketik yelled in the distance. "Come get me!"

Despite his frustration, Zeriel could only focus on his hunger for air. He spotted a slight movement behind a nearby tree, and he focused on that point as he waited to catch his breath. Seconds felt like hours.

Shapes shifted ahead of him and grew larger as they closed in. They were almost on top of him when he finally recovered. He stood and held out his daggers in a fighting stance. "You finally decided to stop running? Good."

The movement stopped for a moment, then one of them stepped out from behind a tree. It was a young man wearing assassin's leathers holding daggers of his own. He had jet black hair down to his shoulders, juxtaposed with ice-blue eyes. Scars lined the boy's face, turning the soft lines of youth into the crags of hard-won experience. He lifted his chin as he spoke to Zeriel. "We'd never run from the Worst One."

"Tell that to your friends outside the walls of Clan Gor."

The boy smiled. "I prayed to Eleshar that I'd be the one to find and kill you. How bountifully she provides to the worthy."

Quiet rustling came from all around Zeriel. Sound that an untrained person would attribute to a light breeze, but he knew better. They were surrounding him, maybe ten more of them. "Worthy? You're a child. I was killing before you were old enough to touch a blade." He drew the shadows around his daggers, turning them into full length swords. "Now where's Ketik?"

The move worked as the boy took a single step back. Fear washed over his features. To the boy's credit, he recovered quickly. The rustling stopped though, which was a small point in Zeriel's favor. "You expose your evil so easily?" The boy was stalling to give the others time to get in position.

Zeriel decided to play along. "Evil? Is that what Veshet told you?"

"Lord Veshet didn't have to tell us what you are. It's clear for anyone with eyes to see."

"And what is that, exactly?"

"Che Eil Ta. Bringer of darkness and destruction."

Zeriel fought back laughter that almost exploded from his mouth. "You think I'm some monster from a children's story?"

"Mock me if you want Worst One, but this is where your evil plans end."

That must have been the cue because assassins burst out of the forest around him, their daggers poised to strike.

Zeriel tried to maintain his composure during the conversation, but even after letting the boy stall, he hadn't fully recovered. With his shoulder injured and the sun tamping his powers, he wasn't sure he would survive such an attack. Instead of crossing blades with them, Zeriel formed his shadow blades into countless needles that he fired in all directions.

Most of his attackers dropped, leaving only two he'd missed. He couldn't dodge in time, so instead he drew a thin layer of shadow around his body and solidified it.

The move worked and the two men's daggers bounced off his makeshift armor, the impact ringing through the trees. Shock spread across their faces. Zeriel took advantage of that opening and planted killing blows on them both simultaneously.

Before he could turn to face the boy who'd been trying to distract him, he felt a hit that opened a deep cut across his side. Zeriel fell to his knees, growling in pain.

"I told you I'd kill you Worst One. Eleshar has deemed it so."

Zeriel shook his head at his weakness. Even with all his powers he was getting beaten by children. "I really am the Worst One." He looked up at the boy who looked ready to launch another attack. "Where's Ketik?"

"It doesn't matter now. All that's left is to accept your death!" he said as he attacked.

Zeriel was injured and exhausted and ready to end this fight. With all the energy he had left he drew a pool of shadow between him and the boy, then shot dark spikes upward as the assassin stepped over it. Four of the spikes impaled the boy from different directions, ending his momentum and his life at the same time. He released the shadows, and the boy fell to the ground, his lifeless eyes staring at nothing.

Zeriel struggled to his feet and turned to continue his chase.

"Zeriel!" Ketik cried from the distance, causing Zeriel to stop short. "Are you done with them yet?"

"I'm com—" he yelled back, but was cut off by the pain from the cut to his side.

"Well, hurry up. I'd like to be untied sometime before the next dark month."

Zeriel walked slowly as the excitement of the fight wore off, replaced by the pain in his shoulder and side.

When he finally came across Ketik, he found the chief tied to a tree, his hands and feet bound. "It's about time," the chief said. He opened his mouth to say something else before he noticed the state Zeriel was in. "Had some trouble with them, did you?"

Zeriel knelt down and began cutting him loose. "It turns out that the sun interferes with my powers much more than I thought. Without those, they're all better than me."

Ketik rubbed his wrists as Zeriel finished freeing him. "I've sparred with you, and I can say with confidence you're one of the best fighters I've ever seen."

"You only think that because you haven't taken Eleshar's Curse. Yes, I'm slightly better than you, but they're still better. They don't call me the Worst One for nothing."

Ketik seemed to ponder that for a moment before he changed the subject. "They came from the north, in the direction of Clan Din. I heard them talking about taking me back there."

"Do you think they went back? Finished off the survivors I saved?"

"Only one way to find out," Ketik said as he stood. "I don't have any of my weapons."

"We're too far away from the camp at this point. Grab what you can from the assassins. We'll push on from here and find out what happened to Clan Din."

Ketik looked Zeriel over. "We're not going anywhere until you patch up those wounds."

He wanted to sprint to their destination and make sure the people he freed were safe, but he knew Ketik was right. He'd be of no use to them if he died from blood loss or infection. "Fine. Let's make this quick."

CHAPTER FORTY-ONE

When Zeriel first imagined what it would be like to care for another person, he couldn't make sense of it. His immediate thoughts were always of what they had done—or could do—for him. The work Ketik described to build relationships felt like trying to lift a mountain. Impossible.

As Ketik stitched him up, he tried to think of something about the man that wasn't grounded in what Zeriel stood to gain from him. After some consideration, he had to admit that he saw even Ketik, the only person he'd ever witnessed put others before themselves, as just someone he could use. A tool to attain what he didn't think was possible on his own. Revenge.

Ketik finished the last suture, and they sped toward Clan Din. Zeriel was exhausted from using his powers, so the chief let him set the pace. Neither spoke, leaving him with nothing but his racing thoughts, yet again.

No, revenge wasn't everything he wanted. Losing Ketik in the ambush made him confront that truth, and the truth of what he'd been searching for all this time. It was a desire in him older and deeper than revenge, and why he'd spent so much time procrastinating at Clan Ra. Acceptance. Admitting it to himself turned his stomach, as if the need was childish, and he was weak for wanting such a thing. Everywhere he went he was shunned, hated, or ridiculed. His father had hated him. His mother, brothers, and even the Clan had turned their backs on him. Even the Te Et Sha, though they made him one of their members, ridiculed him and pushed him to the fringes of the organization. Through the years, he'd come to expect the treatment. Perhaps, in his heart, he believed he deserved it. This desire for belonging felt like a vulnerability he didn't think he could afford. And yet, it persisted.

Jekjarah's faint voice, small and almost imperceptible, echoed in his mind. *While I'm still here, you'll never find acceptance.*

The hallucination was right, in a way. His illness had been in his mind from birth. Or at least that's what every healer had told him. His fall in the mines had just brought it out. There was no healing it, no true cause. Just an unlucky happenstance of his birth.

No, he couldn't have gained acceptance then. Try as he might through the years, someone caught him talking to his hallucinations eventually. Even now, after all the good he'd done for Clan Ra and Clan Gor, and but for a few exceptions, they only tolerated him.

He thought back to the old man from Clan Din who'd been the only one to see him for who he was. Maybe that was the reason he was so determined to protect the survivors. But it was more than that. He'd freed them and sent them back to their Clan. Even knowing they were better off after what he'd done, he felt responsible for their fate. That realization drove him to push through the pain and pick up his pace. Ketik matched his speed without a question or word of protest.

The rest of the trip was a blur, and Zeriel had to empty his mind again, if only to escape his own thoughts. They rested only twice, but still it took most of the day before they arrived. Clan Din's village was nestled up against the mountainside in a huge draw that made it impossible to enter the city from anywhere but the forest to the east.

The Clan was known for its massive wall, easily the height of five men, and made from the enormous logs of the giant ketenki trees that grew in the area. No one knew exactly how old the wall was or how they'd built it, but given the mistrust Clan Din had for outsiders, no one wondered why it was there.

The two men paused at what they saw when the village came into view. The wall, and everything beyond it, was decimated. Piles of ash lay in a massive arc where the wall once stood. What the Te Et Sha had done to Clans Ra and Gor was nothing compared to the state of Clan Din. This wasn't just destruction, it was annihilation. Zeriel's chest tightened as he realized that the survivors, those lives he'd tried to save, could be laying in the ashes.

"We're too late," Ketik said as they stared at the destruction of Clan Din from the tree line. The ground was marred with black and grey, and not a single building stood across the vast land that the Clan once occupied.

Zeriel's eyes were drawn to the waterfall in the distant cliff to the north part of the mountainside. The water flowed, uncaring and undeterred by the destruction around it, and he couldn't help but feel something cold about its indifference. Eleshar, it seemed, had given them over to their destruction.

In the center of the village was a mound, blackened by fire. Zeriel thought he knew what it was, but didn't want to say it out loud, as if somehow it wouldn't be real if he avoided the words.

Zeriel nodded to Ketik as they made their way into the village Just past the remains of a gate and to their left were fields of crops. The ground was blackened, and tiny charred stalks protruded at various heights throughout the fields. To their right were the piled remains of buildings. They continued along the main road, finding small jet-black figures lying among the ashes. Many of those figures were small enough to be children, which stoked Zeriel's anger. His emotions were duller than most, but even he experienced rage at the sight.

There wasn't a single sign of life—other than the two of them—in the village. The unnatural silence around them grated at Zeriel's nerves. The uncomfortable feeling only amplified when the crash of the waterfall could be heard across the desolate remains of the village.

They stepped into the central square of Clan Din. The mound Zeriel had seen was a fountain that stood at the center of the cobblestone, water still trickling through it somehow. His relief at being wrong about the mound was short lived. Twenty bodies hung impaled on spikes driven into the stone. Their throats torn open, the points jutting out their mouths. Among them, propped higher than the others, was the old man. He stood as a warning to any who saw him.

Rage exploded in Zeriel's chest. His throat tightened and he squeezed his fist, knuckles white as he struggled to hold back the inferno. He circled the bodies, inspecting them one by one. By the level of composition, he could tell they had been hanging there for barely more than a few days. "This was my fault," he growled through clenched teeth. "I could have saved them if only we'd left earlier."

Ketik stepped up to him and put a hand on his shoulder. "It's not your fault. For all we knew, they could have been rebuilding this entire time."

Looking around at the buildings in the square, Zeriel noticed that they looked more freshly burned than the rest. He walked across the square and touched a blackened plank protruding from ashes. Charcoal chipped off, revealing fresh wood underneath. "They were rebuilding."

"Don't lose sight of the truth, Zeriel. They would have died in those cages, or at the hands of Veshet's executioners later. Veshet killed them, just like he killed Lavel. This was not your fault."

Ketik's words were right. Too right. Zeriel's pulse quickened as an unsettling realization took shape in his mind. He spun to face the chief. "How do you know that name?" he asked, voice barely above a whisper. The speed of his revelations happened too fast, and his emotions spun wildly. It dizzied him, but they spun faster still, driven by the power of his fury. "I never told you her name."

He's been lying to you, Zeriel, said Jekjarah's soft voice.

"What's going on?" He stepped toward Ketik, pulling shadows toward him on instinct. "What are you?"

Ketik didn't flinch or show fear. Did he look...sad? "I'm not lying to you, Zeriel. And I know Lavel because you know Lavel."

Don't believe him. They're all a distraction.

Zeriel wavered, turning his focus inward. "What are you saying, Jek?"

Ketik sighed. "He's stronger than I thought. Though I should have expected it since he's been with you from the beginning."

Zeriel focuses back on the chief, emotions evaporating, yet confusion remained. "Answer my question. What are you?"

"I'm Ketik, Chief of Clan Gor."

Dying embers of anger stoked again in Zeriel's chest, and he formed his shadow blades without thinking. "No. You're not." He attacked in a flash, cleaving the imposter in two at the waist.

His blades passed through the man without any resistance.

"You can't listen to Jekjarah, Zeriel. He's not a friend. Just the personification of your blood lust."

I'm more than that!

"So what are *you*, then?"

"I'm the part of you that wants to heal. Haven't I been helping you do that?"

That gave Zeriel pause. He thought over everything this version of Ketik had said to him since he arrived at Clan Ra. "You—did help me," he admitted. The shadow blades dissipated from his hands.

"I can't stay now that you know the truth." The hallucination of Ketik started to fade. "I'm sorry for that. Just remember to look outside yourself from time to time. There's a whole world waiting to embrace you if you let it."

Panic hit Zeriel suddenly. "Wait!"

A voice rang out from the edge of town. Deep in tone but clear as a mountain brook. "Zeriel. Come to me."

The fading hallucination of Ketik smiled. "You're going to be fine. He'll take it from here." Then he disappeared completely.

"Zeriel," the voice said again. "Come to me."

Jekjarah stepped up beside him. "I don't...you can't..." Jekjarah glanced at Zeriel with a mixture of fear and curiosity on his face. "Go to him, Zeriel." He turned toward the voice and started walking.

Zeriel lagged, too disoriented to do anything but stand there. "What do you think he wants?"

Jekjarah didn't stop or look back. He just said, "Only one way to find out," and kept walking.

Zeriel stood frozen, mind reeling from the cascade of horrors that had just revealed themselves. The impaled bodies of Clan Din's survivors. Ketik's identity as a hallucination. In all the years he had his illness, he thought Jekjarah was the only voice that showed itself to him. Had he been wrong his entire life? How long was Ketik a figment of his imagination? Since the beginning? Was anything real? Could he be walking into a trap, spun by his own broken mind?

But then Jekjarah turned and held out a hand to him. "Come *on*," he said.

Zeriel hesitated, suddenly unable to trust anything.

"I think he has the answers," Jekjarah said, urging him on, then walking back toward the voice.

Surety overwhelmed him suddenly, and though he couldn't explain it, he knew what he needed to do. Zeriel went to the voice.

CHAPTER FORTY-TWO

That voice called his name again, its tone resonating through Zeriel's body, bringing him a calm he'd never experienced before. His emotions settled, not quite into peace, but closer to it than he'd ever been. Whoever that man was, Zeriel needed to see him.

It repeated its call, patient yet commanding. He followed the voice to the outskirts of the village, moving a little further to the north each time he heard it. Jekjarah walked as if he knew exactly where to go, so Zeriel followed.

He should have felt overwhelmed by everything that had happened, but with each step the discord in his mind settled. Zeriel knew he should be wary of this new voice, disturbed by its sudden appearance and effect, or confused and fearful by his reaction. He felt none of that.

A blanket of calm settled over the area, and all his defenses dropped. Jekjarah mirrored him, his motions smooth and confident.

"Zeriel," the voice repeated. "Come to me." The man behind that voice was close now. He walked down the path that followed the inside edge of the line of ashes that used to be the village's wall. He turned left on that path and saw the man standing near a long bench that looked miraculously untouched. He looked at Zeriel and flashed a grin.

The man's age was difficult to pinpoint. He had brown hair long enough to just brush the top of his shoulders, and a short beard that framed his face in a way that accentuated his features. The Fei En Ar people were taller than most across Eleshar, so Zeriel was surprised that this man who looked like he was from somewhere near The Great Divide given his bronzed skin, was almost as tall as he was. He wore the simple clothes common to the southern clans, and a waist cloth bearing Clan Din's Stripes.

"There you are, Zeriel." He extended his hand toward the bench. "Come, have a seat. We have a lot to talk about."

Zeriel studied the man. The color of the skin on his face, his level of perspiration, even his posture. He carefully inspected every element he'd been trained to observe for identifying deception. All his instincts screamed to remain guarded, yet there was an unexplainable warmth to this man that eroded his defenses. He knew better than to trust so easily, as his mind had betrayed him so many times before, but something about this moment felt different. Even Jekjarah, who so often gave voice to his deepest thoughts and hidden doubts, stood silent and watched.

"Are you real?" His voice was quiet, testing the waters of his ability to believe.

The man smiled patiently and said, "I'm very real," then took a seat on the far side of the bench.

Zeriel shook his head. "But how can you be real, when I'm not sure anything is anymore."

"I understand. You just found out that a man you admired, even bonded with, was a product of your mind."

He looked to the man surprised. "How did you know that?"

"I know everything there is to know about you. I know that your childhood was difficult. That you've spent most of your life killing. That your illness has held you back, and that," he pointed at his chest, "deep down you want a simple life, with people who accept you. Who love you."

Zeriel's eyes welled up, and he turned away. "I'll never have that."

"No, you won't," the man said, his voice strained. "And I'm sorry for that."

When he looked, Zeriel saw tears in his eyes. His chest tightened, squeezing out words he'd held there, never uttered, but words truer than anything he'd ever spoken. "Because I'm nothing. Insignificant," he whispered as the words vomited from his mouth. He'd never meant to say that, but the moment he spoke those words they pulled on the fragile thread that held him together. He unraveled faster than he could stop, and more truths followed.

"I feel like I've lost myself," he said. The weight of this man's presence pressing him to bare his soul. "Before now, I let myself believe that I was an assassin, and I felt comfort in that. It gave me a sense of belonging, though the Te Et Sha hated me.

"I thought Lavel would save me. That someday I'd leave the assassin's life, sweep her up, and take her to some remote place where we would start a life together." He thought back to the funeral and all those people who loved her. He huffed at his own foolishness. "I hadn't realized how naïve I was until it was too late, and now I'll never get the chance to beg for her forgiveness.

"When Veshet tried to kill me, I knew my life as an assassin was over. So, I clung to revenge to keep me going. It should have been a powerful emotion that gave me purpose, but now even that feels pointless." Zeriel met the man's eyes, and for the first time he saw compassion. Not for someone else, but for him, and tears forced their way down his cheeks.

"You're not nothing, Zeriel."

"Then what am I? Because I can't see it."

The man looked out at the mountain side and said, "Life is a series of journeys and destinations. Mankind clings to those destinations because they need something to ground them. But after enough time passes, they get bored. They need something new, and so they strike out on another journey, their mind set on a new destination. And so, the cycle continues.

"What no one tells you—because few recognize it—is that the point of the journey is to allow for your transition from who you were in the last destination, to who you will be in the new one." The man leaned in, as if sharing a secret. "The scary part, Zeriel, is that no one truly knows what the new destination looks like." He settled his back against the bench and twisted his head toward Zeriel. "The fear of the unknown is amplified when the destination at the end of the journey is a mystery.

"You're between destinations, Zeriel. You were thrust onto this journey when Veshet decided to take power. So, you followed the path before you, but the further down the path you went, the more out of focus your destination became. Now you find yourself in a moment of transition, neither the person you were, nor the person you will become, and that's frightening."

"Can't you tell me where it ends?" Somehow, he was sure this man knew.

The man laughed heartily. "I can," he admitted, then leaned back and looked into the sky. "You're coming to a fork in the path, Zeriel. Which direction you choose will affect you for the rest of your life."

"But how do I know which path is the right one when I don't even know where those paths will take me?"

The man met Zeriel's eyes. "One of the paths will be harder than the other, and what you must overcome on that path will feel insurmountable. If you persist through that hardship, you'll change the world. The other path will be easier but it leads to destruction." The man straightened his posture and turned to face Zeriel. "Choose the hard path."

"Choose the—how do I do that?"

"You'll know, when it's time."

"That wasn't very helpful."

The man chuckled. "It will be." He stood and straightened his clothes. "Do you know why you were gifted the powers to control darkness and shadow?"

"Yeah, Plaxes wants to use me."

"Plaxes didn't give you those powers. I chose you. You're pivotal to the events that are just now playing out in the world, and everything hangs on the choice you will soon make. If you walk down the path of destruction, the entire world will fall with you."

Zeriel raised an eyebrow at the man. "A bit dramatic, don't you think."

He flashed a wry smile. "Perhaps a bit, but no less true."

Zeriel's eyes fell to the ground. "I'm no use to anyone. I can't tell what's real and what's not. I struggled just with the idea of saving the clans, I couldn't fathom how to save the world."

"Come here," the man said as he reached out a hand toward Zeriel's face.

A flash of suspicion caused Zeriel to pause, but his concern quickly evaporated in the presence of this man. He slid closer and let the man touch the side of his face. His power-formed blindfold coalesced into a thick coating over his eyes. The sunlight flared, covering his vision. Zeriel jumped back, daggers appearing in his hands.

"It's alright," the man said. "Look around you."

He blinked, disoriented as the world had shifted into indistinct achromatic shapes. As his eyes adjusted, things settled into gradients between black and white. Most of what he saw was an impenetrable mass, but other areas, where the shade of the forest covered the ground, were clear. He turned around slowly, testing the limits of this new perception. Colorless silhouettes moved through trees and under bushes, revealing life around them he never knew existed. The bright form of a tiny rodent caught his eye as it scurried through the brush.

"What is this?" he asked, his voice thick with awe and fear. His world, once a matter of light and dark, had become something else. Yet even this he questioned, unsure if he could trust what he saw.

"There are things your eyes can't normally see. I've used your power to shift your vision to see them. Specifically, you're seeing the heat around you as white shapes. The hotter something is, the brighter it will be in your vision. The colder, the darker."

"Almost everything is white."

"The sun's warmth will make this vision difficult at times. You'll find that I've also given you the knowledge to make the adjustments to see normally, in most conditions."

When the man finished speaking the information came to Zeriel immediately. He knew the subtle shifts necessary to adjust his new eyes. This new ability reminded him of the spectacles he saw some of the wealthy wear in the larger cities he'd visited. What did they call those circles of glass? Lenses, perhaps? A fitting term for his own coverings, he decided. With a tiny effort of will he shifted his lenses, and his black and white vision receded, replaced by a slightly darkened view of the world as he was used to seeing it.

"Good," the man said. "Now one last thing: Do your hallucinations give off heat?"

"Of course not, they're not real."

The man smirked at him and raised his eyebrows.

Excited, Zeriel turned to where he'd left Jekjarah. The hallucination was still standing there.

"I don't like this, Zeriel. Maybe you shouldn't."

"Hush, Jek," the man commanded. Zeriel spun in shock that he could see the hallucination. "Let's not let ourselves get distracted." The man gestured toward Jekjarah.

For a moment he wanted to press the issue, but he'd become increasingly certain that this wasn't just a man he'd been talking to, so he decided not to push. Zeriel focused back on Jekjarah and shifted his lenses again, but only halfway into the other spectrum this time. What resulted was a mixture of his normal vision and the new. It kept the sun's light from blinding him while letting his new vision come through.

Jekjarah was semi-transparent now, the colorless silhouettes of animals behind the hallucination showing through.

Zeriel's throat tightened. "This—"

"You'll never have to worry whether something is real ever again."

"Thank you," he said, then looked back at the man. Even using a small amount of the new vision, he was swallowed by a brilliance so pure that he thought he could see eternity stretching beyond it. He threw his hands up to shield his eyes as his pulse pounded in his ears. Fear gripped him and he instinctually summoned daggers of shadow into his hands.

"Calm yourself," the man said, his voice steady, cutting through the panic building in Zeriel. "You're still in control."

With significant effort, Zeriel took control of his breathing. With an effort of will he shifted the darkness over his eyes and returned to normal sight. Shapes and colors slowly returned, and though he could breathe a sigh of relief, a single question burned in his throat. "Who are you?"

"A friend." He brushed off his clothes, though there was nothing on them. The gesture seemed more for Zeriel's benefit than his own. "I'll give you one last bit of help, though I don't usually go even this far." He met Zeriel's eyes, and the intensity of his gaze caused the assassin to look down slightly. "Your instincts were right about Veshet. Everything hinges on stopping him."

"What if I fail?"

"Then every person on Eleshar will suffer."

Zeriel scoffed. "No pressure, then."

The man gave him a compassionate smile. "I have faith in you." He looked up at the moon and said, "It's time for me to go, and time for you to return to your Clan. Things are about to get harder for you. Just know that you're not alone." He turned his back on Zeriel, then walked away. After a few steps, he stopped and looked back. "Oh, and say hi to El for me when you see her," he said with a wink.

Zeriel stood up to follow the man. He still had so many questions, but a bright flash blinded him for a moment. When he regained his sight, the man was gone. He turned toward Jekjarah who just shrugged his shoulders. Needing a moment to deal with it all, Zeriel went to sit down on the bench, but fell to the ground instead.

He blinked in disbelief, eyes scanning the empty space where the bench had been. For a heartbeat, he thought all of it—the man, the conversation, his revelations—was just another hallucination. A sick joke his subconscious played on him. The lingering warmth in his chest, and the peace it brought him, indicated otherwise.

Everything hit him at once. The weight of the events of the past few hours, the absurdity of it all—Clan Din, the hallucination of Ketik, the impossible weight of responsibility laid on his shoulders. A sudden, involuntary laugh exploded from his mouth. It wasn't an act of joy. It was a release of a pressure that had built up for years. He continued, as if breaking free from the shackles of his past—his father's abuse and family's rejection of him, the Te Et Sha's treatment of him, even Lavel rejection. He released it all. Looking ahead, the path before him came into sharper focus. He had to stop Veshet and his Te Et Sha. As he addressed the frayed threads of his life, the laughter lessened, bit by bit, until there was nothing left but exhaustion and a strange feeling of freedom. He wasn't sure how long it lasted, but when he finished, his cheeks were wet and the muscles in his face ached.

He remained on the ground until his emotions settled, then stood and pulled the nearby shadows to himself. He turned to the south toward Clan Ra and shot forward. It was time to confront the truth.

CHAPTER FORTY-THREE

Wrapped in his shadows, Zeriel could move several times faster than a sprinting horse. Because of this, he covered half the distance back to Clan Ra before the moon had set in the north. Along the way he came across the bodies of the assassins who'd ambushed him on his way to Clan Din.

He stopped amidst the corpses and shifted to his heat sight. Each of the dead assassins gave off a faint white glow at the center of their bodies. It surprised Zeriel, as he'd expected them to be hallucinations.

Jekjarah blinked into existence between two of the bodies near him. "They were probably the ones who slaughtered Clan Din's survivors."

Anger and regret stabbed his gut. Their deaths, and the deaths of the survivors, felt empty. He dealt these assassins the deaths they deserved, but the survivors were still dead, and Veshet still a threat. Even now he tried to conjure some level of catharsis knowing the boys around him had deserved their deaths. There was no satisfaction to be had, though. "Do you think this is what revenge feels like, Jek."

"Your guess is as good as mine. But I'd imagine so. It's not as if one person's death can bring someone else back to life."

Zeriel exhaled in frustration. He knew he couldn't linger much longer, but he couldn't shake the possibility that, in the end, this is how killing Veshet would feel.

When.

It seemed he'd abandoned his previous doubt. For the first time since he was young, he found confidence as he searched through his feelings. He would kill Veshet, there was no doubt, or he'd die trying. Yes, there was no doubt about that.

Something else peeked through from the depths of his mind, something he couldn't dare acknowledge. It stoked his anxiety nonetheless and drove him to act. Now was not the time for introspection. He wrapped himself in shadows again and pressed on. Less than an hour later he arrived at the camp he'd abandoned. Though his urge was to speed past, he had to investigate.

His bedroll—the only one there—lay near the fire pit. The venison he'd packed into his horse's saddlebag lay exposed on the ground, insects swarming it. The horse was gone, and so were the corpses of the assassin that attacked him there. Or more accurately, the ones he *thought* had attacked him.

"How much of my life has been real?"

Jekjarah materialized next to him, studying the abandoned camp. "I don't think you'll ever know for sure."

A sense of dread opened like a pit in the ground under his feet, threatening to drag him in. He pulled the forest's shade around him once again and left, banishing the thoughts that came again. His voices tormented him with the things he tried to ignore.

Nothing is real, not even you.

Your existence is meaningless.

There's no one to care about you.

Kill yourself.

They were always—

"Shut up!" Zeriel screamed as he picked up speed, forcing his mind to focus on weaving through the trees instead of the realities waiting for him. He flew for hours, ignoring the exhaustion of using his powers, or the need to sleep. He had to know.

That man in Clan Din told him it was time to return home. As he began to see the depth of the lies his illness had told him, he thought he knew why they had. It should have brought him joy, this ability to discover the fact from lies. At that moment, it was a burden. A burden to know what could be waiting for him, and that weight crushed him now, almost grinding him into the ground passing beneath him. While he yearned to know the truth, the pain of a lifetime of lies stabbed at his heart.

Despite the pressure of his doubts, he pressed on, flying well past moonset and into the night without stopping to eat or drink. He reached the edge of his abilities as his lungs burned for air and his muscles tired. Just when he thought he would collapse, he saw the forest open to the valley where his village stood.

Coming to a stop at the edge of the tree line, Zeriel put his hands to his knees and breathed heavily, catching his breath. When he eventually recovered, he looked toward the village and saw exactly the thing he dreaded.

Practically every building had been reduced to ash, from where he stood all the way to the village's southern border. A few fresh wooden planks stood among the rubble and ashes. Some newly built walls stood alone in open spaces, and Zeriel saw the monument in the square, larger and thicker than he had remembered. Further out, he could see the windmill, burned and broken, but still standing, its veins thrashed and still. Beyond it the blacksmith's forge stood as well, though no smoke rose from its chimney. The only sound that met Zeriel's ears was the flowing river next to him and the rustling of the leaves from the forest behind.

Jekjarah appeared at his side, his eyes on the village. "You knew this might have been the case."

"I was a fool to hope, I suppose." Zeriel walked slowly down the main road toward the village square. When he arrived at the intersection of the Northern Bridge and the main road, he forced his eyes forward and kept going. His home could wait.

Around him was more of the same. Nothing but ruin, juxtaposed with fresh wooden beams and individual walls that stood isolated among the rubble. The closer he got to the square, the more frequently the new constructions dotted the landscape. A sliver of the moon rose over the eastern mountaintops, meaning clan members should have been busy about their day. Instead, an eerie silence persisted. He tried to cling to hope, but the desolation across the village portended his worst fears.

Zeriel's pace slowed as he passed a newly built wall, the square hidden on the other side. Jekjarah, who'd been walking with him took several steps ahead, then paused and turned to look at him. "You can't put this off, Zeriel."

"I know," he said as he came to a complete stop. He looked around at the freshly erected structures. "Look at these, Jek. I didn't help with more than half of them."

"No, you didn't. Now come on."

Fear overcame his curiosity at the revelation. Doubt crept into his mind about his mission, once again, and for a split second he shifted his lenses to see the heat around him, yet nothing changed. This was real. Thinking back on his conversation with that man, he remembered his words, *One of the paths will be harder than the other.* With a quick shift back to his normal vision, Zeriel stood up straight. "I can handle hard," he said to himself, and stepped around the wall.

When he saw the square, all his tension bled away. Leksha stood at her table studying some papers under her tent.

The Chief looked up at him as he approached, his footsteps echoing on the cobblestone. "You're back." She set her work down and approached him. "Did you find who you were looking for?"

"Not exactly, no."

She looked past him and asked, "Where's Ketik? His people have been a real handful since he left."

That's right. Leksha had interacted with Ketik. Does that mean—Zeriel reached out to touch her shoulder, but his hand passed right through the Chief.

"Hey!" she said stepping back. "What do you think you're doing?"

He remembered the charm she gave him and reached up to feel the string around his neck.

It wasn't there.

Jekjarah appeared next to the Chief. "I've been trying to tell you. They've been lying to you. All of them."

Zeriel shifted his vision and saw the truth. Leksha didn't give off any heat. Even the tent she'd worked under disappeared. He reeled back as the truth bared its ugly fangs, biting him with its certainty.

The Chief sighed. "I hoped you would leave before you discovered the truth."

"That you're just a figment of my imagination?"

"That we're all dead. Look, Zeriel." Leska pointed to the memorial at the center of the square.

He knew what he'd find there, but he didn't want to see it. He turned his head the other way and squeezed his eyes shut. "I can't," he whispered.

"You must," the Chief said.

Still Zeriel hesitated. How much more of his life must he watch crumble? Why must even his most simple of hopes turn to dust?

"Zeriel," Jekjarah said, "it's time to stop lying to yourself."

One of the paths will be harder than the other.

Though he could barely admit it to himself, he couldn't keep living the lie his illness had created for him. The pain was too much to bear, so he steeled himself and opened his eyes.

He didn't see the tall poles adorned with the clothing of the fallen. That was the first lie that he uncovered. The second lie was the hardest. It rammed its blade into his heart so fast and so deep he sucked in a breath in shock.

A pile of immolated bodies stood twice his height and sat atop the blackened cobblestone. When he looked back at Leksha he saw a crowd standing behind her. Laluk was there, along with Altid and Shemua. Every single villager he thought had survived the Te Et Sha attack, along with every visitor from Clan Gor. All hallucinations. What he'd feared all along was true. No one had survived, and no one had come to help him.

Leksha stepped forward with a smile full of pity on her face. "We hoped you'd never find out. That you'd leave to fight the Te Et Sha and find your purpose in the world."

Zeriel fell to his knees as his entire world cracked under the pressure. Everyone and everything important to him had either rejected him or was a lie. The very organization that he'd devoted his life to hated him. Though he could have lived with that if they'd just acknowledged him. Even they were changed, corrupted by Veshet's ambition.

No one wanted him, and he didn't belong anywhere. It was all an illusion, these people willing to embrace him. Those who could look past his illness and his faults. The last week and a half were the happiest he'd even known, and it had been a lie. He had to create a fantasy to find acceptance, community...*love*.

His soul shattered, then disintegrated into nothing. He wept raw, uncontrollable tears. His body bent into itself as if trying to curl into a tiny ball and disappear. Every emotion he'd suppressed or refused to acknowledge, left his body through those tears, leaving only despair behind. It opened a void in his heart so wide it consumed his world, destroying it.

The momentum of that destruction carried through his entire being until he had no more tears to cry. With crisp and frightening clarity everything he'd tried to ignore came rushing to the forefront. The fact that he'd been looking up to Ketik when really, he was looking up to a product of his own deluded mind. How even the villagers in his mind felt pity for him. That he hadn't—couldn't save a single person he'd set out to save. He lost the surety the man at Clan Din had given him.

Am I real? What does it even mean to be real? He could never know.

"Zeriel," Jekjarah said as he put a hand on his shoulder. "Calm down. It's going to be okay."

Zeriel *felt* the weight of that hand. Panic shot through his entire body, and he instantly manifested his shadow blades, slicing Jekjarah through the midsection. The hallucination exploded into a dark mist that immediately dissipated. Zeriel's eyes went wide, and he looked back to Leksha and the others. "What just happened?"

They recoiled from him, fear gripping every face in the crowd. "We...don't know." One by one, they vanished. Then Leksha's tent, her table, and all her papers disappeared.

"No!" Zeriel screamed as he lunged forward and fell to his hands and knees. His voice came out ragged and wet. The pain triggered by his outburst forced him into a coughing fit. He thought he didn't have anything more to feel, but even the loss of his hallucinations pained him. As illusory as they were, they were all he had. All he'd ever had. "Come back!" He let out a ragged scream, born from the emptiness created by the hole they left inside of him. Desperate, he stood and turned in circles, searching for someone who might have stayed behind. "I didn't mean—"

He looked at the spot where he'd struck Jekjarah. "Jek! Jek, I'm sorry. Come back." Tears flowed from his eyes again, and he found himself sobbing in his hands. "Jekjarah!" he screamed, but no one answered.

Zeriel was, for the first time, truly alone. He fell to his knees once more, unable to escape the fear and sorrow.

After a time—he didn't know how long—he fell to his side and curled into the fetal position, his sobbing continuing. The tears finally ran dry, and his frayed emotions flattened like the surface of a pond when the wind stilled. Only despair remained. He knew now that it had always been there, hidden under life's distractions. It hadn't crept up as his world crumbled into dust. It had been lurking below the surface of his damaged existence, ready to pounce the moment it was revealed. And pounce it did, sinking its teeth into his heart then wrenching it from his chest.

He stood, staring at the pile of charred remains. "They've been dead this entire time." He stepped closer, focused on a blackened skull with missing teeth. "What's the point of all this?" He thought back to the man at Clan Din. "Why'd you send me back here?"

Silence.

Zeriel sat with his back to the pile of bodies, unable to look at it anymore. "We all die, I suppose. What does it matter if it's now or later?" He turned his head toward the bodies. "I mean, you guys died, and the world didn't even notice."

The other path will be easier but leads only to destruction.

Slowly, Zeriel pulled one of his daggers from its sheath and inspected the blade. *Yes, this is the easier path.* The blade carried the nicks and scratches of a thousand jobs.

The entire world will fall with you. The old man's words echoed in his mind.

Let it fall. What has the world ever done for me?

Zeriel recalled a memory in each flaw in the edge of his weapon. Despite those flaws, it was razor sharp and shone from the oil he'd used to clean it. A laugh escaped his lips, ragged and unhinged. "A weapon should know how to care for its own kind." Sunlight glinted off the blade and he was reminded of the lenses that gave him sight, thanks to Plaxes's power. That realization replaced sorrow with anger. "I'm no good to anyone, even with this cursed power you gave me."

His vision went completely white as he released the shadows. Pain sliced through his eyes, but Zeriel reveled in it. He deserved every ounce he received for all the pain he'd brought to the world. "You can have it back for all I care."

The tips of his fingers brushed up against the edge of his blade. Blood ran down his hand from the cut it caused, but Zeriel continued to explore the blade with his fingertips. He knew at that moment what had to be done. The only way to atone for the terrible fates his incompetence brought to those around him.

He gripped the handle tightly, and the blade began shaking. He took a breath and clasped the weapon in both hands, steadying the blade, then placed the tip against the carotid artery in his neck. His death would be relatively painless and quick. Neither of those things came close to what he deserved, but like everything else, he was too weak to draw it out. He'd die and no one would know, or care. Sure, Veshet might celebrate for a time, if he ever found out.

Zeriel felt a peace wash over him as he accepted his fate. He slowly increased the pressure of the knife on his neck, waiting for the skin to part and his life to end.

Don't quit, Zeriel. The world needs you. The voice in his head was small, practically imperceptible, but he recognized it just the same.

He released some of the pressure on his neck. "Jekjarah?"

There was no response.

Did he really care about what happened to the world, somewhere deep in his heart? *Impossible*, he thought as he pressed the knife against his throat again. In a moment, it wouldn't matter what anyone said. He'd finally be at peace.

"Zeriel?" came a voice.

He looked up, recreating his shadow lenses to see who had spoken. Ketik was on the main road, sitting on the back of a horse, holding a silver banner mounted to his saddle with the white and dark blue of Clan Gor's Stripes on it.

"What happened here?" he asked as scanned the area. His gaze fell on Zeriel, finally noticing the knife at his throat. "What are you doing?" He dropped the banner and jumped off his horse, running toward Zeriel.

Surely his mind was lying to him again. Sending a hallucination to stop him from ending his miserable life. Just to prove it to himself, he shifted his vision.

Ketik blazed white, radiating the hot light of real flesh and blood. Then more men appeared on horseback, halting behind Ketik. All of them glowing brightly.

"Chief, I don't think anyone could have surv—" one of the men said, cutting himself off when his eyes caught sight of Zeriel, and presumably the pile of bodies behind him. The man pulled his sword from its sheath with a ring.

Ketik put out a hand to calm him. "No need for that." The Chief whispered, putting a soft hand on Zeriel's arm, slowly applying pressure to pull the weapon from his neck. A deep concern was etched deep into his face.

Zeriel let the dagger fall, clattering to the stone beneath him. He wasn't alone. Wasn't hated or dismissed. This man trying to save his life had seen him in his darkest moments, yet he showed him nothing but compassion. For the first time in his life Zeriel felt valued by another person. A *real* person! That alone lit the embers of his dying soul, and he wept painful, dry tears.

CHAPTER FORTY-FOUR

It barely registered at what point Ketik had embraced Zeriel. The Chief's spoke, but it was muffled to Zeriel's ears. His emotions hadn't calmed enough to recognize the words. What did come through was the intent behind them. As he calmed down, Zeriel started to notice Ketik's companions scatter through the village.

Once Zeriel's breathing slowed and his body relaxed, Ketik released him and met his eyes. "Tell me everything." It was a simple command, but carried tremendous weight.

Zeriel exhaled the last of the pain holding him back, resigned—though he couldn't explain why—to telling this man everything. Maybe it was a lingering fog of the vastness of the despair he'd felt. It didn't matter, because the truth was the only thing important to him at the moment, and he had nothing to lose by revealing it. "My mind has been broken since I was a child. I've seen things and heard voices that weren't there." Jekjarah appeared from behind Ketik, waving at Zeriel mockingly. "When I arrived at your Clan, I'd been hallucinating that Clan Ra had survivors. I lived with them for months without a clue that they were only a product of my mind."

Ketik raised his eyebrows in surprise. "And you've had these visions your entire life?"

Zeriel nodded.

"Surely you'd be able to discern your visions from the real world around you."

"It's not as easy as you think. They appear as real as you are to me now. They talk to me like we're talking."

Ketik gripped Zeriel's shoulder. "But surely you wouldn't have been able to touch them. Couldn't you test them in that way?"

"You'd be surprised how little you touch people, especially when they're strangers to you. Until today, I've only identified one of my hallucinations."

"That's me!" Jekjarah said, pointing to his face and sporting a wide grin.

Zeriel glared at him. "Mostly because he's always around and never shuts up."

Ketik turned to see what Zeriel was staring at, obviously saw nothing, then looked back with concern in his eyes. "You see him now."

"I do."

Jekjarah bounced around Ketik, taking up a playful fighting pose. He jabbed Ketik's head several times, his hands passing through the man harmlessly. "Tell him what I'm doing right now!"

Zeriel shook his head. "I really wish I couldn't, though."

"I think I understand. When you told me there were survivors here, you thought there really were. Because you were seeing them."

"I was, yes." Zeriel motioned to the pile of burned remains. "My mind wouldn't let me see them like this."

Zeriel recapped everything that happened since he left Clan Gor. Having to put words to those events helped Zeriel process them. For the most part, Ketik didn't let his face betray his emotions, though Zeriel expected the worst.

Ketik paused in thought before responding to his story. "That's a lot to take in, all at once."

"Look, I'm just starting to get a handle on all of this, and there's no guarantee that I'll be reliable, even now, and especially in a fight. You and your men are better off without me."

Ketik stood and held out his hand to Zeriel. "Why did you come to help us fight the Te Et Sha?"

Zeriel let the man help him to his feet and said, "Their leader,

Veshet, killed someone I cared for, and I vowed to avenge that death. With the mass of allies he's accumulated, I doubted I could get to him on my own. Saving your Clan, getting my revenge, and starting the movement that saved all of Fei En Ar while I was at it...I admit, it felt good to think I could have been part of all that."

Ketik nodded his head. "I can understand that, at least. If you had told me some story about the greater good and personal sacrifice, I wouldn't have believed you anyway."

"I'm no good to anyone, Ketik. I'm broken. I've always been broken."

He turned to find his men moving through the ashes of the village and pointed to them. "Those men who came with me lost everything in only a few weeks. Wives, children, brothers, and parents. Entire family lines were cut off." He turned his focus back to Zeriel. "Do you think they're not broken?"

"Not like I am. I'll get them killed."

Ketik shook his head. "You're the reason they're here today. He grabbed Zeriel's shoulders and looked him in the eyes. "You're not the only one looking for revenge. Not anymore. We're going to dismantle these Te Et Sha, but as broken as you may be, we can't do it without you. Just like you can't get your vengeance without us."

Jekjarah poked his head from around Ketik again. "He's got a point!"

Zeriel gave the hallucination an annoyed look. "I liked it better when you weren't constantly bothering me."

Ketik let him go and searched around them, then turned back to Zeriel. "Jekjarah?"

"As always."

"What's he saying?"

"He agrees with you."

Ketik smiled. "See. There's a part of you that knows I'm right."

One of Ketik's men came running and practically slid to a stop.

"Careful Ietenet," Ketik said, "don't hurt yourself."

"Chief, come see this."

"See what?"

Ietenet was already walking back the way he had come. "You have to see it for yourself!"

They followed him south on the main road to the intersection of the Central Bridge. When the man crossed the bridge, Zeriel knew where he was going. Every building in the artisan's ward was a mass of ashes and rubble like the rest of the village. All but the forge which was built mostly from large stones.

Zeriel's eyes locked on where Shemua's home should have been standing. He imagined her spending hours in that home, crafting her clothing and other textiles, perhaps humming to herself with a smile on her face as she did. She'd never touch another piece of cloth again.

When Ketik passed her destroyed home, he didn't give it a single glance. Zeriel was angered at first, thinking that he should at least pay respects to the girl who cared so much for him. Before he said anything, he remembered this wasn't the Ketik he'd gotten to know. The one that had forged a relationship with the tailor. In fact, he started to wonder if Shemua had been a member of Clan Ra at all before he'd summoned her from his mind.

"Look, sir," Ietenet said, pulling Zeriel out of his contemplations enough to finally notice what the man was so excited about.

Rows of weapon racks and armor stands lined the area in front of the forge. All of them full of newly forged items. Zeriel couldn't believe his eyes.

"It's enough to outfit everyone, sir!" Itenet's eyes sparkled from his excitement.

Ketik turned to Zeriel. "Did you know these were here?"

"I—" He was lost for words.

Jekjarah appeared at the nearest weapon rack and inspected the swords there. "Zeriel, where did these come from?"

"Well," Ketik said.

"I can honestly say I have absolutely no idea how they got there."

Ketik looked back at the trove. "Perhaps the assassins left all this since they don't use swords or wear steel armor."

Zeriel wracked his brain for an explanation, though only one came to him. A conclusion so ridiculous he could barely speak it out loud. Watching Ketik walk though the racks, he felt the need to tell the man his suspicions, but the words didn't come. It was too impossible. The clear answer had to be that the weapons and armor had been there from the moment he first arrived.

"Whatever the reason they were left here," Ietenet said, "we can't let this go to waste."

"You're right," Ketik said. "Go round up everyone and bring them here. Make sure everyone is outfitted and then we'll head out."

"We're not staying, then?"

"There's nothing for us here. We can't continue to let the Te Et Sha run free among the Southern Clans any longer."

"Yes, Chief," Ietenet answered, then hurried to round everyone up.

Ketik turned to Zeriel and said, "Considering what you've already reported about Clan Din, we should be focusing on the last of the southern clans."

"It's a long journey to Clan Bale. We may not make it in time."

"Something tells me it's already too late. Their port is a strategic location and a way to cut off supplies to those of us who've survived."

"See," Jekjarah said. "That's why he's in charge."

"We'll need to be smart about how we attack," Zeriel said. "There's no telling how many of them will be in the village." He caught movement out of the corner of his eye and looked to see Ietenet as he crossed the Central Bridge with the rest of Ketik's men. "You've got what? A little over a hundred men?"

"One hundred and thirty, to be exact."

"I'll work with them on the way."

"They're all seasoned warriors," Ketik said, a little defensiveness in his tone.

Zeriel shook his head. "We'll see how many of them can beat me in a sparring match."

"If they can, you think we'll have a chance?"

"Oh Eleshar, no! I'm the Worst One."

CHAPTER FORTY-FIVE

Clan Bale's village rested on the eastern coast on Fei En Ar and was the center of trade in the Southern Clans. In terms of distance, it wasn't much further from Clan Ra than Clan Din was, but Zeriel had never traveled with over a hundred men before. He felt relieved not to be responsible for keeping the men in line. The work of organizing over a hundred soldiers, ensuring no one strayed, and that communication flowed smoothly seemed an impossible task.

The group traveled slow enough for Zeriel to walk comfortably alongside them, despite most being on horseback. It also meant it would take far more than the two days it would have taken Zeriel to complete the journey alone. Luckily, Ketik's men needed the extra time for Zeriel's training.

The first night, Zeriel chose a nearby clearing in the trees and told the men to meet him there. He watched them arrive from a hiding spot at the tree line. They huddled together in the center of the clearing, quickly losing their composure at having to wait and falling into comfortable conversations.

Jekjarah blinked into existence in front of him. "Look at them, just milling about like there's no danger."

Zeriel planned to show them just how unprepared they were to face the Te Et Sha with an ambush, but he never imagined they'd make it this easy.

In his hand was the makeshift wooden dagger he'd carved during their march, specifically for this occasion. He'd coated the rounded side where the edge of a real dagger would have been with crushed red berries.

Jekjarah looked back at Zeriel. "What are you waiting for?"

I'm waiting for the rest to arrive. He needed everyone to learn this lesson, or it wouldn't leave a strong enough impression. His hand moved to the pouch at his side that held a smoke bomb and a sparker.

A few more minutes passed before the last few shuffled in. Zeriel waited a bit longer to spring his trap. They weren't off guard enough just yet. He didn't have to wait more than a few minutes more before several of them got frustrated and started leaving. It was interesting that the ones who had just arrived moved first.

Zeriel worked his sparker and lit the smoke bomb, then tossed it high so it would sail above their heads and land at their center. A few of them noticed the bomb soaring over them and called out, but before they could react, the bomb fell in the center of the crowd and went off. Thick smoke exploded in all directions and enveloped the crowd. Chaos erupted as they scattered.

With the combination of the speed of his physical enhancements and his training, Zeriel sprinted into the crowd. He stayed low and moved fast, weaving through the group, landing lethal strikes as he went. It took a good thirty seconds to make his way through the entire crowd. By the end of his attack, several caught on to what was happening, but they still couldn't react fast enough to stop him.

As the smoke cleared, the crowd calmed enough to notice Zeriel standing near them, his wooden knife still in his hand. They took several steps back from him in surprise, creating a circle around the former assassin. Then many of the group noticed the red marks Zeriel left on them in his assault.

"As you're starting to notice, I was able to place lethal blows on all of you." He held up the knife, showing the red stain on it. "Had this been a real weapon, you'd all be dead."

One man stepped up from the group. He must have been in his late twenties and some sort of leader considering the courage his initiative gave the others. "Even with your ambush, you shouldn't have been able to kill us all. Your powers give you an advantage the Te Et Sha won't have against us."

"I didn't use my powers. I am—like all Te Et Sha—enhanced by Eleshar's Curse. That means I'm stronger and faster than you, even without my powers."

"How do we know you're not lying?" someone from behind the man asked. "Just to humiliate us?"

Murmurs of agreement rose from the crowd as they watched Zeriel expectantly. He sighed. "If I had used my powers, stopping me would have been impossible. At least this way you had a chance." Zeriel drew shadows from the trees around them and the grass below. Then exploded them into a cloud, engulfing them all. After shifting his vision, he saw them easily. He stepped through the group casually, and silently, whispering in ears and he went. "I can still see you. Standing like livestock waiting to be slaughtered."

Several men swiped their swords at where they heard his voice, but they cut only air. Zeriel returned to his original location and dropped the shadows. Pale faces full of terror stumbled back, trying desperately to get away from him.

"If you prefer a more direct approach," Zeriel said, bringing up the shadows into dark spears that surrounded the crowd, floating just out of reach above them. "I wouldn't have to move from this spot if I didn't want to."

The man who stepped up stifled an angry response, and when he finally spoke, it was through gritted teeth. "Fine. You didn't use your powers."

Zeriel released the shadows, and the spikes puffed out of existence like smoke on a strong breeze. He tipped his head to the man in respect.

"How do we fight these assassins then?" Another voice from the crowd asked.

Zeriel summoned his shadow blades. "First, you fight me."

❖

Through the years Zeriel learned a lot about the art of violence. Some of what he'd learned was taught to him during his time as a trainee, but most was learned through simple experience. Scars lined his entire body to remind him of those lessons.

For the rest of the six days that it took to arrive at Clan Bale, Zeriel taught Ketik's forces everything he knew, and through those lessons discovered something new himself. By the simple transfer of his hard-earned expertise, his knowledge and ability increased. Fundamentals he'd ignored for years were brought to the forefront of his thoughts. Errors he corrected in others shined a light on his own.

As it turned out, teaching broke through walls he'd never realized he had. Coupled with the hours of nightly practice, he'd strengthened along with Ketik's soldiers.

The sun was halfway on its path to setting when Zeriel joined Ketik and his scouts on the edge of a short cliff that overlooked Clan Bale. The village's buildings consolidated at the shoreline, then spread out as the village stretched away from the port. From their vantage, they could see into the streets of the village, but the docks of the port were still obscured, only identifiable from the ship masts that climbed above the roofs of the buildings.

They were waiting for Ietenet—who turned out to be one of Ketik's scouts—to return when Ketik asked Zeriel, "Are the men ready?"

"They're as ready as I can make them."

Ketik nodded. "Good. This will be our first real test. If we aren't successful today, it's likely we'll never be strong enough to stop them."

Zeriel hadn't thought of it that way, but the Chief was right. They fell into silence once again, the coming fight weighing on Zeriel as he assumed it weighed on the others.

A short time later, Ietenet appeared from the trees behind him. Zeriel was impressed by the man's stealth. He'd give the Te Et Sha some good competition.

"They've been there for several weeks, at least. What remains of Clan Bale is enslaved or being held in makeshift cages in the center of the village."

"The Te Et Sha were dependent on slave labor," Zeriel said. "It's likely they plan to take them to Ki Al Tesh, as they planned to do with the survivors of Clan Din before I freed them."

Ietenet nodded. "That checks out. Members of Clan Bale are loading supplies into five ships in the port. They won't be here for much longer."

"Are there any guards posted in the village?" Ketik asked.

"No, Chief. They don't have any defensive positions and there are no patrols. I doubt they expect an attack."

"Good. Did you get an idea of how many of them are in the village?"

"Around twenty."

Ketik's eyebrows raised. "Is that all?"

"Don't forget they'll be as strong as ten of your men—" Zeriel paused to think for a moment. "Well, maybe five with my training."

"Our men, Zeriel. You've trained them for the last week and will be fighting with them. We're together in this."

Zeriel struggled to wrap his head around being part of a team. He'd never fought in a group before and couldn't imagine how it would even work. "Right," he said, then turned to look over the village again. "I take it you have a plan, then?"

Ketik followed Zeriel's gaze. "We can't let them escape on a single one of those ships. Right now, our biggest advantage is that they don't know we exist. But if we let them escape back to Veshet, we lose the advantage of surprise. He could consolidate his forces and wipe us out before we get halfway to the capital."

"Leave the ships to me," Zeriel said. "I'll make sure they don't leave the port."

Ketik nodded. "Good. I'll lead the men from the west. With their focus on the port, we should be able to pin them between us and the water." He turned to Ietenet. "Go ahead of us and tell the men to get ready. Our attack will begin within the hour."

Ietenet nodded and said, "Yes, Chief." Then he disappeared into the forest.

"Make sure you don't destroy those ships, Zeriel. They're key to our success for what comes next."

"Let's stop the assassins here first, then we can talk about what's next."

"Right," Ketik responded. "But while you're stopping them, try your best to avoid unnecessary destruction. Now, go and find a hiding spot near the port. Just before we attack, we'll give you a signal."

"And what will that be?"

"A single flaming arrow shot into the port."

Zeriel nodded. "Don't make me wait too long. I get bored easily." He wrapped himself in shadow and stepped off the cliff.

❖

Zeriel found the perfect hiding spot high in a tree that overlooked the port with enough cover and distance that they'd barely notice him. But he vanished completely, shrouded in the shadows of his power. Ietenet was right. The Te Et Sha were moving barrels and crates into five galleys. He understood now why they'd kept so many slaves among the clans. They needed bodies to man the oars of those ships. He watched as they pulled down the flags on the masts carrying Clan Bale's Stripes: Two silver stripes with two green stripes forming a cross between them on a field of white.

Jekjarah blinked into existence in the air beside him. "I'm usually the last person to say this, but I think we might actually have a chance to pull this off."

"It's a strange feeling."

As if to mock his optimism, the voices returned.

They see you in this tree.

Look below you, they're attacking right now!

The voices droned on, and for once he wished they would speak about something—anything—other than doom.

You're going to die.

Just as he opened his mouth to silence the voices, an arrow, its tip lit on fire, shot into the sky. The voices silenced at the sight of it cresting over the village and hitting a barrel on one of the ships. Several Te Et Sha stepped back in shock and knocked the barrel over. The liquid contents splashed across the deck and the arrow's fire followed. Shouts were raised and most of the Te Et Sha hurried to get water to put out the flames, others sprinted into the village to find their attackers.

Zeriel crouched to leap into action but froze in place when he spotted Lushame, wearing Te Et Sha leathers, and darting from below the deck of the ship that was on fire, screaming at the others who were trying to put out the flames. He shifted his vision and saw a white glow of heat coming from her body.

Jekjarah floated in front of him. "You need to stick with the—"

Zeriel launched himself off his perch, using the shadows to keep him aloft and passed through the hallucination.

"Don't forget the plan," Jekjarah called from behind.

A vision of Lushame holding a knife to Lavel's throat played in his mind. "I haven't."

CHAPTER FORTY-SIX

Over the last month Zeriel had come to understand the extent to which the sun hindered his powers. The contrast between that and the strength he wielded during the dark months was stark. At the end of the light month, he was stronger, but nowhere near at the height of his power.

Driven by vengeance, he sped toward the docks, and a small part of his mind reminded him to be careful. Lushame was dangerous, and he couldn't underestimate her. He'd need every bit of skill and power he could muster to defeat her.

With all that in mind, he pushed on, the long shadows of the setting sun enough to carry him high above the ground. They granted him enough speed to strike with the sudden ferocity needed to catch the Te Et Sha off guard. Once he was in range, he formed shadow spears in his hands and launched them at Lushame as she stood on the deck of her galley trying to organize the firefighting efforts.

The first spear glanced off her shoulder, the momentum sending her spinning. The next two spears followed close behind but missed. The spears tore through the deck, piercing deep into the ship's hull.

Lushame snapped her head in Zeriel's direction in time to see him mere feet away. He dove toward her with shadow blades in his hands, then used the shadows holding him aloft to spin him at the last moment in a brazen attack meant to separate her head from her shoulders.

The third strongest Te Et Sha, in a display of skill few could imitate, dodged out of the way in time to avoid the deadly blow. Zeriel slammed into the deck, cracking the wood beneath his feet. He let the shadows around him dissipate and faced Lushame in earnest for the first time.

She touched her neck and saw blood on her fingers, her face darkening at the sight. "I've been waiting for you, Worst One." She drew draggers from their sheaths at her sides and settled into a fighting stance. "You'll pay for that. And for killing my brother."

At that moment Te Et Sha attacked from every direction. They appeared from hidden positions across the ship, catching Zeriel off guard. He hadn't expected such an attack from the assassins, though he'd been training Ketik's men to do the same. Te Et Sha training didn't cover the proper execution of an overwhelming surprise attack, and what his assailants didn't know was he'd spent the last six days fending them off. He hadn't used his powers against his allies, but he had plenty of time to ponder how he could.

With an effort of will, Zeriel solidified the shadows in a twenty-foot circle around him into arrows, then spun in a circle and sent them through the hearts of every assassin around him. Unfortunately, Lushame once again managed to dodge the one aimed for her. The others dropped, some tumbling into the water, all of them dead.

Zeriel exhaled as he faced Lushame. "Well, that was rude. What were you saying again? Something about making me pay...for what again?"

Lushame screamed and sprinted forward. Her attack was rushed and feral, showing few signs of the precision of her assassins' training, but Zeriel knew he couldn't let his guard down. The deadliest part of that training was still there, ingrained in her muscle memory.

Zeriel dodged her first attack far more easily than he anticipated. The surprise at his own skill blinded him to her next move. She went on the offensive with frightening speed and drove Zeriel back toward the starboard rail of the deck. Even on the defensive, Zeriel was surprised that he wasn't overwhelmed by her assault like he had been in past encounters. His confidence swelled, though they were essentially on an even footing.

Zeriel's back hit the rail, leaving him nowhere else to go as Lushame lunged for the killing blow. Just as he tried to parry her strike, the ship listed port side and threw them both off balance. Zeriel's blade missed the parry, but gravity wrenched Lushame away, leaving her blade hovering inches from his chest.

Swinging with his offhand blade, Zeriel managed to turn her dagger aside. He went for a lunge of his own in the hopes that the fall would give him an advantage. Their fall caused his own thrust to fall short by inches.

Lushame recovered before Zeriel, quickly kicking off the deck and twisting into a backflip. A second kick mid-air knocked Zeriel's blade aside. Her flip sent her high into the air, allowing her to sail over the water to land safely on land. She moved quickly, addressing the few Te Et Sha left at the port. They had been frozen in shock at the exchange. "Untie those ships and cast off now!" she screamed at them. Each one looked at her in confusion for a second, then jumped into action as her command sunk in.

Zeriel's feet met the ship's deck, but its steep angle sent him sliding toward the port rail that hovered inches above the surface of the water.

Jekjarah appeared in front of him, panic written across his face. "You can't let them take those boats!"

Zeriel growled, pulled the shadows to form a dark mass around him and sent out several tendrils from the mass to slam into the wood of the deck and halt his fall. "I know that!" he screamed at Jekjarah as he used the tendrils to launch him in the air with enough strength to send him soaring above the mast. The deck of the ship shattered under the strain of it and the entire galley snapped in half.

Near the crest of his jump, he could see the five assassins left on the dock, four of whom were running to the remaining ships. As his momentum ran out and he hovered at the peak of his jump, Zeriel desperately reached out with his senses for whatever shadows he could find. To his surprise, he found a vast reserve of shadows in the depths of the water below and summoned them in a desperate panic. Tendrils of shadow erupted from the water and slammed into him, joining with those around him to become a huge cloud of darkness that enveloped the docks.

Zeriel quickly shaped parts of the cloud into huge spikes, and with a swipe of his hand, fired them across the port. Every dock exploded in a mass of wooden shrapnel and all four of the assassins were impaled on his spikes, unable to escape the sheer size of his attack. Once again, Lushame defied all odds, dodging every projectile. She looked up at him, a fire in her eyes he'd never seen before.

Gravity wrenched him downward. As he plummeted, Zeriel hurled ropes of shadows at the walls of the nearby buildings, embedding them in the wood and plaster. With an effort of will he used them as a tether to yank him toward the shore.

At the last moment he drew his shadows back and forced them downward, softening his landing. He didn't feel the impact, but the sound was like a thunderclap, and the ground around him exploded outward.

To her credit, Lushame didn't flinch, instead facing him with defiance in her eyes. Her knuckles turned white as she gripped her daggers. "I see you've picked up some new tricks since we first met. That explains how you got the better of Denetek."

"If I'm honest," Zeriel said, reforming his swords from the darkness, "he should have killed me. His arrogance created an opening he probably didn't think I had the strength or skill to exploit."

"That, I believe. But don't get your hopes up, Worst One, I won't present you with such an opportunity." She sprinted toward him with her daggers held out.

For a moment Zeriel thought she was baiting him. Surely, she saw what he'd just done. Maybe she simply acted on instinct, not taking the time to realize that a direct assault wouldn't work on him. Not anymore.

Zeriel relaxed.

"Don't mock me!" she screamed, jumping from the edge of the crater he'd made, her daggers falling only a few feet away.

He found shadows under his feet, and with an effort of will, speared her on spikes made from his power. Her momentum shoved her further down the spikes. Her eyes went wide, and she twisted awkwardly trying to free herself. She slid to a stop inches away from Zeriel before her entire body went limp.

He released his blades along with the spikes and reached out to catch her. In that moment he expected to feel satisfaction, but all he felt was sadness as he formed a dagger in his hand. "This is for Lavel," he said, then rammed the weapon through her ribs, causing them to shatter as he sent his blade through her heart.

Lushame met Zeriel's eyes as she cried out in pain. He saw the rage and unbelief swirling in her irises. She didn't say a word, just let the intent of her gaze tell Zeriel everything she wanted him to know, then she went limp and died in his arms.

This, like Denetek's death, left him hollow. He fought a strong and sudden urge to abandon his quest. But the words of the old man at Clan Din rang in his ears once again, reminding him that he'd been giving a mission, even if he didn't know by who.

He dropped Lushame's corpse and turned away from the port, ready to head into the village and reinforce Ketik's men. Jekjarah materialized in front of him as he did. "That was easier than Denetek. Maybe all that time training Ketik's soldiers helped you."

Undeterred, Zeriel walked through the hallucination and responded, "Training never helped me before, why would it now?"

"I don't know, but something *does* feel different."

Zeriel scoffed as he gathered shadows around him and launched himself through the buildings, toward the sounds of battle beyond. Though he didn't want to admit the hallucination was right, something was indeed different. He felt more in control than he ever had, and things just...fell into place.

The battle was close. In seconds, he reached the remaining Te Et Sha fighting Ketik's men to the south, near the outskirts of town.

The tactics he'd taught them were working. They attacked in groups of no less than four, focusing on defense, only striking when a clear opportunity arose. There were roughly five assassins left, each fighting groups of at least ten soldiers, but when he looked around them, he saw the corpses of Ketik's men on the ground.

Rage surged through him, pushing him faster than ever as he sped through the village streets in a blur. A small part of him wondered why he got so emotional. He'd seen plenty of death, most of it delivered by his own hands, and never felt a thing. This time, though, something powerful stoked more passion in him than anything he'd thought he felt for Lavel. He'd trained these men, invested in them in a way he'd never known was possible. They weren't just random soldiers any-more. They were *his* soldiers.

In a flash he caught the rest of the assassins off guard, cutting them down one by one. He became a streak of darkness, delivering death so swiftly that the last of them died before the first one hit the ground. A shocked silence filled the air for several heartbeats, then cheers erupted.

For the first time since fighting the Te Et Sha, the Southern Clans had won. They'd retaken Clan Bale.

CHAPTER FORTY-SEVEN

The final count was thirty dead. A staggering number considering they faced only ten Te Et Sha. Ketik had told him that the casualties were expected. That sentiment hadn't quelled the growing anger inside him.

He overlooked the graveyard in the southwest edge of the village and watched as soldiers dug graves for their brothers in arms.

The heavy footsteps he'd come to associate with Ketik approached Zeriel from behind.

"You should help them," the Chief said. "It'll help you process everything."

Zeriel studied the Chief's face, trying to understand what he must be feeling, though he couldn't interpret the man's expression. He knew how he felt, though. Angry. If he'd been a better instructor, able to train those soldiers better, maybe they wouldn't have died. He looked back toward the graveyard where a score of men dug graves and said, "They have enough people down there. They don't need me."

The ones that lived hate you for letting the others die.

Zeriel gritted his teeth.

Ketik put a hand on his shoulder. "The voices?"

Zeriel met the man's eyes. "How'd you know?"

"There's a...darkness that comes over you when they speak."

"I failed them, Ketik. Didn't train them hard enough. Embedded my own incompetencies in them, somehow. I should have been faster at the port. I could help sooner, then none of them would have died."

"Stop that. You single-handedly killed nearly twenty Te Et Sha and managed to save four of the ships."

"If I'd controlled myself better, we'd have all five."

Ketik shook his head and faced Zeriel. "Those voices tear you down on a near constant basis, right?"

"They do," Zeriel whispered.

"I couldn't imagine the strength it would take to push through that and come out the other end as capable as you are. You're perhaps the strongest person I've ever met, Zeriel. *You* just need to believe it."

Zeriel scoffed. "If you had met me before I received these powers, you wouldn't have said that. There's a reason they call me the Worst One."

"They may call you that, but you let it define you." He let out a deep sigh. "Take a walk back to the port and see what's happening in the village. As you do that, I want you to remember that without you, we would have failed here." Ketik walked toward the men in the graveyard. "You can't stop every bad thing that happens in this world. Don't let yourself take responsibility for what you can't control." He approached the men digging, grabbed a shovel leaning against a tree, and joined them.

Did he still believe he was the Worst One? He'd never considered how he felt about the title, he'd just accepted it as his role. Thinking through recent events, though, he was confronted by the amazing things he'd achieved. He'd fought scores of Te Et Sha and won. Even killed Lushame in a one-on-one fight. In the past, such a stark shift in how he saw himself would have sent him into a mental spiral, but somehow this new reality made him feel strong. He was no longer the Worst One, and surprisingly, he believed that to his core.

Zeriel eyed the Chief as he dug. How could a few simple words from the man shift his perspective so profoundly?

Jekjarah appeared next to him suddenly. "He's not the Ketik you hallucinated, is he?"

"No, he's not. But he seems somehow more...real." Zeriel turned away from the graveyard and did as the Chief told him.

He traveled across the village and saw the men and women of Clan Bale picking up the pieces of their lives. The destruction left behind was typical of Veshet's Te Et Sha. Men were busy cleaning the ashes of homes burned to the ground. Women moved busily through the village gathering water, food, and other materials to help with the rebuilding efforts already underway.

These villagers had been held captive, waiting to work as slaves in the galleys. The despair of that lingered, and sadness blanketed them all, pushing their heads down. Even saved from that, the devastation left behind was immense. They hadn't found a single child alive in the village, though why the Te Et Sha felt the need to end the next generation was anyone's guess. In twenty years, the clans' numbers will have dwindled. Their traditions would be lost, and soon after there would be nothing for Veshet to rule over.

Jekjarah materialized walking next to him. "These people are already a remnant of what Clan Bale was just a month ago."

"That's not what I see."

Jekjarah looked at him skeptically.

He met the man's gaze, then shook his head. "Fine. That's not *all* I see."

"It's all I can see. I mean, this might be the end of Clan Bale."

"Look at them, Jek. Mere hours after being rescued, after their lives were decimated, they're hard at work rebuilding. Yes, they feel sadness and unimaginable grief. But they haven't let it stop them."

A woman had been walking by, holding a bucket of water, had stopped near him and was staring with a mix of fear and curiosity on her face. She startled when he noticed her and hurried away.

Jekjarah chuckled. "Oh yeah, they're very resilient."

"This won't be the end of them, Jek," Zeriel said as he watched the people. Clan Bale's resilience inspired him, and he found a motivation he hadn't felt for a long time, imparting energy to his steps as he made his way to the port.

❖

They remained at Clan Bale for another week, helping them rebuild. In that time, they'd convinced the new Chief to let them take the ships. And while she wasn't happy about it, she eventually let them recruit new soldiers from Clan Bale's survivors..

The sun touched the western horizon, casting enough darkness across the village that the plant life was aglow with its polychromatic brilliance and people moved around by the light of white vine lanterns. It was even dark enough that Zeriel didn't need his shadow lenses, except to check what was real around him. He'd gotten into the habit of checking every few minutes, just in case.

Zeriel stood next to Ketik, the two facing the four galleys at port. Soldiers hurried to load the ships in preparation for their journey.

"How many joined?" Zeriel asked.

"Close to eighty men," Ketik said, "and roughly twenty women."

"It'll be difficult to train them on these ships."

Ketik eyed him. "You plan to continue your training then?"

"We can't have nearly a hundred people join us and not know how to fight."

Ketik grinned slightly as he nodded. "I just thought, after your reaction to the last fight, you wouldn't be too excited to go through that experience again."

Zeriel scanned the port, watching the people work. A deep connection to them grabbed hold of him, though he didn't have the words to explain why. He'd struggled to grasp these new emotions over the last week, but they were too unfamiliar. "We can't lose that many again. At that rate, we'll have lost before we even make it to Veshet."

"You've trained about half of our forces already. It might help to speed things along if you pick the most skilled soldiers—those who picked up your training the fastest—and let them train the others."

Zeriel lifted an eyebrow. "You really think that'll work?"

Ketik laughed and clapped him on the shoulder. "It'll work better than you spreading yourself to thin trying to get to everyone personally."

"We'll probably need to organize better to accomplish what you're proposing. Institute formal ranks." Though Zeriel had no idea how to do that.

"Right. That reminds me. I've been trying to think of a title for little army."

"What?" Zeriel said. "Why?"

"Well, we're not just Clan Gor anymore, and we're fighting for the sake of all the clans. We need to call ourselves something. A title people can rally behind."

"And what have you come up with so far?"

"Nothing good. I was hoping you'd have some ideas."

Zeriel spread out his arms. "Do I look like someone who comes up with names for things?"

Ketik laughed. "Still, if something comes to mind, let me know."

Surprisingly, a few ideas did come to mind. One of them stuck out, but he struggled to understand why. "What about The Liberators?"

"Kind of on the nose, don't you think?"

Zeriel shrugged. "I told you I wouldn't be any good at this."

Ketik's eyes stared into the distance for a moment. "The Coalition." He said, finally.

"Isn't *that* kind of on the nose?"

"You don't like it?"

Zeriel shrugged again. "It's probably better than my idea."

Ietenet approached them and Zeriel found himself glad to see the man had survived the battle. "Excuse me gentlemen, but we're almost ready to depart."

Ketik looked to the sky and Zeriel followed his gaze to find the moon showing midday. "Good. Take the rest of the afternoon, make sure everyone's ready. We'll leave first thing in the morning."

"I'll be joining you, as well," came a feminine voice from behind them. They turned to find Odinte approaching them. She was a young woman, her light brown hair cascading in waves over her shoulders.

Her eyes were a piercing green that contrasted with her hair and the simple brown dress she wore. A circular patch was sewn into the dress over her left breast, embroidered with the Stripes of Clan Bale. She'd tied a braided leather cord around her waist that held a small dagger on one side and a pouch on the other. She spoke firmly, but she held the bend of one arm across her back, and only met their eyes briefly.

The remaining members of Clan Bale had named her the new Chief, though Zeriel couldn't understand why. "Don't your people need you here?" he said, not keeping the annoyance from his voice.

Ketik shot him a reproachful look and said, "Of course, *Chief*." He turned back to her. "But my friend Zeriel here has a point. Shouldn't you focus on the rebuilding efforts?"

"Shouldn't you be at Clan Gor doing the same," she met Ketik's eyes, "Chief?"

Zeriel raised his eyebrows. Perhaps she wasn't the demure flower he'd assumed.

Ketik sighed. "Of course, the matters of your Clan are your own. I won't stop you from accompanying us, if that's truly what you wish."

"Good," she said, standing up a little straighter and letting her arms fall to her sides. She gave a terse nod, then spun on her heels and stalked away.

"You sure that's a good idea?" Zeriel asked.

"Don't be fooled by how she looks. There's a reason they named her Chief. She'll be an asset for what's next."

"If you say so," Zeriel said, then headed toward one of the galleys to help finish loading the last few barrels of supplies.

CHAPTER FORTY-EIGHT

One of the trademarks of being an assassin is silently slipping into the shadows and disappearing. To master this, one must understand their surroundings, building layouts, street configurations, and guard patrols. This ability alone gave Zeriel the edge he needed to succeed at his missions. It was also the only thing that got him away from the inevitable danger of failing his mission or being detected. As the Worst One, he often spent time struggling with his targets or alerting others to his presence.

All that failure has taught him one simple fact: Never get on a ship. There was practically nowhere to hide, and even fewer places to run. So, as he stood on the deck of one of the galleys, muscles he'd never used before ached as they fought against the motion of the ship. His stomach churned as he felt its contents slosh back and forth.

The Gulf of Plax met the eastern shores of Fei En Ar, opening to the Hama Sea in the distant south. They had turned north, where the Otehep River poured into the gulf and marked the border between the Central and Southern Clans. Clan Ke, one of the Central Clans' two port villages, sat on the riverbank several miles upstream.

These facts replayed in Zeriel's head over and over as he tried to distract himself and wrestled his stomach into submission. A sudden and fierce nausea hit him, and he leaned over the side to vomit. The sound of Ketik's boots colliding with the wood of the deck approached. He briefly wondered if the chief purposefully walks that loud on purpose. He couldn't answer his own question as the nausea returned and he was over the rail again.

Ketik laughed and clapped Zeriel on the back. "Not accustomed to sailing, I see."

Zeriel finished his retching and glared. "You seem to be doing just fine."

"The motion of a ship on the water never bothered me."

"Why am I not surprised."

"Hang in there. It's going to be a long day for you, I'm afraid."

Zeriel finished and set his forehead on the rail. "Day?"

"It's a full day's journey to Clan Ke."

He looked up at the moon, which was still in the southern sky. They couldn't have been sailing for more than a few hours. "Now he tells me."

Jekjarah blinked into existence next to him. "How many times did I tell you to travel by ship? If nothing else, so you could get used to it."

Zeriel turned to Jekjarah. "I don't need an 'I told you so' right now, Jek."

"Still feels good to get one in though," the hallucination said with a smile. He laughed as he faded and Zeriel leaned over the railing again. With nothing left to give, his muscles struggled painfully to squeeze something, anything out.

"I'll uh—leave you to it, then." Ketik stepped away, his footsteps uncharacteristically uncertain. He paused and said, "You should drink plenty of fluids. That dry heaving isn't good for you."

"Th—thanks," Zeriel managed.

⁂

The day crept along with agonizing patience. Even though Zeriel had stopped throwing up every ten or so minutes, he was left with a steady feeling of nausea that gripped his stomach and wouldn't let go.

He'd finally managed to handle the discomfort as he stood on the bow with Ketik, looking out at the port in front of him. Black banners carrying Clan Ke's Stripes—two white vertical stripes with another white diagonal stripe crossing them—hung torn and ragged across the port. Ships burned at every dock and people stood around them, silent and unmoving.

"That doesn't bode well," Zeriel said.

"No," Ketik replied, "it doesn't. There seems to be a good number of survivors though. Perhaps they repelled the Te Et Sha and never needed our help."

"It's possible. They may not have committed a large force by land, anticipating Lushame would arrive with more by ship."

"Could be. But if we thought of that, you can be sure someone in Clan Ke did as well." Ketik pointed toward the port.

Zeriel looked where the Chief was pointing and saw a group of villagers crowding on the docks nearest to where they were approaching.

Several of the people raised outstretched arms, and though they weren't close enough to see details, Zeriel knew what they were doing. "I guess we can't hope that they want to welcome us with open arms, then." Just as he finished that sentence, an arrow whistled through the air and splashed into the water a short distance in front of them.

Ketik sighed. "I don't think so."

"Should we stop here, then? We'll be in range of those archers soon."

Ketik turned to face the crew. "Lower the sails and drop the anchor!"

The crew complied, and thankfully, as the ships behind saw what was happening, they followed Ketik's lead. Unfortunately, they didn't stop fast enough to stay out of range of the archers, which forced Zeriel and Ketik to step back as arrows impacted the bow of the ship.

"What now?" Zeriel asked.

"We take a lifeboat to port and see if we can convince them we're on their side."

"Should be simple enough." Zeriel glanced at the nearest lifeboat.

Ketik turned and called out to Ietenet, who was directing the crew as they finished tying everything down.

"Yes, Chief!" the man said, who immediately dropped what he was doing and approached.

"Select a few of the men to join us. We're going to port."

Ietenet looked past Ketik toward the arrows in the bow just as another one plunked into the wood there. He opened his mouth to object, paused, then shook his head slightly. "Right away," he said, then turned to two men and redirected them. Ketik walked to the lifeboat and Zeriel joined him.

"I thought for sure he was going to tell you how crazy you are," Zeriel said.

"He's a good man. I wouldn't have blamed him if he did." Ketik looked back and watched Ietenet give final orders as the two men hurried toward them.

Ketik looked to the stern where Chief Odinte leaned against the rail, watching them. "I'd like you to join us. It'll be good for Clan Ke to see that we're united in our cause."

The Chief surprised Zeriel again when she didn't object. Instead, she nodded her head, said, "Agreed," and walked over to join them.

The three stepped into the boat, joined by Ietenet's crewmen. The two crewmen untied the ropes holding the boat in place and lowered them into the water.

The current immediately pulled them away from the village, and the two crewmen hurried to the oars.

"I've got this," Zeriel said to them. The shadows were deepening with every passing day, so he had plenty to call forth, especially the ones he could feel lurking on the riverbed. The effort of commanding the shadows was becoming automatic, like moving a limb. So, with barely an effort, he willed the darkness to obey, and it did.

Dark tendrils lashed their way out of the water, attaching themselves to the bow of their boat, then extended into the distant port and attached to the docks there. The crowd that had accumulated there ran off at the sight. Zeriel didn't waste any time; he shortened the tendrils and drew them into port.

"You don't think that was a bit much?" Ketik asked. "They're going to think you're some kind of monster."

"They'll find out about what I can do eventually. At least this way they won't be shooting at us as we approach."

"Good point," Ketik said.

Zeriel pulled them the rest of the way to port and released the tendrils once the crewmen had tied them to the dock. The villagers watched in stunned silence as all five of them climbed out of the boat.

A group of archers rushed in with arrows drawn. "Don't move!" one of them said.

Ketik raised his hands in a placating gesture. "We're not here to attack you. I'm Ketik, Chief of Clan Gor."

The man who had addressed them looked at their ships in the river, then back at them. "Those are Clan Bale ships."

"Right," he said, then gestured to Odinte. "This is the Chief of Clan Bale. We departed from there early this morning."

"Liar!" The man said, the tip of his arrow trembling. "Why would the chiefs of Clan Gor and Clan Bale be sailing together? Not to mention that the Southern Clans have been wiped out, so you couldn't be from there anyway."

"We were very nearly destroyed, yes. But enough of us remained to fight back."

"Impossible."

Zeriel stepped up. "You survived. Is it any surprise that some of us did as well?"

The man's eyes narrowed. "The Southern Clans aren't skilled enough fighters to defend against the ones who attacked us."

One of the crewmen stepped toward the archers, "I'll show you unskilled—"

Ketik put his hand out to stop the man in his tracks. "The Te Et Sha are formidable. We probably would have been wiped out if we didn't have a secret weapon." He nodded toward Zeriel.

Taking that as his cue, Zeriel called shadow tendrils from the water around them, sending them high in the air like the arms of some gigantic sea creature. The archers lowered their bows as they gazed at the sight, several stepping back reflexively. Pleased with their response, he released his powers and let the tendrils dissipate.

When Ketik saw the shock on their faces, he added, "He also has some...unique abilities." He stepped closer to them, hands at his sides, but they stepped back as he did. Ketik sighed and said, "We weren't in time to save everyone in Clan Bale, but we had hoped to arrive here in time to help you. Perhaps stop the Te Et Sha in their tracks right here." Ketik looked out at the boats across the port, each engulfed in flames.

Zeriel followed the Chief's gaze and saw wrapped corpses piled onto the boats.

Ketik bowed his head. "We're sorry we were too late."

A man pushed through the crowd and stood in front of the archers. He was young, in his early to mid-twenties, and stood taller than the rest of his clansmen by a finger-width or two. The cotton shirt he wore stretched tight over his muscles, a juxtaposition to his round face and friendly smile. "No apologies needed, Chief Ketik. I'm sure we've all suffered losses at the hands of these—Te Et Sha, you called them?"

"Correct. They're a secret order of assassins who have decided to come out of the shadows. Their leader, Veshet, means to commit genocide across our lands and take control of Fei En Ar."

"*Only the strong survive*," the young man said.

Zeriel squeezed his hands into fists at the words. "Veshet has sent his forces across the land with their only mission to cull the weak from Fei En Ar," he said, practically growling the words.

The man nodded. "We surmised as much, though we didn't know their leader's name. I'm Aleber. I was made Chief of Clan Ke after my father was killed fighting these Te Et Sha." He turned to the crowd. "Clear a path for them. They're not our enemy." The crowd parted at the man's words as he turned back to Ketik, Odinte, and Zeriel. "Come, join me in the village hall. We've got more to discuss, I'm sure."

Ketik turned back to the two crewmen. "Head back to the ship. Let them know what's happening."

The men nodded and got back into the lifeboat and started untying it from the dock.

"Alright," Ketik said. "Lead the way."

❖

Aleber led them to the village hall. It was a large building to the north. By the look of it, the building had survived the attack mostly unscathed, save for a significant hole in the western wall covered by a large canvas that shifted in the wind. Inside, the center of the building came to a point, the rafters unhidden. A large seat at the back of the hall—the Chief's seat—faced inward and overlooked large tables with benches that filled the rest of the space.

Aleber took them to a spot near the front of the hall but didn't sit in the Chief's seat. Instead, they sat at one of the long tables in the front. Zeriel wasn't used to powerful men avoiding the chance to flaunt their power. This man's actions raised Zeriel's suspicions to an anxiety inducing degree. When he looked to Ketik, however, the Chief seemed more at ease by the gesture than bothered by it. Odinte seemed her normal skittish self, though now Zeriel knew not to completely trust that impression. He'd begun to wonder if the woman did that so others would underestimate her.

"How long has it been since the attack on your Clan?" Ketik asked.

"They attacked two days ago."

"How'd you fend them off without any warning?" Zeriel asked.

"Word had gotten to us about the attacks on the Southern Clans a month ago. Rumors about something happening in the Southern Clans bothered my father, so he sent scouting parties to the south at the outset of the light month. The party headed for Clan Din returned early, having encountered the Te Et Sha's army on their way north."

"How exactly did you find out about the Te Et Sha?" Ketik asked.

Aleber glanced at Zeriel before he answered, "Someone from Clan Din who claimed to have been captured by the assassins showed up one day. She spun an unbelievable story about being captured and thrown into a cage deep inside one of the Te Et Sha's camps. Then one day, a man who could command the shadows was caught, only to free himself and decimate the entire camp. He freed them, and instead of returning home, she fled to the Central Clans hoping to escape any more fighting."

"There were only a handful of barely trained young men in the camp," Zeriel said, waving off the Chief's implications. "They weren't exactly *elite*."

"Yes, well, at the time I didn't believe her stories about powers beyond the imagination. But when I saw you draw shadows from the depths of the river itself." The new Chief shook his head. "Let's just say that's why you're sitting here with me right now."

"Sounds like the advanced noticed kept your Clan from complete annihilation," Ketik said.

"Yes, but we aren't without our casualties."

"None of us are," Chief Odinte said, her face a mask of stoicism, though Zeriel knew the pain she felt underneath. He felt it too.

Ketik bowed his head. "My condolences. We've all lost much to these assassins. Your informant was being mostly truthful. Almost every survivor of the Southern Clans is either sitting in front of you or on our ships anchored in the river."

"I see," Aleber said. "I had hoped the report had been exaggerated." He paused in thought for a bit with a finger to his lips. "So, you're refugees then?"

"Not quite," Ketik responded. "Thanks to Zeriel here, we were able to eliminate all the Te Et Sha from Clan Bale before we sailed here. We were hoping to arrive in time to help you."

"If you've had him with you, how did they manage to practically wipe you all out."

"These powers are still relatively new to me," Zeriel said, "and I'm just starting to master in them."

"That," Ketik said, "and we've been one step behind the assassins from the start. Hence our tardiness arriving here."

"Assuming you would have arrived in time to protect us, what was your goal after that?"

"We hoped to convince your Clan to join us."

Aleber raised an eyebrow. "Join you to do what?"

"Destroy every last assassin in Fei En Ar," Zeriel said, "until we reach their leader Veshet and put him in the ground with them."

Aleber stared at him for a moment before addressing Ketik. "Is he always like that?"

"You have no idea," Ketik said with a smirk.

Aleber chuckled, which lightened the air around them, but then his face turned serious. "If Zeriel here is actually capable of what I've heard, and if it were in my power, I would lend you our strength, but things being the way they are right now, we need to focus on rebuilding."

"I understand. That's exactly what I told Zeriel when he arrived while the Te Et Sha were attacking our village. He helped us drive them off and I sent him away. It didn't take the Te Et Sha long to return to finish the job."

"We didn't get a second chance," Odinte added. "They swept in and overwhelmed us. Half of Clan Bale was put in cages, while the other half were slaughtered or put to work. The only reason we're still alive is thanks to these men and the soldiers they brought with them."

Zeriel leaned forward. "They're not going to stop just because you fended off one attack. Veshet doesn't just want to cleanse weakness from Fei En Ar, he wants to rule every clan."

"I believe you, but I can't force my people into another fight." Chief Aleber paused in thought. "I won't stop them from joining you, however."

"I wouldn't ask for anything more. Thank you Chief Aleber."

The young Chief stood up. "Now, as your first recruit, I have just one question. How are we planning to take out these bastards?"

CHAPTER FORTY-NINE

Another two hundred soldiers joined from Clan Ke. With their addition, the Coalition was formalized, and Aleber, after seeing how Ketik led the Southern Clans, decided not to challenge him for leadership. He and Chief Odinte formed a war council to make sure the wellbeing of all the clans was considered. Zeriel thought the move was ridiculous. Neither of them was a warrior, so why would they think they knew what should be done better than Ketik?

Given that the Te Et Sha had a two-day lead on the coalition, Ketik marched their forces toward Clan Pey the day after they'd arrived. Though he did leave behind a contingent of soldiers with their ships. Ketik wanted to hit them with their own tactics, sending half the men on the galleys to sail up the gulf while the other half attacked on land. It worked, and they drove the assassins out with minimal casualties.

Afterward, Zeriel pushed ahead of the Coalition, following the remaining Te Et Sha forces in a bid to wipe them out before they crossed into Northern Clan territory. He scoured the countryside, searching every forest, road, and hill for any sign of the assassins. He didn't find a trace of them before getting to Clan Nor in the Central Plains. The village had no walls despite being settled among the hills without any natural barriers. Banners showed two light blue stripes with a brown stripe crossing them diagonally against a white background—Clan Nor's stripes. The banners were untouched by violence and every building stood untouched.

Zeriel met with the Clan's Chief, Mishteel, an aged man with white streaks visible in his wheat-colored hair and wrinkles across his face. Despite that, the rest of his massive body was full of tightly packed muscles. The man confirmed that the Te Et Sha had never come to their village. Zeriel kept watch for an attack until the rest of the Coalition arrived, just in case. When they did, it was with nearly four hundred soldiers, thanks to their recruiting efforts in Clan Pey.

Momentum was on their side now, and after seeing how the clans were coming together, Clan Nor boosted the Coalition to six hundred strong. With those numbers, Zeriel started to believe they could succeed.

Their efforts in Clans Pey and Nor took the remaining weeks of the light month, giving Zeriel the transitioning shadows of twilight to power him. The darkness held him aloft and allowed him to soar northward over the treetops of the forest on his way to scout Clan Eten. He knew the village well, having visited often since it was the closest to the Te Et Sha stronghold. It also served as a major crossroads between the Central and Northern Clans, which meant that the largest road in Fei En Ar—the one that traveled from the northern tip to the southern shores—passed through it. All he had to do was follow that road and he'd find the village in no time.

Jekjarah appeared next to Zeriel, flying next to him in perfect sync to his movements. "Do you really think the village is still standing? Veshet would have gone straight through that village on his way to Ki Al Tesh."

"True. But he also needs that village standing if he's going to have strong trade between the Clans once he's done with his genocide."

"Ha! You really think Veshet is thinking that far ahead?"

Zeriel eyed the hallucination, who flashed his usual smug look when he thought he had made a good point. He often forgot that anything he said was something Zeriel was already thinking. "Probably not. But even he wouldn't abandon such a strategically important location."

"Twenty gold zaxes says the village is burned to the ground, without any survivors, just like the rest."

"You don't have any a single zax to your name, Jek."

"*I* happen to be a very successful merchant. *You're* the one without any money."

Zeriel smiled to himself and shook his head. "Fine. Make it fifty gold zaxes, then."

"Deal! Easiest coin I've ever made." With that said, the hallucination blinked out of existence.

Zeriel spent the rest of the journey with his attention on the colored lights of the forest. They would glow brighter each day as twilight transitioned to the next dark month. Eventually he saw the structure of Clan Eten's wall poking up from the forest canopy ahead of him. What would have taken him a little more than a day's travel on horseback took only a few hours with his powers. The wall that surrounded Clan Eten was as tall as the one in Shyal, forming a complete circle around the village. As he approached, the steady glow of white vine lanterns that emanated from inside the wall became visible, turning the Clan into a beacon in the middle of the forest. Closing in, he noticed the first sign of trouble. Two torn banners flapped pathetically on either side of the main gate. They were torn haphazardly, but Zeriel could still make out the Stripes of Clan Bale on what was left—three wide teal stripes with a diagonal teal stripe crossing them on a white field.

After spotting a point on the top of the wall, Zeriel drew more shadows from the forest to surround him. He gathered them underneath him and pushed off his tether, launching himself into a wide arch that deposited him on top of the wall.

Once he landed, he quickly shifted his vision to check for the heat of the guards posted on the wall. Nothing appeared.

"Shouldn't the top of the wall be guarded?" Jekjarah asked after materializing close by. He saw nothing more than a subtle shift in his amplified vision where Jekjarah manifested. "I was hoping to see a little bloodshed."

Zeriel had an idea of what the answer to the hallucination's question was, but he'd have to verify. The southern gate was close to his landing spot, so he leaned over the outer edge of the wall to search for it.

Just a short distance to his left, he saw the giant gates closed and flanked by two Te Et Sha, identifiable by the black leathers they still wore. They were young men, obvious by the way they passed the time in conversation instead of staying vigilant on their guard duty. A clear sign these were Eililta's trainees.

"I wonder what they're guarding," Jekjarah said, giving voice to Zeriel's thoughts.

He stepped to the inner edge of the wall and looked out into the village. With his heat sight, the light of the white vine lanterns was surprisingly diminished, making it easier to distinguish the white glow of bodies below. People moved through the streets as though nothing was wrong, and street vendors sold their wares openly. The buildings that showed signs of recent damage also showed patches where repairs had been attempted. Despite all that, something still felt off.

"Have you noticed there are no children?" Jekjarah asked.

Zeriel looked up to the sky to find the moon showing just past mid-day. Jekjarah was right, there should have been children around. Clan Eten had a problem with its street urchin population the last time Zeriel had come through. They should have been causing their mischief by now. Zeriel shifted to his normal vision and realized immediately what he was missing.

Most of the people moving through the village were Te Et Sha. Those carried themselves with relaxed confidence. The others were all men, and they moved about with tense muscles and avoided gazes. Likewise, the shop owners were tense when interacting with the assassins. They made clear efforts to complete transactions quickly and send them on their way.

"Looks like you owe me fifty gold zaxes, Jek," Zeriel whispered.

"Do you offer a payment plan?" Jekjarah said, standing next to him. "Something that doesn't start for at least, say one hundred years?"

Zeriel used his shadows to sneak across the top of the wall toward the northern gate. He kept his eyes on the village inside as he moved but saw only more of the same. "Where are all the women and children?"

"Do you really want me to answer that question?" Jekjarah asked.

"No." Zeriel knew what the assassins had been doing, he didn't need the hallucination to speak it aloud.

When the northern gate came into view, Zeriel looked past it, letting his eyes scan over the main road to the north. He skidded to a stop, frozen in terror at what he saw.

Jekjarah stepped beside him. "How?"

"I—" Try as he might, Zeriel found himself lost for words. He could only watch as a line of white vine lanterns stretched down the main road from Clan Eten's northern gate all the way to the horizon. Hundreds, perhaps thousands of men were approaching. "That can't be Veshet's army. Can it?"

Jekjarah turned toward him, fear written all over his face. "What else would it be?"

"Where would he have gotten all those men?"

"There's only one explanation, Zeriel."

The hallucination was right, and it meant Zeriel had precious little time to return to the Coalition. He jumped off the outer side of the wall and called on his shadows to carry him southward, pushing his speed to its absolute limits. And there was only one reason he needed to, something that caused his heart to pound in his chest. A realization that was obvious when he asked himself how Veshet could have built his army so large in such a short amount of time. He couldn't accept until he'd said the words out loud.

"The Northern Clans have joined the Te Et Sha."

Jekjarah appeared flying next to him. "There's no way our forces can stand against that."

"We may still have a chance," he said, grasping for any reason to hold on to some glimmer of hope. "Few of them are Te Et Sha. Most of them are recruits from the Northern Clans."

"Recruits that outnumber us five to one. Even if they aren't assassins, that's too great an advantage to overcome."

Zeriel's thoughts raced almost as quickly as his body flew over the trees. Chromatic streaks of the forest's lights passed below him as he tried to grasp onto a solution. As much as he tried there was a single thought that he couldn't shake. A desperate gambit that quickly became the only solution he could fathom.

Jekjarah looked over to him with wide eyes. "You can't be serious. There's no way—"

"It's our only chance," Zeriel said, then abruptly turned to the west.

CHAPTER FIFTY

The moon hung just above the southern horizon by the time Zeriel arrived at the Coalition's camp. It stood against the tree line of the forest on the northern edge of the Central Plains. He landed at the edge of the camp where guards kept watch, careful not to jostle the contents of the pack he was carrying.

The guards jumped as he landed in a blast of black smoke, pulling their swords halfway out of their sheaths. When he stepped into the light, they relaxed and returned their swords. "Lord of Shadows," one of them said, with a bow. The men began calling him that since their victory at Clan Pey. He hated the name.

The guard straightened at his approach and said, "The leaders have been waiting anxiously for your return."

Zeriel interpreted the message underneath those words. *They want to know why you're so late.* "I'm headed there now," he said, as he stalked past the pair. Just inside the camp, hundreds of men trained in an open field. They'd shortened the grass there, removing the bioluminescent part of the plant and plunging the area into darkness. To compensate, they'd posted white vine lanterns around to light the area. The soldiers trained in groups of five, shifting through the formations he'd taught them. After the battle at Clan Pey, he'd refined their strategy, confident the changes would make a huge difference in the coming fight. He'd been wrong.

Images of the vast army marching their way into Clan Eten haunted him. Though he didn't know much about the tactics of war, he knew that at some point, numbers overwhelmed even the most skilled soldiers. The Coalition's forces were better, stronger, and more equipped to fight the Te Et Sha than ever before, but he wasn't sure that would matter anymore.

Working with the men, passing down and deepening his own knowledge, had become one of the most fulfilling things he'd ever done in his life. Walking by them now, he ached to join. Instead, he turned away and headed straight to the command tent. There were more pressing matters, for now.

The command tent loomed in the center of camp, its towering wooden poles rising higher than those around them. Its thick canvas shifted reluctantly as the wind tried to bring it down. Two guards flanked the tent's entrance to keep those inside unbothered. As he approached, one of them opened the flap of the tent. "They've been waiting for you."

Zeriel nodded to the man and entered.

A large table positioned in the middle of the tent was the only piece of furniture inside. Behind it, against the canvas on the far side of the tent were seven banners, six of which more the stripes of the clans who joined the Coalition. He eyed Clan Ra's banner. They'd insisted on including it, despite his objections.

Between the clans' banners, larger than the rest, stood a seventh banner with a new set of stripes—gold, blue, and silver vertical stripes crossed by gold and silver diagonal stripes over a field of navy blue. They were the newly christened Stripes of the Coalition, a symbol of the clans joining together.

On the table lay a large and detailed map of Fei En Ar, held down at the edges with simple rocks. Hastily carved wooden figures were strategically placed on the map to represent the various armies involved. A wooden ship sat in the Gulf pointing north.

Around the table were five Clan Chiefs. Ketik stood at the center of the group, carefully analyzing the map. The others followed Odinte and Aleber's lead, collectively naming Ketik the High Chief of the

Coalition.

Aleber from Clan Ke was next to Ketik, wearing a long tunic covered in his Clan's stripes, brown pants and leather boots. His signature smile stretched across his face as he watched the High Chief carefully.

Odinte stood next to Aleber. She wore a dark blue dress and wrung her hands nervously, showing much less patience than Aleber. She looked like she could barely stifle the millions of questions that fought to burst from her lips.

To Ketik's other side, Mishteel held a lazy posture as he gripped a war hammer slung across his shoulders and yawned.

Finally, the Chief of Clan Nor, Quatesh, leaned a hip on the table next to Mishteel with her arms crossed. Her raven black hair was pulled into a tight ponytail. Her stern expression couldn't mask the elegant beauty of her features. Likewise, her leather armor failed to hide her perfect curves. Indeed, Zeriel found it hard not to stare for several beats longer than was appropriate. Strapped to her armor were two swords on her hips, accompanied by daggers tied to her sides, starting just under her arms and continuing down to her calves. Those blades, and the dangerous way she carried herself, helped to keep the men in the tent on their best behavior.

All eyes fell on Zeriel when he stepped into the tent. Odinte took a single step back as he did.

"Finally, you're back," Ketik said. "Did you run into some trouble out there?"

"Nothing like what you're probably thinking," Zeriel answered as he approached the table, "but we do have a problem."

Mishteel smiled broadly. "A problem for my hammer, I hope."

"I wish that's all it would take to solve it, Chief Mishteel," Zeriel replied, then launched into his report.

"That's not a problem," Mishteel said after he finished, "it's a suicide mission."

"Beggars can't be choosers, Chief," Quatesh said, slapping the old man on the back.

"This changes everything," Aleber said. "We can't possibly win against an army of that size."

"Even so," Odinte said. "We can't just do nothing."

"We could join them," Aleber suggested, frowning. His smile had disappeared during Zeriel's report.

Ketik reeled back in surprise. "Just roll over and let them get away with everything they've done?"

"They left many in your Clan alive after you showed them strength. Meanwhile, they decimated the rest of the Southern Clans?"

Ketik huffed. "They returned to Clan Gor weeks later to finish the job."

Aleber gestured to Zeriel. "The Northern Clans are clearly alive and well. What did they do differently than us? Perhaps it's time to accept the inevitable, rather than sprint toward a pointless death."

"Coward," Quatesh said, her voice low and dangerous as her hands inched toward the blades at her sides.

"Call me what you want," Aleber responded, undeterred, "but the way I see it, I'm the only one thinking rationally."

Ketik sighed and held up a hand to Quatesh. Her posture loosened, and she crossed her arms again. "I hate to say this, but Aleber might actually have a point."

Mishteel glared at Zeriel. "So, everything we've done, and everyone who died fighting them, was all for nothing?"

Ketik faced him, standing his ground against the Chief's challenge. "That's not at all what I'm saying. I simply believe we should consider every alternative before deciding our path."

Mishteel didn't move a muscle and spoke through gritted teeth. "We will never surrender to tyrants and murders, High Chief."

Zeriel sighed at the Chiefs' drama and set his pack on the table, knocking down the wooden figures. All eyes fell on the bag as glass clinked heavily inside. "We have an opportunity, but it's probably our worst option. But, it's the only thing I can say for sure will even the playing field."

Ketik grabbed the pack and poured its contents onto the table. Hundreds of tiny bottles rolled out, their contents an aggressive red-purple color with swirls of black. "Is that what I think it is?"

"What is it?" Odinte asked as she grabbed a bottle and inspected it.

"We could turn nearly half our forces into soldiers on equal footing with the Te Et Sha."

Odinte gasped. "Eleshar's Curse," she whispered.

"What is that?" Mishteel asked.

"It's the potion that gives the Te Et Sha their enhanced bodies," Zeriel responded.

"Then what are we waiting for?" He snatched a bottle and moved to pull out the stopper.

Ketik seized Mishteel's hand and met his eyes. "What's the survival rate of those who take this, Zeriel?"

"Thirty percent. On Average."

Mishteel released the stopper and slowly set the bottle back on the table.

A brief silence flowed through the tent as the Chiefs eyed the potions.

"We couldn't possibly sacrifice so many," Odinte said. "We're not barbarians."

"It would be voluntary," Ketik said. "Every man would be made aware of the risks."

"Are we really considering this?" Aleber asked.

"Every soldier in the Coalition will die if we attack without this," Zeriel said. "At least this way, some will live, and have a chance at victory."

"Are we forgetting that we have the Lord of Shadows on our side?" Odinte asked, then faced Zeriel. "Surely your powers would be enough to tilt the odds in our favor."

"I'm only one man. In every battle we've fought, I've been a deciding factor in the outcome, I admit that. But I still needed others to play their part. Against several thousand men, I'm sure I'd be overrun with the rest of you."

Quatesh leaned a hand on the table. "If we cut our entire forces down by seventy percent, I can't imagine the rest will be enough, enhanced or not, to tackle the numbers you're talking about."

"You'd be surprised," Zeriel said. "The Te Et Sha aren't trained to fight like normal soldiers. They're assassins, used to stealth and subterfuge. In traditional combat, our forces have found ways to capitalize on that, tip the scales ever so slightly in their favor. With a large group of soldiers, enhanced by Eleshar's Curse, we'll have a decisive edge."

Quatesh snorted. "Those are a lot of assumptions to bet hundreds of lives on."

"It's that, be completely wiped out," Zeriel gestured to Aleber, "or join them."

Mishteel shook his head. "No good choices, then."

"We're all Chiefs here," Ketik said. "We should be accustomed to choosing the best worst option."

"Enough chattering, then," Odinte said. "The way I see it, if we're going to fight, we have no choice but to use Eleshar's Curse. It's that, or surrender, and Clan Bale will not surrender."

"Nor will Clan Nor," Quatesh said.

Mishteel stood tall. "Clan Pey will drink whatever poison you give us and crush those assassins, and any traitors that join them."

They all turned to Aleber, who sighed. "Fine, you can ask my men if they want to take your potion."

Ketek nodded. "It's decided then." He turned to Zeriel. "How many bottles do you have?"

"I took everything I could find in the Te Et Sha stronghold. I'm not sure exactly how many there are, but I would guess somewhere around three hundred."

"That would leave us with less than a hundred soldiers, by your math," Mishteel said.

Aleber appeared visibly shaken. "Eleshar help us."

"Let's gather our forces," Ketik said, "and hope we get three hundred volunteers."

∴

The moon set on a hundred and fifty pyres, radiating their flickering orange light across the camp. It overwhelmed the glow of the plain's flora, casting a garish light on the macabre scene. The heat of their fires combined to create a near burning touch onto Zeriel's exposed skin.

This wasn't the first time he'd watched hundreds of people die after taking the Te Et Sha's potion, but this time felt different. He thought back to the aftermath of the battle at Clan Bale, watching men burying the dead. The helplessness he felt in that moment mirrored what he felt now, yet somehow stronger than before. His fingernail bit into his palms as he clenched his fists. The responsibility he'd felt for these soldiers had deepened. He'd known them. Trained them. Taught them to be better soldiers. And though each one volunteered to take Eleshar's Curse, he couldn't shake the feeling that he'd failed them.

He stood next to Ketik and four Chiefs. Mishteel, no matter how much the others argued, insisted on taking Eleshar's Curse. Even Zeriel felt anxious over the decision. Now wasn't the time to lose a key leader. But no one would take away his right to make the choice.

"How are the survivors?" Odinte asked.

"Being watched over by the healers," Ketik responded.

"And Mishteel?"

"He's with them. One of the few who remained conscious throughout the process."

"How soon will they recover?" Aleber asked.

"Several days for most," Zeriel said, "though some might take longer."

"Half survived," Quatesh said. "More than you predicted. Their recovery might be quicker, as well."

He studied the Chief, a darkness covering her features, deeper than usual. "In my experience, those who choose to become assassins are broken in some way. It could be that our soldiers are made from something stronger and more capable. If this outcome is anything to go by,

I'd expect they'll outperform even the Te Et Sha when given the chance."

She seemed to ponder that for a moment. "That's an uncharacteristically positive opinion from the Lord of Shadows." She shifted her gaze back over the sea of burning bodies. "I pray to Eleshar you're right. This sacrifice cannot be in vain."

"What will we call them?" Aleber asked.

The others regarded him questioningly.

"You can't expect soldiers to risk their lives and become the tip of our army's spear, then not be given a title."

"Zeriel has already given them a title," Quatesh said.

"I did?"

She turned to him and nodded. "You called them enhanced."

"The Enhanced?" Aleber asked, touching his fingers to his chin, considering the name. "A bit boring."

"Zeriel," Ketik said. "I expect you to work with the Enhanced as soon as they're able. You'll have only a few days to get them ready for battle." Clearly, he wasn't in the mood to debate the title.

Zeriel swallowed nervously. A few days were too few to prepare them properly. The weight of those lives settled on his shoulders, and his doubts grew. "I hope that'll be enough."

Ketik turned around to leave. "It'll have to be," he said as he marched away.

CHAPTER FIFTY-ONE

Zeriel stepped onto the training field with Quatesh, staring out at the tall grass at its edge, watching the soft amber glow of its inflorescence as it wavered in the breeze. The entire army was already spread throughout the area training. It had taken some time, but they'd finally structured the Coalition into three different companies. The Enhanced formed one of those companies and dubbed themselves Vanguard Company. They were half the size of the other two but just watching them train in proximity, the difference in abilities between them was obvious. The other two groups were content to simply be called First and Second Company.

"They seem eager," Zeriel said.

"I don't think that's the right word," Quatesh responded. "In your early days, how did you feel in the days leading up to an assassination job?"

"Terrified." Zeriel glanced at the Chief. "I ran through the plan in my head a thousand times."

Quatesh nodded. "It's more like that. Though they're seasoned soldiers, most of them have never fought a force as large as what's waiting for us at Clan Eten. Many have never faced the Te Et Sha, only having the accounts of others to go by, which feeds even more into their anxiety, and drives them to train."

"Makes sense." Zeriel said. He shifted his vision and hundreds of glowing bodies appeared. Satisfied, he shifted back to normal. Checking those around him became a habit since he'd left Clan Ra. Anytime he started to question who was real and who wasn't, he'd shift his vision and check.

With that done, Zeriel stepped away from Quatesh. "I better get to Vanguard Company. We don't have much time."

"We never do," she said. "I'll start with First Company and see how they do today."

"Good luck," Zeriel called.

The Enhanced were in the process of testing their new abilities. Mishteel had them jumping, sprinting, striking training dummies with wooden practice swords, even seeing how far they could throw rocks. The entirety of Vanguard Company seemed to be having the time of their lives as they became acquainted with their new bodies. Zeriel remembered feeling similarly. For him, it faded quickly once he discovered that everyone else could outperform him.

Once Mishteel noticed Zeriel coming, he stopped what he was doing and sprinted to him. He stopped clumsily, jumping on one foot from the momentum, and laughed at his awkwardness. "You've been like this the whole time?"

"Almost. I'm—"

"Race me," Mishteel interrupted.

"What?"

"Race me, Zeriel. I want to see how I compare to one of the Te Et Sha."

"You want to compare yourself to the Worst One?"

Mishteel was taken aback for a moment, then laughed heartily. "Worst One or no, you were faster than me before." He took a starting pose and pointed. "To that training dummy," he said pointing. It was about fifty yards away.

Zeriel took a starting pose himself and nodded.

"Ready. Go!"

The two sprinted and, as expected, Mishteel quickly pulled away. It lasted one, maybe two seconds, but the Chief beat Zeriel by almost ten yards.

"Would you look at that!" Mishteel said, clapping Zeriel on the back. "I feel twenty years younger!"

Zeriel breathed an exasperated sigh. "We should get to the training."

"Right." Mishteel called the Enhanced to form up. They hurried into formation in front of Zeriel and the Chief. "The Lord of Shadows here will be giving us all some training to help us get used to our new abilities."

"Well, mostly to help you better understand how the Te Et Sha fight. It looks like you're already getting the hang of being enhanced." Zeriel inspected the formation and pointed at the first person he noticed with a practice sword. "You there, come up here."

The man started at the attention and nervously jogged up to Zeriel. He misjudged his speed and stumbled when he tried to stop, almost falling on his face. Several snickers sounded from the formation.

"Quiet!" Mishteel chided. The men quickly obeyed and straightened up.

"Strike at me." Zeriel said to the man.

"Okay," he said. He steeled his nerves and took a standard sword fighting stance, both hands holding the sword with the tip held out in front of him. When he moved it was quick and sure. Zeriel could tell he'd had years of practice with the weapon. His enhanced body still threw his off, and when he brought up the sword over his head to strike down, he over swung and left himself open.

Zeriel stepped into the strike and executed a perfect takedown, slamming the man on his back. He followed the Enhanced to the ground and held a wooden knife to his throat.

The man had the wind knocked out of him and was struggling to catch his breath, unaware of the knife at his throat. By the looks on the rest of the Enhanced's faces, they all understood what had happened.

Zeriel stood up and put the wooden knife back in his belt. "Until now I've shown you how to overwhelm your enemy, which was effective in the past. But you're on the same level as the Te Et Sha now. That means you need to know how to fight them one on one, and to do that, you need to remember the most important thing about how they fight.

"They'll never come at you straight, as your friend here just did. Everything is about deception. If it looks like they're unarmed, they're more armed than you. If you're reacting to an attack, it's just a distraction for the real strike." He gestured to the man still on the ground, a sour look growing on his face. "Now, I'll start with showing Chief Mishteel everything I know, then the two of us will work with each of you individually."

Mishteel stepped up. "Right then, back to your training, men. We'll call you up when we're ready."

The Enhanced shuffled away and the man Zeriel had demonstrated on stood up, and furrowed his brow at him before joining the rest of them.

When they were a sufficient distance away, Mishteel turned to Zeriel. "You've never been part of a team, have you?"

Jekjarah appeared behind the Chief and stepped in front of the man. "What a weird question," he said as he studied Mishteel's features, his face mere inches from the Chief.

"I can't say I ever needed to," Zeriel responded, trying his best to ignore the hallucination.

Mishteel nodded his head as if he expected as much. He pointed at four different men, each wearing a red cloth from the left side of their belts and standing at the front of four distinct groups of soldiers. "Those men there. Can you tell me what their roles are in Vanguard Company?"

Zeriel studied them, hoping to glean something from watching them work, but he couldn't figure it out. They'd decided when they created ranks for the Coalition what those red cloths would mean, so he went with the obvious. "They're the platoon leaders."

"Right. What is his name?" Mishteel pointed at the man second from the right.

"I have no idea," Zeriel answered.

Mishteel huffed and pointed at another. "What's his wife's name?"

"*What?*"

"What's his wife's name? It's a simple question, Zeriel."

"How in the depths of Eleshar would I know that?"

Mishteel faced Zeriel with a serious look. "By talking to him. Not as a soldier, but as a man."

"As a—" Zeriel was flabbergasted. "Why would I need to do that?"

Mishteel put a hand on Zeriel's shoulder, directing him away from Vanguard Company. "Let's take a walk."

They circled the training area close to the tall grass border in silence for a time before Mishteel spoke up. "Who are you?"

Another confusing question. Zeriel started to wonder if those were the only kind Mishteel knew how to ask. "What do you mean?"

"Are you an assassin? A Coalition member? The Lord of Shadows? Who is Zeriel?"

Jekjarah appeared on the other side of Mishteel and leaned forward to look around him. "That's a good one. I don't think you've figured that out yet."

The hallucination had a point. He wasn't what he was, but, like that old man had said, he hadn't quite made it to his next destination. Hoping to discover something new about himself, he took an inventory.

Was he an assassin? No. He'd left that life behind him when he left Shyal after Lavel's death.

Coalition member? As he thought about it, he never really felt like a member of the Coalition. More like a mercenary that helped along the way. But no, that wasn't right, it was just his feeling of inadequacies coming through. He was there from the beginning and had a hand in its formation. So yes, he was a member of the Coalition.

What about the Lord of Shadows? The name still grated on him, but he supposed others, after seeing what he could do, would see him as that. It wasn't wrong to say his power had quickly become a part of who he was.

To Mishteel's credit, he waited patiently as Zeriel worked through his answer before he finally turned to the Chief and said, "Some of all of those, I guess. And probably more. Murderer, kidnapper, and insane man rejected by his family and his home. Probably more things that I can't name."

A smile crept onto Mishteels face. "Good." He pointed back at the Vanguard Company. "And just like you are a product of all those things, so are they a product of their successes, failures, loves, and losses.

"You see them as soldiers and nothing more. I want you to look at them as men, with lives and experiences that have shaped who they are."

"Okay," Zeriel said, turning to watch the Enhanced. He tried to see them as Mishteel described. It hadn't been obvious to him before, but now he noticed how they all looked the same to him. Not individuals, but a single organism of war. Soldiers.

They'll kill you if you give them the chance.

Why does Mishteel want you to let your guard down?

Zeriel grimaced.

Wait, why is the Chief looking at you like that?

Zeriel looked up at Mishteel and saw a soft expression on his face.

How dare he pity you!

Kill him!

"Shut up," Zeriel hissed through gritted teeth, his eyes squeezed shut as if that would banish the voices. His fists clenched reflexively.

"This is difficult for you, isn't it?"

He couldn't risk losing focus to reply or he might give in to his voices. It took a while before they quieted. "It's nothing I haven't dealt with before."

The Chief put a hand on his shoulder. "But you don't have to carry the burden alone anymore."

Not once in Zeriel's life had he considered someone carrying the burden of his insanity *with* him. Others either abandoned or abused him, but no one stepped in to support. Yet, here was someone who wasn't walking away from or trying to exploit him. No, Mishteel was *helping* him. It defied all reason.

Zeriel was distracted when he caught a glimpse of Ketik in the distance talking with men in the other companies. They looked comfortable around the High Chief, but their body language was still respectful, and they even laughed together for a moment. Ketik took time to correct some of their techniques, and even sparred with a few of them briefly. He'd known it from the start—felt the air of leadership the man exuded without effort—Ketik truly cared about his men. There was something more there that Zeriel had just now noticed. Ketik stewarded these men; made sure they were properly cared for, trained, and grew on a personal level.

With a deep breath Zeriel nodded to Mishteel, finally understanding what the Chief was trying to get him to see. So, he watched Vanguard Company. He noticed one of the men struggling more than the others. It was obvious to Zeriel what the man was doing wrong, and he could easily correct the mistake.

Another of the men crossed his sight and Zeriel noticed a thick, ugly scar that traveled down the left side of his face and down part of his neck. He wondered what the story was behind it. The whisper of a smile pulled at the edges of his mouth as he finally understood. "Thanks Chief," he said as he stepped toward the men. "I know what to do now."

"It seems you do."

Zeriel walked up to the man he saw struggling a moment ago. He'd been trying to scale the twenty-foot wooden wall obstacle but was consistently several inches short of grabbing the ledge. The man kept trying, though, which went from laudable, to sad that he couldn't accept the truth, to admirable in his determination.

"You," Zeriel called to the man.

He looked at Zeriel and snapped to attention, breathing heavily. "Yes, Lord of Shadows?"

Zeriel waved away the comment. "None of that. Just call me Zeriel."

The comment put a nervous look on the man's face. "Yes Lord—

er—Zeriel."

"At ease and relax. I'm not going to bite you."

The man relaxed his posture, but still looked uncertain.

"I noticed you're having a hard time getting over that wall."

The man huffed. "I've been trying all morning, but I just can't seem to get the height necessary. I'm starting to think I'm just not as strong as the others. Everyone else cleared this so easily."

Zeriel understood how that felt. "Your technique is off, that's all. Here, let me show you." For the next half an hour Zeriel walked through how to use momentum and the natural mechanics of his body to launch him up. It took several tries, but eventually the man got the right combination of both and launched himself so high he hit the ledge with his chest and hung there for a moment with his arms hooked over the top.

Cheers erupted from the men nearby and the man threw a triumphant hand in the air which caused him to lose his grip on the wall and fall backwards, landing on his back and knocking the wind out of himself. Laughter erupted from those same cheering voices, but Zeriel couldn't detect a hint of ridicule in them.

Once the man caught his breath, Zeriel helped him up. "Good work. What's your name?"

"Jetsuda," the man said as he brushed the dirt off his clothes.

"I'm Zeriel."

Jetsuda paused and looked at Zeriel with a strange expression. Jekjarah appeared behind the man. "What, is this the first time you talked to another person?" he hallucination said to Zeriel.

A wave of embarrassment slammed into Zeriel and his mind went blank.

"Right, I know." Jetsuda said finally.

"Okay," Zeriel said hurriedly, "well...keep up the good work." He turned and hurried away just as some of the other Enhanced jogged up to congratulate Jetsuda on his success.

A few feet away, Mishteel stood having watched the entire

interaction, an infuriating smile plastered on his face. "What, have you never talked to another person before?" he said playfully.

Jekjarah blinked into existence between the two men. "That's what I said!"

"Shut up," Zeriel said to Jekjarah.

"Sorry," Michteel said with his hands up in surrender. "You don't have much experience connecting with people, do you?"

He was bad at everything, so it only made sense he would be bad at that, too. "I guess not."

"Well, not bad for your first try." Mishteel looked across the field of training Enhanced. "There!" He pointed at a man training on a sparring dummy. "Let's go talk to him!" He put a hand on Zeriel's back and all but shoved him forward.

Jekjarah followed, skipping along behind them. "Oh, this is going to be *fun!*"

CHAPTER FIFTY-TWO

The underbrush of the forest around Clan Eten was aglow with a strong radiance now that the sun had disappeared completely from the sky. This didn't restrict Zeriel's use of his powers, not like the bright sunlight of the light months.

Zeriel took a step toward the tree line, his feet cushioned by shadows to make them completely silent. He'd come up with the idea when reflecting on how he cushioned his landings after taking flight. To his delight, it worked perfectly to silence his steps. With the rest of his body wrapped in a dark mist, he was silent and invisible.

He stood about a hundred feet from where the forest ended and the wall of Clan Eten rose out of the ground. Crossing that distance would seem endless for attackers when arrows, rocks, and other defensive weapons were raining down on them from the top of that wall. The work to keep that field clear had a consequence that tilted in Zeriel's favor. It removed the bioluminescence and left the distance covered in a near-complete and natural darkness.

Jekjarah appeared next to him. "This feels good, sneaking around, stalking and killing like an assassin again. I didn't realize how much I missed it."

"It's different this time, though," Zeriel whispered.

"Because you never had an entire army behind you, their chances of success or failure hinging on you executing your mission?"

A spike of nervous energy ran through Zeriel at the thought. "Exactly." He took a deep breath to calm himself and thought back to the last few days of training with the Enhanced. They'd turned out to be some of the best soldiers in the army and as a result took to their new abilities quickly. They'd stretched Zeriel to the limits of his skills for those three days. And with Mishteel's prompting, got to know some of them quite well.

The intensity of that training instilled a confidence in his abilities he'd never had before. Not because he won every sparring match, but because he didn't lose them all. He'd decided not to use his powers in the training, relishing the challenge for the first time in his life. By the end, the sparring moved in slow motion and his awareness in combat had expanded.

Zeriel stepped forward, ready to sprint across the field when his voices exploded in his head.

You're weak.

You'll die.

The men you trained will die with you!

It's what you deserve.

Never be strong enough!

Driven to his knees, Zeriel's chest tightened and every muscle in his body tensed. The voices hammered at the walls of his sanity, and he covered his ears to try and shut them out. It had been years since the voices had overwhelmed him like this. "Enough," he hissed through clenched teeth.

The voices, unbelievably, fell silent as Shemua appeared before him. She wore her stained clothing exactly like the last time he'd seen her, but this time her face was twisted with anger. "You're too weak for this, Zeriel."

"Go away," he whispered.

"No!" she screamed as she reached down, grabbed a rock, and threw it at him.

Zeriel watched as the hallucinated rock flew toward him. When it touched his forehead, he thought he felt pressure there and ripped his head back in shock. He righted himself and when he looked back,

Shemua was gone.

"What was that?" Jekjarah asked.

Zeriel flinched at his voice, eyeing the hallucination warily. "Just some new tricks my mind is playing on me." For the time being, he couldn't dwell on what had just happened. A growing anxiety that told him he was running late. Still, he hesitated, wondering if a hallucinated rock had really touched him.

"Go Zeriel," Jekjarah prompted. "You'll have plenty of time to figure that out when this is over."

He closed his eyes and refocused, tensing and relaxing one muscle at a time until his head was clear again. "And if I die tonight, it won't matter anyway." Zeriel's focus closed in on the task at hand, and Jekjarah disappeared.

A quick shift changed his lenses to heat sight, and he sprinted to the wall. With his feet still cushioned and a cloud of darkness for cover, he became a phantom, streaking imperceptibly across the field. It took seconds to cross the distance and just as he reached the wall, he summoned more shadows to carry him into the air.

He flew inches from the wall, eyes locked on the edge ahead of him. He slowed his ascent until he could peek just barely over the top and hovered there. A quick scan revealed nothing. Not a single guard patrolled that section of the wall. Zeriel lifted himself over the end and stepped on the top of the wall.

One of the advantages of his heat sight was he could see anything that gave off heat, even at a distance, and even in the dark. That's how he knew that not a single soul stood on the walls of Clan Eten.

"Mud and stones," Jekjarah said from his left. "I was looking forward to some glorious bloodshed."

"Something's wrong." Zeriel whispered.

"You're just being paranoid."

Zeriel stalked to the inner edge of the wall to spy on the village. The streets were empty save for a single drunk, presumably stumbling his way home.

"Doesn't look like anything's wrong," Jekjarah said.

"It's hard to believe they'd be so incompetent as to leave the wall unguarded when they have plenty of manpower to cover it."

"Hubris, plain and simple."

Was this what he thought, or just another example of his inexperience in the tactics of war? "You're probably right," he said, deciding he couldn't let his fears stop him. "Let's get back on track." Zeriel hurried to the southern gate. This part of the plan relied on him clearing the guards on the wall, then taking out the ones watching over the southern gate. With the first part unnecessary, he focused on the second.

A single lantern lit the gate below and the two guards there. Their own shadows were enough for Zeriel, even at this distance, to do his work. He pulled them into several points and brought them upward into a mass of spikes under their owners' feet. The move was so quick the guards barely let out a sound before they dropped dead.

"Bah," Jekjarah exclaimed. "All this murder from a distance. It's just so *boring!*"

It was hard to admit that his bloodlust still existed, but the deaths of those men did feel empty. Zeriel released his power and let the men fall to the ground. After a few heartbeats, dark figures emerged from the forest and stalked toward the gate. Mishteel led the Enhanced to begin the infiltration of the city.

His anxiety grew with each success. This was too easy, and as he gathered a dark cloud around him, pulling it tight and springing forward, he started questioning the next part of his mission. He rose a few inches from the wall and flew, moving faster than he would have dared before. Concentrating on speed, he followed the wall in a circle. As he approached the northern gate he looked out past the walls and saw a field of tents covering the northern field and stretching north along the main road. Strangely, the camp didn't look nearly large enough to hold thousands of soldiers.

When the scouts had reported this back to Ketik and the Chiefs, they'd assumed either Zeriel had exaggerated his initial estimate, or most of the forces were garrisoning inside the village walls. Whatever the truth was, it didn't matter. His mission was the same either way.

The moment he reached the northern gate he launched himself off the wall, eliminating the gate's guards as he fell with spikes made from their shadows. At about thirty feet above the ground, he launched forward, calling up a field of spears from the ground that decimated the tents in a twenty-foot circle around him. Shifting to his left he continued his flight, inky black lances erupting before him and disappearing behind as he swept across the enemy's camp.

Once he got to the north edge, he turned in a circle, going the other way to continue his sweep. After his third sweep, he'd decimated every tent in the northern field. That done, he flew over the main road and started clearing the tents pitched farther along it.

"Is this a bit...easy?" Jekjarah said.

A look to Zeriel's right showed only a slight waver in the air where Jekjarah was manifesting. He turned his focus back on his task. "Things can't always go against us, Jek. Luck owes us one at this point. Doesn't it?" He didn't have to look at the hallucination to know the face he made.

"They knew we were coming."

"Damn it!" Once again, the hallucination gave voice to his own thoughts, but Zeriel didn't change his course.

"What are you doing?"

"I can't leave my job unfinished on a hunch. We'll wrap up here and find Ketik."

The camp stretched northward for a mile. When Zeriel reached the last of the tents, his anxiety was at its peak. Each second that passed stretched into an agonizing eternity as he became increasingly certain they were playing right into the Te Et Sha's plans.

When he finally arrived at the northern gate, the Coalition's soldiers were rummaging through the remains of the tents, the telltale sounds of battle painfully absent from the field.

After a quick scan, Zeriel found Ketik. He adjusted his path and landed near him. The High Chief snapped his focus on Zeriel and he immediately knew the truth.

"The tents are empty," Zeriel said.

"We haven't checked them all, but it would seem so."

Until that moment he hadn't believed his fears, but Ketik's words made him certain. "They knew we were coming. These tents are a trap."

Ketik looked out across the field. "But where are they?"

A deafening silence filled the air as both Zeriel and Ketik came to the same realization together. Zeriel's pulse quickened as the sounds of the Coalition army sifting through the tents grew in his ears.

Ketik broke the silence, spinning around and screamed, "Ambush! Retreat!"

As if in direct answer to the High Chief's warning, hundreds of soldiers burst from the forest all around them. Their battle cry was practically deafening.

Ketik spun to Zeriel "Clear our eastern side!"

He was flying before Ketik finished speaking.

CHAPTER FIFTY-THREE

A never-ending stream of soldiers poured out of the forest on the east side of the road. Hundreds of them appeared, with more following behind.

The soldiers of the Northern Clans must have been told to expect Zeriel, because none of them flinched at the sight of him in the air, encased in shadows and speeding toward them. As he neared, he noticed most were holding small glowing white orbs. To his heat sight the glow was severely diminished, but the fact it gave off any light gave him a clue to what they were planning. They were working on old information, though.

Before he got into their throwing range, Zeriel formed hundreds of shadow spears that hovered in the air around him and shot them toward the enemy force. They barely saw what was coming until it was too late. The spears tore through their front lines and deep into their ranks, reducing their numbers by almost a third in the blink of an eye.

Panicked streams of arrows flew toward him. Zeriel formed a half-sphere of hardened darkness in front of him to deflect the counterattack. Then, as if they'd been waiting to play a trump card, the remaining soldiers lobbed their glowing spheres at him. He caught one in mid-air and inspected it.

The globe was a wooden mesh with a piece of white vine inside. He dropped the ball and flew on. They worked well to light up the area, and if they'd used this strategy on him months ago, it would have put him at a significant disadvantage. His knowledge and skill of his power had grown exponentially since then.

What these soldiers didn't know was the brighter the light was, the harsher the shadows it cast. He faltered for a split second before he called on those concentrated shadows to keep him aloft and his shield in place. The men before him would have seen a wraith, with dark tendrils evaporating for a moment, then reattaching to the ground and keeping it aloft.

Zeriel smiled as the failure of their strategy was finally enough to shake their resolve. Some in the front lines froze, others turned and ran. A much smaller number screamed and charged.

They were feet away when Zeriel landed. He molded his shadows into blades and went to work. Even without his powers these soldiers were no match for him in a real battle, not after Mishteel's instruction. Zeriel used his shadows as thick armor around his back and sides, protecting from a surprise attack as he sprinted through their lines.

Jekjarah appeared next to him, floating through the air as if laying on solid ground. "Finally! Blessed carnage!" He held his arms out to his sides as if inviting the shower of blood that erupted around them.

As it always did, the hallucination's glee bled into Zeriel and the bloodlust took over again. Instead of quick kills, he focused on arteries that would project large amounts of blood into the air. He wanted it to cover his body; to paint the earth with the beauty of his killing.

The battle became a blur of parried blades, turned aside arrows, and death. It was the first time he'd fought at this scale. The first time he discovered the pure joy of war.

A sword caught his side, drawing a line of fire across his ribs. The suddenness of it sobered Zeriel immediately. He turned toward his attacker and locked eyes with Elilta, upside down in the air as she flipped across his vision. She smiled, distracting him, which caused his momentum to send him crashing to the ground. His powers faltered, evaporating around him. Zeriel managed to plant his hand on the ground and vault himself back to his feet just as Elilta brought her sword point down where he'd just been.

With a quick swipe of his hand, Zeriel brought a shadow spike upward from underneath the assassin. She managed to dodge it before it impaled her, but not enough to stop it from cutting into her side.

She landed, then put a hand to the wound, which came back bloody. "The Worst One's finally learned a thing or two."

"As it turned out, I just needed the right training." Zeriel reached out to his sides and grabbed shadow blades as they formed in the air. "I'm not the Worst One anymore."

Elilta grinned widely. "Is that so? Then show me what you've learned."

Without hesitation Zeriel formed and threw shadow spikes at the assassin's right side, then sprinted to attack her left.

As expected, she dodged to her left, but before Zeriel could connect with his attack she jumped and twisted over him. He barely brought up his swords in time to block her strike. With a quick twist, he eyed her trajectory and formed shadow spikes in the ground where she would land.

Somehow Elilta contorted her body around them. As impressive as the move was, she failed to avoid them all and was caught in the left arm. With a quick effort of will Zeriel caused the shadow spikes to explode into a dark mist. His old trainer would be completely blind inside that cloud. He covered his feet with cushioning shadows once again, hiding even the sounds of his footsteps from her. Elilta saw and heard nothing. Zeriel, on the other hand, could see the white glow of her body heat in his shifted vision perfectly.

She spun in jerky motions, trying to anticipate from which direction Zeriel would attack. "As much as I hate to admit it, I can see that I failed you as a teacher."

Zeriel kept his distance from the woman. "Hmm, a year ago, that admission might have meant something to me."

She twisted to face his direction and attacked with a wide swipe of her sword, but Zeriel had already shifted to the side well out of her reach.

He moved around her in a wide circle as he said, "I guess you just didn't mean that much to me."

She attacked at the sound of his voice again, completely missing again. "Funny," she said through her teeth. "I feel the same way about you."

"I guess we're done talking, then. Ready to finish this?"

Elilta relaxed out of her fighting stance. "Quite," she said, then turned and sprinted away.

Surprised, Zeriel followed quickly, pulling the shadow cloud along with them.

Every child in Eleshar learned at an early age that no matter the form that light took, whether the orange wavering of a flame, the plants' bioluminescence, or the sun in the sky, it all produced some level of heat.

This simple fact let Zeriel see the soft white glow of the forest's bioluminescence ahead of them. He needed only to let this play out.

Her steps adapted a panicked quality as she failed to escape the darkness. She changed directions multiple times, but the trees rushed inevitably closer. The moment came when Elilta ran full force into a tree she couldn't see, and the impact produced a wet snapping crunch more visceral than Zeriel expected.

Her body stiffened and she fell backward with arms outstretched. This was the moment he'd been waiting for, but just before he made his move, Jekjarah appeared standing over the woman. He pulled the sword from his cane and stabbed Elilta in her heart.

Zeriel stared at the place where the hallucination's sword entered Elilta's chest and saw blood escaping the wound. He froze as the pool of white-hot blood slowly lost its glow as it cooled in the cold air of the dark month. The realization of what was happening threatened to crush the little sanity he had left as he tried to make sense of what he saw.

Jekjarah just killed someone.

He looked up at the hallucination's face and saw it twisted into a feral glee that sent sheer terror through Zeriel's body. With an involuntary step back he asked, "Jek?"

Once the question left his lips the vision faded, replaced by a dark spike, jutting upward through Elilta's chest. The spear dissipated as if in a strong breeze.

Carefully Zeriel stepped up to Elilta and watched as her life evaporated from her body. "Jek?"

The hallucination appeared in front of him again, his cane sword sheathed and a perfectly normal expression on his face. "You're not done yet. There're some stragglers to clean up."

"How?"

"She distracted you before you could kill them all."

"No," he said, shaking his head, "not that. How did you kill her?"

"What are you talking about?"

Zeriel formed a shadow blade in his hand and held it up to the hallucination's neck. "How'd you kill her?"

Jekjarah looked at Elilta's corpse. "Oh, you got her, did you?"

Zeriel inched forward, putting the tip of his blade inches from Jekjarah's neck. "Don't play games with me! *You* killed her!"

Jekjarah stepped forward, letting the tip of Zeriel's blade pass through his neck.

Zeriel flinched back, but the blade passed through the hallucination harmlessly.

"Get a grip, Zeriel. The entire Coalition army is going to be wiped out if you don't pull yourself together."

Zeriel released the blade in a puff of dark smoke. He looked around and saw the Northern Clan soldiers Jekjarah warned him about. Maybe two hundred of the soldiers survived his assault. They'd let Elilta handle him and were sprinting toward the rear flank of the Coalition's forces who were barely holding their own against the enemies attacking from the west.

Jekjarah was right, he had work to do, but when he tried to move a flash of the hallucination's deranged expression flashed in his mind and caused him to hesitate. Zeriel growled then shook the image out of his head. There would be time to worry about his murderous hallucination later.

With a barely clear mind, Zeriel lifted himself into the air and shot toward the remains of the eastern front. He turned in wide curves, forming dark lances and striking down bodies from the sky. They were too focused on the army in front of them to see him coming.

After a few passes he finished the rest of the eastern force, leaving them all to die screaming.

CHAPTER FIFTY-FOUR

Ketik's forces were locked in battle with hundreds of forces from the western tree line. They'd done an exceptional job holding them off, but from the air Zeriel could see they were moments away from being overrun.

The sight inflamed something deep in his chest. He'd risked his life for every soldier in the Coalition, then he'd poured every ounce of his skill and knowledge into their training. Those were his men down there struggling just to survive. And by the very thing they'd feared: Superior numbers. It was more than he could bear.

A quick shift of his trajectory sent him toward the left flank of the clashing forces. He turned to fly over the enemy, parallel to the line of battle. The soldiers from the Northern Clans threw their impotent balls of light at him as he passed and died on the wave of spikes that followed under him. In mere moments he'd covered the entire force, but just as he started his turn for another pass, his powers failed.

Weeks of training the Coalition—and the days training the Enhanced after that—did wonders to increase Zeriel's endurance with his powers. So much so that he hadn't noticed he was at his limit until it was too late.

Gravity ripped him violently from the sky and his vision shifted back to normal. Light exploded across his vision from the globes he'd dismissed only moments earlier. He hit the ground suddenly and with incredible force. The impact sent him into an uncontrollable roll then the shin bone of his right leg snapped and sent pain shooting up his leg all the way to his hip.

At some point he hit his head, and his vision swam through the tumble. Vaguely he felt himself settle and slide across the ground to a stop. The pain seeped into every inch of his body, overwhelming his senses.

The screams of soldiers and the clashing of their swords grew louder, but Zeriel had no way to tell whether they were friend, foe, or both. It barely mattered since he could do little more than lay in the dirt and prepare for his inevitable death.

The sounds of battle continued to increase. Zeriel closed his eyes, giving him a small reprieve from the daggers stabbing into his brain from the light of the globes. Then a voice, quiet but forceful, cut through the rest of the noise. It was familiar, but Zeriel's thoughts came slowly so he couldn't place who it belonged to.

Seconds, or hours, or an eternity later, the voice grew louder until he heard it scream as it flew over him. Swords clashed nearby as the world started to make a little more sense. "Grab him!" the voice cried frantically.

Hands seized him under his arms and dragged him across the ground.

"Cover our retreat!"

Awareness returned and Zeriel finally recognized the voice. "Ketik. Tell me you didn't just risk your life to save me."

"Of course I did, you idiot. How many of us could cut down nearly a thousand soldiers in mere moments?"

"My power is spent, my leg's broken, and I'm completely blind."

"Take him to the rear," Ketik said, presumably to the ones dragging him.

They lifted him off the ground, causing Zeriel to cry out in pain.

"You've done well, Lord of Shadows," one of the men carrying him said. "We'll take it from here."

"No, wait," Zeriel said, then the men carrying him stopped. He looked toward Ketik who was already beyond his vision. A tight ball of pain squeezed his chest. "Did I kill enough of them?" he called after Ketik. "Can we win?"

Ketik's voice came from a distance. "Let me worry about that."

Zeriel relaxed and let the men carry him. They jogged to the rear of the formation, every agonizing jolt a torturous shock as they went. As they gained distance from the light spheres, Zeriel's vision cleared until he could finally see again. When he looked toward the battle to the west, he saw nothing but piercing white light. Turning to the east he saw more of the same. Only the small area around him seemed unaffected by the light of those cursed globes. Once his porters set him down, Zeriel heard the crunch of their footsteps fade away toward the fight.

Jekjarah stepped over Zeriel as he lay there, looking out at the battle. "How many did you kill?"

Zeriel pulled himself up on his elbows. "I don't know. Maybe a thousand from the East and another five hundred at the front." Sounds from the battle nearby made it clear the fighting was far from over. "How many more are there, Jek?"

"I have no clue. I see the same white blob you see."

Instinctually, Zeriel tried to create his shadow lenses and shift to his heat vision. A lance of pain carried from his right eye, over his head, and into the base of his neck. His torso hit the ground as he grabbed his head.

"You really are spent," Jekjarah said.

The sounds of battle grew louder. Zeriel looked out at that white blob, Jekjarah follow his gaze. "That doesn't sound good."

Jekjarah turned to him. "It might be time to abandon this fight. You're strong enough now, you might be able to take Veshet on your own." The hallucination glanced back at the sounds of battle. "If you stay here, you'll die."

Zeriel's reaction to Jekjarah's comment was quick and visceral. It shocked even him. "No! Those are my men out there!" The emotions had been there for a while now, hidden deep in a place he hadn't yet confronted, but he hadn't had time for that in the last few weeks. The conversation with Jekjarah had done that for him, in a single explosive moment.

"What about Lavel? You'd rather die for these men than avenge her death?"

His thoughts, manifested from Jekjarah's mouth were marching him toward something. Was saving these men more important than his duty to Lavel? It was true that he needed them to get his revenge, but there was more to it than that. A truth he would never have discovered had he remained an assassin.

"You can't believe what you're thinking," Jekjarah said, responding to the decision he was making.

Zeriel held the hallucination's eyes for several heartbeats. He'd accepted the truth. "The living are worth more than the dead." Such an obvious statement. Why had it taken him so long to realize it?

The battle crept closer, and he couldn't ignore the cries of the dying anymore. Zeriel grabbed the part of his shirt that protruded from the bottom of his leather armor. "I'm going out there, Jek," he said as he ripped off a strip of cloth and began tying it around his eyes. With that done he could see slightly better. Assessing his surroundings, he noted that they'd laid him amidst the destroyed tents that were set up against the main road. The one closest to him, destroyed from his initial assault with all the others. "Because if I can help save some of them, I have to."

The tent poles were shattered, perfect for what he needed. He ripped more cloth from his shirt and used it to tie the pole fragments to his broken leg. He grunted through the pain of applying the makeshift splint. "They *trusted* me, Jek. For the first time in my life, someone trusted me. And before I knew what was happening, I started learning from them, too." Zeriel struggled to his feet, putting weight on his leg as a test. Pain shot through it again, but he'd expected it, and was able to push it out of his mind. Just as he had with the agony of Plaxes' training.

"You're going to kill us both, Zeriel."

He looked at the hallucination and calmness washed over him. Peace followed a surety he'd never felt in his life. "Maybe. If I do, then my death would have meant something."

The hallucination's face stretched with anger. "How are their lives worth sacrificing ours?"

"Because something else happened during my time with them that I didn't expect. I didn't notice it while it was happening, and it took me until this moment to realize. I started to care for them." Zeriel walked forward, limping awkwardly on his broken leg.

"I'll stop you, Zeriel." The words choppy in the hallucination's mouth.

"No," Zeriel said as he pushed himself to a wavering trot, "you won't."

Jekjarah screamed in frustration, but the noise faded as Zeriel continued toward the battlefield. His makeshift blindfold barely cut through the white haze of those light balls. At most, he gained three—maybe four feet of visibility. Though it wasn't much better than stumbling around blind, it was enough to keep him on his feet, following the sounds of the battle until the soldiers of the Coalition appeared in front of him.

When they noticed him, many looked with mouths agape. Zeriel was sure his broken body was quite the sight, but their impressions of him didn't matter, only the purpose he'd set himself toward. Soon soldiers from the Northern Clans appeared in his visible space, locked in combat with his men.

One of those men turned his back to Zeriel. He reached out to grab a shadow blade but it wouldn't come, and pain lanced through his arm. It was the first time he felt completely naked in the middle of a fight. Luckily, he wasn't as unprepared as he felt, having tied daggers to his sides as a backup. He drew the weapons and attacked. The strike was poorly placed, and it took several more to finally connect with the man's heart.

Jekjarah appeared above the man as he fell to the ground. He shook his head, then knelt and breathed in the scent of the man's blood. "If we're going to die, this is *definitely* the way to go!"

Once the enemy noticed their fallen comrade, they turned their attention toward Zeriel. Several of them appeared from out of the white haze, rushing toward him with weapons drawn. He moved without thinking and without any care for his injuries. It was enough to dodge the first attacker, and a lucky swipe of his dagger caught the man's carotid artery. The second one didn't go as smoothly. Zeriel dodged a second time, but his body didn't respond as quickly as the first. He had to bring up his dagger to parry the incoming blade.

The block was poorly placed, and pain lanced across his hand, sliced against the edge of his attacker's sword. The man shifted his momentum for another quick strike. Then Zeriel's leg gave out. The enemy stumbled past him in surprise as Zeriel fell to the ground.

He propped himself up with one hand and used the other to bring his dagger into a defensive position. The man swung wide and brought his sword down on Zeriel, then stopped short as a blade escaped from his stomach. The blade disappeared, then the man dropped to the ground. One of the Coalition's soldiers stood behind his attacker, gave Zeriel a curt nod, then turned back toward the battle.

Hands grabbed him from behind as the other man disappeared into the haze. Zeriel struggled at first, then the man who grabbed him spoke. "I've got you." The hands hauled him to his feet.

He craned his neck around to find Ietenet standing behind him. The man turned to watch Zeriel's back.

"Thanks," Zeriel said.

"Around me!" Ietenet called. The next thing Zeriel knew he was surrounded by four other men. The group created a circle around him exactly as Zeriel had trained them to do when one of them was wounded.

"I didn't think we'd been pushed back that far," Ietenet said, "but we'll make sure you get back to safety, Zeriel."

"You haven't been pushed back," Zeriel said as he sheathed his daggers and grabbed swords off the enemy corpses on the ground. He shuffled up to the line and pushed into the circle. "I've come to fight with you."

The men closest looked at him and grinned.

"Doesn't look like we have much time to argue," Ietenet responded. He was right because no sooner had he spoken, than enemy soldiers appeared in front of Zeriel. The tactics Ietenet's group were using was a strategy Zeriel had developed to fight more than one of the Te Et Sha. When he rushed forward to dispatch the man closest to him the others moved in concert with him to maintain the integrity of the circle. This meant none of them had their flanks or backs exposed at any time. It also meant each man had to be aware of the movements of the others, allowing the circle to pull them away from combat when necessary.

The group dispatched their attackers in moments. Ietenet surveyed the field and yelled, "They need help closer to the front. Follow me!"

They shifted into the next formation quickly, a wedge with Ietenet near the tip. Zeriel took up a position near the outside edge. The group moved through the battle, engaging the enemy only when necessary.

They were moving at Zeriel's pace to maintain the integrity of their formation. "Ietenet," he called out. "You've got to leave me behind. Your team is slower with me in your ranks."

"We're moving as fast as we can, you've got nothing to do with it. Just maintain formation."

Looking around, he saw that Ietenet was right. The formation was working exactly as intended, he just wasn't on the part facing the largest resistance. "Right," he said with gritted teeth. The pain was nearly unbearable, but Zeriel was determined more than ever to fight until his body stopped working.

His new squad continued their march forward, and the fight took on a sort of rhythm for Zeriel. The pain of his broken leg faded away, and the blinding light around him pushed into the background of his consciousness.

Jekjarah started dancing in front of their formation, making a show of his glee at the carnage. Zeriel smiled, feeling comfort at the familiar sight.

Then an enemy appeared, passing through Jekjarah and surprising Zeriel. The enemy stabbed the soldier on Zeriel's right directly in the throat. His teammate eyed him with shock on his face. When the enemy pulled his blade back the man fell to the ground, gurgling for air through the blood that poured from his wound.

Red filled Zeriel's vision, and he moved without thought or concern for himself—or anyone else. He slipped forward of the formation, spun, and cut the man's head clean from his shoulders.

Another enemy soldier appeared from the haze with his sword outstretched. He landed a blow into Zeriel's left shoulder, digging into the cartilage of his arm's socket.

His left arm went limp as Zeriel pulled away before the man had a chance to finish the move and take the limb completely off. A quick duck and spin allowed Zeriel to open the man's stomach, leaving him to die on the ground with his entrails in his hands.

The squad moved up and defended Zeriel from two more attackers as he struggled once more to get to his feet. "You need to stay in formation Lord of Shadows," one of them said. "We might not get to you in time again."

Zeriel met the man's eyes and nodded. He silently cursed himself for losing control. These were the tactics he'd developed, after all.

The battle continued as Zeriel took special care not to lose his cool, even as more of his squad mates fell to the enemies' blades. Time fell away as the fight went on, and his muscle memory took over, thoughts turning to nothing. Though he knew he was in control, a piece of his mind felt disconnected from his body, as if watching from afar. Even Jekjarah's form dancing around him felt removed from his consciousness, like a play being acted out by someone else.

The clash of blade on blade quieted, replaced by the moans of the dying until finally he heard Ietenet call out, "The battle is over. We've won!"

Cries of victory rose into the air around him, but all Zeriel could do was collapse to the ground.

CHAPTER FIFTY-FIVE

For the second time, Zeriel woke up to the worn features of a grumpy old healer. The man's face was close to his shoulder, applying stitches to the wound that almost took his arm off.

"Hi Odenuk," he said. "Still bald as ever I see."

The old man stared at him flatly. "You're on bedrest for at least the next two weeks," he said, bluntly. Nothing about the man had changed at all. "Depending on your progress, it may be longer."

Zeriel tried to sit up in his bed, but his left arm didn't seem to want to respond. He grunted through the effort, using only his right arm. "That bad, was it?"

The healer put in the last stitch, then straightened his back in his stool. He turned to wash his hands in a bowl of steaming water. "You probably should have died. I'd wager your powers do something to strengthen your body." He stood up as he grabbed a cloth off the table and wiped his hands dry. "That injury separated your shoulder. I expect you can't move your arm much."

Zeriel pushed through the pain, trying harder to move the arm. It moved slightly, but a jolt shot through his shoulder and made him give up the effort. "Damn that hurts," he growled.

Odenuk nodded. "I've done everything I can. It'll either heal, or it won't, but don't expect to get full range of motion back. Ever."

"How will I know when I can use it again?"

"When you can move it without any pain."

Zeriel gave him a flat stare. "How long do you think that will take?"

"Give it a couple weeks, then spend some time every day stretching it out at much as you can. The range of motion you have after about a month is likely all you'll get."

"Any good news?"

"Your broken leg didn't penetrate the skin. With time, and considering your age, that should heal just fine."

Zeriel looked at his leg and found it wrapped in a proper splint. "When can I walk on it again?"

"That will take longer than your arm. You should stay off it until at least the next dark month." He walked to a corner and grabbed a pair of crutches Zeriel hadn't noticed were there. "Until then, you can use these to get around. Just don't put any weight on the leg."

Zeriel was about to complain when a knock came at the door.

"He's awake," Odenuk said. "You can talk to him if you want."

The door to the room opened and Ketik stepped through. "It's about time."

"I didn't mean to keep you waiting," Zeriel responded.

Ketik smirked. "You've been out for a week. I was starting to think you weren't going to make it."

After the report from Odenuk, Zeriel's concern shifted elsewhere. "The casualties?"

Ketik's expression shifted and he said, "We lost close to half of our forces."

Sudden and ferocious rage flared through him. "Damn!" Zeriel exclaimed as he slammed his right fist on the bed. He'd done so much to help those men survive, had he only been able to save half? "This happened because I was too weak."

"Are you joking? When we surveyed the battlefield for survivors, we counted the number of soldiers you killed from the eastern side."

"I estimated close to a thousand."

"Just over twelve hundred. Another seven hundred on the western side. You single-handedly took out half of the enemy forces, Zeriel."

"That still left us outnumbered at least two to one."

"The Enhanced reinforced us at the end. They soldiers took out the Te Et Sha in the city without much difficulty, then joined with the main force."

"They were that much better than the assassins?"

"It turned out that our campaign through the Central Clans had nearly wiped them out. Only about fifty were left in the village."

"That's still a lot of highly trained assassins to contend with."

Ketik smiled proudly. "Not for them. And your training helped prepare them for the assassins' fighting styles and tactics."

A long sigh escaped Zeriel's lips, and he let himself fall back to the bed. "It's about time something went our way."

"Indeed. They arrived shortly after you swept across the enemy line. With their help, the remaining soldiers from the Northern Clans were overwhelmed."

"Great. We won." Zeriel met Ketik's eyes. "Why doesn't it feel like a victory?"

The High Chief's face softened. "Did our other victories feel like victories?"

"They did."

"Then what's different about this one?"

Zeriel didn't want to admit what he was thinking. It felt like exposing a weakness. *I cared about them this time. I knew their names!*

Ketik nodded though Zeriel said nothing. "Leadership is a heavy burden, Zeriel."

"I'm not a leader. A leader would be able to save the people who follow him."

"You think you didn't save anyone?" Ketik stepped closer. "You're the one who brought Eleshar's Curse to us. Convinced us to use it, then helped to prepare the survivors. You expended every ounce of your power to wipe out thousands until you couldn't use it anymore."

Your men still died! Zeriel's voices screamed.

"My men still died," he repeated. It was the first time in his life he gave voice to the whispers in his mind.

"Then," Ketik said, ignoring him, "you wrapped up your broken leg and fought alongside Ietenet and his men, powerless and injured. He told me about it, and enough of the men saw you that the story of it has already become legend."

The faces of men in that formation flashed through his mind. "Yes, and they're lost too."

Ketik raised his voice. "How many did you save because of what you did, Zeriel? How many are still standing? Or maybe you're incapable of doing anything wrong? Are you a *god*?"

The questions were like punches to his gut. Of course, he knew the answers, but he couldn't shake the feeling he hadn't done enough. Still, he spoke the truth Ketik was driving toward. "You're right," he whispered. "I saved people's lives."

"Right! And don't forget, you're not the only one risking his life for this fight, Zeriel. Wallowing at your inability to do the impossible spits in the face of men who gave the ultimate sacrifice so we could be alive today." The High Chief's face was bright red, and he was breathing heavily. "We have a meeting in an hour in the center of the village. Get your ass on those crutches and be there."

Zeriel had never seen Ketik that angry before. "Yes, High Chief," he said out of reflex.

Ketik spun on his heels and stormed out of the room.

Odenuk followed but paused before walking through the door. He looked back at Zeriel. "Idiot," he said, then closed the door behind him as he left.

❖

Roughly an hour passed before Zeriel managed to figure out how to use a single crutch to keep weight off his leg and get around. He couldn't use the other one while his shoulder was still healing.

Once he felt confident enough, he opened the door to his room and stepped out. Just outside his door was a small cobblestone street. He was in Clan Eten, and the people moved about the village with their heads held high. It was a welcome change to what he'd seen when he first scouted the place.

The light of the white vine lanterns in the village cast a pale haze over his vision. A week without using his powers had caused his sight to begin returning to normal. He went to his powers again and a band of anxiety wrapped around his chest. Some part of him worried he'd lost them for good.

He reached out gingerly at first, and when he felt something there he strengthened his call to the darkness. It obeyed as it always had, and his vision flared white as he drew in the shadows to create his lenses once again. Able to see normally once more, he was ready to head out in earnest.

Ready as he was, and despite his scouting before the attack, he had no idea how to get where he was going. A quick look down both directions of the road showed him he was close to the nearest arterial. He made his way there and caught the attention of the first person that crossed his path—a man, no older than twenty, with the scrawny frame of someone who spent their life doing anything but hard manual labor. He shifted to his heat sight and the man glowed white. "Can you tell me how to get to the center of the village?"

The man gave Zeriel a casual glance, then looked back as he sucked in a shocked breath. "You're the Lord of Shadows!"

Zeriel sighed. "Some have taken to call me that. Yes."

He pointed behind him. "Head that way. It will take you straight there."

"Thanks."

The man bid him farewell excitedly, something Zeriel didn't quite know how to take. The journey was slow on his crutch, and many approached him along the way. Men who'd survived the battle shook his hand, some of them telling the story of how they thought all hope was lost until they saw him flying overhead or fighting with Ietenet's squad.

It was all a bit much, so he felt relieved when he finally made it to the center of the village and saw Ketik standing there impatiently.

"It's about time."

"Almost like I'm barely managing on a single crutch."

Ketik responded with a grunt, then turned toward a nearby building. "They're waiting for us."

Zeriel followed without protest.

Inside the building were the four Chieftains surrounding a table with papers strewn across it. They were focused on Odinte, who was reading from a piece of paper in her hand. She quieted when they entered, and all eyes shifted to Ketik and Zeriel.

"Ah, just in time," Odinte said. "I was just telling the others about what I found."

"Why don't you start from the beginning," Quatesh said.

"Right. We interrogated the two Chiefs we captured. They were from Clans Ori and Fi. If they were telling the truth, then it seems the combined forces of the Northern Clans were comprised of four out of the eight. Their two clans as well as Clans Yul and Amm. They were told the other four clans had been wiped them out for their resistance, though none of them believe it."

"If our experience holds true," Ketik said, "it's very possible they were."

"They claim their four clans surrendered immediately, and Veshet let them live as long as they join his army."

"That's unlikely," Zeriel said. "I've never known him to avoid a fight. Even an unnecessary one."

"Let's review what we know before assuming the Chiefs are lying," Aleber said reproachfully. "Veshet *did* send the might of those four clans to Clan Eten. Granted, it was probably to establish a forward base and push back our efforts in the Central Clans. As far as he knew, our army was too small to win against the four clans united. Given that, it would make sense he'd use them."

"He was right," Mishteel said. "we are smack, but he overestimated the Northern Clans' strength, and the extent to which Zeriel would contribute to the battle."

"Right," Aleber said with a deeply aspirated tone. "We all

underestimated that. But there's likely a deeper motivation to Veshet's tactics. Let's assume his primary goal had been met. The four clans would have wiped us out. Anyone who died in the effort would have been considered a desired casualty to him."

"*Only the strong survive,*" Zeriel quoted.

Aleber pointed to him in agreement. "Secondarily, if they failed, he succeeded in reducing our strength and the Northern Clans were, again, desired casualties."

"A win-win in his eyes," Ketik said.

"A good hypothesis, but impossible to know for sure," Quatesh said. "What do we gain from all this theorizing, exactly?"

Odinte set her paper down. "We can use it against Veshet. Roughly seven hundred survived from the Northern Clans. We tell them what we've *discovered*, and *let* them fight for us."

"Not a chance!" Mishteel said. "Those traitors can't be trusted."

Ketik shook his head and said, "I'm sorry, but Mishteel's right. They betrayed us when they joined forces with Veshet."

"We give them an option," Odinte said. "Join us, or face execution."

"What a stupid plan," Mishteel said. "We should just execute them all and be done with it."

"Shut up and let her finish," Quatesh said, then addressed Odinte. "I assume you have some way of mitigating the risks."

"I do." The Chief pulled out a tiny bottle from a pocket hidden in the folds of her dress. The dark purple and black liquid was unmistakable.

"Eleshar's Curse?" Zeriel said. "I thought we used it all."

"All but one bottle," Odinte said, then turned around to grab a nearby crate.

"How is one bottle supposed to help us?" Aleber asked.

In answer Odinte set the crate on the table and opened the lid. Inside were perhaps a hundred small bottles of the potion. "I used the last bottle to figure out what it was made of, and I made more."

The other Chiefs were dumbfounded, standing silent for a long moment.

"Odinte," Mishteel said, "I owe you an apology." He flashed her a toothy grin.

"But we can't just give hundreds of potential enemies the means to destroy us," Ketik said.

"Of course not. We offer them a choice to redeem themselves, take the potion knowing it will likely kill them, then fight Veshet with us. If not, we execute them."

"I'm sorry," Aleber said, "that sounds like a terrible plan. You want to give our enemy the power to destroy us?"

"It's a risk, but we have time to keep them under watch, feed them our suspicions about Veshet's motives—though they will think them facts—and test their loyalty before we make our final move."

"We only give them the Curse once they've proven themselves?" Ketik asked.

"Exactly."

"Then they belong to me," Mishteel said. He'd become the defacto leader of the Enhanced.

"It's a risk," Ketik said, "but it's hard to argue the value of gaining more of our strongest soldiers."

The six of them stood in silence for a time. This was a tremendous risk, Zeriel knew that. They all did. Yet they were all considering it. He was coming to understand exactly where Odinte's strengths lay, and it frightened him.

"We vote, then?" Quatesh asked, finally breaking the silence.

"All in favor?" Ketik asked. Everyone raised their hand. Everyone but Zeriel. They all looked at him and Ketik asked, "You disagree?"

"I didn't think I got a vote."

"Ha!" Mishteel exclaimed. "As if The Hero of the Coalition wouldn't get a vote."

"The...what?" Zeriel asked.

"Just raise your hand," Odinte said.

Zeriel sighed. "That better not be a new name I have to deal with," he said as he raised his hand.

Odinte nodded. "It's decided, then."

Mishteel approached Zeriel with a grin plastered on his face. "Stop doing impossible things, and perhaps others will stop giving you new names." He patted him on the good shoulder and walked out.

The rest of the Chiefs left behind him, their path was set. It wasn't the first time they'd made a decision that had the possibility of destroying them, but Zeriel did wonder how many of them it would take before that destruction finally came.

CHAPTER FIFTY-SIX

Roughly five hundred soldiers from the Northern Clans agreed to take Eleshar's Curse. A hundred of them survived.

It was a stark reminder of the human cost of the Enhanced. To Zeriel it felt like he was back in the Te Et Sha stronghold watching scores of recruits die. The care Ketik had taken for the remains of the dead reminded Zeriel of the utter ruthlessness of the Te Et Sha.

On Mishteel's suggestion, they lingered at Clan Eten for a full month to train the new Enhanced. Zeriel had agreed immediately since he needed the time to heal. The rest of the Chiefs supported the decision. While Ketik didn't like the thought of lingering after the momentum of their victory, he eventually agreed the delay was necessary.

The month passed quickly for Zeriel. He healed faster than Odenuk had anticipated, which allowed them to move out in just under a month. With Clan Yul on the direct path to the Capital, they had no other option but to fight their way through it.

The sun had risen halfway up the sky by the time they arrived at the Clan. Its village was set on the top of a ridge surrounded by fields of tall grass. The normally prominent display of the Clan's Stripes was nowhere to be seen. Zeriel stood on a distant hill with Chief Odinte and the other support members of their army. Though he'd healed well, they agreed he should sit out this fight so he could be at full strength for the fight with Veshet.

He and the Chief watched as the Enhanced made first contact with the Te Et Sha outside the village walls.

Odinte eyed Zeriel for a moment before she asked, "Do you wish you were with them?"

That's a strange question. He took his eyes of the battle to look at her, but her features didn't betray her thoughts. "Should I?"

"I find that most soldiers long for the fight. Is that not the case with you?"

Jekjarah appeared on the other side of the Chief and looked around her to give Zeriel a conspiratorial grin as he bobbed his eyebrows. "Should we tell her?"

Zeriel turned his eyes back to the battle. "The opposite, actually. I probably long for the fight a little too much."

"This must not be easy for you, then."

"For most of my life I've fought alone. Stalked my prey from the shadows. It's a different kind of fighting than what we've been doing. It's all too new for me to long for it, I think."

"I see," she said, then let silence pass between them for a time.

The two watched as the Enhanced broke through the wall and into the city.

"Mishteel seems to trust our new Enhanced soldiers." She turned to face him. "What do you think?"

"I only spent a week with them in the training field, but I think he's right to trust them. Many were just following their Chiefs' orders. The ones who took the Curse felt like they'd betrayed the Clans and were eager for redemption."

"That seems very...convenient."

Zeriel shrugged. "It doesn't always have to be complicated."

"When it comes to people, it's always complicated. But since you have to fight next to them, I'm glad you feel that way. We can't be fighting amongst ourselves right now. Perhaps a little outside skepticism isn't a bad thing, either." The woman turned back to the battle.

Zeriel felt like he was truly seeing her for the first time. His first impression of the woman was of a demure pushover. Over time he'd come to see the brilliance of her mind and thought that was the only reason Clan Bale followed her. Now he saw the truth. She *was* all those things, but she held a deep wisdom and shrewdness that none of the others possessed.

If Odinte was keeping watch over the new Enhanced, he suddenly felt supremely confident she'd ferret out any dissenters that might have slipped through the cracks.

In only a few minutes Mishteel emerged from the broken section of wall and raised a fist. The fight was already over.

❖

There had only been a handful of Te Et Sha in Clan Yul. Just enough to keep the population not out fighting for them under their thumb. Their Enhanced had wiped them all out before even breaking through the wall.

In the days that followed the Coalition had settled around the village. Many of the new Enhanced were from Clan Yul and being back with their families had a noticeable effect on their morale.

Their army continued their morning training routines in the fields outside the village. Zeriel took to walking through the training groups, providing advice, assistance, and sparring practice. He'd gotten better at getting to know the men, taking time to talk to them about their personal lives as well as the progress they made in their training. They were noticeably more relaxed around him even if they maintained an air of respect.

The men who'd been training with him the longest started to take the newer ones under their wing and formed their own training groups. The pride Zeriel felt in them was so foreign that he suppressed it at first. Eventually he allowed himself to feel little sips periodically. The idea of letting the emotion flow freely was too frightening, so he took solace in his meager portions.

One morning, just as the moon was peaking over the horizon, Ketik found Zeriel on his usual patrol through the training fields.

"How are you feeling?" He asked.

Zeriel rolled his shoulder a bit, feeling the stiffness there that had settled into place in the last week. "As good as I'm going to feel, I think."

"Walk with me for a bit." Ketik put his hands behind his back and turned toward where the Enhanced were training. "Do you think you're ready for Veshet?"

"I was going to talk to you about that."

"You want to wait for the dark month before we move."

"I should have guessed you'd already worked it out."

Ketik smiled. "It wasn't hard. Your powers are strongest in the darkness."

"That puts us out at least another several weeks."

"It might surprise you, but I don't plan for us to sit around the entire time." As he finished, they'd neared the Enhanced. Ketik raised a hand in the air and called for Mishteel.

The Chief broke off from his sparring and approached. "High Chief." His tone lacked any trace of sarcasm or displeasure at the honorific, a fact which surprised Zeriel.

"I'm sure you know we're several weeks away from our final assault."

Mishteel eyed Zeriel. "I assumed as much."

"I have a mission for you and your Enhanced."

"The rest of the Northern Clans."

"You figured it out already," Ketik said, "good."

"I read the report from our scouts. Ki Al Tesh is filled with nearly two hundred Te Et Sha. I figured you'd want some extra muscle to ensure our victory."

"If there's muscle to get out there. It could be that the reports were true, and they were all wiped out."

"Wait," Zeriel said. "There are that many in the capital?"

"We think it's the reason we've only encountered small groups of them lately. They sent one large force to the south. They conquered the Central Clans and left just enough behind to hold the territory. We finished off the main army at Clan Bale."

"Just when I think I'm getting used to large scale strategy, you prove me wrong."

Ketik put a hand on Zeriel's uninjured shoulder. "Leave the strategy to me, Zeriel. We'll need your specific expertise before this is over."

Just then a young man approached. "Excuse me, High Chief. I've come with a message from Captain Jetita. The blockade is in place."

"Excellent!" Ketik said. "Find the Chief of Clan Yul and let him know if you need resupplied. He'll make sure you have everything you need."

"Thank you, High Chief," the man said, then jogged his way back to the village.

"It looks like your plan is starting to come together," Mishteel said.

"For now. But plans are like lines drawn in sand. Wiped away by the steps of even the smallest of feet."

Later that day, Zeriel stood among the waving stalks of grass—dead in the heat of the light month sun—on a nearby hill and watched as the Enhanced disappeared over the horizon on their way to Clan Enla to the northwest.

Jekjarah appeared next to him. "Is it me, or is it starting to feel like they don't need us anymore?"

"Should we want them to?"

"You certainly do."

"I feel responsible for them. They took the risk to gain their new strength and the only guide they had to master it was me. *The Worst One.*"

"It wasn't long ago you told me you cared about them. You risk your life to save them."

Zeriel thought back to that moment and a well of emotions built up inside of him. "I do care for them."

"Even though they don't need you?"

"I..." The answer didn't come immediately. There was a small piece of him that hated the thought of being cast aside because he'd outlived his usefulness. Another part of him felt a sense of accomplishment at the role he'd played in helping them become self-sufficient. After a short time of contemplation, he realized one of those emotions was stronger than the other. "No. I don't care for them just because they needed me. I genuinely want what's best for them."

"Then you're a fool."

Zeriel smiled broadly. The effort of the stretch pulled painfully at the corners of his mouth. "What's new, Jek?"

CHAPTER FIFTY-SEVEN

The march to Ki Al Tesh took the Coalition a full day. The road from Clan Yul to the capital was wide and well maintained as it cut through forests and weaved through rolling hills. Of the marches that Zeriel had taken part in since helping to form the Coalition, it was one of the easiest. He traveled next to Ketik, who marched in the center of the formation, ready to give orders to the front or rear in case of an ambush. The other Chiefs were scattered throughout to avoid an attack wiping out all their leadership at once. Up and down the formation were banners bearing the Coalition's Stripes, sewed by the members of Clan Yul.

Without the Enhanced, they had just over two hundred men in their army. That number felt large when on a day's long march, but it was nothing compared to what they were likely to need. When their formation broke through the last tree line, and Zeriel saw the strength of the capital's defenses, his concern deepened.

While the height of Ki Al Tesh's walls was nothing near that of Clan Eten's, they were far more magnificent. Ancient stonework covered the outside of the wall. Depictions of their people's histories, representation of each Clan, and beautifully rendered images of Eleshar as an omnipotent goddess spanned the distance between towers and gates. Crenellations topped the artwork. Few walls built by Fei En Ar included those types of defenses. They'd been added decades ago, when Kloren stonemasons were brought in to repair and reinforce the wall. Projecting from inside was a tower, its flat top rising high above the top of the walls.

Ketik stopped the march at the top of a hill about four hundred yards from the city, well out of range of any archers on the wall. From that distance, they could see the farmland against the north portion of the wall, as well.

Surrounding them was shin-high dried grass and rolling hills, leaving Zeriel feeling overexposed as he kept his eyes locked on the city gates. "Help me understand why Veshet won't just send the two hundred Te Et Sha at us right now," he asked Ketik.

"I doubt he'd take the risk to attack a force that just marched all the way from the Southern Clans, and through all the soldiers he threw at us."

"That's one hell of an assumption. We're not exactly as intimidating as the thousand-man army he brought against us."

"We're not going to win this without taking risks."

Zeriel eyed Ketik and said, "obviously." He turned back to the city gates, "But not knowing what awaits us behind those walls has me nervous." No sooner had he said those words than the Eastern Gate opened, and a group of five on horseback rode out and turned in their direction.

Ketik looked at Zeriel with a smirk. "That's not a hundred men coming to kill us." He walked out to meet them.

Zeriel followed and whispered, "Not yet."

They met the Te Et Sha at the bottom of the hill. All five of them were men in their mid-twenties. They each wore black assassin's leather armor, and all looked like they'd barely killed ten men. Zeriel didn't recognize them, which meant Veshet had likely sent his most experienced into the Central and Southern Clans. Ketik's gamble seemed to be paying off.

The group stopped their horses, then one of them coaxed his a little ahead of the group. "Veshet is impressed that you've made it this far. Though strength is its own reward, he would give you one himself."

"A *reward?*" Zeriel asked.

The young man sneered. "Yes, Worst One. In his divine wisdom, Veshet has even deigned to give you a reward."

Zeriel laughed. Genuinely laughed for the first time in his life. It hurt.

The man drew his blade.

Ketik stepped between the two. "I think what Zeriel's trying to say is he's surprised at the offer of a gift, given how ferociously Veshet sought to kill us."

The young man squinted at Ketik, then sheathed his sword. "*Only the strong survive,*" he said, as if that was all the explanation they needed. "You are hereby given the opportunity to join his Great Society."

Zeriel guffawed. "Oh, we *get the opportunity*, do we? Why don't you take your *opportunity* and shove it—"

"Enough," Ketik said as he snapped his head back at Zeriel. He then turned back to the Te Et Sha and said, "We'll pass, thanks. But I have a gift of my own for your leader."

The man shuffled uncomfortably on his horse. "What's that?"

"I will allow him to surrender. If he does, we won't bring destruction upon you so complete that your memory will be wiped from the face of Eleshar herself. Your ancestors won't cry out in pain at the horrid retribution we've inflicted upon you."

The man glanced at Zeriel. "You haven't been listening to the Worst One, have you? I would advise you not to put your trust in him. He was assigned the worst jobs. The ones that didn't matter if they failed. And it was a good thing, because he returned to us a failure more often than not."

Ketik looked back at Zeriel. He simply nodded to the High Chief. *It's all true.* A thought came to him, suddenly. *If they still think I'm the same as I was back then, they must not have gotten a single report about what happened in Clan Eten.*

Ketik raised his eyebrows. He seemed to understand what Zeriel was thinking and turned back to the man. "Him?" He threw his thumb back and Zeriel. "We just keep him around for laughs. If I were you, I'd be more concerned with the men behind him. They're the ones who tore through your generals and their armies in the Southern and Central Clans. They fought through thousands of the Northern Clan members you sent to destroy us in Clan Eten."

All five of them looked up at the top of the hill and at the line of soldiers standing there. The young man in front was the first to look back at Ketik. "I find that hard to believe."

"Then how are we standing here in front of you now?"

He eyed Zeriel again. "The skills of the Te Et Sha can be taught, even by the Worst One. You could have snuck a small force such as this past the Ori twins. Even Elilta has her blind spots."

"I killed the Ori twins and Elilta on my way here," Zeriel said. Something about their dismissal made his blood boil.

"An obvious lie," he said then turned to Ketik once more. "See how he can't even lie convincingly? At least it seemed he believed that one. I suppose there is something he's good at." The man smiled and the group behind him sniggered.

Ketik let out a sigh. "I'm the one who lied, assassin. Those soldiers weren't the only way we gained victory against those odds."

The man smiled as if he knew what was coming.

"We won because we have Zeriel on our side."

He didn't know how he knew it, but Zeriel recognized that as his cue. Shadow mist exploded into existence around them, and he shifted to his heat sight. With his feet covered in darkness he sprinted around the horsemen silently, the only one able to see the bright white glow of their body heat. "Denetek died on the blades I forged from darkness." He created a shadow knife and threw it at the lead man, opening a small cut on his cheek, and kept moving.

The man pulled his sword out and swiped in the direction Zeriel's shadow knife had come from, but nothing was there. The speed at which it all happened caught the others all off guard. The ring of their leader's blade exiting its sheath caused them to draw theirs as well.

"What's happening Kilite?"

Zeriel took the opportunity to forge another shadow knife and throw it at the one who just spoke. He made sure to hit the artery in his neck at just the right angle so the blood would seep into his throat. "Lushame died by my power, much like you will."

The man died choking loudly on his own blood. Three of them abandoned their leader and turned their horses around to ride away. They shot out of Zeriel's shadow mist, then sprinted back to the city.

"But you're the Worst One!" The leader screamed.

"Yes," Zeriel said in a manic, high-pitched tone. "The worst storm you'll ever encounter. The worst calamity to ever befall you." He shifted the shadow mist into hundreds of shadow spears floating in the air. Their tips pointed at the man.

The man's eyes opened wide as he saw what surrounded him.

"I am your worst nightmare," he said, then shot every spear into the man's body. The speed and ferocity of the attack didn't give him enough time even to scream before he died. His corpse rolled to one side and fell off the horse.

Zeriel let the shadow spears evaporate, then turned to walk back up the hill. "That should keep them from attacking us for a while," he said to Ketik.

The High Chief's eyes were locked on the young man dead on the ground. "I should think so."

CHAPTER FIFTY-EIGHT

Two weeks passed, and it seemed Zeriel's intimidation tactic had worked. The Te Et Sha hadn't left the city, even when Ketik moved the Coalition to the eastern side of the wall, cutting them off any possible shipments from Don, their neighboring country to the east.

In the time since they arrived, the sun hit its zenith and was on its way to the western horizon. Zeriel stared over the field between the Coalition's army and the capital. His eyes scanned past the walls and focused on the tower. Before the Veshet's coup, it was where the Ai Jel, Fei En Ar's rulers lived. He tried to see through the open windows for any sign of movement inside, hopefully Veshet himself.

"Wondering why he hasn't shown himself yet?" Ketik asked, as he stepped beside Zeriel.

"I find it surprising they haven't tested us even once since we arrived. I doubt the impression I made would have lasted this long."

"Yeah, I was wondering the same thing."

"Really? I thought you'd have a theory and a fleshed-out plan by now."

Ketik smiled warmly. "Normally you'd be right, but I'm in the dark on this one."

"Action is more valuable than plans anyway."

Ketik chuckled. "True." He grabbed a letter from his pocket and offered it to Zeriel. "A messenger arrived with this today."

Zeriel took the paper and read its contents. "The other clans weren't destroyed?"

"The Enhanced are on their way back with them and should arrive any time. That'll probably provoke Veshet to make a move."

Zeriel handed the letter back, his eyes falling on the farms against the north wall. "We may have to stomp on some ground hornets before then." He pointed at the farmland where small figures worked the fields. "If we let them cultivate those fields, then this siege will have been for nothing."

"What happens if they attack all at once? We can't win without the Enhanced."

"We can't take and hold those farms even with them. They're too close to the wall. And if we let them finish their planting, the siege will have failed."

"What do you recommend, then?"

Jekjarah appeared between the two and jumped around excitedly. "Finally! Some old-fashioned fun!"

"Let me do what I do best."

❖

The Coalition soldiers were more than happy to help Zeriel. They were getting bored with the constant training, and he gave them something to look forward to. They'd spent the entire day gathering ingredients and helping him create the firebombs he'd need for his mission. After a few hours of work, they'd crafted around fifty.

Zeriel stood on a ridge, looking out toward the farmland as Ketik helped him put the bombs in a pack. Zeriel gingerly swung it onto his shoulder.

Ketik inspected the last one and asked, "Are you sure these are going to work?"

"Being an exceptionally bad assassin forced me to adapt. I developed these, and other devices like it, to help me out where my skills were lacking."

Ketik placed the last one carefully into his pack, then looked toward the farms in the distance. "How do you plan on getting there without being seen?"

Zeriel checked that the bag was secure, then spied the distance he was about to cross. The little bits of shade around him would make this particularly difficult. Most of the dead grass had fallen flat, creating very little shade. "I don't."

"I was hoping for something more...magical."

"Not many shadows to work with out there. It'll be better if I put my focus on crossing the distance with as much speed as I can muster, dropping the firebombs in one pass, then retreating as fast as I can."

"Hopefully they'll be too busy trying to put out the fires to retaliate before the Enhanced return."

"They sent their messenger from Clan Amm early this morning, right?"

"They did."

"That village is closer than Clan Yul. If our timing is right, they'll arrive before things get too slippery."

Ketik slapped him on the shoulder. "Good luck."

Zeriel nodded, then reached out with his senses in every direction, as far as he could, and gathered every shadow to him. They trickled in until he finally had enough to cover himself in a thin layer of darkness and lift into the air.

With a deep breath, Zeriel pushed everything but the mission out of his mind. He put the full force of his power to quicken his flight and shot like an arrow over the field toward the farmland. The ground sped by just beneath him, and for a heartbeat, he thought he'd arrive before anyone on the wall would even notice.

Then a cry sounded.

In seconds, arrows rained down around him. Zeriel hardened the darkness around him, the projectiles bouncing off harmlessly.

Then the farms were upon him, and he waited for a break in the arrows to focus his power underneath him and launch himself into the air. He sailed in an arch over the farms, quickly swinging the bag around to gain access to the firebombs. He snatched his sparker from his pocket, lighting the loose wicks in the bombs. One by one, he hurled them at his targets.

Fields exploded into fire, spreading quickly through the dead plant life. Bombs crashed against farm buildings, lighting up their wooden structures. By the time Zeriel began his descent, he'd already set half the area on fire.

He focused, spinning his bag to his back and calling the darkness to coil under his feet, cushioning his fall. Luckily the fire cast long harsh shadows that assisted in the effort. By the time he crashed to the ground in a puff of dark mist, the north gate was already open, Te Et Sha running out.

Luckily, the fires cast enough shadow for Zeriel to create a strong tether that held him high in the air. Then he shot forward, deciding to make a second pass. Arrows came from assassins on the ground now, but with his new reserve of shadows, he managed to counterattack with spears. He completed his second pass while multitasking between attacking the assassins below and throwing his remaining bombs into areas not yet on ablaze.

Zeriel touched down on the eastern side of the farmland and spun around to survey his work. An inferno raged across the fields and buildings. He'd done enough damage to accomplish the mission. Those farms wouldn't produce food for the next two months. Unfortunately, a huge group of maybe twenty Te Et Sha had seemingly decided the farms were a lost cause and had given chase. They were already too close for comfort. Zeriel formed shadow spears and released them at the assassins, but they all dodged in stride and kept coming.

With his mind racing, he could see only two options: Run and hope they gave up the chase, or fight and hope he could take twenty assassins on his own. He looked behind him at the Coalition army. They could take maybe twenty on their own, but not without suffering a tremendous amount of loss. That could put their entire plan in jeopardy. He knew this plan was risky, but facing such a catastrophic failure was unacceptable.

Jekjarah appeared in front of him. "You can't let them through," he said, mirroring what was building in Zeriel's thoughts. "Not if you want to get your shot at Veshet."

Zeriel mustered his determination, covered himself in shadow, then put pressure on it. Until now he hadn't even thought to do it, but necessity pushed him to a solution. The dark fog around him coalesced into hardened armor, and he summoned blades to match. It was all he could manage with the darkness he had available.

They advanced quickly, and just before he was overrun, Zeriel propelled himself into them. Though he was at the limits of his resources, Zeriel found that the shadow armor supported his body in ways he hadn't anticipated, effectively enhancing it a step above what he already had from Eleshar's Curse.

With that boost, he blasted through the Te Et Sha. His blades passed through five of them in the blink of an eye. It was too fast for the others to react, their blades slicing nothing but air as he went by. These were not inexperienced assassins, however. They organized quickly and surrounded Zeriel, closing and cutting short his movement bit by bit.

Their strategy hindered his speed, but not the defense of his armor. They attacked all at once, trying to put an end to him in a single desperate attack. His armor did its job, turning aside their daggers. It didn't arrest their momentum though. Their collective force drove him to the ground, sending a wave of agony ripping through his body.

They pressed their advantage, stabbing and slicing his armor in an unrelenting flurry of blows. He could feel his fatigue growing as they attacked, and knew he had to do something. Fast. Getting his hands and feet underneath him he shoved downward, launching his body into the air and knocking his attackers back. That gave him the space he needed. Coming down on his feet, he released his armor, exploding it outward into a shadow fog large enough to cover himself and his remaining attackers.

He shifted to his heat sight, revealing them as glowing white forms that stopped in their tracks in confusion. Zeriel didn't hesitate, he found the current of the darkness and weaved through the group, opening arteries before they could even get their bearings.

When the last one fell, Zeriel released his power, only to be met with a sight that made his stomach drop. At least a hundred Te Et Sha were sprinting toward him, each with blood in their eyes.

This was it. The limit of what Zeriel could accomplish on his own, especially with the sun high in the sky. Not wanting to lead them back to the Coalition army though, he gathered up his power and flew north. Nearly half of the assassins followed him, the other half sprinting straight for the Coalition forces.

Zeriel crested a hill north of the city and spotted a forest to the northeast. He changed his trajectory, hoping to take advantage of the shade under the forest's canopy. There was little he'd be able to do for the Coalition forces, but his heart ached being forced to leave them to fend for themselves. For the time being, however, they were on their own.

Suddenly a huge crowd crested a hill farther to the north. They sprinted toward him, and a powerful collective scream carried over the hills. A jolt of terror shot through Zeriel, then he spied Mishteel's outline running out in front of the group, his war hammer held high above his head. Zeriel smiled broadly and let out a cry of his own. He knew the timing of their arrival was close, but he couldn't predict just how close it was.

Another quick change in trajectory sent Zeriel toward the Coalition's Enhanced. Behind them were more soldiers—another thousand at least. The rest of the Northern Clans had joined the Coalition.

He pushed his speed to the limit and got to Mishteel in seconds, well ahead of the Te Et Sha. "It's about time."

"No time to talk," the Chief said as he ran past Zeriel. "There are assassins to kill!"

Zeriel spun around to catch up, which was difficult now that the Chief was an Enhanced. "That's only half of them. The rest are on their way to the main Coalition army to the east of the capital. In fact, they're probably already fighting."

"We kill them quickly, then. That works for me!" Mishteel let out another war cry, and the other Enhanced replied with their own.

Zeriel ran with them, only then realizing that, though he hadn't felt like one of their ranks, he was their equal. The only difference between them was his power, but the reality he hadn't considered until that moment was, he *was* one of the Coalition's Enhanced.

Jekjarah winked into existence running next to him. "Yes! More blood!"

Zeriel smirked, reformed his shadow armor and blades, and joined his brothers in battle. It wasn't long until the two forces collided, and to his surprise he felt the force of that impact in his bones. Death came in a flash for many on the front lines. After a few seconds, the fighting settled into group skirmishes, and Zeriel found himself back-to-back with Mishteel. Together they were a spinning force of destruction. Blood flowed freely to the ground around them and Zeriel caught glimpses of Jekjarah rolling in it.

The fighting ended much faster than Zeriel anticipated. The warriors from the Northern Clans had caught up and joined them toward the end. The Enhanced didn't have the luxury to sit still, though.

"The Coalition," Zeriel said.

Mishteel nodded, looked out at the others, and raised his war hammer in the air. "We're not done yet! The rest of the Coalition still needs us!" Cries rose up in response around them and everyone broke into a sprint.

They crested the hill Zeriel had come over and saw the Coalition forces locked in combat. They were barely holding their own using the formations they'd developed, but there were too many assassins to hold off for much longer.

"Zeriel!" Mishteel screamed.

"On it!" he responded, then drew enough darkness around him to lift into the air and hastened toward the fight.

Every second of his approach was an agonizing eternity. He felt like he had during the battle at Clan Eten. Like he was failing those men because he was too slow, and too weak to save them.

Ketik's voice rang in his head. *You're not the only one risking his life for the fight.*

Zeriel steeled himself, pushed his speed to its limits, and in a matter of a few heartbeats, arrived at the next battlefield.

There wasn't enough shadow to wreak the havoc he had in the battle at Clan Eten, but every person on that battlefield had a shadow. So, he landed on the northern edge of the fighting he used each assassin's shadows against them, bringing them up into spikes that impaled them.

He sprinted through the fighting, focusing on the Te Et Sha doing the most damage. Effective as he was, each time he'd kill an assassin, a new one seemed to appear in its place.

Then the Enhanced arrived behind him and swept through the battle like a storm. As they washed over Zeriel he let himself get caught up in the wave of their destruction, adding his own strength to theirs.

The assassins retreated in the face of their assault. Many of the Enhanced tried to follow, but stopped when Mishteel screamed, "Hold! Let them go!"

Zeriel spotted Ketik running toward Mishteel and he sprinted to join them.

"You couldn't have cut that any closer," Ketik said to Mishteel.

"Do we really need to do all the work for you? Didn't I leave you with the Lord of Shadows?" He eyed Zeriel with a smirk and winked.

"Did you forget I'm just one man?" Zeriel asked.

Mishteel's face turned serious. "How did we end up?"

Ketik scanned the battlefield. "It looks like we lost half." Then he saw the crowd cresting over the northern hill. The Northern Clans had finally caught up. "It looks like you brought some friends with you, though."

Mishteel clapped the High Chief's shoulder. "And once again, the Enhanced have come to your rescue."

"Perhaps," Ketik said, "but could you come to our rescue faster next time?"

CHAPTER FIFTY-NINE

After things settled, they took inventory of the battle. The Coalition had reduced the Te Et Sha to about half the numbers they had before the fight. This meant their Enhanced now outnumbered the assassins by almost two to one. However, with the danger Veshet presented, the Chiefs thought it best to continue with the siege as planned.

It was mid-dark month when they finally decided to make their move. By that time, the assassins inside the walls would be running low on food—if they hadn't run out already. Ketik argued to wait even longer, allowing the hunger to soften their numbers further. Ultimately, they decided that utilizing Zeriel when his power was at its peak would provide the greatest advantage.

That's how Zeriel ended up standing on the riverbank that ran along the capital's southern side, staring at the city's sewer outlet, watching the black water belch out into the currents below.

"This brings back some memories, doesn't it?" Jekjarah said.

Zeriel scrunched up his nose from the smell. "Not good ones."

The hallucination stuck his head into the outlet. "At least this time you're not running from the nobility of Kloren. Remember that mess?" He pulled his head out and gave a nonchalant shrug. "But you could always just turn around and tell Ketik you didn't want to get stinky."

"Would you shut up, for once? I'm just working myself up to it." Zeriel eyed the moon in the south. The stars in the sky shone bright around it as it crested the horizon on the other side of the Epreva

River. He had work to do, a deadline to do it by, and he was already behind.

Much to his chagrin, Zeriel had come up with the idea to infiltrate through the sewers. On a normal mission, he wouldn't have chosen that path of entry given how the resulting smell would linger, giving him away. So much had changed since then that he'd thought of a way to avoid that downside, allowing him to penetrate deeper into the city than the Te Et Sha were probably expecting.

With his plan now in motion, and no time to waste, Zeriel gathered the now plentiful shadows and created a wedge. The result split the flow in front of him, giving him a stop to walk clear of the sludge. As he willed the wedge into place, he was pleasantly surprised when he saw the single flow of black water split into two.

"Wait, that worked on the first try?" Jekjarah said. He gave Zeriel a worried look. "That's a bad sign."

"For once in our lives, would you just shut up while I'm on this mission."

Jekjarah's eyes widened. He leaned back and placed a hand on his chest. "Well. I'm sorry to be such a burden on you."

His nerves were building, and the hallucination wasn't helping. This was the moment he'd been working toward. The struggles, the battles, and the risks. They drove him here. He pushed down the worries and that little piece of him that still thought of him as the Worst One. It was time to make good on his promise to Lavel and save the clans in the processes.

With a deep breath, he steeled himself and focused on the mission. He covered himself in his shadows armor, hoping to put yet another barrier between him and the stench of the black water.

He gave the hallucination a terse nod then stepped into the sewer.

Jekjarah snorted in response.

As if on cue, the voices started.

They'll know you're coming!

They're waiting to kill you!

You're not good enough. You never were!

Zeriel winced at their appearance but managed to shove the voices to the back of his mind and push on. The inside of the sewer was pitch black, even when he shifted to his heat vision. The only thing he could see was the occasional glow of the rats that scurried through the tunnels. He kept his heat sight, though, not willing risk attacking enemies that weren't there.

After a time, he came to an inlet large enough to crawl through. He peered through its grates without worry of being seen, considering he was covered in shadows in the pitch dark.

Zeriel had been inside the walls of Ki Al Tesh many times, on many missions. He'd killed people inside these walls. Some would have rebuked him for it, even call him a traitor for turning on his people. None of them could fathom the sewer that is politics. It stinks more than the one Zeriel stood in now.

He looked out of the inlet at the cobblestone streets, flanked by stone-constructed buildings. The emptiness, not just on the roads, but in every window, made the city feel dead. A quick shift of his vision to normal then back showed him the dim light of dying white vine lanterns was all that was lighting the streets. Images of Shyal flashed through his mind. *I guess this is what it looks like when cities are brought to ruin.*

His thoughts were interrupted when two Te Et Sha entered the street. They looked—tired?

A spot in the street next to the inlet wavered like the air in the heat of the mid-light-month sun. "You think they're stretched thinner than we thought?" Jekjarah said.

Perhaps. Zeriel sent shadows slowly creeping along the ground toward the men.

The assassins walked toward Zeriel's inlet, unaware. Neither of them spoke, nervously checking their surroundings instead. One of them startled at something in the distance Zeriel couldn't see or hear. He whipped his sword from its sheath and faced the invisible threat.

The other one did the same. When they realized nothing was there, they each relaxed and put their swords away.

Zeriel struck. The shadows on the ground shot up into a mass of dark spikes that impaled the assassins. They died silently as he used the spikes to drag the bodies toward the inlet. He stepped to the side as his shadows pulled them into the sewer, then pushed them downstream.

Though time was short, Zeriel waited for a moment longer hoping to catch additional patrols. Time passed, and the street remained empty, so he crawled out of the inlet and slipped into the shadows of an alley. The pungent stench of the sewer latched to the inside of Zeriel's nose. He hoped that was the only place it existed. He couldn't afford to give himself away because he chose a poor infiltration point.

After a moment to get his bearings, he caught the sounds of the river to his left and immediately dashed toward it. He lifted himself on his shadows mid-stride and deposited himself on the nearest roof. He bounded from rooftop to rooftop. Disturbingly, there were few sounds in the city except the quiet echo of the port's ambiance. The Te Et Sha must have had the citizens locked down in their homes or killed months ago.

In seconds he was standing on a roof overlooking the port gate. It was closed and barred, and two assassins stood guard atop the wall across from him. They faced outward watching the river.

The air next to him wavered again. "Looks like they anticipated an attack from the river after all," Jekjarah said.

It was Ketik's plan to start the assault from the river, even though Veshet had been posting men there for weeks anticipating their attack. That's why Zeriel suggested his infiltration. He would eliminate any defenses by ambushing them from behind, opening the way for the Coalition to infiltrate with limited casualties.

A quick scan of the wall showed only those two men. Zeriel gathered his shadows and launched himself from the rooftop. He manifested spears and threw them in mid-air, hitting his targets moments before he landed between them. A quick flair of his shadows grabbed the falling corpses then set them down without making a sound.

On the other side of the wall were roughly twenty Te Et Sha. Even knowing this was what he'd be facing, his heart raced at the sight of them.

This was the moment the first stage of the attack was supposed to start, but Zeriel hesitated. He grabbed the single firebomb hanging from his belt and inspected it for a moment. Thankfully, the glass hadn't cracked and none of the contents had spilled after all his jostling. Something nagged at his mind, though. Assassins didn't stand in groups out in the open, waiting to be attacked. He'd already been with the Coalition too long, fighting like a standard soldier. Still, he cursed himself for not recognizing the trap sooner. Zeriel crouched, scanning the port.

The terrain was rocky where it hadn't been cut away for the docks. Tall stones jutted up into the air around it, making it practically impossible to tell if anyone was hiding among them, even with his heat sight.

"It's kind of obvious, not that you're looking for it," Jekjarah said.

"They're in those rocks," he whispered.

"What are you going to do, then?"

Zeriel thought through his options, none of which he liked. He shook his head to clear away the distraction. "It doesn't matter. I'll just have to handle them when it comes to that." He pulled his sparker from his pocket, lit the firebomb, and tossed it over the edge of the wall.

It landed and caught three assassins on fire immediately. The others reacted quickly, but not fast enough. Zeriel was already falling from the wall and casting shadow arrows by the time they thought to look for him.

He'd killed all but two of them before he landed on a cradle of shadows. To their credit, they attacked immediately. They were no match for Zeriel. Not in the middle of a dark month.

Two shadows blades coalesced into his hands and with the additional speed he gained from his shadow armor, Zeriel moved in a flash and dropped them both.

The hair on the back of his neck stood on end and he spun to face the craggy rocks. Assassins, at least twice as many as were guarding the port, appeared from behind their cover.

"And there they are," Jekjarah's voice came from behind him.

A field of arrows with their tips on fire appeared from the river and sailed over their heads. Zeriel looked out into the water to see the Coalition's ships, their starboard sides facing shore. A tall figure directed the fire from the closest of the ships. Captain Jetita looked like a man out of legend, standing with a foot on the railing of the deck, hand outstretched directing the fire, and lit from behind by two large braziers.

Volleys of fire arrows were loosed from the ships in deadly waves, illuminating the port as they sailed overhead. This was the signal they'd agreed on. The Coalition's assault on the capital had officially begun.

CHAPTER SIXTY

The Coalition ships approached the docks, and just like they planned, the assassins on the port were solely focused on Zeriel. A torrent of conflicting emotions flowed through him. Fear that he couldn't fight them all on his own. Hope knowing all he had to do was hold them off until the reinforcements on the ships arrived, and a bit of pride that the Te Et Sha finally saw him as enough of a threat to ignore everything else to try and kill him.

Zeriel went into action as fire arrows continued to sail over his head and into the city. He burst forward, caught the front of their group off guard, and killed them in an instant. The others moved in to surround him, but he simply spun in a circle and impaled them onto inky spikes from the ground. At the sight of the carnage he'd wrought, the rest pulled light globes from pouches and threw them at him.

He let out a sharp curse for not anticipating they'd use those again. Luckily, he was already using his heat sight, so it didn't affect his vision as they'd expected. Somehow his eyes still strained painfully as if it did, though.

He pushed through the pain with an outburst of speed and the flow of battle took over. His consciousness withdrew into the back of his skull and his head felt suddenly wrapped in an invisible blanket. Everything shifted into an unreal dream state as his body took on a life of its own. His hands felt as if they grew ten times their normal size. Anxiety and panic set in as Zeriel tried to will the feelings away. It didn't work, so he focused instead on surviving.

The muscles of his body seemed to rely on the memory of his training. The use of his powers was too new to him, though, so they barely persisted, faltering in key moments. With all the will he could muster, Zeriel managed to hold onto his shadow weapons and armor. The effort was probably what saved his life.

The strangeness slowly faded as Zeriel rotated, and landed killing blows on all the Te Et Sha around him. He released his blades and grabbed his head, then breathed deeply and sank to his knees. The emotions of what happened lingered, and it paralyzed him as they too faded.

The crunching sound of dirt shifting underfoot sounded behind him, then came the clang of a blade hitting the stone. He spun and summoned a blade as he did. By the time he'd turned around he was taken aback by the sight of an assassin standing over him, the man staring at his chest. Blood oozed bright white from his sternum. Zeriel shifted to normal sight in time to see a wisp of shadow evaporate from the center of his chest then the man fell to the ground.

Jekjarah stood behind him. "That was close," he said, reaching out a hand to help Zeriel up.

He tried to take the hallucination's hand, but they passed through each other.

Jekjarah looked at his hand puzzled. "Huh."

"What are you?" Zeriel asked.

The hallucination puzzled over the question, but before he could answer, more Te Et Sha appeared from the outside edges of the port, sprinting toward Zeriel.

There were at least a hundred of them, practically the entire remaining force of assassins the Coalition knew about, and they were carrying large steel kite shields. Jekjarah winked out of existence as Zeriel stood to face them. He grabbed his shadow swords, and gathered up as much darkness as he could, forming hundreds of spears in a circle around him. Then with a spin he launched them at the oncoming horde.

In response, the first two rows interlocked their shields. The spears deflected off the steel with a deafening crunch. Several assassins were knocked back at the impact, but their defense held. After the impact they launched back into a sprint.

"Zeriel," Jekjarah said. "I don't think that's going to work."

"I can see that," he replied. He shifted tactics, flattening his shadows into a pool on the ground, then sent them across the cobblestone.

The enemy stopped and interlocked their shields again, but those shields couldn't stop his power from leaking under them. While they waited for his attack to impact their shields Zeriel stretched his power to its limit and created a sudden field of spikes, shooting upward from the ground.

In that single moment Zeriel cleared the field of assassin to a handful. At the same time, he felt a wave of exhaustion run through his body.

The remaining assassins quickly recovered from their shock and sprinted toward him. When he got to his feet, he knew he didn't have the strength to defend himself, but that didn't stop him from trying.

For the first time in his life, Zeriel knew—really knew—that he was going to die. He'd always expected some sort of peace to fall over him— much like when he passed out in *The Pick and Shovel*. Or maybe at least the feeling of a burden shed. Instead, what he got was every negative emotion he'd ever had and bottled up, every failure he'd endured, and every struggle he'd failed to overcome, all exploding out of him in a fierce war cry. There was no controlling the sound he made, it was a concoction of pure force.

The assassins slid to a stop at the outburst, fear plain on their faces.

Zeriel met the eyes of those ahead of him. "Come, fools! Meet your end at the hands of my blades!" The statement felt foolish, and over-dramatic, but also somehow *right*. He added shadows into his swords, expanding them to an almost impractical size. To his surprise they didn't increase in weight or become unwieldy in his hands.

For the first time in his life, he saw members of the Te Et Sha hesitate at the thought of fighting him.

"Yes!" Jekjarah cried. "Kill them, Zeriel!"

As he prepared to launch himself into his final battle, men flooded the port from the docks and attacked, Mishteel leading their charge. It caught Zeriel off guard, and when he tuned to see where they'd come from, he realized he'd completely forgotten about the Coalition ships. The Coalition's Enhanced and several hundred of their soldiers poured from their decks into the port.

A figure with raven black hair tied into a braid falling to the middle of her back appeared out of the group. She wore thick leather armor and felled assassins with her cutlass as if it were no more difficult than cutting grass. She stopped in front of Zeriel, and he finally recognized her.

Quatesh looked him up and down and said, "We can take it from here. Focus the strength you have left on finding and killing Veshet." She turned and reengaged the remaining Te Et Sha. For a moment the Chief mesmerized him. She wasn't one of the Enhanced, yet she fought side by side with them, and with a speed and skill he'd never seen from any normal person.

In that moment a lance of fire split the sky and rammed into the lead ship on the docks. The ship exploded in a ball of smoke and flame.

Zeriel twisted around to find the origin of the attack and saw a figure on top of the tower, framed in a wavering orange glow, gathering a ball of fire above its head. Veshet, it seemed, had finally decided to join the battle.

As the man prepared his next attack, Zeriel gathered the darkness to himself once again. Though he'd felt exhausted only a bit earlier, he was surprised to find he'd pushed past that barrier. When he gathered shadows this time, they responded more swiftly. It felt like his breath was easing, like when a weight was removed from your chest.

He created a ball of his own and launched it at the same moment Veshet sent his next fireball. His ball impacted the center of Veshet's fire, and the point of impact turned in on itself. Then the fireball exploded in mid-air.

When the blast cleared, Zeriel saw Veshet looking down from that tower. For a moment he felt the assassin's eyes on him.

Veshet spun around suddenly and disappeared.

"What are you doing?" Quatesh yelled at him from the fighting. "Get moving. We've got this handled."

The Chief was right. It was time to get his vengeance.

CHAPTER SIXTY-ONE

In a single leap Zeriel launched himself in the air, gathering enough shadows underneath him to soar over the wall. The streets inside the capital were glowing with the wavering orange light of fire. To his left and right he could hear the fighting at the gates as he passed.

The entirety of the Te Et Sha was now completely focused on repelling the Coalition's assault, which left Zeriel free to continue his flight toward the tower. Unmolested as he was, it didn't take long.

He sent a tendril of shadows high up the tower and as soon as it connected, used it to pull himself upward. The angle of it pulled him into the side of the structure. With a quick motion he pulled his legs up in time to land with his feet on the outer wall. Zeriel sprinted upward, pulled by his tether. When he got close to where it connected, he sent a new tether high up to continue his ascent. As focused as he was, nervousness still twisted his guts as the fight with Veshet approached.

Lines of shadow from the darkness below reached up and connected with Zeriel as he collected as much power as he could. It built into a mist around him that dripped darkness like a cloud about to burst with rain.

The top of the tower was only a few steps away when Zeriel shifted to his heat sight. He rushed up the wall, his foot planting on the top ledge, and jumped. The momentum of his speed and the force of his leap sent him high in the air.

The roof of the tower came into sight. It was only about as large as the small village square in Clan Ra. In the center was a huge pile of wood that smoked and turned to ash, though there was no detectable flame.

Veshet stood at the north edge of the tower, waving his arms wildly as he drew fire from the city below. Tendrils of flames streaked through the air and into another ball over his head. Zeriel followed the direction Veshet was focused on and saw the North Gate in ruins. The Coalition forces were flooding into the city, and Veshet was about to unleash his fireball at them.

Zeriel had come to understand the inner workings and limitations of his power, and as he watched Veshet, it was clear his fire must follow some of the same principles. He thought back to their fight in *The Pick and Shovel* and remembered the man reducing a piece of wood to ash when fueling his power.

The pile in the center of the tower's roof made sense now, so when he spread his shadows out into a mass of spears, he made sure to fire plenty at what he could only assume was Veshet's power source.

A full third of the spears headed toward the wood, while the others went after Veshet. When they connected, the wood in the pile exploded, sending most of it over the edge.

Somehow, Veshet sensed an incoming attack and spun his head around in time to see Zeriel's spears. He dodged the initial attack but couldn't avoid the shrapnel of the wood pile. The force of it almost sent him over the edge.

When Zeriel landed, he had his blades in his hand on the opposite side of the tower from Veshet. He made his move quickly, leaping over the remaining pile of wood to execute a powerful strike on Veshet from above. But the assassin recovered more quickly than Zeriel had expected and drew a sword in time to block Zeriel's attack.

He landed and rolled away, narrowly avoiding Veshet's counterattack. In a flash he was back on his feet facing the man.

Veshet's sword burst into flame, causing smoke from the wood pile to thicken as it rose to the sky. The man was dressed in the pearl-white robes of the Jel, the supreme ruler of Fei En Ar. He didn't look like a ruler, though. The robe was torn and stained with dirt and blood. Veshet's shifting eyes were ringed in dark circles that Zeriel could see even through his heat sight. His posture was unsure and movements erratic, matching his hair that stood on end, wild and disheveled. "It seems you've proven me wrong, Zeriel."

"I haven't come to prove anything to you. Only to kill you."

He burst out laughing. It came out in high-pitched tones and went on far longer, and with more intensity, than the comment could have possibly demanded. *"Only the strong survive."* He said the words in the same way all the others had, but on him they felt...*wrong.*

"You've gone insane," Zeriel said. It wasn't an accusation, just the recognition of someone who knew the signs.

Jekjarah's presence began to waver next to Veshet. "Maybe he's easier to kill, now? I do want to see what his blood looks like."

"I guess you would know," Veshet said, "wouldn't you?"

"I would." Zeriel took a step forward, forcing the man to deepen his fighting stance. "That hardly matters now, though. I've waited a long time to avenge Lavel's death, and your insanity won't stop me."

Veshet's face snapped into confusion, and he tiled his head erratically. "La—who?"

Zeriel growled. "The woman you killed when you came after me in Shyal."

Veshet's features turned dark, and he grinned. "Oh, right. That one. I barely remembered her. I killed her, you say? Well, it's possible, I've killed so many, it's hard to keep track of them all." He met Zeriel's eyes for a split second, his own wide and shifting. "You wouldn't know what that's like, though, would you?"

"Oh, I wouldn't say that. The faces of the thousands of your men who I've killed in the last few months are starting to run together."

"Yes, you've become a true killer for the first time in your life. Someone strong enough to fight through my men and make it to the top of this tower. You're truly worthy to die at the hands of the greatest man in all Eleshar." He puffed up at the last part.

An uncontrollable burst of laughter flowed out of Zeriel. He struggled to contain himself, but when he did, he saw Veshet frowning. "Are you ready to die?" The assassin asked.

"I was just about to ask you that same question."

Zeriel exploded his shadows into a huge fog of darkness that covered the entire roof.

The white heat-form of Veshet responded almost immediately by flaring the flames of his sword to huge proportions. The move evaporated enough of the shadow fog to expose Zeriel again, and without hesitation, Veshet shot forward.

Flames jetted from his feet, causing him to skim across the distance in a split-second. In that time, he'd somehow produced another sword that instantly caught aflame.

Zeriel barely had enough time to bring up his own swords and block the attack. The force of it was something fiercer than he'd ever encountered. It threw him backward and crushed him against the tower's crenellations. The shadow armor around his back cracked, then exploded into mist that immediately dissipated.

"That was too easy," Veshet said as he stalked forward. "The Te Et Sha are far weaker than I thought if they were no match for you."

Zeriel bared his teeth as he stood up and brought his swords to bear. Veshet rushed forward again, and as Zeriel pushed off with his foot the roof beneath him sank several inches, then the entire tower shuddered.

There was no time to worry about that as Veshet and Zeriel's blades clashed again. This time, Zeriel was ready, and deflected the flaming blades to the side. He spun to face Veshet who had swung around for another pass, still propelled by the flames under his feet.

Then the roof collapsed.

Zeriel's stomach lurched into his throat as he fell among the stone and wood. Smoke wafted upward into the air. The cause of the collapse became apparent when he noticed every beam in the tower had been reduced to ash and coal. Since Zeriel had thrown his supply of wood off the tower he'd been using the building's rafters to power his fire.

Unsupported stone collapsed under Zeriel's feet, turning the inside of the structure into a hollow tube. It was dark save for a few white vine lanterns that still clung to the outer wall. They glowed softly, struggling to stay alive. He consumed the shadows around him, fusing them to his back, then formed them into long, spider-like legs with spear-tipped points. Zeriel reached out with those legs and found the wall. The contact was enough to change his trajectory, pulling him into the wall.

Zeriel slammed all the legs into the wall, slowing his descent to a stop. He used the legs to right himself and put his back against the wall. Looking up he saw the hole at the top of the tower, stars twinkling in the sky above.

Veshet dove into the tower, propelled by his jets, holding his flaming swords outstretched. "Impossible!" he screamed.

Bracing himself, Zeriel reformed his swords and brought the spider legs closer to his body. As Veshet neared him the man spun to right himself and slow his descent. At that moment Zeriel pushed off the wall and launched himself at the assassin.

Veshet veered back in surprise, but it wasn't enough to completely dodge.

Their swords crossed again, but this time Zeriel sent Veshet spinning from the impact. His shadow legs connected with the wall on the other side, as Veshet slammed into the wall near him. The structure shuddered, cracks echoing through the hollow space.

The building was going to collapse on top of them, and their time was running out. But Zeriel would do everything he could to finish this before that happened. He launched himself at Veshet once more, and once more his attack was defended.

He didn't wait to attack a third time, instead rebounding off the wall the moment he hit. Veshet was also getting the hang of the fight, regaining more control after each of Zeriel's strikes.

Again, Zeriel hit the wall, rebounded, and attacked. And once more

Veshet defended. They continued that dance moving up and down the tower until pieces of stone started to peel off from above. They avoided the falling debris, then continued their struggle.

Sure they'd run out of time, Zeriel started bounding upward in hopes to take the fight outside.

Veshet appeared to understand his plan and shot upward quickly, getting to the top before Zeriel could, and gathering a fireball as he went.

There was no way to block what was coming. Instead, Zeriel released the spider legs and brought the shadows underneath his feet as he fell to the ground. He landed on a wooden floor that shattered from the impact. Then everything around him lit up with the orange glow of fire.

Zeriel looked up, seeing nothing but fire filling the whole of the tower. It rocketed toward him at incredible speed. In the blink of an eye, he ripped every shadow from every nook and crevasse around him, and created a black dome to cover himself. Every scrap of darkness that he had left, and every ounce he could summon from the tower's floor poured into the dome adding to its thickness and hardening it.

Debris from the collapsing tower collided first. Zeriel felt the strength of the impact in his body. The light of the fire approaching brightened and the falling debris multiplied. The chunks of stone wall began piling up on the dome until it covered it completely, dimming the intensity of the fire, giving Zeriel more darkness and helping him hold the dome in place.

His luck was short-lived as the fire rolled closer. Its light brightened and brought with it heat that washed out his vision. He released the heat sight, but even his normal site went completely white.

The fire impacted, and the strain it put on his power was practically unbearable. Force and light threatened to shatter his control. The moment stretched into eternity and his body and will were at their utter limits, when suddenly the light and heat faded.

Like a swimmer who'd been underwater too long, Zeriel exploded the dome outward and freed himself from the rubble. Just as he scanned upward, the light of the jets on Veshet's feet washed out his vision again and something collided with his nose.

The force knocked him off his feet as a wet crunch exploded pain across his face. Stars shot through his vision. Zeriel heard Veshet's feet his land on the rubble next to him and his vision slowly cleared.

The fire on his blades faded into nothing as he reached down and grabbed Zeriel's hair. The leader of the Te Et Sha lifted his head, forcing him to meet the man's eyes. "You're strong, there's no denying that. But you're also dangerous. So, despite that strength of yours, you will die today."

Jekjarah appeared behind Veshet suddenly.

"Jek," he said, "please. Kill him."

Veshet turned to look behind him, then shook his head and turned back. "Sometimes I forget how your insanity undermines you. Reduces all your strength to nothing."

"Please!" Zeriel pleaded. "I know you can. You've done it before."

The hallucination turned his head to look away from Zeriel.

Veshet raised his blackened sword to land the final blow. "Goodbye, Zeriel." He thrust the blade forward.

"No!" Zeriel cried out. He called the shadows to form a blade, but they didn't come.

Instead, Veshet looked to the side suddenly, his eyes went wide. "What? No!"

Another blade swiped Veshet's away, then a form slammed into him and knocked him to the side. The unmistakable, almost hollow knock of a skull against stone sounded. Veshet was unconscious.

Jekjarah smiled. "I figured he should be the one to save you."

The man standing over him was the last person he'd expected to see. He looked at Zeriel and smirked. "Why do I feel like I always have to save you from the stupid stuff you do?"

"How?" Zeriel said. "You're not."

"Not real? No, I guess not. But right now, I'm real enough to kill this guy." Laluk stepped past Zeriel and unceremoniously lopped Veshet's head clean from his shoulders.

Zeriel shifted to his heat sight and confirmed two things. Veshet was dead, and Laluk was a hallucination.

His old friend looked back at him and winked, then faded. His form was replaced by a shadow figure holding a dark blade in its hand. The form nodded to him, then evaporated in an invisible breeze.

Zeriel laughed as he let his head rest on the ground. Sudden and overwhelming exhaustion covered his body, and his eyes began to close. "At least it's over," he said.

The last thing he saw as the darkness closed in was a red gem appearing out of Veshet's chest and falling to the ground. It was thin, and as long as one of his fingers, and it rolled on the stone for a bit before it disappeared down a crack in the floor.

CHAPTER SIXTY-TWO

In all the years Zeriel considered what death would be like, he never once expected it to be so *painful*. His entire body—if he had one—pulsed with it. Vaguely, he realized two things: First, he had eyes, and second, they were closed. When he opened them, he was surprised by how bright the afterlife was.

After a moment, his eyes adjusted, and he saw the truth. He was lying in a bed inside a small room. An open window let in the brightness of the early light month sun. Next to that was the bed he lay in, and a chair sat on the opposite wall. Ketik sat in that chair, slumped over and snoring loudly.

"Would you keep that down?" Zeriel said. His throat grated as he spoke, sending him into a coughing fit.

Ketik startled awake. "Zeriel!" He bolted up and ran out the door and shouted, "He's awake!"

"Can't a guy have some time alone after rising from the dead?" Zeriel asked the empty room.

Jekjarah appeared sitting in the chair. "That was rude. He didn't even wait for you to get your joke out."

Zeriel looked at Jekjarah. When he saw the hallucination, his mind could focus on only one thing. Thinking back, he could pinpoint hints of the truth along the way, but even now it seemed such a ridiculous thought, how could he have been expected to piece together what was happening. "Laluk saved me."

"You mean when you fought Veshet?"

"But, how?"

"I shouldn't have to be the one to tell you this, but you're kind of insane."

"You know what I mean. He killed Veshet."

"Oh, that," was Jekjarah's only response.

Zeriel recalled the clues he'd been given over the last few months. Times when his hallucinations appeared to interact with the world. "Shemua threw that rock at me. Twice you killed people to save me. Then Laluk..." He let the statements settle in the air for a moment, then said, "What's going on, Jek?"

The hallucination exhaled slowly and said, "While you were distracted with your imaginary friends at Clan Ra, I saw something change inside you. You didn't notice because you were too distracted, but as time went on, I started to cultivate that change. It took a while before I could make anything happen."

"Make what happen, Jek? What are you talking about?"

He stood up and stepped closer to Zeriel's bed. "Do you remember the state Clan Ra was in when we left?"

Zeriel thought back. They'd been rebuilding for months, but none of the villagers were real. Still, there had been construction standing that he couldn't account for. His eyes went wide at the realization. "How could all those buildings have been repaired? I never touched most of them."

"You gave the villagers substance."

"How?"

"So many times, you've used those powers to create arrows, spears, tethers, and other *real* things. Did you not once imagine you could make a shadow *person?*"

Zeriel opened his mouth to respond, but paused before he said, "No, I guess I didn't."

Laluk appeared next to Jekjarah. "It's a good thing Jek did, or I wouldn't have been able to help."

"You created him?" he asked Jekjarah.

"No, he's your invention, Zeriel. You formed us all."

"Then why torment me?"

Laluk's head dropped, and he disappeared.

Jekjarah's face softened. "Haven't you been listening? *You* made us. Me, the voices, the Clan Ra villagers. Your hopes. Your fears. Your insecurities. Your darkest thoughts. We've always been a manifestation of the deepest part of you."

"And now my hallucinations have access to my power." The revelation sent a chill down Zeriel's spine.

"Which saved your life more than once."

"But those voices," Zeriel said, a shiver coursing through his spine. "They would never save my life. What if they used my power to—" The idea was too terrible to put words to.

Jekjarah stepped forward and opened his mouth to speak but was interrupted as the door to the room slammed open. Mishteel ran in, stepping through Jekjarah as the hallucination disappeared.

"I knew the Lord of Shadows wouldn't let a few burns kill him!"

Odinte, Quatesh, and Ketik entered the room behind Mishteel. All of them flashing genuine smiles.

"They are more than a few," Odinte said. She looked over Zeriel's bandages and nodded to herself. "You were covered in severe burns across your entire body. Healing is going to take a long time. Don't rush it."

"Where's Aleber?" Zeriel asked.

"He didn't survive," Ketik said, and all the Chiefs' heads bowed at the admission. "He led the assault on the north gate and died in Veshet's first attack."

"How many did we lose?"

"Two thirds of the army," Odinte responded, "and more than half the entire population if all the clans. The devastation Veshet brought to Fei En Ar will be felt for generations."

Silence passed between them for a moment before Zeriel noticed that Ketik was wearing the same robes Veshet wore during their fight—though his looked new. "What's with the robes?"

Ketik stood a little straighter. "There was a vote, and the Chiefs named me the new Jel."

"It suits you," Zeriel said with the best smile he could muster.

"We're uniting the clans," Odinte said, "to help prevent something like this from happening again in the future. We needed someone with experience leading us all."

"I see," Zeriel said, then eyed Ketik. "You got the job by default."

Ketik barked out a laugh. "I like to believe I proved I was capable."

"That you did," he said.

An awkward silence sat in the air before Ketik finally asked, "What about you? The Te Et Sha are gone, and you got your revenge. What's next for the Lord of Shadows?"

Zeriel's thoughts turned to Plaxes, images of her in the dark void of his mind, offering him power. "It turns out I still have one debt I haven't paid back."

"Well," Ketik said, "if you can pay that debt back and stay here, I have a proposal for you." The other Chiefs smiled knowingly.

Zeriel looked at them all in turn and shook his head. "Okay, out with it, already."

"I want you to be a general in our new army."

"Me? The insane Enhanced with strange powers?"

"The man whose idea it was for the Clans to fight together, trained our men, sprinted far ahead of our forces to strike at our enemy first, and the one who founded the Enhanced? Do we need the man who did all that, and defeated the greatest threat Fei En Ar has ever faced?"

Embarrassment crushed Zeriel. "I'm not as amazing as you make me sound. I'm clumsy and selfish. I barely know how to interact with people."

"You're exactly that amazing, Zeriel," Quatesh said. "If you ask me, Ketik downplayed your contribution."

Ketik stepped forward. "So, what do you say? Will you be one of the generals in our new army?"

"Now, now," Odinte said, "don't put so much pressure on him after he just woke up." She turned her eyes to Zeriel. "You can have as much time as you need to consider it."

Tears came to Zeriel's eyes. The desire to be part of something greater than himself was still there, deeply rooted in his being. It was one of the driving forces that kept him in the Te Et Sha for so long. It was the reason his mind created such a grand illusion when he returned to Clan Ra. Now here it was, offered to him in earnest by people he respected. No, not just respected. Loved.

He pulled the scant shade around the room to his eyes and shifted to his heat sight. They all glowed white with their body heat. More tears welled up at the confirmation and his throat tightened. This was what he'd been missing his entire life.

Thoughts of Plaxes crashed back into his mind. *When you've gotten your revenge, you'll serve me without question or complaint. Once I've achieved my goal, only then will you be free.*

It was the condition of her training, and at the time he'd agreed without hesitation. A twinge of regret penetrated the joy he felt, and quickly turned it to sadness.

"Thank you, everyone," he said through the tightness of his throat. "But my debt won't allow me to stay. Once I'm healed, I'll be leaving Fei En Ar."

CHAPTER SIXTY-THREE

The transition sky had faded, and the sun was a day away from breaching the eastern horizon. The morning moon hung low in the south as El stood at the port and hugged her mother for what she knew might be the last time.

"I still don't understand why you have to be the one to fight him," her mother said through her tears.

"We can never know why," El responded through tears of her own. "Just that the responsibility was thrust on me, and I can't walk away from it."

"You could," her father whispered as he put a hand on her shoulder. Despite everything that had happened, that gesture still made her feel safe and protected.

She released her mother and smiled at her father. "I wouldn't, though."

A sad smile stretched across his face. "No, I suppose you wouldn't."

El looked around. "Where's Oete?"

"I haven't seen your grandfather all morning," her mother responded, scanning the port.

El sighed. "Well, give him my love."

"I will," her mother said. "Now, your father and I need to see to the hunters. Make sure you send letters home."

"Every chance I get," El responded. She brought her parents into a group hug and then they departed. She watched for a bit before she stepped on the main dock. Two caravels were moored on either side of her and crew members hurried to finish preparations for their respective voyages. Several docks over she could see the hunters preparing to set out for the first hunt of the light month. She had gone on several expeditions with them before they discovered the Uklak's new home, much farther east than they expected. Luckily, other than adding a few extra hours to the hunts, finding them meant they had stable hunting waters again. Unfortunately, the larger Uklak remained too deep for the hunters to capture without El, but the smaller ones that favored the shallower waters were more the size they were used to, anyway.

El glanced down at the bracelet on her wrist, idly feeling the too-smooth crystal. Spikes on the inside of the bracelet penetrated her skin. She activated her powers to peer inside, marveling at the fibrous tendrils that extended from the points of the spikes, reaching their way up her arm. Though she had expected her body to reject the foreign substance, it accepted it instead. Releasing her power, she regarded the blue lines the tendrils created on her skin.

"Your ship is loaded up with everything you asked for," Ki said as she appeared next to El. "It's not too late to change your mind, you know."

El flashed Ki a warm smile. "No, it's actually far too late. But thanks," she said with a wink.

Reon appeared on El's other side. "Well, I still don't like this plan."

El bumped his hip with hers. "You're welcome to come up with something better." That elicited a huff from Reon that deepened her smile. She turned back to Ki and said, "After this morning, Baharkar Trading Company will be yours."

Her friend shook her head. "It's grown so much. I don't know if I can manage the entire thing alone."

"Ki, you've been running the company on your own for months. It's *you* that this company couldn't run without."

Ki blushed. "I guess you're right. Maybe I just don't *want* to run it without you."

El swept her up into a hug. "If I could stay, I would. You know that."
Her friend hugged her back and squeezed tightly. "I know."

What El could never bring herself to say was how much better Ki
had become at leading the trading company. As much as every fiber of
her being wished she could stay, she knew that handing the company
to Ki would have needed to be done, regardless.

After a moment they broke away, wiping tears from their eyes, and
that's when El noticed a group of women standing at the beginning of
the dock, bundles in hands and smiles on their faces. They ran up to
her the moment she noticed them.

Luti led the pack, eyes glistening from tears as she approached. "You
didn't think we'd let you go without saying goodbye, did you?"

"I wouldn't have it any other way," El said as her own vision blurred.

They exchanged many hugs, and each one piled their bundles into
El's arms. Gifts for her voyage. Reon took them from her and called
one of the crew members over to help carry everything to her cabin.

"Thank you everyone," she said, voice cracking. "Remember everything you learned, and don't hesitate to teach it to others."

"Yes, yes," the oldest woman there said. "'The healing arts are for
everyone.' We haven't forgotten."

Another woman from the group piped up and said, "How could we?
She said it so many times I hear it in my dreams." The group laughed,
and after another round of hugs, they departed, the din of conversation
following them.

"I need to go as well," Ki said. "Travel safe and may whatever powers
in this world that are on our side protect you."

The image of that priest in Shyal flashed in El's mind. "I hope they
are." The friends hugged and El watched as Ki left, the two waving at
each other like children.

Loud footsteps sounded behind her, and she spun to find a stout
Nuuian man, shorter than her, approaching. His name was Durdrin,
and he wore a simple tunic, trousers, and pair of leather boots, topped
off with a brown short-brimmed hat that he tucked his silver hair into.

He had a wide chin and perpetual stubble across his scarred face. She'd hired him as ship's captain for his years of experience, though they made him hard as stone, and often difficult to work with. "We're ready to cast off, mistress. Can we expect more..." he glanced at the direction Ki had just disappeared into the trade district, "delays?"

"Yes, you can." She wouldn't neglect a proper sending off for Reon. He approached them just then, and she said, "And here comes the most important delay."

Durdrin grunted and walked back to the ship. Reon watched him go with a cocked eyebrow. "I still don't know why you hired that man. Don't you find him as insufferable as everyone else does?"

"Of course I do. But underneath all that, he's passionate, and incredibly good at what he does. I can manage a little insufferable."

"If you say so," he said, pulling her into his arms. The two shared a long kiss, both understanding the implications of what was about to happen. When they broke it off Reon's expression softened. "You're sure you don't want me to come with you?" He looked up at her ship, a thoughtful look on his face. "I feel like I'm abandoning you."

A smile tugged at the edges of her lips at the admission. She felt the same but would never admit it to him. He was immensely capable and treating him otherwise was an insult to his reliability and skill. "Nonsense. You're the only one I trust to make sure everything goes smoothly in Shyal. And you'll join me in Ferrix as soon as you're done, anyway. This is temporary."

His shoulders slumped a bit. "You're right, of course."

She grabbed his chin in her fingers and pulled his mouth to hers. After breaking off the kiss she said, "Don't make me wait too long, though."

He smiled at her and nodded. "Don't get killed by any ancient gods while I'm gone."

"I wouldn't dream of it."

The two separated and she watched him as he boarded his ship. After months of preparations, there was nothing more she could do to prepare her island for life without her. She reminded herself that it had managed just fine for thousands of years before she came along. But what really worried her—that they would come to rely on her powers—is what had driven her to spend months preparing for this moment. Still, she felt nervous for her people and hoped that she'd given them a gift that would last generations.

Not wanting to add to Durdrin's delays, she boarded her ship, spotted the captain giving orders to one of the crew, and waved to him. "We can set sail now, Captain." The man gave her a nod and started barking orders. El stepped to the starboard side of the ship, eyes scanning the northern horizon.

"What do you think we'll find out there?" came a familiar voice from behind her.

El spun to find her grandfather stepping up to the rail and looking out at the water. "What are you doing here Oete? We're disembarking right now!"

He spun around and leaned on the rail with his arms crossed. "I spent most of my life focusing on what's best for the village, and I found fulfillment in that, but now that your father's the Chief—" He glanced at her and flashed a smile.

Looking at him now, she was surprised by the vigor and strength she saw there. His presence alone bolstered her confidence and settled her nerves. Suddenly, she couldn't imagine confronting the cosmic challenges ahead of her without his support.

"You want to race toward certain death at the hands of a god you used to worship?"

He laughed heartily. "I want adventure!" He spun back around and gestured to the ocean. "I want to see what's out there, El. Experience the world before the end of my days." He turned to her and his face turned more serious. "And if I can help my daughter save the world in the process, then my life will have truly meant something."

She thought about throwing him off her ship right there but couldn't bring herself to do it. Instead, she shook her head and smirked.

"I never could say no to you."

"No, you couldn't," he said as he turned to leave her. "But it looks like adventure may be a few days away, yet. Come find me in my quarters if something exciting happens." He shot her a wink then stepped below deck.

El huffed at the old man but found comfort in his presence. Remembering what it was like when she last stepped foot in a foreign city, alone and surrounded by enemies, she would have given anything to have someone there with her back then.

"Everything feels like it's leading me toward this," she said to her memory of the old priest in Shyal. "You told me it wouldn't be up to me to save the world, but right now it sure feels like it is. I wonder, if you knew everything that had happened since then, if you'd say the same thing to me now." The old priest wasn't there to give her his wisdom, though, but she found she was okay with that.

She'd accepted the burden of the fate world, so she'd either save humanity or die trying.

CHAPTER SIXTY-FOUR

Months passed before Plaxes returned to Zeriel's mind to give her first instructions. He'd barely healed enough to travel but wasn't about to go back on his word. Everyone in the capital gave him a send-off he didn't feel he deserved, but he didn't argue with them either.

Ketik handed him a heavy bag of four thousand platinum Kloren zaxes and another two-thousand gold ones. They'd explained that it was his payment for everything he'd done for the Coalition. They'd gotten it from the hoard of riches the Te Et Sha had stolen from the clans and were now using to build their new monarchy. The weight of the money in his pack was the easiest burden he'd ever carried. Unlike what he felt when leaving everyone behind.

It was the height of a light month when Zeriel stepped out of the western tree line of the forest near Shyal, and once more marveled at its massive walls. The main road into the city was busy with merchants and travelers who passed him by as he stood on the side of the road.

Jekjarah appeared next to him. "It'd be nice to know why Plaxes sent us here."

"Serve without complaint or question. That was the deal." Several people who heard him shifted to the opposite side of the road and hurried along. He ignored them and continued down the road.

"Still," Jekjarah said, "you'd think she'd at least give us a hint."

The final stretch of road felt short compared to the distance he traveled to get there. Zeriel paid the gate tax and entered the Guild District and was shocked by what he saw. If he hadn't been there during the slave uprising, he wouldn't have known anything had happened there.

The buildings were intact—though there were some obvious repairs—the streets were clean, and the people looked happy. He turned south, heading for the Lower Market and was pleasantly surprised to find the changes they'd made in the face of calamity had persisted. Before the uprising, the area was dirty, and clearly catered to the poor and less than reputable. Now, the fresh cobblestone roads and well-kept buildings told a different story. The residents of this area had changed, and it showed.

It didn't take long to arrive at his destination. An empty field of dirt between two buildings. Remnants of the inn that once stood there remained as blackened charcoal mixed in the dirt. Zeriel walked over the area as a reverence fell over him. He hadn't known it at the time, but his life changed in that place. He'd risen from that fire a new man, or, at least a chrysalis of the man he would become.

A child walked by the road and stopped to look at him. When their eyes met the child started, then ran away.

Jekjarah appeared, stepping toward the road to watch the kid. "It's those black eyes of yours," he said.

Zeriel turned away and knelt, then grabbed a handful of the dirt, and let it fall between his fingers. A piece of charred wood was left in his hand. He turned it over to inspect it. Thoughts of Veshet filled his head, memories of the ash he left behind, and not just from the powers he wielded. Though the man was gone, he hadn't felt like he'd accomplished his mission.

"I almost avenged your death, Lavel. Unfortunately, I survived."

Jekjarah turned to him and asked, "do you really think we have time for what you're planning?"

Zeriel dropped the charcoal and stood. "Plaxes never said when she'd meet us here. And considering how long she goes without talking to us, I think we can indulge a bit."

Hurried footsteps sounded on the cobblestone. Zeriel turned to watch as a Donian man practically slid to a stop in his hurry.

Suspicion and anger played across his face. "What are you doing?" he asked. "Someone owns that land you're standing on!"

"I know, Aketen," Zeriel said. "I do."

The man reeled back and asked, "Zeriel?"

"I know. I'm as surprised as you are."

"Is he still there?" yelled a voice from down the road. A moment later a Donian woman appeared. "Did you make him leave?"

"Hi Pihuanata," Zeriel said. "I take it you two have been guarding this patch of dirt for me?"

She looked at him for a moment before recognition flashed across her face. "Zeriel."

The two didn't look happy to see him. It had been a long time since he'd seen that look on someone's face. He didn't blame them, really. The person he was the last time he was here wasn't someone he liked either. Somehow, their presence comforted him, if for nothing else than their familiarity. "Did you guys take the land for yourselves?" He knew he shouldn't have asked it the moment the question left his lips.

"We would never!" Pihuanata said. "You of all people should know we couldn't disrespect Lavel's wishes like that."

"Of course," he said, raising his hands in surrender. "Then how do you feel about helping me rebuild the inn?"

Aketen raised an eyebrow at him. "That would cost nearly ten-thousand gold, assuming we would do such a thing with you."

Zeriel smirked. "I've got it covered."

EPILOGUE

It wasn't easy sleeping on the cold stone of her dungeon cell, but over time, Lavel had gotten used to it. So, it wasn't the hard stone, or the chill it tried to inject into her muscles that woke her. It was the thunderous explosions that rocked the ceiling of her cage, and the dust and debris that fell on her that did it.

Those were all minor inconveniences compared to the agony and torment Veshet and his army had visited upon her from the moment that *mudborn woman* had pulled her from her burning inn. She'd clutched onto the seething hatred that grew in her through it all. Hatred for those who treated her like a plaything. Hatred for Veshet and those twins who followed him. But the hatred she felt most of all—what kept the embers of loathing that emanated from the very core of her soul from extinguishing—was for that blighted assassin, Zeriel.

He was the one to blame for it all. For murdering her family and leaving her in that Obe forsaken inn, cared for by a pair of lizard-loving abominations. If she lived long enough, she would see them all suffer, but Zeriel most of all.

So no, the cold stone could never cool the fires of the hate that heater her very soul.

Another explosion sounded above, this time rocking the walls of her cell. The stone above cracked open and burning debris fell through. Lavel rolled to the side of her cage to avoid it as a wave of heat followed the debris. A voice echoed through those cracks that she knew all too well.

"You're strong, there's no denying that," Veshet said, and though he wasn't speaking to her, she squeezed herself into a tight ball in the corner to distance herself from him. "But you're also dangerous. So, despite that strength of yours, you will die today."

She'd watched Veshet kill before, but never had he sounded so disappointed to do it. The instincts that she'd learned since being taken squeezed her eyes shut and kept her pulled into her corner, not willing to risk moving until she knew Veshet couldn't hurt her.

"What? No!" Veshet screamed.

Lavel opened her eyes and looked up at the ceiling. Embers of burned wood continued to fall through the crack like water leaking from a basin. No more voices came. Hesitantly, she got to her feet, stepping nearer to the cracks. *Dare I hope?*

Nothing stirred for a long moment, and doubt crept into her mind as the seconds passed. *No, there's no one who could challenge him. I'm sure he killed whoever he was talking to and walked away without a second thought.*

Lavel dropped to the floor and sat cross-legged, cursing that little piece of her that still thought good things were possible.

Then something else fell from the ceiling, and at first, she barely noticed it until several sharp clicks echoed through her cell as it hit the floor. She crawled forward, inspecting the object as she got closer. It was a thin, red gem, pointed at both ends, glowing a soft red light. The hint of a red mist emanated from the jewel and traveled a short distance across the floor before dissipating.

Something about that crystal *felt* right. It called to her in a way she'd never felt before, as if her true home existed inside that gem, waiting for her return. She found herself unconsciously reaching out and taking it. The gem immediately melted into her skin, and heat flashed across her body. It felt like molten steel coursing through her veins, but she didn't feel burning, nor any pain. Instead, that heat had mixed with the fire of her hatred and the two became one.

Then something grabbed the base of her spine and ripped her spirit from her body.

✧

White flashed across her vision, and Lavel found herself sitting in a soft leather chair in the corner of a dimly lit room. The walls of the room were bare except for a square patterned molding and an open window to her right. A small bed was pushed against the wall to her left, with a single nightstand holding a covered white vine lantern.

Before she could take in any more of the room, her head turned toward the door as a figure opened it slowly and slipped inside. Panic rose in her chest as she recognized Veshet, but when she tried to get up to escape, she couldn't move.

"You're all so predictable," she said, except that it wasn't her voice, and those weren't her words. The voice that came from her mouth was on the high side of masculine and changed intonations constantly in a way that set her on edge. Her hand moved of its own accord, and she caught a glimpse of the ash-white color of its skin. The hand moved in front of her and snapped its fingers. Fire erupted from several pots that were arranged on the floor around the room.

Veshet moved with supernatural speed and in a flash had a knife dug into Lavel's chest. The pain was immediate, and excruciating, and she wanted to cry out but couldn't.

The person controlling the body she was in didn't flinch. He just looked down at the knife, then back at Veshet. "At least you live up to your reputation." He produced the red crystal Lavel had grabbed and placed it on his attacker's chest.

Veshet's eyes widened and went out of focus for several moments. When he regained consciousness, he looked at her differently. "It can't be."

"Oh, but it is," the voice said from Lavel's mouth, and with a quick motion shoved the assassin across the room and into the far wall. Veshet created an indent where he hit, then slid down the wall to a seated position where he remained, trying to catch his breath.

The body Lavel was in stood up and walked closer to Veshet. He slowly pulled the knife from his chest, then dropped it on the floor behind him. Lavel felt the wound close in a few heartbeats. "You're mine now, Veshet."

The assassin's face betrayed his fear. "No—I'd nev—" he was cut off suddenly by his own screams. His entire body tightened, and he writhed on the floor in excruciating pain. After a few moments, his muscles relaxed suddenly, and he went quiet and wept uncontrollably.

"Did you think you had a choice in this? Now that you're mine, I can do what I please with you, and from anywhere on Eleshar."

Veshet took some time to collect himself. All the while the body Lavel was in remained uncomfortably close, looking the man in the eyes from mere inches away.

"What do you want from me?" Veshet finally managed to say.

Lavel clapped and spun in a dancing circle and said, "Excellent!" Glee laced the man's voice that came from her.

Then she abruptly stopped, face turning immediately serious. "I want you to kill." The words came out cold and even, a strange departure from his mercurial tone.

That pulling sensation ripped at the base of her spine again and she was torn from the body of whoever that man was.

❖

After another white flash she was back in her cell. Lavel jumped up retreated, pressing herself back into the wall in a vain attempt to get away from whatever had just happened. Fear gripped her throat as the answers eluded her. She frantically searched her cell, looking for any clue, any sign that she'd been ripped from her body. There was none.

Well, it looks like you're my slave now, said a voice in her head. It was as clear as if someone had spoken right next to her and had the obvious intonations of the man she'd inhabited in her vision.

"My mind finally broke," she said out loud. It was the only obvious conclusion. After all the torture, all the torment, it had clearly been more than she could handle.

If your mind is broken, would you know that your mind is broken?

"I'm insane, not stupid. Zeriel knows that he's a Splintered Soul, so why wouldn't I know about my fractured mind."

See that glowing ember next to you on the floor? Take it in your hand.

"And burn myself, I don't—"

Take it! The voice boomed through her head and her hand involuntarily reached out and grasped the red-hot piece of burned wood. She flinched in preparation of the pain, but none came. Curious, she opened her hand and inspected the coal.

Could you do that if all of this was in your mind?

"I...guess not." She was transfixed by the fact that she held that coal and wasn't being burned.

You know what to do.

She did. It surprised her, but she activated her power by pure instinct. Fire erupted from the coal, reducing it to white ash. The act expanded her senses and everything near her that could provide fuel for her fire entered her consciousness. She used that fuel, and her fire grew larger. Hotter.

A grin spread across her face as she realized the opportunity this power gave her. That vengeance that she was lamenting as impossible just moments ago was now in reach. She'd never be at the whim of another person again. *Ever.*

An image of Zeriel filled her mind. At first, she wondered why she hadn't thought of Veshet, or those twins first. But deep down she knew. He was the cause of all her suffering. The catalyst of destruction that stole her very soul. Yes, he would be the first to feel her wrath.

Don't get too ahead of yourself, slave. If you behave, I may allow you your revenge. For now, you need to get to Ferrix. Since Veshet failed, we'll need to move on to my next plan, and there's lots of work to do.

Despair gripped her as she realized she had not found freedom. No, she'd been freed from one cage, only to step into another.

THANK YOU!

I hope that you enjoyed *Forged in the Chasms of Darkness*!

I would be honored if you would **take a moment to leave a quick review on Amazon or Goodreads**. Reviews are one of the best ways to help other readers discover this story and keep the series going.

Want more? **Join my newsletter** at therichinman.com to receive *The Last Warden*, an exclusive novella that tells the tale of El's ancestor and how his actions rippled through time to change Eleshar forever.

AUTHOR BIOGRAPHY

 RICH INMAN grew up in Spokane, Washington where he spent most of his life until 2022 when he moved to south Florida where he lives now.

He self-published his first book in 2014, then took a break from writing when he changed careers to take a project manager position in software development. After Covid, he found his passion for writing again and in 2023 published The Storm's Approach.

https://www.therichinman.com

@TheRichInman

https://www.facebook.com/TheRichInman/

Read on for the exciting opening of the next book!

The Beast Unleashed
The Records of Eleshar Book 3

Available on Amazon!

CHAPTER ONE

Jaden Beyford rode up the switchbacks of the Glittering Mountains in the pouring rain, chasing the answers to secrets he'd been pursuing for nearly a decade. He'd spent the last year convincing his father to purchase the foreign estate that contained the mine inside those mountains on a hunch; one fed by the memory of a blue crystal he'd seen at a ball a little over a year earlier. After that grueling effort, today was the day he'd find out if it was worth it.

His mount navigated the last leg of the switchbacks, its dirt turned to mud in the downpour. At the top of the incline, the road flattened, giving him a perfect view of the mine's entrance. Rainwater flowed away from the opening, cutting rivulets through the ground and down the mountainside.

Vaie, Jaden's personal steward, emerged from the mine's entrance and approached him. She looked to be in her mid-twenties—though he knew she was older—especially with her clothes accentuating her slender frame and her deep auburn hair done up in a braid. But it was her striking, soft pink eyes that always drew the eye.

"Shouldn't you be in a meeting right now?" she asked.

"It's not until later this afternoon. I have plenty of time to see the state of things here," he replied while dismounting his horse.

She raised an eyebrow at that. "We both know that's not why you're here."

Jaden waved the comment away. "Well, I can see to my duty and do some investigation at the same time, can't I?"

"Maybe, but I doubt you'll find what you're looking for in that cavern. Might as well see for yourself, though." She spun her heels in the mud and stepped toward the entrance.

Some of the miners wore shocked expressions at the way she addressed him, but Jaden had known Vaie for over ten years. She had been one of his squad members in the war, and of those that survived, she was the only one who stayed with him. He ignored their stares. She'd earned the right to speak to him however she wanted.

His chest tightened in anticipation, quickening his breath as they approached the threshold of the mine. Men worked through the miserable weather, eager to fulfill his father's orders to get the mine operational within a week of their arrival. The soldiers he'd stationed there stood guard, a precaution given they'd had to run a group of bandits out of the place when they first arrived. From the reports he'd seen, they'd been in those tunnels for a long time. Probably having moved in shortly after the Hisks were killed back in the slave riots.

A man near them carrying a crate of tools slipped in the mud and knocked into the man next to him. They spilled their equipment down the damp slope next to them as they fell to the ground.

Jaden hurried over and helped them up. "Are you gentlemen alright?"

The two perked up when they saw him and scrambled to their feet. "Yes, sir, Prince. No need to worry about us."

"No injuries, then?" He looked down the slope and saw the tools strewn down it.

"No, sir."

"Good to hear." Jaden scanned the area, then pointed to boxes of tools just inside the mine's entrance. Vaie gave him an annoyed look from just inside the mineshaft, having left him behind to get out of the rain. "Grab a rope and make sure you tie yourselves off before going after what went over the side."

"Right," one of the men replied. He clapped the younger one on the shoulder and gave a quick order. The younger man rushed toward the tools at the mine's entrance, slipping in the mud along the way.

Jaden followed in the young miner's wake, unable to keep the amusement from his face. He watched Vaie smirk as the boy's gaze paused on her for just a moment too long.

Jaden neared the pair and said, "He's too young for you."

The young man's steps hitched at the comment, then he hurriedly snatched a length of rope from a crate and practically sprinted back. The other miners laughed as they watched the exchange.

She pushed herself off the side of the entrance as she watched the man get good-natured gibes and slaps on the back. "They always are." She shot Jaden a brief glance.

"You ready?"

"Are you?" she asked, turning to step inside without an answer.

He shook his head and followed. White vines clung to the ceiling, casting their bright light throughout the tunnels. The Hisks must have spent years growing, trimming, and guiding them through the mines. The effort and expense were clearly for show. Still, he enjoyed the luxury of exploring the tunnels without the need for a lantern.

The walls dripped with the humidity brought by the rain outside, filling the mine with a pleasant earthy aroma. His mind drifted back to the secrets held deep inside the mountain. "So, there are no crystals in there at all?"

"I'm not even sure I believe you about the first one."

He huffed. "I was at the ball, Vaie. So was Alaya. You think we're both lying?"

"No, I believe you saw something. I just don't think it was what you think it was."

"It's not just the crystal. From your initial report you said there were twelve pedestals down there. There were twelve gems in the diagram on the walls of that cave back at Stonerest. Both aligned in an oval? Found on opposite sides of the world?"

She sighed. "I really don't understand your enthusiasm for rummaging around dirty caves." She turned right at a fork and the light from the mine's entrance disappeared around a corner.

"There's a connection to the diagram in this cave, Vaie. And if I can prove it, then the Hisks didn't just pull a single crystal from this mine. They stumbled upon something bigger, something that existed across Eleshar millennia ago. Maybe even a lost civilization!"

"I've seen the pedestals. They didn't seem all that grand to me," she muttered.

He let the comment go. Vaie hated what she called his "little side project." She never understood just how important this was to him. His thoughts barely had a chance to settle before a voice echoed from behind them. "Bandits!" it cried. The fast-paced rhythm of boots pounding on stone echoed around them. The world around him darkened as he slid his sword from its sheath. Somehow, he knew they would attack when he arrived. Not that they waited for him specifically. No, just that life was never so benevolent to let him escape his nature.

Vaie grabbed his arm. "You don't have to help them," she said solemnly. "You posted guards there for a reason."

She was right, of course. He should trust the men he hired to do their job. But he was here, and he could stop the attack before it took those men's lives.

"Yes, I do," he said, gently pulling his arm out of her grip. Steeling himself with a breath, he sprinted back the way they came and toward the battle, but there was no excitement for what was coming. Just the pain and sorrow of knowing he'd be taking more lives that day.

In moments the man that had called out the warning appeared. "They're at the entrance!" he yelled as Jaden sped by. The ring of metal on metal echoed through the mineshaft, and he could now feel the vibrations of the fight through the earth.

Jaden exploded into the rain once more, the vibrations of the combatants' footsteps revealing their location to Jaden as if viewed from above. Four enemies attacking workers while the bodies of the guards lay lifeless, riddled with arrows. The workers were desperately holding onto their lives with the tools of their trade. Two enemy archers hid in the woods. They loosed arrows sporadically at the miners.

The bandits and miners fought as their feet slipped in the mud, some falling, others managing to stay upright. In contrast, Jaden's footsteps were as sure as they'd always been. A miner died and the loss drove him forward. The part of him he couldn't bury took control once more.

The bandit who slayed the miner died first, his head spinning through the air, that disgusting grin still plastered across his face. The next enemy barely reacted in time, swinging his sword wildly in a panic. A quick move and a single swipe of Jaden's sword left the man holding his own entrails.

Two more swordsmen remained, but they barely managed to put up a defense before he slit their throats.

A ping vibrated through the ground. Jaden spun, snatching an arrow from the air. He continued his spin and launched the projectile into the head of the archer who had fired it.

Then he locked eyes with the other archer. The man had an arrow knocked but was shaking so hard he would have had a better chance of hitting the moon than Jaden. A quick feint forward caused the archer to jump, misfiring his arrow high into the air. Panic flashed across his face and he ran.

Instinct dropped Jaden to a crouch. His prey was about to escape, but it knew little of what hunted it. Just before he launched into another sprint, something made him hesitate. A small voice growing louder every moment. One second stretched into two.

He stood up, in control again, then bent down to use the clothing of the nearest bandit corpse to wipe the blood off his blade.

Vaie appeared a moment later, surveying the scene. "We didn't think they'd attack so brazenly."

"We pushed them out of a home they'd held for over a year. One that held platinum they could sell for higher-than-normal prices. Why would no one think they'd fight to get it back?" He shook his head, unable to wipe the sneer from his face as he studied the corpses of the guards he'd stationed there. "I suppose even I underestimated the threat. Triple the guards. If I wasn't here, the enemy might have killed everyone and taken control of the mine again."

Vaie's eyes lingered on the corpse lying among the trees, the arrow Jaden had thrown pierced deeply into its forehead. "I doubt they'd try anything after this," she said in a quiet voice. She'd seen him do far more impressive feats than that, so it wasn't awe that gave her pause. Perhaps it had stoked a memory from the war they'd fought together. When she looked at him her expression was soft, almost apologetic.

Jaden suppressed a growl and barked, "Let's go." Whatever excitement he'd felt before was gone.

When he turned back to the entrance, he stopped short as he saw shock on the miners' faces. He'd forgotten they were there, and they obviously had never seen him in action. They recoiled at his attention.

This.

This was what chased him his entire life. An unmatched warrior. A terror in combat.

He was those things. But was it too much to ask for a prince to change the world with discovery instead of death?

There was nothing to do about it, though, so he marched past all those men with his head held high. They parted as he did and a single whisper met his ears, one that pierced every defense he had and shredded his insides.

"The Beast of the Desert," it said.

www.ingramcontent.com/pod-product-compliance
Lightning Source LLC
Chambersburg PA
CBHW051534250626
47157CB00001B/49